C000092739

THE PACT

HILLY BARMBY

BLOODHOUND
— BOOKS —

Copyright © 2022 Hilly Barmby

The right of Hilly Barmby to be identified as the Author of the Work has been asserted by her in accordance with the Copyright, Designs and Patents Act 1988.

First published in 2022 by Bloodhound Books.

Apart from any use permitted under UK copyright law, this publication may only be reproduced, stored, or transmitted, in any form, or by any means, with prior permission in writing of the publisher or, in the case of reprographic production, in accordance with the terms of licences issued by the Copyright Licensing Agency.

All characters in this publication are fictitious and any resemblance to real persons, living or dead, is purely coincidental.

www.bloodhoundbooks.com

Print ISBN: 978-1-5040-8007-1

ALSO BY HILLY BARMBY

From My Cold Dead Hands

1

ELE

EPPING FOREST – 15 DAYS AND COUNTING

*I*s that really you?

Facebook was just the best, wasn't it? You know, sometimes Ele wanted to write back: *No, it's not me, so bog off!* There were times when she wondered why she'd even set up an account. Work-related, a necessary evil and most definitely not for social contact. But this time she saw the name. He had to be joking. After all these years? Michael. Michael Storm. Not Mike, or Mickey, or Mick.

'You wouldn't call one of the greatest archangels Mickey, now would you?' he'd said.

'It's got a ring to it,' Ele had said. She could never work out if he was being ironic, comparing himself to the most beautiful of God's creatures. Or if he believed it. Believed his own hype. She wouldn't put it past him. And he *was* so beautiful.

'Bastard!' It was as if she'd suddenly stuffed a handful of bird's eye chillies into her mouth, cheeks burning, eyes watering but not crying. No, never crying. She felt as though the room had filled with sand up to her chin, ready to smother her. Breathe now. Breathe.

Ele leant back into her computer chair, her fingers tweaking a long twine of chestnut-hued hair free from where she'd scraped it back into a ponytail. Why now? *Jesus wept!*

'*Fuck you,* Michael Storm.'

Ele got up from the desk to make a mug of tea, leaving the friend request sitting there, sort of pulsing at her.

Is that really you?

Filling the kettle, Ele threw a tea bag into her mug and opened the fridge door. Don't cry. Never cry over him. It was strange. By the time she came to make her cup of tea, the milk in the bottle in her hand was warm and the kettle had cooled. Ele shook herself. Cobwebs filled her head; tiny spider legs tickling inside her skull, cocooning her thoughts. How much time had she lost? Ten minutes? An hour? More? Please God, not this again. *Not now.*

Closing the fridge door slowly, she reached for a tin on the side. Salted caramel cake. Not bothering to take it out, she pushed her hand into the soft sponge and sticky icing, stuffing more and more into her mouth until it became hard to swallow and there were only crumbs and smears of cream left.

Head pounding with pain, Ele glanced at the computer, but the screen had gone dark. She knew the message was still there. What should she do? Who could she talk to? Mum and Dad? No, they'd take it the wrong way. Maria? Hell no. Hadn't she learned her lesson yet?

Wondering how much time she'd lost, she had to boil the kettle a second time. It couldn't be starting again, could it? Just when she believed she'd climbed out of the mire that'd been dragging her down. Was God having a laugh then?

Schrodinger, her cat, was pawing at her leg, although it wasn't suppertime yet.

'Get off me, Schrody.' Hooking her foot under his stomach, she heaved him halfway across the room. Staring at the cat, now flicking his tail, his mottled black and umber fur spiky, she held out her hand.

'Sorry, *carido*,' she mumbled. 'Mean Mummy.'

It must be about the pact they'd made all those years before, when they were eighteen and naive, not tainted by the world. To meet when they were thirty.

'Oh, Schrody, my head hurts so much.' Sucking the icing out from beneath her fingernails, she tried to focus on the cat. 'You hungry, *carido*?'

Pouncing onto the worktop, the cat surveyed the inside of the tin, licking the remnants and bouncing it until it clattered off the edge. The sound made both Ele and the cat jump. Schrodinger slipped quickly under the sofa. She could see amber glints from where he watched warily from the safety of the dark, sat on the softness of the dust that never got hoovered.

It seemed to take an excessive amount of time for her to open a tin of cat food.

'Don't look at me like that, you ungrateful fur-bag. You're lucky to have this. I don't feel well, and I'm going to bed.'

A troubled night's sleep meant forcing herself out of the flat the next day was hard, but now Ele was absorbed by deciding whether to splash out on a yellow-skinned corn-fed chicken or a cheap pack of pallid chicken thighs. There was still an obstinate tap-tapping inside her skull that she had to ignore. Was Michael contacting her about their stupid pact? Tap. *Tap.*

Tinkling, tinny music and the odd blare of a blurry voice over a loudspeaker, with soft muted burbles of tired shoppers, was similar to white noise in the background.

She was startled when a voice shrieked right in her ear. A

moment of disorientation overwhelmed her. *That* voice shouldn't be here.

'*Oh my God!* Hey there, sister?' said a woman, standing in front of Ele. Her basket full of Christmas chocolate bars and festive crisps clattered to the floor. Startled Morrisons' customers hovering by the frozen ready meal aisle peered and tutted but moved away.

'Ele! Long time, no see.' Arms were flung around her, a sharp-nailed grip digging into her neck and back, more akin to strangulation than a hug. Over her shoulder, Ele could see the advertisements hanging jauntily across each aisle. Basted turkey crowns. Bottles of Baileys and Green's Ginger wine. The ubiquitous stalk of sprouts like a mad jester's wand. Christmas was overwhelming the shops, and spangly adverts on telly bawled at her daily about things she didn't want, yet *they* somehow knew she needed. Suffocating.

Ange. Long hair still dyed a most violent red, as if she'd dipped it in dried blood. Kohl-smeared eyes and black-painted nails, a tattoo curling from her shoulder up to beneath her heavily pierced ear, a stud through her lip. Looking twenty years older than the last time she'd seen her, although it couldn't be more than six or seven.

Had the air solidified?

The grip around her neck tightened. 'Christ! Ele. How long has it been?'

Ele felt the spit drying in her mouth. Dragging air into her lungs, she blinked rapidly. 'Ange. Jesus, what can I say? It's been a long time.' Not long enough. A million years wasn't long enough.

'How you doin', Babe? You're looking good.' There were cracks in Ange's voice as though it had shattered under duress. 'Still so beautiful. Just as I remember. How do you do it?'

'Wow, Ange.' There was a stutter to her voice that she

couldn't hide. 'Beautiful? Thanks, but I don't feel beautiful right now.' Ele focused and stared into the other woman's bloodshot eyes, aware of her breath reeking of stale alcohol. Bile rose up her throat. 'You're looking great too.' A lie. Always lies.

It'd never occurred to Ele she might bump into Ange in the Morrisons in Epping Forest. *How did she stay looking good now? By keeping away from the likes of her.*

The myriad bangles on Ange's thin wrists jangled discordantly as she moved to sweep hair from Ele's face.

'I've missed you, Babe. Not a day goes by when I don't think of you and, well, him.'

Ele resisted the urge to bat her hand away, shove her hard and run.

'I know. Me too.' The only way was to lie. How could she tell this woman that she'd spent years erasing every tiny detail from her mind? Didn't want to remember her, let alone *them*. How they'd *died.*

'*Fuck!*' Ange wiped her cheeks, smudging more kohl. 'I haven't dealt very well. Still can't believe it.'

'No. I know.' She had to get out of there. Could she shoulder her way through the sea of frazzled dead-eyed women, with trolleys piled skywards dragging small wailing children in their wake, pelt to the automatic doors and get lost in the fine drizzle that was now misting the windows?

'Oh, Babe.' Ange clung to her arm as though she sensed Ele might bolt. 'It's so good to see you. Do you live near here? Can we go back to yours, have a drink? Catch up?'

'No, I don't.' Ele's mind was turning a bright white. *Think.* 'I'm on my lunch break. I work close to here.' More lies. Her breath trickled out of her. 'Listen. Have you got a mobile? I'll give you my number, and we can arrange to meet up properly.'

'Yeah. Right.' Ange rummaged in her old stained leather bag and pulled out her phone. Wafts of patchouli oil belched out.

'Shame you can't make it now.' Hands trembling, she punched in the number that Ele reeled off, careful to change the last two digits. 'I'll call you now to check I've got it right.'

'*No!*' Ele swallowed. 'I mean, my phone's at my desk.'

'Really?' Ange squinted at her. 'You don't take it with you?'

'No. Not always. After all, it's my break, and sometimes I just need a bit of peace, you know?'

'Yeah, right. Can we meet after work? I need to talk to you. I'll walk back with you, so I know where it is.'

'Why not. That's a great idea.' What the hell was she going to do now, considering she didn't work anywhere near here?

Ange pointed. 'Is that what you have for lunch then?' The laugh that followed was sharp and hysterical. 'We used to snack on Nutriment cans, and chocolate washed down with a bottle of voddy or two. Looks like things have changed.'

Ele peered down at the contents of her basket. A lettuce, two tins of cat food and a can of tomatoes. 'I was just about to grab a sandwich.'

Ange bent to pick up her basket. 'Me too, same old, same old, when the munchies hit, you gotta do something about it.' She stared at Ele. 'You remember that, don't you, Ele?'

'Sure. Good times.' She saw the look on Ange's face. 'I mean us, before...' There was a sour smell in her nostrils.

'Yeah. Before.'

Ange's trembling fingers were stained a deep yellow. 'I've got some smoke if you want some?'

'Cheers, but I'm okay.' Waving her hand indiscriminately, she said, 'Still at work. Got to be a bit more professional now.'

'Professional? You? Hell. Things have changed, haven't they.'

Yes, they had, and her new life didn't include this ragged woman in front of her. There could be no going back. Ever. She couldn't bear the thought her life might spiral out of control again.

Carrying their plastic bags, they walked side-by-side up the main high street. The rain was easing off, leaving tiny drops like shiny crystal beads in their hair. As they passed a prominent solicitor's firm, Ele ducked in behind a man who'd already buzzed himself in. 'Thanks.'

He gave her a slightly startled look but no challenge. Maybe God was on her side, if just for a moment.

Turning to Ange, who stood in the same way as a lost child on the pavement, she said, 'Well, this is me. Don't get the wrong idea. I'm not a solicitor, merely a legal secretary.'

'That sounds way better than still being on the dole, like me.'

'It's just a job. It sounds more glamorous than it is. Pays the bills, that's all.'

'Okay. So, what time do you finish?'

'I'll be out close to six. Don't wait for me, Ange. That's a terrible waste of time. I promise we'll meet up.'

'Promise? Cross your heart and hope to die?'

Ele had to strap batons of steel across her heart to combat Ange's forlorn and helpless expression. Block her out. Completely. Then maybe she wouldn't be haunted by the *others*.

'Cross my heart.' She made the obligatory motion. Surely a little white lie was better than the hateful truth? She never ever wanted to see this woman again. Never wanted to remember that time.

Ange looked at the ground for a moment and nodded her head just once. 'Goodbye, Ele. It's been great seeing you again. We'll meet up soon, eh?'

'Yeah, sure.' As Ele let the door slide closed behind her, she heard one small sob. Waiting in the brightly lit foyer for a few minutes, she ignored the frowns of the woman seated at the reception desk.

'May I help you?' called the woman. Focusing on the

woman's blue-rinsed hair helped to block the thoughts swirling in her mind.

'No, I don't think anyone can help me. Thanks, though.'

'You need to sign in, get your visitor's badge.' She beckoned Ele over to the desk with arthritic, swollen fingers. Ele didn't move.

'I'm sorry, young lady. You either have to sign in if you've got business here or go. I'm afraid you can't just hang about in here.' The woman peered at her. 'Are you alright? You don't look well.' She was beginning to stand, to come over.

'I'm fine, thanks.'

Ele's body was slightly to the left of her as if she'd slipped out of it sideways. She saw her hand move. Was she moving it? The hand reached for the handle, the door opened, and her body stepped onto the pavement.

2

ELE

SOMETHING TERRIBLE

The memory hit her as though she'd driven at speed into a skip. Images, bright and sharp as splinters of glass, as if she'd gone through the windscreen.

Even though it was Sunday morning, the whole of London seemed to be on the move. The tube journey took far too long, and Ele had the beginnings of a migraine, lights spiralling at the corner of her vision and the promise of pain to come. She had to get back home fast before it hit properly. She rubbed at her temples. Where had she been anyway? Realising she was clutching a small holdall, she rummaged inside. Overnight stuff. Make-up, wash gear and her sleep T-shirt. She must've stayed over somewhere. But that was the point. Where?

Lingering in the next street, Ele took a deep breath and walked into her road. Somehow she already knew that something had happened. *Something terrible.* She stopped and stared. Fire engines were still there, although they'd put out the blaze. An ambulance was just that moment pulling out from the kerb. The lights and siren were not on. Was that a bad sign?

Ele stared up at the blackened carcass of the house. The front door was gone, all the windows blown out by the heat, the stairs, as she peered in, were smoking shards of burned wood. She took a step in, then another, seeing what was left of the kitchen. Half the wall tumbled down to show a view of the garden, melted things dribbling, a ghastly stench. She was turning as someone pulled her back.

'You're not allowed in here, miss.' A police officer was behind her, rigid and shocked.

'I live here.' She'd glimpsed Rab's room. The heat-scorched walls, the crisped sheets and duvet. She reeled, but he held her up.

'Come out of there,' he said. 'You need some air.'

Ele perched on the small wall outside, getting soot on her trousers, except now she didn't care. People were aimlessly milling about, some dirtied and some merely staring with mouths slack. She recognised a few of them. Their neighbours.

'Ele!' Ange was standing in front of her, trembling hands held out. 'He's dead. My Dave's dead!'

Ele stood, though her legs felt like they were made from rubber. 'Oh God, Ange. I've just got back. What the hell happened?' She pulled Ange into her arms, and they stood there, clinging to each other.

Ange reared back. 'Fuckin' Rab and his fuckin' eggs and toast!' Spittle sprayed from her mouth, now an ugly slit painted black. 'He fuckin' murdered Dave. Oh God, poor Dave.' Great sobs wracked her thin frame, and kohl was smeared like soot down her hollow cheeks.

'This is Rab's fault?'

'Fuckin' Rab! If the bastard wasn't already dead, I'd have fuckin' killed him.' Snot dribbled from her nose in stringy globules. 'Dave said so many times that one day we'd all burn to death in our beds, and now he's dead. Rab's killed them both.' Swinging around, she gripped Ele by the shoulders, her bony fingers digging into her flesh. 'That could've been us too. They could be carting our bodies off in an ambulance.'

Ele's gaze flicked to the shell of the house, an acrid stench creeping from it. 'Jesus wept! You're right.'

'I know you don't believe in angels, Ele.' Ange wiped her nose. 'But I think we had angels guarding us last night.'

Ele shook her head rapidly. What? Didn't believe in angels? Oh, she believed in them, alright. It was just that she hated them.

3

ELE

EPPING FOREST

Somehow, it was dusk by the time she stumbled up to her front door. How had that happened? It was definitely light when she'd stepped out of that solicitor's. There was a horrible taste in her mouth. Had she been sick? A faint memory of lunging over, vomit splattering. Her head was floating off towards the pile of pewter-coloured nighttime clouds glowering along the horizon. There was the tang of iron in the air.

Was Ange on her tail, accusations and recriminations on her tongue? She'd have to lock the door, shout for forgiveness through the letterbox. Or just scream, scream and scream until all the pain and darkness had enveloped her, and she'd pass out on the floor. She didn't want to remember, didn't need to be reminded, wasn't able to cope with the past. Today was the only day she was interested in, not even tomorrow until it too became today. Too much investment.

There were times when she felt she was in a small dark room and couldn't find a door or window. Patting round and round the walls made it worse, as she could never find her way out. It used to be Michael and Tiger who'd showed her how. They had always been the light that led her back. But neither of them had been there for her for years. Not after Michael's betrayal and Tiger's death had left her totally alone.

Dropping the Morrisons bag on the floor, the tins rolled out, the cheese and tomato sandwich greasy and wilting in its tiny plastic casing. It seemed to take forever to prise off her shoes, then she stood immobile on the rug in the middle of the living room. Renting a tiny one-bed flat at the edge of Epping Forest, she was practically as far out of London as you could get and still, ostensibly, be in London. And no, she wasn't a legal secretary. She'd built up a small bespoke business selling handmade chess and backgammon sets in the Covent Garden Craft market. And yes, she did live here, though that wasn't something to tell Ange, now was it.

Apart from her cat, she lived alone in her flat. She wasn't sure if the cat counted as a permanent resident as he was absent so frequently. Probably thieving from the neighbours. Rising up through the torpor, she poked at the mess on the floor with her toe, wondering if she had the strength to prepare dinner tonight. Once in a while, she'd tentatively open the pristine Nigella Express book she'd picked up in The British Heart Foundation's charity shop along the high street a couple of years earlier. From the look of it, its original owner had made as much use of it as she had so far. She expected a few species to flap out of it that hadn't been seen since the dawn of man. She'd been planning to cook something Italian from it. But the ability to read, concentrate and actually cook had been blasted away. Surely there must be a ready meal in the freezer?

As yet, there'd been no knock on the door. Had Ange taken her for her word, expecting a text or call? Or had she intrinsically understood that they'd shared too much, and now there was a barrier that couldn't be surmounted? Closing the curtains against anyone prying, she went through the motions. So now a dinner for one that didn't take a great deal of preparation, usually involving taking the outside carton off, punching holes into a thin sheet of plastic and microwaving the contents until thoroughly heated. No more than fifteen minutes to prepare and less than that to eat it.

Taking a deep breath that filled her lungs until she thought she might burst, she looked about her. She'd painted all the walls in her flat, some might say, rather startling colours to brighten it up (the hall was blue, the bathroom lilac and the main room a sunny yellow), but it couldn't disguise the fact that it was still damp, with a black furry mould that crawled towards the ceiling as the winter months drew in. Certain things never seemed to change. No, don't think about that either, as it reminded her of Michael. Now he'd come back into her life, she felt her little world shift. She knew he was waiting for a response, but what answer could she give him? And why so soon after had Ange rematerialised? It was unnerving. Both within the same week.

Had Michael contacted the others? Would they all go even if she decided not to? Of course, and they wouldn't even notice her conspicuous absence. No, no. Best to think about something else, more mundane and ordinary. What to do for Christmas, which was now only a week or so away. Should she visit her parents and pretend to be happy or huddle here, bah-humbug, with a box of chocolates and a big slab of Stilton? As a handicraft market stall trader, she'd still have to work Christmas Eve to catch all the disorganised, forgetful, 'haven't got a clue what to get her and now I've run out of time, and I'll have that and *make it snappy*' crowd. What! Not going to gift wrap it? Sometimes she loathed these people (who admittedly put the food on her table and paid her rent).

Her room was filled with knick-knacks; a fragile Chinese lantern that blocked the harsh glare of the spot lamp in the corner of the minuscule kitchen, battered leather suitcases picked up from flea markets, acquisitions bought or swapped from the market, not to mention the faux sycamore veneered wardrobe and dresser, with its large tarnished mirror from the 1930s. Standing in front of it, the woman it reflected back at her looked different. Twelve years had etched lines that scattered outwards from eyes and mouth. What did that say about her? Pulling her hair free, she tugged it, smoothing the curls down until she could no longer see herself. Is that how other people saw her too? Faceless? Ange had called her "beautiful". How could she be beautiful after all that had happened?

Draping a shawl over the mirror, she opted for a bit of telly, sat quietly in the dark, with only the flickering of the screen illuminating the room. David Attenborough and a bit of wildlife. None of the reality TV shows as she couldn't see the point of watching other people living their lives, albeit upgraded for the delectation of the prying audience. She'd seen too much of real life to be able to stomach the puerile antics of the fatuous would-be famous.

The bottle of vodka sitting on the side by the kettle called to her, but she chose not to listen to it. Not that route ever again. Especially with Ange. It was her warning.

Schrodinger nudged at her ankles. He was a coffee-table cat, completely square with four legs, one at each corner. If she didn't give him some grub soon, he'd be climbing up her trouser leg and clinging to her flesh; needle talons drawing blood as he clambered up to her shoulder to meow loudly into her ear. He usually shared what she ate, though, on occasions, she had the backup tins of expensive cat food. There were times when he ate better than she did.

'Here you go, *carido.*' She scratched him under his chin.

Ele scraped a big blob of meaty goo into his bowl. The rest she secured in a plastic bag and then stuck it on the lower shelf in the fridge. She'd got him as a rescue cat; needy and meek with grateful pawing. Now she knew that was just a ruse as he seemed pretty set in his ways, living a life of thievery and deceit. He cultivated the humans in the area until he won their confidence, and then he *struck*. Anything that could be stolen was far more interesting to him than being given something.

Now his baleful stare flicked to the mess in his bowl, then back at her. She could almost hear him say, "It's not worth it." Disdainfully he waddled off and flopped on the sofa, flicking his tail. She knew he was biding his time. She sure loved that cat. You always knew where you were with him. And that was under his furry little paw.

She went back to the computer. Maybe she could put it into perspective. After all, it had been a long time ago.

4

ELE
WIMPY GIRL

Michael Storm. Next door neighbour. Friends since childhood. Attended the same school. Lovers...

How long had it been since Ele had last seen Michael? Some memories were emblazoned in her mind in glorious Technicolor as though they were embroidered in rich threads, and others had faded to grey and fuzzy like an old worn doormat. At eighteen, they'd both moved to London, the Big Smoke, to become who they wanted to be, their real selves and not the mirage that was their teens. Ele's decadent, wood-panelled and balustraded design school was around the corner from where he was learning to be a hack, a bloodhound, a dealer in smut and lies. *A journalist.*

'Don't you revile my most esteemed profession,' he'd say. 'It's nearly the oldest, after prostitution.'

'And as revered,' she'd say.

There was no student campus of paid-for services to cushion them from the world of paying rent and utility bills. Of wondering where the cleaning fairy had nipped off to as dust in corners grew to the size of a cat and probably needed naming and putting a collar and bell on. They'd made the executive decision to rent a flat together. Then had the slit-eyed, grit-teethed arguments as to whose turn it was to wash up the pyramid of rancid bowls and grease-spattered pans stacked in the sink, who had to sort and put the rubbish and recycling in the allotted places and who had control of the TV remote.

But they were in love. Deeply, passionately and unashamedly in love. She remembered the wooden bed that creaked and rattled when they made love, spilling half-drunk tea perched on the bedstead. She could still see the black and sulphurous damp crawling up the wall in the living room towards the ceiling, even though they were paying a small fortune for this privilege. The view of Russell Square outside their flat window, where at night, the drunks slept on benches, curled into nests of newspapers. As the sun crested, the scenery changed, much as if the whole park had been spun around to show the happy families that chucked frisbees and picnicked on Moroccan blankets. So much falafel and hummus, and elderberry cordial. So cosmopolitan and sophisticated. How very *them*. Spreading their blanket too, picked up in a flea market in Camden, they'd open their tubs of olives and feta and pull the cork on a bottle of fruity red. Pretend to be adults. And they'd talk about anything and everything: from the immensity of the universe to the life cycle of a mayfly.

How things had changed.

Is that really you?

Staring at that friend request again, Ele admitted her heart did a somersault to rival that of any American cheerleader. Her finger hovered uncertainly. She finally hit 'accept' and waited. The green dot by his name meant he was already online. His response was fast.

Do you remember the pact? he asked.

Of course, I do.

I've arranged it all. The meet. New Year's Eve. I'll give you the details and don't worry, it's my treat.

Ele bridled a bit at that. Did he, after all these years, still think she couldn't look after herself? That she needed paying for? It was like holding out his hand and then hitting her over the head with a wooden mallet hidden in a woolly glove. And add to that the fact he assumed she'd go, that she didn't have more tempting offers. Even if she hadn't.

She read his next line. *I've got a story.*

Ele could easily visualise the expression on his face; silver-blue eyes lit up in excitement as though it was Christmas and Santa had filled the stocking to overflowing.

It's a big one, and it's utterly crazy

Are you going to tell me?

Now, where would be the pleasure in that. No, I'll tell you face-to-face.

This was the crux. *Have you contacted everyone else?*

Not yet. You're the first. What would be the point of sorting it all out if you decided not to come? You are going to come, aren't you?

She hesitated. Her fingers had become dunked in liquid nitrogen. If she moved them, they would crack off.

You are, aren't you?

I'll let you know tomorrow.

After two years of paying for damp and squalor, she and Michael had been told about co-operative housing in London.

Ele knew she shouldn't admit to fear; still, she'd blurted out: 'Doesn't that mean we have to live with other people?'

Michael had squinted at her as though she'd suddenly

spoken in Russian. 'Yes, but we have our own room, and it's really cheap. We need that right now if we're going to save for our own place.'

That clinched it. Saving for their own place. She'd walk every day barefoot on burning coals if this co-op house meant that.

It was Ange who'd shown them both to the house, where they were to sign on the dotted line. Central location in London and the minimal rent was not to be sniffed at, was it?

Ele discovered that Ange, living in another co-op house further up the street, was dating Dave, one of their prospective new flatmates. Judgements and book jackets. She'd been frightened of Ange and her untamed looks and crazy ways, never realising that in time she would surpass her.

She appraised the house. Staring suspiciously at the cracked windows and grubby walls, she noted the sticky heaps of crisp packets and Mars bar wrappers adorning the bin bags packed on top of each other in the tiny yard that fronted the building. This was to be their new home? *Jesus wept!* But they still moved in, as money was money after all.

Ange would be there sporadically with Dave. Their relationship was as fiery as the colour of her hair. Doors slamming and screaming meant they'd fallen out again. Just the screaming meant they'd made up. Big Dave, usually a quiet, unassuming man, unfortunately, turned into a monster after eating, drinking and smoking as many drinks and drugs as he could. Three degrees under his belt but still living much like a squatter. Being so bloody clever, he constantly thought about the state of the world, was terrified by his conclusions, and so turned to whatever could console him.

Often, Ange would join him in his revelries, and Ele couldn't work out which one of them was the worst. They sang songs into the night, sounded similar to animals howling from the bad trips they had, banged about in the kitchen when they had the munchies and were trying to find something sweet to eat, and then the very loud and boisterous lovemaking.

And then there was Rab, their other new flatmate, threatening violence in every movement, and none of them wanted to be on the receiving end of that.

Of course, Michael acted as though he'd always been living the city life. Unafraid of the myriad ways to get lost on the tube, unfazed by the sheer volume of people crowding and pushing along the pavements, able to negotiate his way across the city, whether topside or in the bowels. Ele tried to put on a mask, to pretend that she was okay. The problem wasn't even the state of the house they lived in. States can be altered if not for the better, then at least for the tolerable. The problem was the people you lived with. If they were intolerable, they more than likely remained intolerable no matter what your address. It was no good being scared of the loonies who paced the streets outside if most of them had keys to your house and lived in the room next to you. But Ele loved Michael so much, that she made a decision. Wimpy Girl had to be crushed underfoot, as if she was a deadly poisonous Brazilian wandering spider that leaps out of bananas and scares the shit out of you.

In hindsight, *Wimpy Girl* should've been listened to.

Clicking out of Facebook, she noticed she was shaking. Michael Storm. Where have you been all these years? Could she really meet him again?

Stripping off her clothes, she wiggled into an old, black, baggy T-shirt with the words 'the truth is out there' printed on it. Then she drank a glass of water and cleaned her teeth. But she didn't go straight to bed. She stood and stared at the street light glinting off the bottle in the corner, accentuating its curves, shimmering in its depths. Don't fall now, not after everything. Not quite closing her bedroom door, she pulled the duvet up tight around her neck and rolled over, except she could still see Michael like he'd been projected on the wall in front of her. As though she'd only seen him yesterday. Hearing Schrodinger snoring, she found comfort in that sound.

5

LIANG

SAN FRANCISCO

Life had been pretty tricky. Liang wasn't complaining as she'd brought it on herself. Sometimes you have to fling your hands up in the air and admit, loudly, you made a stupid mistake. The absolute worst mistake of your life. She guessed she was still in shock, waking at night with a terror enveloping her akin to being wrapped in a sodden death shroud, but she wasn't dead. Someone was shovelling earth over her until she couldn't drag in another breath, and she was suffocating.

Days were better when she could find space under a tree in the Golden Gate Park close to where she worked. She would lay on her back to spy the vast sky above her through the ever-shifting leaves, her naked toes scrunched into the cool wispy grass, wary of shadows around her but she kept them at bay. Since she'd got out, it was as if she experienced the smell of early summer, the scent of flowers, newly mown grass, barbecues, for the first time. Today, winter was creeping in. Crisp, clean, the brilliant colours of life dying back. Kicking through the fallen leaves and watching for thunderheads building up and the smell of metal in the air. Doused in scent, Paul Smith's *Rose*, not that it could dilute the stench that was still in her mind, her memory. She couldn't expunge that. After all she'd experienced, six months of liberty couldn't ever wipe out the seven previous years.

San Francisco, with all its exotic vagaries, was like ascending to heaven. Being brought up an atheist by Communist parents, she'd never believed in God. Yet in those seven long years, she wondered if he did exist. Would it have made it easier if she'd believed in God? Or would it seem as though he'd also turned his back on her?

Now free, Liang had to fight daily, sometimes hourly, to push the images out of her consciousness that threatened to overwhelm her. Her freedom. That was all she should concentrate on. Nothing else. Her beloved uncle had found her a job, pulled strings and called in favours, as they say. After all, who'd want a woman with her record? But big companies needed translators, and there weren't that many who could fluently translate back and forth between Cantonese and English. They could turn a blind eye to that. The pay was more than enough to live off as her needs were so minimal now. Food, water, shelter. Basic and functional. Somehow it felt indecent to have her nails done, to wax her bikini area and have a facial, when before she'd been scrabbling in the dirt, fighting for scraps with other women who looked at you as if you were prey. Sometimes it was only the grass under her feet and the scudding clouds overhead that stopped her wanting to die. Perhaps freedom was never about walls and barbed wire; it was the space in your head.

San Francisco was gearing up for Christmas. Gorgeous holiday lights were being erected, ballet, musicals and even the Cirque du Soleil were being advertised. Crowds bustled down Lombard

Street, visiting the Japanese Tea Garden, or were entranced by the murals in the Mission.

Liang, though, was standing on the Golden Gate Bridge, staring at the water glittering below, only remembering the horror of b*efore*. Seven years of her life spent in a hell of her own making. She did survive; maybe she went a little mad too. Well, who wouldn't? Freedom has its own price if you can't forget. The anxiety is always there, making you hoard food in your room in case, suddenly, for whatever reason, it isn't there one day, and you're back to having your ribs stick out much as a child's glockenspiel.

Her life now should've been filled with wonder, yet somehow each day got heavier and heavier to bear. She must've been moving, starting to reach up onto struts, clamber, zombie-like, upwards to get to that sweet oblivion below. Was she seriously contemplating jumping?

'Hey,' said a deep voice, 'I wondered if you'd like to have a coffee with me?'

His voice brought her back as though she'd been in a tight elastic band, pulling it as far as she could. Now it'd snapped, and she was catapulted into the present, red-faced with shame and fear. It took a moment to be able to see clearly. She felt his hand lightly on her shoulder, ready to grab and hang on should she… change her mind? Liang looked up, and there he was: eyes akin to looking into a wild sea, dark hair with a smear of grey at the temples. She recognised that soft Irish accent. There were many Irish here with their clover leaves and Guinness and dark bars full of laughter and heavy fists. He stared at her, and there was a strange look on his face.

'I'm sorry,' he said, 'but you look like someone I know.' He winced. 'I mean someone I knew.' Pain flitted across his face as though he'd been stung suddenly by a wayward wasp.

'I don't get that often,' she said, 'unless I'm in China. Then I don't seem as though I'm the odd one out. But I'm not who you knew. I'm not that person.' Was that a ridiculous thing to say?

'I know you're not.' He blinked rapidly and stared somewhere above her head.

Liang peered swiftly over her shoulder. 'I wasn't going to jump. I just want to make that clear.'

'Of course not.' He pulled his hand from her slowly, and it was as if the sun had slipped behind a cloud.

'I'm Michael.' He extended his hand again, formal, courteous. 'Michael Storm.'

'Liang.' She shook his hand, feeling the texture of his skin against her own, watching the tendons flex, noticing the tattoo on his forearm of a yin-yang symbol. She knew what that signified. Complementary forces interacting to form a dynamic system in which the whole is greater than the parts. As in the natural world, light cannot be light unless darkness shows it off. She'd been in the dark. Now she searched for the light.

'So,' he said, 'do you fancy coming for a coffee with me? Or do you have better things to do?' He glanced at the water sliding greasily past below the bridge.

'I only drink tea, but that aside, I'm quite free at the moment.' She laughed, and he looked surprised. 'I'm sorry. That's kind of like an inside joke. With myself.'

'Okay,' he said, 'maybe you'll tell me later.'

But that's it. How much could she tell him? This beautiful Irish man in front of her, who came with wings outstretched, her guardian angel to save her from herself. They started to walk, and the pull of the river lessened its hold over her. So what should she tell him over sweet tea and a Danish? The truth? Watch him make excuses and flee out the door, the tea half-drunk and cooling on the smeared table, two bites from his pastry. The truth is not easily digested. It has to be broken down into little easy to swallow chunks. But two cups of tea and cakes later, he was still sitting at the table, with empty cups and plates.

'Tell me, Liang,' he said, and his eyes were now flinty grey, 'have you ever been to England?'

She nodded. 'Once. A long time ago.'

'Do you want to go back?'

'Every minute of every day.' Liang frowned. 'That must sound mad. It's more I want to go back but in time as well as place. Can you understand that?'

'Yes. I know that feeling.' He looked downwards. Was he also remembering something? 'You want to go back to change the things you did, but time travel doesn't exist. Yet.'

'Not for want of praying for it.'

'Was it really that bad? What's happened to you, Liang?'

'More than you could believe.'

'I'm here if you want to talk about it.'

'No. That part of my life is over. A fresh start.'

'I *will* see you again tomorrow.' Michael had his phone out to punch in her details. There was no brooking defiance, no letting a false number sneak out of her mouth. She gave it to him. They parted with a demure air kiss and a shake of the hand.

'Tomorrow?' He smiled at her, teeth just showing, a little bite of his lip. Liang nodded because she couldn't risk her voice in case no words came out. Tomorrow. There'd been a time when "tomorrow" meant so many things. Days that expanded, seconds morphing into the next, each minute an agony and her heart crying out for release. Times when she could see that tiny glimmer of hope that she might leave that dreadful place. She knew that hope was something she could ill afford, would make her more vulnerable than she already was.

Wasn't she free? She'd paid the price for what she'd done. It was over now. Surely she could start to live again?

She found her voice. 'Yes, tomorrow.'

6

HOPE
BRIXTON

Standing with the other mums and a couple of dads by the school gates, Hope felt that creeping uneasiness that radiates from the pit of your stomach when she saw who was emerging from the front entrance. *Please, not again.* Hope focused on all the little kids running towards waiting outstretched arms, some with shoelaces trailing, coats half on, even though it was cold enough for her breath to *huff* visibly in the air. She saw some of the children were bearing gifts made in their art lessons. She hummed, *'Tis the season to be jolly.* Hope knew that soon, they would be swamped with badly cut and stuck together Christmas decorations, giant floppy Christmas cards and the odd unidentifiable plaster object that was supposed to be a reindeer or an elf. Or something.

'Mummy?' Her daughter Mia, who was nearly five, trotted up to her, and Hope enveloped her in a great big hug. She pulled Mia's coat tighter around her and zipped her up to her neck.

'Hello, gorgeous.' Cupping her daughter's face, she smoothed back the mass of dark curls.

'Look what I made.' There was such pride in her voice. Mia waved a painting. 'Miss S said it was very good.'

'It's wonderful, darling.'

'It's Rudolf, you know, the red-nosed reindeer.' Hope felt relief that she'd been enlightened as to what it was supposed to be. It looked a mass of coloured daubs. More impressionist than realistic.

'Of course, it is. I can see his big red nose there.' She pointed.

'That's Santa! He's there.' Mia indicated a strange brown and red blob and scowled.

'I knew that.' Hope pinched at her cheeks. 'Silly.'

Mia giggled and glanced across the playground. A strange look crossed her face.

'Mummy?'

Hope turned. She could see movement; first a ripple and then a swelling. The crowd of parents parted, moved aside, all, Hope knew, quietly relieved that *she* wasn't heading like a cannonball in their direction. *She* being the headteacher.

'Mrs Klaus?' The woman puffed up to Hope.

'Miss Dunbar?' said Hope. 'I hope there's nothing wrong?' But of course there would be, else why would the headteacher be barrelling her way towards her? The woman stomping up to Hope always reminded her of Agatha Trunchball from Roald Dahl's book *Matilda*. And she had the same sunny personality. She ground to a halt inches from Hope and swayed as if the sheer momentum of her bulk couldn't be stopped that fast. Mia clutched her hand hard and stepped behind Hope. Hope wondered who *she* could step behind.

'Mrs Klaus, is it possible to have a couple of minutes of your time. We need to talk to you about George.'

'Yes, Miss Dunbar, but where is he? I've come to pick them both up.' Hope waggled Mia's arm to show that at least she had one of her kids. But she knew where George was. He was where he always was. In detention. George. Eight years old. How could an eight-year-old cause as much trouble as he did?

The headteacher, Miss Dunbar, led Hope and Mia across the playground into the brightly lit reception area. Hope could hear the muted mutterings of the other parents behind her. Making judgements, naming names. Blaming. The diminutive woman behind the front desk waved, and half smiled at Hope. 'Mrs Klaus.'

Everyone knew Hope at school. *She was George's mum.*

'Miss Sensier will look after Mia.' Miss Dunbar indicated a slim, pretty brunette who was sat waiting patiently in the foyer. Hope knew that Mia adored this sweet young teacher, Miss S as she called her, and she'd be in good hands.

'Come this way.' Miss Dunbar lumbered down the corridor, and then up a flight of steps that made her wheeze. Hope followed behind, hanging onto a polished but slightly sticky bannister, and was ushered into the headteacher's office. Hope longed to turn tail and run. It must be mega serious if she was in the Head's office and not the usual interview room downstairs. Photos of school productions adorned the walls, with kids in wild costumes against wobbly looking backdrops. Sometimes Hope had the urge to lob a brick at all the self-satisfied faces smiling brightly out at them. George would never be in one of them. Would never have the chance, never be allowed.

'Mrs Klaus,' Miss Dunbar cleared her throat. 'It's always difficult to have these conversations with a parent, especially ones that work as hard as you do to accommodate your son's... needs.'

'Okay, I appreciate that. So, what's he done this time?' She really didn't want to know.

'I don't know how he got hold of it, but he had a flare.'

'A flare? What... *what?*'

'Similar to the sort we usually have in our roadside emergency kit.' Miss Dunbar closed her eyes briefly. 'They produce light through igniting something similar to a firework, so it doesn't so much explode as burn.' She sighed loudly. 'Exploding or burning, it's still serious. We have no idea where George picked it up or what he thought it was. Unfortunately, the thing is, it is still counted as a weapon. The fact that he launched it into the main corridor moments after the bell to sound the end of school–'

'He did what?' Hope was out of her chair. 'Oh my God! Was anyone hurt?'

'Apart from setting fire to the canteen door and us having to deal with a lot of frightened children, unbelievably no one was injured, although it was a potentially lethal act. This was wilful and malicious destruction of school property and add to that the threat to the safety of the other children, this is serious indeed. I will have to talk to the Board of Governors on Monday, but as we are so close to Christmas, I'm excluding George for the rest of this term and pending investigation, there might well be a recommendation for expulsion. We'll let you know if this is permanent or if he will be allowed to return in the spring.' Miss Dunbar shook her head. 'I'm also sorry to say you might well be billed for the damage caused by George's actions.'

Hope bit her lip hard. Swallowing, she said, 'I understand completely. I'm so sorry.' Hands shaking, she fumbled in her coat pocket, but the headteacher was ahead of her. She was handed a paper hankie from a box on the desk. 'Thank you.'

'I'm sorry too, Mrs Klaus. This is an extremely grave situation. We have to think of the welfare of all the other children in the school.'

Hope nodded. 'Where is he?'

'He's in the Science block. Mr Collins kindly took him. I think he's trying to instil in George how dangerous this was.'

'He'll be lucky. George doesn't understand the concept of danger, not to himself or others.'

'He'll need to get to grips with this before too long, or it'll have a terribly detrimental impact on his wellbeing.'

'That's something we're aware of, and we're working on it. Again, I'm so sorry.'

Miss Dunbar looked down at her desk and shuffled a few bits of paper around. 'We try our best here, Mrs Klaus. You know we're a small school in the heart of Brixton, catering for every ethnic group, speaking at least five different languages, and usually English isn't the main language spoken at home. We just don't have the resources to look after a child with your son's needs. I wish we could. I heartily wish we could cater for every single one of them. As they keep telling us, every child matters, but not when it comes to funding, it seems.'

'Thank you for trying.' Hope rose. She'd seen another side to the usually choleric Head. Perhaps she'd misjudged her. Mind you, they probably saw more of George than she did. What a thought that was.

'I'll call through to Science, and Mr Collins will bring George out to reception.' Miss Dunbar held out her hand. 'Merry Christmas, Mrs Klaus.' There was a layering of sadness in the other woman's voice as she shook Hope's hand.

Hope smiled as best she could, even though all she longed to do was sob her guts out.

'Merry Christmas, Miss Dunbar.'

Walking back to reception, Hope felt as though she was sleepwalking. George had let off a flare in school at the time when it was at its most packed. What if he'd hurt another kid? What if someone had *died?* What if he'd killed Mia? Why would the school even contemplate allowing him back next term? She couldn't envision any of the parents condoning that. She wouldn't, and she was his mother! She wiped the wetness from her face.

Mia was sitting with Miss Sensier, looking through a picture book.

'Well, Mia,' said Miss Sensier, rising in one fluid motion, 'I have to go now. Have a lovely weekend. I'll see you Monday. Only three more days to go after that, and then you'll be on holiday.' The teacher raised an eyebrow. 'Will we be seeing George on Monday?'

Hope shook her head.

'Okay. Then have the best Christmas that you can.' She looked a little embarrassed. 'You know what I mean.'

Hope watched Miss Sensier pass George as he was led up towards her with a huge, burly man in a white coat with glasses and usually a big grin. He wasn't smiling now.

'Mr Collins.' Hope could barely look at him.

'Mrs Klaus. We've been having a little talk about thinking things through before doing something, haven't we, George?'

'What?' George's leg was jiggling, and he was looking around the room. 'What are you gawping at, Mia?' George pounced on the book, pulling it from Mia's hands.

Mia tried to hang onto the book. There was the sound of ripping. 'I was looking at that, George! Give it back.'

'I've got it now.'

Hope reached out to part them. 'George, you've broken the book. Oh, Mr Collins, I'm so sorry–'

'That's okay. We'll try to get it mended.' He nodded at George. 'Best to get him home now.'

But George spent only a minute flicking through it before chucking it aside. The spine snapped, and pages fell out onto the floor. 'Are we going home now, Mum?'

'George? You were listening to what Mr Collins told you, weren't you?'

'Yeah, sure. Whatever. I want to go home now. I want to play on my X-Box.' The fidgeting was worsening. Hope knew that if she didn't get him home soon, then she'd have a full-blown meltdown to deal with. Grabbing him by the hand and shooing Mia out ahead of her, she turned and called over her shoulder. 'I'm so sorry, we'll deal with this when we get home.'

As she pulled her children out the main entrance door, she could see the relief on the teaching staff's faces. They didn't want to have to deal with her son either. This was definitely a red alert situation. Paul would still be at work, but she needed the "heavy guns". Whatever she said to George tended to whizz over his head, although there were times, maybe only moments, when he might listen to his father and understand what was being said. But now, she had the spectre of George not returning to school. Homeschooled? Not in this lifetime. She still had at least a couple more years left until her son would be attending the local comprehensive. She didn't think she'd be able to last that long. She could scarcely do the six-week holiday in the summer, and she still had a two-year-old at home, as well as Mia.

Happy *blooming* Christmas. Hope lit a cigarette as they walked back, exhaling out the side of her mouth. Maybe now was not the time to give up.

7

ELE

EPPING FOREST – 13 DAYS AND COUNTING

A tap on the door was scary enough at any time, but now it made Ele crouch down by the side of the sofa. Not that she expected visitors at any time, nevermind Sunday evening. This was usually a 'no-go' period for most people, as the glowering presence of work the next day was hanging above them all.

The curtains were still closed, although there were cracks where anyone could peer through. Could she be seen hiding? Was she able to slink to the bedroom like a ferret on its belly? Hang on, get a grip here. Was she a grown woman or what? Straightening her shoulders, she inhaled deeply. There, better.

The tapping became more insistent.

'Ele? Ele, it's me. Maria. Let me in. It's so bloody cold.' The voice had a rich accent, full of rolled r's and soft lisping.

Maria? *Maria!*

Envisioning that it was Ange at her door had left no room for this. Ele couldn't even remember the last time she'd seen Maria. Even though it was cold enough in the room for her breath to show, her face felt hot and sweat prickled at her temples.

'*Ele!* Come on now, *carida.* You know I hate your awful British winters.'

It took a moment to command her legs to move. Her toes seemed to be rooting in the carpet, not wanting to let go.

'Okay. Just give me a moment.' Fumbling at the lock, she dropped the key twice before opening the door a crack. 'What are you doing here, Maria?' There was a deep and fast thumping in her head.

'Nice greeting there. Let me in, *tonta!*' Maria pushed past Ele, gave her a brief hug and went to perch on the edge of the sofa.

Jesus! How stunning she was. Her sister, sometimes more her twin. Long dark wavy hair, curves in the right places, eyes as if gazing into a summer woodland pool reflecting the trees and leaves above. She never changed, not really. Maybe if you looked closely, you might find tiny lines radiating out, but they were laughter lines. Not the sort of lines that Ele saw on her own face. They were similar in many ways but yet different in so many more.

'Maria, don't call me stupid. You know I hate that.' The door slammed. It was amazing how Maria could come in and take over any place she walked into. Much as where she put her feet was automatically her space and sod anyone else in the vicinity.

'Then don't be stupid. I've come a long way to visit you. You should be a little more gracious, no? I presume you have coffee, I mean real coffee, not that powdered rubbish the English drink.' Draping her coat over the back of the small chair by the sofa, she fingered at Ele's CD collection in the shelving unit that ran down one side of the room. '*Madre mia!*' She made the sign of the cross over her chest. 'Please tell me you're not still listening to all this crap.' Pulling out a case, she waved it at Ele. 'The Pet Shop Boys? How old are you, Ele? Where is Jaga Jazzist and Ellie Goulding?'

'First off, yes, I'm still Spanish, so of course, I've got coffee.' Rummaging in the cupboard, the silver coffee percolator was on the stove in only a minute, the aroma of fresh coffee wafting across the room. 'And if you look a little closer, you'll see I've got Rihanna, so don't judge me yet.' She smiled. There was never going to be a "please" or "thank you" from Maria. There was the inherent assumption that she expected to be waited on hand and foot.

'Brrr,' said Maria. 'I have to put the heating on. God, Ele. How can you live in such a cold, damp place?'

Ele saw the old oil radiator hauled out and the *click* as it was switched on. Again, no consideration of cost. Maria was cold, so Maria must be warmed up.

'It's where I live, you know that.' Two sugars were ladled in. They both enjoyed their coffee sweet and dark.

'Where's Schrody? That old cat will warm me up.' She whistled the sharp tune she used to attract the cat's attention, which always annoyed the heck out of Ele.

'He's probably under the duvet in the bedroom.' Ele handed a mug of coffee to Maria and sat on the other corner of the sofa. 'I haven't seen you in ages, so why are you here?'

'I got a feeling about you. You know?'

'What sort of feeling?'

'That you weren't in a good space.' Maria blew on her coffee.

'How did you know that? I haven't spoken to you in so long. I can't even remember if it was this year or last.'

'I just know. Tell me what's going on, Ele.' Tucking her long hair behind her ears, she stared at Ele. 'And don't hold out on me. I can tell when you're lying.'

'Okay. You're not the only person who's suddenly materialised back into my life. I bumped into Ange yesterday.'

'Ah. That explains the hiding.'

'*Joder!* You saw that?'

'You're the Mistress of Skulking.' Maria sipped at her coffee, steam twisting in front of her, obscuring her for a moment. 'What did she want?'

'To talk.'

'Why didn't you invite her back here. Tell her the truth?'

'I can't do that. Not after everything that happened at the house.'

'Not surprising. But maybe you should tell her. Maybe she has the right to know?'

'If I say anything, her whole world will shatter. It'd destroy her. I know it will, and I can't be responsible for that.'

'But *your* world was shattered. Doesn't that matter then?'

'Not in the great scheme of things. I'm over it. You sorted that out.'

'She may not know about Dave, but she knew about Rab. She knew what that scum did to you.'

'Yeah, she was there, so of course, she knew.'

'What did she do about it?'

'What could she do? Who in their right mind would go up against him, for God's sake? He was a total nutter!'

'A friend. A true friend would.'

'We're not all as strong as you, Maria.'

'No, but she knew you hated Rab, so would she not suspect that something was off, especially as you weren't there the night it happened. Convenient, eh?'

'I was with you. Anyway, why would anyone think that I had anything to do with it? That's ridiculous. I may have hated the both of them and wished them a horrible death, though I wouldn't go *that* far.'

'You're absolutely right. Nothing to worry your pretty little head about.'

'That's really condescending.'

'But it proves a point. Looks as though my intuition was spot on. Good thing I dropped in to see if you were okay. As you say, it's been a while.'

'Listen, I'm fine, well, terrific actually...' Ele paused. 'Mostly.'

Maria kicked off her shoes and wiggled back into plump cushions. There was a streak of black and orange. Ele noted Schrodinger was now draped amicably across her. Unbelievable! Maria even managed to monopolise the damn cat.

'Mmm, good coffee.' Maria tickled Schrody, and he stretched, long legs pointing, then he nestled into a ball in her lap. 'How's work? Still selling okay at the market?'

'Are you changing the subject?'

'Yes. For the moment.'

Ele sighed. 'I have good and bad days, like anyone.' The heat from the radiator made her relax. 'It's crazy that my livelihood depends on a whim. That someone passing will find the colours of the boards and the shapes of the pieces I've chosen to put out that day attractive. That it will be enough to put their hand in their pocket and pass a wedge of money to me.'

'You look as if you're doing alright.'

'I think I need a backup plan. I might teach the cat to steal–'

'He does that already, doesn't he?'

'I meant for me. He can sneak into the neighbours' and nick their cuppa soups for me.'

'Push the boat out, why don't you.' Maria rubbed at her neck. 'Are you okay?'

'Slept badly last night. So what are you going to do about Ange? A. Spend the rest of your life sneaking about? B. Try to avoid her? C. Move completely? Or D. Kill her?'

'Yes to the first two and hopefully no to the last two. I'm happy here, and I don't want to be forced out of my home. Why should I? I haven't done anything wrong except try to get my life back together.'

Maria looked at her with that special look she seemed to reserve just for her.

'I haven't done anything wrong, have I?'

'No... ' The word was drawn out, playful. Maria smiled. 'No, not you.'

'What's that supposed to mean?'

'Only that we need to keep you as far away from Ange as possible. It didn't end well, did it.'

'That... that day. Was I staying around yours? It's strange because sometimes I can't quite remember.'

'Well, der. We had nothing to do with the fire.'

'Who said we had something to do with it?'

'It was insinuated.'

Ele stood up. 'By whom?'

'Now, don't worry. It was all taken care of.'

'You mean *you* took care of it?'

'Don't I always?' Maria stroked Schrodinger's tiny head. Ele could hear deep rumblings from inside of him.

'Yes, but that's what people don't like. It's the way you do things.'

'I don't care about other people. You should know that by now.' Maria suddenly shifted and leaned forward. 'Sit down, Ele and tell me if there is anything else going on.'

'What do you mean?' Ele tore her gaze from Maria.

She sat back down heavily. Both Schrodinger and Maria were staring intently at her.

'I don't know, I've still got that feeling. As though you've missed something out. What haven't you told me?'

'Nothing.' There were moments when it felt that Maria could see inside her head, was able to run her fingers over her soul and read her as if she was braille. Sometimes, it was too much, and she wasn't amused by it. They might be sisters, but certain things should remain private.

Maria swept her long dark hair from her face. Amber glints shone in her eyes as though they were beginning to catch on fire. 'Are you holding out on me, *carida?*'

'No. Listen, I don't like it when you get so nosey–'

'Nosey is it? I'd term it being protective, caring for someone I love–'

'Okay. Still, I want you to go now, Maria. I've got a migraine coming on, and I need to go to bed.'

'Another migraine? Okay.' Maria uncurled slowly, unceremoniously shoved the cat to the floor and retrieved her shoes. 'You know where to find me. I'll be there when you need me.'

'*If* I need you.'

'No. *When*. You know I'll always be there for you. As I always have been.'

'I know, Maria. Please, you have to let me sort out my own life. You can't do it for me. I have to do this myself. I'm not a kid anymore.' Ele could hear the whining tone in her voice. How could Maria always bring her to this point?

'*Bueno*. One final thing. I shouldn't have to remind you but don't tell Mum and Dad that I'm around again. You know they don't understand about us.'

'As I said, I'm not stupid.' Ele watched as Maria shrugged into her coat. 'Where are you staying?'

'Oh, around and about. Are you feeling bad that you're sending me back out into the cold? You should be.'

Ele thought about it. Maria was right. Her parents would be mad if they knew that Maria was with her. But she was here, wasn't she? Having gone to the trouble of visiting, how mean would it be to turf her out the door. And yes, it was bloody cold. What a crappy sister she was.

Ele sighed. 'Do you want to stay the night? We can share like we used to?'

'Sense at last.' Maria's coat was whipped off in a second. 'But you put the light out. You know I'm afraid of the dark.'

8

ELE

SO MANY 'WHAT IF I'D JUST…'

As Ele drifted off to sleep, an image of Rab came unbidden into her mind. She squirmed. Rab. The short, wiry and feral Glaswegian who lived on the ground floor at the front of the house. Nobody picked on Rab twice. Surely the broken nose, the myriad tattoos and the ample scarring should have been a clue, but no, there was always some idiot in the pub that felt inclined to have a go, and Rab, bless him, felt inclined to lump them back. Many times. Ele gathered from Ange and Dave, who'd seen this happen before, that it was as if they were watching a tiny typhoon that sucked up and smashed anything in its path.

At least once a week, usually on a Friday or Saturday, she'd open the bedroom door and be hit by a wall of heat. Rab would come home late, very, *very* drunk, put two boiled eggs and two slices of toast on, return to his bedroom where he turned his music on loud and passed out, leaving his food to char. Quite often, she crawled down the stairs as early as five in the morning to creep into his room to turn off his music. Manoeuvring the oven away from the wall to lessen the scorch marks, the toast was always tiny rectangles of carbon. Once the pan had cooled off, popping sporadically, the eggs resembled grey marble when peeled, even down to the consistency. Rab always denied all knowledge of these events, not that she dared to challenge him. But she had often heard Big Dave shouting at him about it.

There was something about Rab that made you want to avoid him as though he had a miasma of violence that hung about him like a heady perfume.

'Keep out of Rabbie's way.' Big Dave told her. 'He's not the nicest guy in the neighbourhood.'

How ironic that in the end, it was the eggs and toast that killed them both.

Her overactive mind brought the memory to the forefront, even though she'd tried to bury it deep. Soon, she was worrying at it like poking with your tongue at a loose tooth.

'It was Ele's idea to leave it in your room,' said Big Dave.

Ele was listening, her bedroom door slightly ajar. It'd never occurred to her that taking an envelope from some dodgy-looking bloke on their doorstep and leaving it in Rab's room could cause this much trouble. How was she supposed to know that he was a plainclothes copper? And he was out to get Rab?

'*Was it now?*' By the tone of his voice, she knew then that it would not be good.

Ele heard Rab's footsteps coming up the uncarpeted stairs, hard and heavy. This man wasn't going to stop.

'Ele?' Such a soft voice, so quiet. The quieter he was, the more it was going to hurt.

She looked around her for something to wedge up against the door.

'I know yer's in there, so doon't make me keck the feckin' door en.'

'I'm really sorry.' Leaning with all her weight against the door, she held the handle up, but it was as though she was a child as he pushed through. She'd never been hit in her life. The blow across her face sent her reeling backwards until she crashed into a wooden sideboard. Pain shot up from her elbow. Her cheek was on fire, and something wet dribbled down her chin.

'Don't ye eva do something es stupid es that agin, or you'll git more an' this.'

Ele slumped to her knees, clinging to the leg of the sideboard. 'I said I was sorry.' She wiped at her mouth, blood daubing her hand. She held it out to him: an accusation. 'Holy shit, you didn't have to hit me, for Christ's sake.'

'Ye shut the fuck up, now girly.' And then he got her by her hair and cracked her face against the edge of the sideboard.

'Help me!' The words caught in her throat as the pain ricocheted down her neck and up across her skull. 'Dave! Please help me!'

And then Rab said it. The crux of everything. 'Ye've no got no big man te look afte ye now.'

Hindsight is a wonderful thing. She should've called the police. She should have taken her battered face and her swelling elbow to be photographed and catalogued, but she was as scared as a mouse with the shadow of the hawk above her. And surely Big Dave had heard her call, at least knew what Rab was like. He'd even dropped her in the shit by saying it was her in the first place. Had he merely turned his back and walked away?

Ele should've gone running home that very second to her mum and dad, crying out for help and curling up in her old bed in her old bedroom with the familiar childhood posters still blu-tacked to the walls. But she couldn't. It was tantamount to admitting defeat and saying that she couldn't survive in the world without Michael. What a stupid cow.

Now she remembered how much she'd hated Michael Storm.

———

It wasn't as though she'd forgotten about the pact. It was more she'd stuck it in a box marked 'the future' right at the back of her memory cupboard, under a pile of old clothes, a tennis racket with a string missing and a few ancient teddies that had clothes moth damage and the odd missing eye. She'd tweaked at the box a couple of times, but then more things must've been stacked on top of it, and it slowly disappeared from her mental view.

She couldn't blame Maria for the night she spent thrashing like a shark caught by its tail, as Maria always slept as though dead, barely moving. Perhaps it was Schrodinger's fault, draped across her head in his favourite position, as toasty as a hot water bottle.

Was Michael actually going through with this? And why hadn't she said anything to Maria?

Is that really you?

In the morning, Maria had slipped out, and there was only the cat in her place, washing his nether regions, one leg high in the air. He stopped and glared at her as if she was being rude by watching his ablutions. A cat voyeur.

'Sod you.' She struggled out of bed and flicked on the heater. It might be expensive to run, but she needed that warmth now that the bed was empty. The smell of freshly brewed coffee was strong. A note scrawled on the back of an envelope was propped against the bread bin. It read: *Don't do this alone.*

———

Alone. Alone. Always alone.

Ah, Michael. How she'd loved him *once*. She'd dreamed incessantly of *that* ring on a certain finger and when and how it would arrive. The fact that they'd been living together in that horrible house for nearly two years meant it had to be winging its way to her soon. It never occurred to her that they'd never be married. Ever.

Sure, it'd been years since she'd spoken to Michael. Christmas cards to their respective families had been duly popped in the post. She always heard from her parents when Michael's card arrived, except she never got one herself. It'd gone way past that by then.

Is that really you?

They were all now thirty. Before she'd got married, Hope Jackson was the cool girl with her Jamaican heritage and saucy mouth. She and Hope were still in touch, sort of, and that meant she knew about Paul. Hope had started dating Paul Klaus back in high school, sandy-haired and rangy, the opposite to Hope. With the prospect of universities in different parts of the country, they'd clung together at eighteen in the same way drowning men grip onto a single lifebuoy. First love and the vista of a relationship that the rest of them knew probably wouldn't last six months, what with months of separation. They'd try, but they'd ultimately fail. That was the consensus. Even they knew it. There was nothing to say. Not like her and Michael. Forever. But against the odds, *their* love did survive. Marriage and three kids later, Hope and Paul were still together. Well, how about that! Perhaps "forever" did exist. Just not for her.

Looking back, they'd nearly made it out of that house. Ele thought about it. Would anything have been different if they had? Maybe. Didn't they say a miss of an inch was as good as a miss of a mile? They'd been within a hair's breadth.

Their degree courses had finished, and they'd joined the ranks of the great unemployed. Or at least Ele did. Michael was snapped up as though he'd fallen into the mouth of the nearest Nile crocodile. In fact, it was more akin to a feeding frenzy, great jaws crunching and scaly bodies rolling to get at him. She'd never realised how good he was at his job. A post at the *Guardian*. How very "him". But her world was shrinking to the size of a dried-up pond with not even a guppy in sight.

'Any luck yet?' he'd say when he returned from work, and she'd shake her head. They'd never envisioned a life where one of them wasn't working, was a "sponger" on Benefit Street.

'I'll do better,' said Ele, clutching at him. 'I won't let you down, Michael.'

Michael prised her hand from his arm. 'Ele, you'll get a job, easy. It's only a matter of time, but you have to stop saying things like that. You don't have to do better for me. Whatever you do, you do for yourself.'

'But I want to be the best for you, Michael.'

'You are already.'

Did he mean it? Or did he despise her for not being as good as him?

'Come on, *mi carida. Mi amor.*'

Ele wiped the tears from her cheeks. When he spoke Spanish to her, a sense of calm crept over her.

But they were in love? They were, weren't they?

At that time, Tiger also lived in London. One of the friends who'd made the pact with her when they were eighteen. Her best friend. In fact, her *gay* best friend, not that he'd leapt out of the closet or anything. Not with *his* family. Hu "Tiger" Sung was the "Asian aesthete", so emotional that he'd cry through the Kleenex advert with that cute blonde puppy. Aged eleven, the moment Hu had blurted that his name meant "tiger" in Cantonese, it had stuck to him like gum under a school desk. It was their inside joke as you couldn't get someone who less resembled a tiger than Hu. She'd never been sure if he'd moved to London because of her. After all, she was his best friend, too.

He was always around their place, having been given his own house key. Michael didn't object. In fact, he seemed relieved that she had someone else who was equally supportive. Sometimes she suspected that Michael relied on Tiger taking the brunt of her feelings of inadequacy. It was as though she stepped into quicksand, dragging her down, unable to move or think for herself, brain mired in hopeless thoughts. Then when it had passed, she was herself again, wondering why she couldn't fight these feelings, why wasn't she strong enough? She always spoke to Tiger about how she felt. There were times when he felt more akin to a sister than a *bestie*. She knew he hated the house and its occupants as vehemently as she did, eloquently bemoaning all their faults behind Michael's back. Like she did. United front.

Tiger was making toasted sandwiches on the main table, as all of them had stopped using the filthy kitchen, except Rab. Condiments were lined up neatly, and wafts of melting cheese and something spicy curled invitingly from the sandwich maker.

'I can't believe the state of that kitchen,' Tiger said. 'It's a death trap and no mistake. It'd be nice to be able to cook in a real kitchen for once. I hate having to wash plates in the bathroom sink.'

'I know,' Michael said. 'It's gross. We'll move out of the house once Ele gets a job.' He started to flick through a discarded magazine on the table.

Tiger made a *tsk* and then went back to the sandwich toaster. Ele knew her *bestie* was doing his best to avoid looking at her.

Just Michael saying those words made Ele feel as though he'd doused a blanket in petrol and thrown it over her. She could practically hear the scratch of a match being lit. She must have made a sound.

Michael looked up suddenly. 'Oh, Ele, I didn't mean anything by that. It's just this is convenient, isn't it? Cheap and central? We can think about moving to somewhere really snazzy and upmarket if you get a job and we can afford it. Somewhere you'd be happy to live.'

Ele sucked in a breath. 'What you're really saying is that we're stuck here because of me being ineffectual and lazy. Any idiot could find work.' She'd been judged and found wanting.

Was she wrong to keep trying for the job of her dreams? She wanted a career that'd grow with her, build up to be something, to be *somebody*.

'Ouch, hot, hot hot.' Tiger prised a smoking sandwich from the machine. 'Ele, babe. I'm sure Michael didn't mean to insinuate anything like that.'

'No, I wasn't implying that.' Michael snapped the magazine closed. Was he angry? She hated it when she'd made him angry. 'Ele. You know I wasn't. You've worked hard for your degree, and I want you to find the job you want. As I said, it's only a matter of time.' That was a lie. It had to be.

'I'm just a nobody.' Tears splashed; she couldn't hold them back. Ele tried not to rub at her eyes, as she always smudged her kohl. That would make her ugly, unattractive.

Michael stood and pulled her into his arms. 'It'll be alright, Ele. You don't have to worry about anything. We're here for you.' Ele felt Tiger's arms encircle her over the top of Michael's. She focused. The two men she loved with all her heart were holding her up. They weren't judging her. They were trying to help her.

Try listening to them, she scolded herself, and stop being so stressy.

'I'm sorry,' Ele said. 'Sometimes, I feel useless and dumb.'

'You are,' whispered Tiger into her hair, 'gorgeous and funny.'

'And,' said Michael, 'adorable and clever.'

Now she knew how false they'd been to her face. How she loathed the both of them.

―――――――

What would her life be like now if she'd got a job? If they'd escaped? Would she still be with Michael? Have a lovely house in the home counties and two adorable kids? They'd have a dog, as Michael was not a cat person. But no, *tonta!* Not after what she'd seen. That memory broke her every time.

She had to get to work. Concentrate on something else. Her mind was spiralling outwards so fast, that she thought she might disintegrate completely. A puff of wind and she'd disappear. Forever.

9

LIANG

SAN FRANSICO – 12 DAYS AND COUNTING

Tomorrow became today. And then another day and another. Liang tried not to stare, except she couldn't help it, lost in the immensity of the depths of his metallic eyes. Each time, a new street, a different café. Today they had black tea and lemon drizzle cake.

Having worked their way through the "chit-chat", they had now come to an impasse. Silence settled around them, a spiked fence, and neither one of them could break through it. Seconds ticked on past, turning into minutes. Words filled her head, but not one could scrabble past her throat. Would he get up and go now? Nod his head and say, 'Well, that was fun. See ya around.' Would she sit and watch him walk away, a silhouette that slowly disappeared to a dot and then nothing? She couldn't bear it.

Michael was a journalist for the *Guardian* newspaper, he told her, working there on a major scandal that'd erupted in the middle of the pro American football season. Managers accused of bribery and corruption. It wasn't news in her view, as she believed this happened every second of every day in all walks of life. Football, whether here or in England, had the status of a religion, and you don't mess with that.

She had to say something, break down the barrier that'd grown, separating them. 'Are you really going to print what you've just told me?' Liang hung onto the look on his face, the fervour and excitement. He loved what he did. She could always engage him on this level. She knew that.

'I've already sent the copy through to my editor. He's happy, and so I'm happy.'

'Is it ever dangerous? I mean,' she swallowed, 'have you been threatened at all?'

'There have been moments. But that's part of it, isn't it? Telling the story, no matter the consequences. We have the right to know what's happening around us, especially if it affects us and probably even more so if it doesn't. We shouldn't be complacent. We live in a tiny bubble, here in the West, coddled and fat. The real world is out there. One day, and I think that day is coming fast, it will explode into our little lives like a grenade, and then we'll be forced to take note. It might be too late by then.'

'That sounds very serious.'

'It is. I've seen a lot of what's out there, and most of it isn't nice.'

Liang had a flash of what she'd seen. Her face must've shown it.

'Liang? God, are you alright?' Reaching over, he touched her lightly on her shoulder, and she remembered that first time on the bridge.

'Sorry,' she dabbed at her mouth, hands shaking. 'Just a memory.'

'Looked like a pretty bad one.'

Liang nodded.

Michael pulled his hand away slowly. 'I've told you about me over the last few days, can't you reciprocate? Even a little bit?'

She tried to fill the widening gap between them, although

what could she say? Is now the time to drop in that she'd just got back from a delightful trip to Thailand, where she spent seven years in a hell of her own making? That she ran drugs for a triad gang, that she walked into it of her own accord because she was incredibly stupid? Bye, bye, Michael Storm.

'I can't. It's as simple as that.' She waited, gazing into her lap at her folded hands, waiting for the moment he realised that he wasn't onto a good thing here and moved on. The worst bit was if he thought he might have a story, that she might be his next *meal ticket*. Did she really believe that he'd be that callous? Quite frankly, she'd realised she couldn't read other human beings anymore. She used to think she knew what motivated a person, how their mind worked, but since her stint in prison, she'd been surprised and deeply saddened.

Clearing his throat, he leant forward. Liang could barely look at him, fearful of the "goodbye" that must be coming. 'Come back to England with me, Liang. Come home to London.'

The look of stupefaction on her face must've been much as a punch in the gut. He looked as though she'd physically hit him.

'Back with you?' she said. 'I've only just met you. Are you seriously asking me to do this? Why? Because I look like someone you used to know? I told you, I'm not that person, Michael. Don't get me muddled up with them.'

'No. I'm not.' He ran his hand through his hair. A lock flopped over his forehead. He looked more boy than man. 'I know we've just met. I'm not stupid, and I'm not usually rash, but I know this could work.'

Liang wanted this so badly. What did she have there in San Francisco, such a light and boisterous city, but her own darkness and fear? To be alone amongst so many people. What was this man offering her? Did she even care? But she still had to ask. 'How would this work? Surely you have a life that you're going back to? How do I fit in there?'

'I'll make it work. Trust me, Liang.'

Trust? Ah, there's another word that shouldn't be bandied about, shouldn't slide off the tongue coated in sugar syrup. Trust is something that must be earned, cherished and never forgotten. She didn't know who to trust anymore, least of all herself, as she had betrayed trust and thrown it all out, just garbage underfoot, kicked it from her and walked on by. Is that what sentient beings do? They have the choice and often choose poorly. As she had.

Liang waved at herself. 'Do you think I'm pretty?'

He looked up, puzzlement creasing his forehead. 'Yes.' His voice was husky, and in the fluorescent lights of the café, the shadows under his eyes were the colour of new bruises.

'What I'm trying to say is that this might look pretty,' She indicated her body, her face, 'on the outside, but the journey has been far from a pretty one.'

'We've all got things we wish to hide, things we don't want others to know. We've all got a bit of Dorian Gray in us.' He held out his hands. 'I mean, most people have skeletons in the closet at some point in their life.'

'Some more than others.'

He raised an eyebrow. 'Maybe so.'

Liang could see a different picture in her mind. A long time ago but not forgotten. The time before. She wondered if he also had a "before" and "after" time? A life filled more with regrets than successes? Probably not. A man such as him lived in the "now". Maybe she should try that for a while.

'When are you going back?'

'This Thursday.'

That soon! She somehow expected longer.

'So,' said Michael, 'we only have a few days to sort out a ticket for you.'

'You're that sure this is a good idea?' Trying to still her

breathing didn't work. She felt she was panting like an overheated dog.

'Never been more sure of anything in my life.'

'Then let's do it.' She heard the words as she said them as though someone else had moved her lips and caressed her throat to make a sound. But she needed to be helped, longed to be held up by strong arms, ached to be wanted by another for herself and not what she could provide for them. Did she have a chance here?

Stretching across the table, he took her right hand in both of his, leaning in to kiss each of her fingertips.

'Liang,' he said as if savouring the sound. 'What does it mean?'

'It means "strong woman" in Cantonese.'

'It's an apt name.'

10

HOPE
BRIXTON

Hope listened. She was sitting at their shared desk tucked under the bedroom window, with the laptop open in front of her. It was just getting light. Sneaking a peak on Facebook was a bit of an addiction, just to see if anyone had posted something funny, usually to do with cats in boxes or dogs on ice. The snoring emanating from the bed behind her was regular and loud, so she knew she could have a few more minutes scrolling up and down, liking this and that, maybe making a comment to her internet friends, the closest she now got to any real friends. She needed a laugh. Sometimes it felt like a tiny lifeline to the outside world, a world she barely remembered and rarely saw nowadays.

Three kids. It was incredible how such small people could take up every minute of your life, not that she resented it, although Paul acted as though looking after them must be a piece of cake and that when she said she was exhausted, it was an excuse or something. The resentment was when he said that "working" for a living was far more tiring than being a mum and that when he came home, he expected to be looked after. There were moments when she could've swung for him.

When the only "adult" conversation she had was when she received a text on her mobile from her eldest son's school, kindly informing her that her son had a detention and then the reason for that detention, (usually involving disobedience, violence and/or plain rudeness,) it was no wonder she felt as though her brain was turning into the same consistency as the baby food she shovelled into her youngest son's mouth. No ambiguity there. No chance of mistakes or misunderstandings. Bam! This would be closely followed by the not-so-adult conversation with her son, giving her lip and denying all culpability. That would then be accompanied by "the throwing of whatever comes to hand" and "the swearing" using any new and exciting language he'd picked up in school. What was worse? Sending him to school and facing the consequences or having him home? At least it was the school Christmas holidays. That was normal. But now, depending on the Board of Governors' decision, she might have him home for good. Lord help the lot of them.

There was a red icon on her Messenger box. Ooh? No one sent her messages anymore. They knew not to bother.

Hope. Well, here we all are. Thirty years old and I really can't believe it, can you? Do you remember our pact when we were all kids?

Hope felt like she'd licked her finger and then stuck it in a plug socket. Michael? Cupping her head in her hands, she breathed in noisily through her nose, pushing unwanted images from her mind. No, she couldn't afford to remember.

Michael? Haven't heard from you in ages. You're not serious, are you? Her hands were trembling violently.

The glowing green dot by his name showed he was online, and he was quick to respond.

Long time, no see. Serious? Never more so. I know it's short notice, but I've arranged it for New Year's Eve. I'll send you the details. You will both come, won't you?

At least he remembered she had a husband. Hope craned to see if Paul was still asleep. *Where are you? Still in America?*

San Francisco. Got some pretty crazy news to tell you all.

Have you contacted the others?

There was a pause as though he was thinking. *Do you mean have I contacted Ele?*

Yes.

She'll come, I'm sure of it. I think she's in a good space right now.

'Well, maybe not for long,' whispered Hope under her breath. She typed rapidly.

I'll see what Paul says.

What she meant was: I won't say a word to him, and then I'll tell you we can't make it. Other commitments.

Sabine will be there. We'll all be there. Let me know. M x

Sabine? Like that's tempting. She watched as the green dot by Michael's name blinked out.

Now what? If she did ignore it, would he push for them to go? Contact Paul and ask why he didn't know about this meet? Hope sighed loudly. She really didn't need this right now. Or at any time.

'I don't understand what you're doing on your computer at this time.' Paul was reading over her shoulder. 'Why can't you stay in bed and give me some of that hot lovin' we've not had in nigh on two years due to pregnancies, breastfeeding and temper tantrums?' He paused. Ah, the words had sunk in. 'You've got to be blinkin' kidding!'

So immersed in her own thoughts, she hadn't heard the warning bedsprings creak.

Paul laughed, although there was an uncertain quality to it. 'What the fuck? Michael's contacted us about that stupid pact we made?'

Hope scrabbled to close the laptop lid, but it was too late.

Why hadn't she shut it down faster? 'Paul? Yeah, it's unbelievable.'

And he shouldn't be reading her private messages. That's what it meant. Private.

Paul groaned. 'It's Sunday morning, the kids are at Monique's, God bless her sweet and patient soul, and I, for one, would like a lie-in. Maybe with some extras?' A shaft of sunlight illuminated his red-gold hair as if he had a glowing halo. 'We don't have to answer yet, do we?'

'No. I think we need to seriously think this through.'

Stroking rapidly at his goatee, his movements expressed stress, not curiosity. If she had a beard, she'd also be pulling at it now. This might be the proverbial straw, and she was already pushed to her limits.

Paul continued to twiddle at his beard. What was wrong with him?

'It seems he's arranged it all.' She poked at him. 'Are you alright? You're acting a little weird.'

'I'm fine.' He lunged clumsily and pecked her on her cheek. Hope could smell last night's curry on his breath, but there was something else too, more overpowering. They'd had a bottle of red, some organic Merlot, yet now he smelt as though he'd also drunk twelve whiskies on top of that. She turned her head away.

Paul snorted. 'The pact? Really? Sabine? Ele? I can't believe he'd get Ele to come.' His movements relaxed.

'He says she'll agree. I suppose it's been a long time.'

'Water under the bridge and all that?'

'Maybe she's over it all?'

'Like fuck!' Paul pulled a chair up close to the computer. 'You remember when we all met up in our old sixth form pub after Michael phoned us about Tiger?'

'I remember', said Hope, 'it'd only been a few months since

Ele had split from Michael. We were all creeping around her as though we were walking on the proverbial eggshells.'

'Yeah, and then being told straight afterwards that Tiger was dead.'

Hope scratched at her head, nearly shaved back to her skull to stop her youngest, Alfie, getting his grasping fingers hooked in her tight curls. 'Never understood it then, and quite frankly, I still don't understand what happened. We never did find out what he died of, did we?'

But she knew the impact it had had, far too close and personal.

'And that awful, bloody letter. What was it again? Hu's dead, so fuck off the lot of you? We were his friends, and they may have been inscrutable, but I think we had the right to know what'd happened to him.'

'They wouldn't tell us if I remember correctly.'

'No, they hated us. Not Chinese enough for them.' He grinned. 'Or rich enough.'

Hope nodded. 'Bigoted bunch of pricks. I remember the look on Ele's face after we'd handed the letter back to her. She reacted like it was going to sting or bite her.'

'Well, yeah! Just sending her a note, a scrawled message that was so cold and uncaring, of course, she felt like that.' He paused. 'For me, it was more the effect on Michael. He looked so grey. You know, I didn't ever twig that he and Tiger were that close. I always thought they were friends by default 'cos of Ele.'

'I heard he was around their place all the time, so I don't suppose it's weird.'

'Yeah.'

'Sabine, the Ice Queen of all people, cried', said Hope, frowning, 'but Ele seemed to be made from granite. Not a peep out of her.'

'Shock can make you freeze up like that.'

'Was it something the family were embarrassed about? Aids? Syphilis?'

'Aids would have shown, and syphilis is cured by a dose of antibiotics. If it was a long-term illness, then Ele would've known, surely? He was her best friend. So it must have been an accident.'

'Poor Tiger. He was such a sweetie, wasn't he.'

'I think the word you're looking for is *gay*.'

'You don't know that for sure. He was pretty girly, yes, but look at a lot of the top designers. Come across as gay as a row of pink tents but have wives and kids at home. You never can tell nowadays.' Hope grinned at him.

'Anyway, I think Ele was angry that she hadn't had the chance to say goodbye. I mean, she must've felt cheated.'

'She said she loved him when she walked out, just after you suggested we have a wake–'

Paul yanked his dressing gown off the back of the chair in the bedroom and wrestled his way into it. 'That was Sabine. But as I remember it, Ele said something along the lines of, 'I have many things to say to him, but I can say them anywhere. I don't need a special place or time to do that. So, if you want to have your "wake", go ahead. I won't be there. He knows how I feel about him.' Then Michael hugged her. That was the bit that got me. Did you see the look on her face then?'

'No. It's all a bit hazy.'

Paul shook his head. 'I did, and if I didn't know better, it was pure hate.'

'Hate? I wouldn't go that far. I know they didn't split amicably, so it must've been hard losing Michael and Tiger within weeks of each other. But hate? No.'

'Listen, I don't know what happened between them, except that look, I'll tell you it frightened me.'

'It was years ago, and we were all in a bit of a state. Don't dwell on it.'

'Do you want to go? Meet up with them all again?'

Hope shrugged. 'Not really. It's been too long. How about you?' *Please say 'no'.*

'I'm not bothered, but I am intrigued. I wonder what they're all like now.'

'Older and richer, I would presume.'

Paul cleared his throat. 'Yeah, maybe. So,' he slipped the dressing gown down over his shoulders and wiggled his hips, 'how about we go back to bed and try to make another little baby?'

Hope wondered what the look was on her own face now.

'I'm going to put the kettle on.' She pulled her dressing gown tighter about her. 'Do you want French toast?' She ignored the pleading in his eyes.

Make another little baby? Hope had taught herself not to swear. Not even in the sanctuary of her own mind. It was for the sake of the children. If they learned words, at least she knew it wasn't from her lips. But this time, the words blazoned as though they were surrounded by a glorious pyrotechnic display: *Fuck no!*

11

ELE

EPPING FOREST – 11 DAYS AND COUNTING

W hat was this feeling? Ele peered down. Slivers of pain were ricocheting up her calves. Was she treading on glass? Trying to walk, she nearly fell as her feet dragged, screaming in pain, numb from cold. Where was she? Teeth chattering. Her head filled with clattering sounds and a clammy grabbing mist. She looked about her. Bright white and orange illumination at intervals in the distance. The same in the other direction. Street lamps? Stumbling, she looked down again. A kerb. Was she on a pavement? There was a haze of softer luminescence above her. Sky. She was staring upwards. Pre-dawn. A siren wailed, and she flinched, though it was far away and muffled.

'Jesus! Where am I?' It took a moment more to realise that not only were her feet bare, but so were her legs. She was stood somewhere in only her T-shirt and knickers. Trying to cover herself, willing herself to move, she lost her balance and crunched down onto her knees.

'Fuck. *Fuck!*' Every part of her was deadened.

Shadows shifted, undulating. Anything could be hidden in that murk. A dog barked, and Ele jumped. Crawling to the next lamp post, she hauled herself up. Pins and needles stabbed at her toes, so she stamped to try to get some feeling back. Clinging to the post, she focused on what was around her. It took a while, but she finally recognised the houses across the road, swinging her head around; even though it felt as though it was made from lead, there was the next-door neighbour's overhanging bush, here was the driveway for her own block of flats.

Her legs moved much as rusted machinery, her feet trailed clumsily. Step, step, step. Grasping along the wall, fingernails snapping, she rounded the bend and could see her flat door was wide open. No lights were on. Creeping down the steps, she hesitated at the door. How long had she been outside? Could anyone be in her home? Had someone spotted her open door and slipped in? Ele picked up a terracotta flowerpot that was on the small wall fronting her flat. Commanding herself to step across the threshold, she switched on the hall lamp, blinking in the glare, and brandished the pot in front of her. She didn't pull the door closed behind her in case she needed to run, but then her feet were barely moving. The pain from them warming up was crippling. Tremors batted at her body. Reaching into the living room, she found the switch. The sudden light revealed it was empty. The bathroom was also just as she'd left it, but the bedroom door was shut. She always left it slightly ajar, so Schrodinger could move around easily and not yowl at the entrance to be let in or out. Was there someone in there? Ele backtracked slowly to the living room. A metal candlestick was on the bureau, and she traded it with the flower pot. Holding it tightly, she opened the bedroom door as quietly as she could, her heartbeat pounding in her head. A streak of russet shot out, and Ele screamed and fell backwards, the candlestick knocked out of her hands. Her shoulder hit the bookshelf and a blossom of agony unfurled.

'Jesus wept! Schrody! You scared the shit out of me.' The cat was skulking in the corner of the living room, eyes as big as dinner plates. Clambering upright and rubbing at her shoulder, she picked up the weapon and kicked the bedroom door open. Her duvet was scrunched down into the headboard, and clothes were scattered, but apart from that, there was nothing untoward in there. Hang on, wasn't the front door still open? Scouting around again, in case she locked herself in with someone who'd just snuck in, she pulled the door shut with a bang and slid the lock on.

Resting her head against the door jamb, she took a deep, shuddering breath. Sleepwalking? She thought she'd grown out of it. Years of waking in strange places, freezing and vulnerable, her parents' frantic calls usually the trigger to rouse. They'd been perplexed as to the cause of her nighttime wandering, although Ele knew. Not that she could tell them. Not then because of the fear and shame and not now because it would destroy them.

Her arms and shoulders ached when she pulled off her T-shirt, damp from perspiration and early morning dew. Pulling on a clean one, Ele left the lamp on as she climbed back into bed and yanked the duvet up to her chin.

The cat plumped himself down on her stomach and settled himself.

'I don't like this, Schrody. There's something wrong.' The cat shifted, tucking his paws beneath him, lazily opened one golden eye and then started to purr.

'What's happening to me?' Ele was convinced that sleep couldn't ever come that night.

The seven o'clock alarm was insistent. Ele had definitely had a bad night. Futons might be allegedly good for you, but hers seemed to have developed lumps and bumps that materialised from nowhere. She crawled from the heavy embrace of the bed covers, feeling like a giant had been sleeping on top of her, squeezing the air from her lungs until she woke, sweating and fighting for breath. She put a coffee on the hob, washed and got dressed slowly. There was a fragment of memory of being cold and wet. Dreams? Her neck was hurting and her shoulder throbbed. Had she strained it in the night? Maybe she'd been sleeping in an awkward position? She looked down. It was strange, as she didn't remember being in that particular T-shirt when she went to bed last night, and why was her usual sleep T-shirt hanging out of the washing machine?

'Urgh, Schrody. I've got such a headache.' Holding onto the front of her head, she rummaged in the cupboard for paracetamol. There were luckily three left in the pack. She downed them all and hoped they'd kick in fast.

Clutching a steaming coffee, she wiggled her mouse to wake the computer from its sleep.

'If I've got to start work, then so do you.' Accounts had to be sorted, money moved around to balance the books, the ins and outs checked. Her head drooped over the keyboard. Doing accounts with a head stuffed full of mashed potato possibly wasn't such a good idea. If she got it wrong, there could be nasty consequences. When she wasn't trading at the market, her time should be spent doing something for her business, making her boards and pieces or building up her marketing strategies and online presence. So what to do now?

She couldn't help it. *Michael.*

What's the first thing you do after accepting a friend request? You see how many friends they have. If less than twenty, then they're either too old to have got the hang of social networking or worse, they're "Billy-no-mates", and you can pity them with impunity. More than a thousand, as Michael had, and that's taking the piss, abject showing off. What? Did he give out his details whilst drunk at a club on Saturday night? No one can truly keep on top of over a thousand friends. Ele could barely keep on top of five.

The green dot by his name showed he was online. The question waited for her. *So are you coming, Ele?*

Hell, what would she say? Could she do this? See him again, see them all again? Schrodinger deigned to sit in her lap at the computer desk, but he was so heavy, her leg went numb. And his breath stank.

I'm coming. Wouldn't miss it for the world.

Perhaps someone else had control over her mind, as that wasn't what she meant to put. She stared at the words on the screen.

Great.

Where are we going then?

Maybe she'd misconstrued what he'd written earlier. Perhaps they were going on a trip to Butlins.

Somewhere fantastic. It's called The Siren Inn. It's in Rye.

I know Rye. Went there as a kid. It's along the south coast.

It's supposed to be one of the most haunted places in England.

Her heart lurched as if it'd missed a couple of beats and had trouble kick-starting itself again.

It's full of stories of smugglers. The place dates back to fourteen hundred and something. Really old.

So not a five-star hotel in Mayfair?

Would you prefer that? I didn't think that was your style. More Sabine.

'Yeah, right,' said Ele. 'What? More like a cheap B&B for me?'

Sucking on her bottom lip, she hit the keys hard. *I didn't think even Mayfair was upmarket enough for Sabine nowadays.*

LOL. I take it you're up for smugglers, ghosts and log fires? And tales to tell? You'll find it so incredible.

So you've finally got your big scoop, then?
I have a story.
And you'll only tell us if we go?
You'll love it.

After you've searched through their friends to see who you can recognise from school, so you can snigger and point in a supercilious fashion at anyone who has put on weight or looks ten years older than they should (ha!) or if they haven't aged a day and give the impression that they've spent the last ten years down the gym for six hours a day and only eat sprouting beans and miso soup (boo!). What do you do? You avidly peruse their photos. At least it would take her mind off her creeping headache.

Michael's albums were labelled with dates and locations. Wow! He'd sure visited a load of places. It reminded her of when she'd been with Michael, and he'd come home from some exotic country the *Guardian* had sent him to. Gradually though, his wonderful foreign gifts dwindled to small mementoes that ended up on the bottom of the wardrobe floor. Each time the lovemaking no longer consumed them as much as it used to. Now, it was more a candle wavering in a draft, whereas before, it was akin to being tied to a stake, and the flames burned and crackled up their blistered bodies, leaving them gasping for air and believing they would die. Then the arguments grew, though over what, she was never really sure.

'He says there's nothing wrong,' shouted Ele at Tiger, 'but I know there is.'

'If he says there's nothing wrong, then believe him. Don't you see that you're making the whole situation worse by insisting there is something? If you're not careful, you'll make it happen.'

'Me make it happen? How?'

'Xiao dong bu bu, da dong chu ku, which means "A small hole not mended in time will become a big hole more difficult to mend".'

'What the hell does that mean? Sod your bloody Chinese proverbs. Life can't be lived by quoting stupid things all the time, Tiger.'

Tiger pulled his fingers through his hair as if in exasperation. 'What it means is if you carry on being so negative about yourself, you'll drive him away. He loves you so much, Ele, but sometimes, you know you can be difficult to cope with. Just have more faith in yourself.'

'You sound like all the reports I had from school.' Was he compounding all she knew about herself? *'Elena should try to be more forthcoming and have more faith in her own abilities.'*

'Then do it.' He was holding out his hands.

'That easy, eh? Clap your hands, and all will be well in the world?' Ele felt the tears prickling. 'I love him so much, Tiger. I'd just die if he ever left me.'

'It'll be okay,' Tiger said, pulling her tightly into his arms, and she had to believe him because if it wasn't, how could she exist anymore?

'Will it? Swear it. Swear it'll all be okay.'

Tiger's eyes scrunched shut. His next words were squeezed out. 'Ele, the man *loves* you. He's just a bit confused or something. I don't know.'

'Confused whether he loves me?' She twisted away from him.

'Just confused.' It was a whisper. Tiger looked down at that point. She knew it hurt him when she was in pain as though they were twins that could feel what the other felt. She'd always thanked God for her beautiful Tiger.

. . .

Not anymore.

By then, Michael was busy, busy-*busy*, and she was still wrapped in the weekly job adverts. Had she now become one of the derelicts on the park benches outside their little world?

'I hardly ever see you,' she said one day, 'and when I do, it's still like you're not even there.'

'Then,' he said, 'maybe I shouldn't be.'

And that was all it took. Michael's leaving tore a hole in her as though she'd been strapped over the mouth of a cannon and the cannon lit. Her heart was gone. She never thought she'd ever find it again. Young love, first love. What do they say? The first cut is the deepest? *Well, it sure hurt.*

———

Trawling through vistas of mist-enveloped temples on rocky mountains in Thailand, then images of India splashed with so much vibrant colour, it was as though they'd had the whole bloody spectrum thrown at them. She saw exotic faces of many differing hues, wearing the attire of the world, from Peru, Mozambique, Nepal, Finland. All the great cities were in there too. New York, Paris, Berlin, Tokyo. Was there anywhere that this man hadn't been? Wasn't Scunthorpe on the list? She thought not.

Ele leaned back in her chair. Where had she gone in the intervening years? Magaluf. And she spent most of that drunk as a skunk and shagging the barman. Or possibly men. These pictures reminded her of the postcards that Tiger sent them. *Wish you were here.* He'd gone travelling after they'd all left school while the rest of them prepared for uni. She heard the words he'd said to her as he stepped into the taxi for the airport,

'*Hua you chong kai ri, wu zai shao nian,* which means "flowers may bloom again, but a person never has the chance to be young again," so don't waste your time. I'm not going to waste mine.'

She'd never been sure what he meant. When he finally settled back in London, Ele had felt relief that her best friend had returned to her. That was until...

Then she saw something in one of Michael's photos, and felt sharp-nailed creatures skitter all over her skin. A face in the crowd. A face that shouldn't be there.

'Jesus wept!' she said. '*What?*'

Schrodinger scrabbled off her lap as if she'd pulled hard on his tail.

There was such a crash that Ele cowered. Her breakfast bowl lay smashed, the last slosh of milk up the wall in a wave with a delicate spattering of soggy cornflakes round it. It was her best bowl, a treasured item given to her by her Nana years ago. Blue ceramic with swirls of green and gold. Hand made by artisans. Unique, and now she'd destroyed it. No, *that face* had destroyed it, made bile rise in her throat, made her reach out with clawed fingers, ready to scratch. Heat rose up and flooded her cheeks and neck, she was an incendiary, and now the top of her head must be aflame. Not possible, she kept saying. Not possible: a mantra to build a wall between *that face* and her shrivelled heart.

12

LIANG

A CATASTROPHIC MISTAKE

W hat was she thinking? Liang knew instinct had been over-ruled by her heart, and thinking never came into it. Daydreaming about a life she could never hope to have had skewed her sense of self. So there were two options here, go with it, live the dream and never tell him about the past, or, front it out, be brave and hope beyond hope that he would understand, forgive her, and they'd move beyond it. Move past the past? Now that was it in a nutshell. That moment when she'd met him, what had she been doing? She hadn't even admitted it to herself. Would she really have jumped? Suicide was a sour word in her mouth. It made her want to spit. If she told him and he rejected her, would she be up that strut again, wanting to hit the water so hard below that she'd never be able to rise, be dragged down until there was no more of her? No more pain. No more *guilt.*

Liang had seen the darker side of so-called "tropical bliss", and it wasn't pretty. Bangkok. Not her first time there, but the times she'd visited before, she'd been in a different state. It was vibrant and alive, full of noise and stinks and a great animal hunger. Whereas she was broke, miserable, probably feeling she needed to fight the world, scratch at it with her beautifully manicured nails. Her hurt and rage at the way her life had turned out, how she'd been disowned and humiliated by her own family, had been broiling similar to the hot geysers that spew forth burning liquid. Bad at any time but especially bad here, in Thailand, as a woman and a woman alone at that. It meant she *wasn't paying attention.*

A sharp-faced girl with a short skirt and skyscraper shoes stood on the corner of a street Liang didn't know, as she'd just been wandering. The girl seemed to detach herself from the wall as if she'd been previously glued to it.

'Wha' you want?' The girl fingered at Liang's clothes, her arm tweaking around her waist.

'Karaoke.' Liang fumbled to get her probing hands off her. Having downed a couple of beers in the hotel bar, she'd ventured out, hoping to find a place where she could sing out her troubles.

'You come wid me.' Liang was dragged in by her elbow up to a small room at the back of the building. She glimpsed a large smoky room filled with men and the untuned sounds of singing. What does it take to wake up and smell the coffee? Liang focused. The girl's eyes were bloodshot to the point of being primarily red. Devil hued. Why hadn't she seen that out on the street? She wouldn't have walked in here with her. The room felt claustrophobic, only a small table with a well-thumbed songbook and stained settee, especially as the unshaded bulb strobed sporadically. Liang felt a little sick.

'You want?' Her hand shaking as though she had some form of palsy, the girl offered Liang small orange and green pills. She picked one up and sniffed it. It smelled of grapes, and there were letters or numbers stamped on them, though she couldn't see clearly in the gloom. Oh hell, where was she?

'Good no?' The girl stuffed at least three in her mouth. Her head lolled back for a moment, and the tremors increased. She suddenly looked down at her arm, hanging languidly in her lap, and started to pick at her skin. There was nothing there that Liang could see. Handing the pills back to the girl, Liang stood up.

'I have to go now. Not up for singing much tonight–'

Having already ordered tea as they entered, the waitress returned just as Liang had her hand on the door handle. Two men in obscenely short boxer shorts with identical tattoos on their arms pushed in behind her. Any idiot would recognise them. Triads. They spoke in Thai, but Liang knew enough to realise that she was in deep trouble here.

Her family name caused a lot of excitement until her beloved father refused to pay the ransom. Then came the threats against her influential family. How could this be happening to her? How stupid and naive to have walked in here. It was then a simple choice. Prostitute or smuggler? No choice, really. Being a drug mule was considerably more appealing at this juncture than being chained to a metal bedstead in a lonely guesthouse in the mountains, where long-distance drivers could take a rest and fuck a pretty whore at their convenience. She'd take too long to die.

At the airport, walking through customs, she'd taken "the fall" for them. She realised that now. Set up, so another more bountiful smuggler could slip by. Primed with faces to watch out for at customs, two women who were supposed to let her pass, turn the other way, well they were actually the ones who "fingered" her. X-rayed, they could easily see the tied off condoms she'd swallowed. She was the patsy with just under the amount of drugs inside her not to get the death penalty but more than enough to be sentenced to a few years inside a Thai jail.

13

HOPE

MEMORIES

I t'd been a long time since Hope had opened the photo albums of their wedding. The years had whirled past her, except she felt she was stuck on a carousel. Maybe the landscape around her had changed, but she remained on that candyfloss-coloured horse, with its garish gold paint and huge-teeth-filled grin. Up and down and round and round. There were times when all she could remember was her belly obscuring her feet, then the pain of popping another baby out into the world, closely followed by breastfeeding at one, two and three in the morning but having to be up to make lunch boxes not only for her real children but her surrogate one, her husband. Loving them all beyond belief still didn't preclude the overwhelming need, once in a while, to pack a rucksack and run off to the teepee village in Wales, to contemplate her navel for a bit.

The album smelt musty, stuck in the bottom drawer of their wardrobe. Hope blew a thick layer of dust off and then sneezed three times. Did that signify good luck? There they were. Ubiquitous group photos of grinning family, a little awkward, too posed by the official photographer and then the more fluid shots, snapped by friends on the day. There were pictures of a bored Sabine, looking like royalty, Ele looking dead and devoid of any emotion, she and Paul, glazed with too much excitement and perhaps shock. But of course, no Tiger and Michael. Her finger trailed across them all. Tiger because he couldn't be and Michael because he wouldn't be. She'd been so wrapped up in planning that she never really considered how it might affect Ele. Nearly nine years ago, yet with the photos in front of her, it felt as though it was yesterday.

'You are cordially invited to the marriage of our daughter Hope Jackson to Paul Klaus on the 28th of April.'

Hope shook her head and waved the invite at Paul. 'Ele's not going to like this.'

'Fuck her, Hope. We've been creeping around her since she split with Michael. There's no way we're going to postpone the wedding 'cos of her.'

'Maybe she'll decline.' Hope sighed loudly. 'I know it sounds really selfish, but some part of me wishes she would.'

'I know. It's supposed to be our day, and I don't want it ruined 'cos we got us a moper.' Paul scratched at his burgeoning whiskers.

'She's not a moper, she's...' Hope cleared her throat. 'Okay, she's a bit down at the moment. I don't want her to feel as if we're rubbing her nose in it.'

Paul pulled a face and put on a slight Spanish accent. 'You know I've just lost the love of my life, and my best friend is dead. All my dreams have been shot to pieces, but you'd like me to come and witness your eternal bliss. You'd like me to hear you make your special vows and watch you walk down that aisle as man and wife. You'd really like me to endure your mothers as they cry with joy and your fathers as they slap each other on the back in hearty congratulations. Like I'm never going to in my life.' He raised his eyebrows at Hope, 'Thanks for that.'

'Don't be mean. She's going through a bad patch.' Hope looked away. They'd all gone through a bad patch at that time. There were things she'd needed to forget.

He stood and pulled Hope into his arms, resting his head on top of hers. 'We're going to be married, and it'll be the best day of our lives.' He smiled down at her. 'So far.'

Hope waited four days from when the invite had been sent before she dialled Ele's number.

'Ele? It's Hope. Have you got our invite?'

'Yeah.'

'I know it must be especially hard for you right now, but I need to say that the wedding has been planned for over a year now. It's not as though we decided to get married *after* you and Michael...' Her voice petered off.

'Okay.'

Hope could hear in her voice that it wasn't okay. At all.

'The dates had been set, and it'd all been paid for. We can't call it off now, although we understand if you don't want to come. You've had a rough time of it recently.' *Please say you're not coming!*

'I hadn't noticed.'

'Oh, Ele. We'd both love you to be there. We're your friends, and if there's anything we can do, you must let us know.' *Except ask for the wedding to be called off. Don't ask for that.*

'Sure.' There was a weird wet sound. 'Will Michael be there?'

'No. He's got a job in the States somewhere. That's what he says. I'm not sure if it's true, but we think he's trying to give you a bit of space.'

'Space?' Ele's voice drifted as though the phone was held away from her. 'I've got the whole fucking universe now.'

'I'm so sorry,' said Hope. 'Think about it and get back to us.' In reality, it was Hope who needed space. She had to sort her head out. Work out the best thing to do without hurting anyone. Tell the truth and watch her world shatter? Lie and pray it never comes to light? What a dreadful, heartbreaking dilemma and one she'd never believed could happen to her.

Hope had spotted Ele as she walked down the aisle on her father-in-law's arm, as her own father had been conspicuously absent all her life. Ele had obviously made an effort. A dress and hat that Hope had never seen before, her long dark hair loose about her shoulders. She was sat next to Sabine on the shiny, worn pews. At least she had a friend here when she and Paul spoke their vows. She shouldn't worry about Ele now. As she neared the front of the church, Hope lost herself in the look in Paul's eyes, such unquestioning love and devotion. Her tears were just as real but for other reasons. She'd opted for lying. She never noticed the traffic roaring outside for the roaring inside her head. She spoke the words loudly for all to hear.

The reception was in their local pub, The Anchor. Hope looked around her. Paul's parents, Axel and Liesel, had helped as best they could, but they'd just moved back to Dresden a few months before and been hit by unexpected bills. They'd all done their best on a shoestring budget. Everything was dressed in white as if the whole place had been smothered in snow. The food was barely more than pub fare, but they'd got a reasonable price for it. Anyway, if people only came for the grub, sod them.

Hope listened to the speeches, brimming with salutations and congratulations, and sipped her champagne. She'd promised herself half a glass and if anyone judged her, then again, sod them. Paul leant over and patted the protruding bump sticking out beneath her bodice.

'How are you? Happy, Mrs Klaus?'

'Very.' It was difficult to lean forward, but she managed to kiss the end of his nose. Yes, she was happy, although there was still the fear, biting at her like a tiny viper.

It was quite a while later before she found Ele sat at the back of the pub. Sitting awkwardly on the wooden stool, she draped her arm across her shoulders, feeling the slight tensing. Maybe Ele couldn't bear to be touched anymore? Sabine was nowhere to be seen. Typical, had she legged it already?

'You're going to be alright, Ele. It might not feel like it now, but you will be in time. You're a strong woman, don't forget that. You have friends.'

It was as though Ele was coming out of a dream. 'Do you believe that, Hope? Or is that merely the rhetoric you think you should be saying?'

'You doubt that? You've got two choices here. Either wallow in self-pity and go under or rise above it and say, "blow this, I'm going to be stronger than all of this. I'm going to win." I think you'll do the latter.'

Ele raised an eyebrow. '*Gracias.* It's not easy.' She motioned around her. 'I always thought this would be mine.'

'It will be, but maybe not with Michael. I know I shouldn't mention fish and sea, but it's true. You will find someone else.' Easier said than done. Hope knew that now.

'But I don't want anyone else.'

'Maybe you'll get back with Michael.' Some secret part of her hoped this wasn't an option.

Ele shook her head. 'I don't ever want to see him again. I wouldn't go back with him if you paid me a king's ransom.'

'Point taken.' Hope thought that was a strange thing for her to say. Didn't she love Michael to the moon and back? Not that she could blame her... she didn't think through her next comment. 'I wish Tiger was here, though. He'd have loved all this.'

'*What?*' Ele blinked rapidly. Her breathing speeded up.

'Sorry...' Maybe mentioning Tiger wasn't a good idea. From the look on Ele's face, it was as if Hope had punched through her chest, reached in and ripped out her heart.

Ele glanced at the empty seat beside her. Hope supposed she was seeing the space for Tiger.

'One day, babe,' she whispered. 'There were so many things I wanted, I needed to say to him. And now I never can.'

Something with tiny sharp claws skittered down Hope's back. It wasn't so much the words. It was the way she said them. And the look on her face.

Hope shut the album with a *snap* so loud it woke the baby in his cot. Alfie started to wail. She reached in and hauled him out, settling him on her lap, making comforting sounds. Teething was never a good time for any of them. Fat tears were caught in his eyelashes, but at least he'd stopped crying and was looking around the room. Snuggling him close, she breathed in deeply, that talcum powder baby smell soothing her senses.

'I could eat you right up,' she kissed his tiny hands, and he chuckled. 'Yes, I could. Yum, yum, yum, lovely scrummy baby.'

An image of Ele popped into her mind. Ele as she had been when they were eighteen. So sweet, so funny, *so* needy. She fully understood why Michael had finally left her. You couldn't support someone every minute of every day. You just couldn't. It wore you out, all that massaging another person's ego, all that reassuring and encouragement. It wasn't as if she needed it. Did she? Hope would've killed to be as funny as Ele, who could make them all roll around, holding their sides they ached so much. But she also knew there was a darker side. Michael had hinted on more than one occasion that Ele had symptoms of depression. Really? What the hell could she have been depressed about? Beautiful, witty and loved by the most gorgeous man in the whole bloomin' universe.

Ah, Michael. She'd often wondered what would have happened if she'd met Michael first. Probably more times than she should have. If she'd married Michael and not Paul, would her life be better? Have lots of beautiful kids with the faces of angels? Was she glad it hadn't panned out that way? With his looks, he was a contender for the runway, strutting his stuff, showing off his chiselled chin, being admired and lusted after by both sexes. Even at school, the boys had idolised him, wanting to be on his team in the football squad, be next to him in the canteen, be near him, *be him*. The girls had adored him, made goo-goo eyes at him, lisped with little girl voices, licked their lips at him. It was funny; out of all of them, he should've got off with Sabine. Sabine Delacroix. Uber fashionable and *chic* "French chick". A blonde ice queen, forced to this uncultivated land of badly dressed savages at the tender age of ten by selfish relocating parents. He was so dark, she so golden. A match made in heaven. No wonder Ele was always on edge around her. If Hope had gone out with Michael, she'd have been the same. Oh, the green-eyed look of jealousy and Sabine lapped it up, made sure that Ele felt every glance, every accidental touch. Sabine had been a bitch to Ele and no mistake! And Michael, with his easy smile and random caresses, didn't exactly help matters. But with *her*, it was his vulnerability, his pain that had done it. Michael Storm got them any way he could without even knowing he did it. It would've killed her, knowing that she couldn't trust him.

'No,' Hope said to the baby, 'I'm glad I'm with your daddy, else I wouldn't have you now.' Hope shook her head. 'I still don't think this is a good idea, Alfie.' She tickled him on his chubby tummy, until he chuckled. 'Some part of me doesn't want to meet up with any of them. It's been too long. Yes, it has. Far too long and so much water under the bridge, as they say. What do you think, eh?' Smiling at him, she hefted him onto her hip. 'I think you agree with me.'

Having placed Alfie in his high chair, Hope peeled and microwaved an apple, adding a slosh of milk. While rummaging for a salad dressing jug in a cupboard, she knocked a pot of growing basil off the shelf above it. The soil fell everywhere, and the poor plant looked naked and straggling in the middle of the kitchen floor.

Hope gazed up at the ceiling and counted to ten, forwent swearing loudly and then scooped up the plant. It was so dry the soil hadn't managed to hold together. Watering the house plants was the one thing that she'd asked Paul to do. She tended to get overzealous and then swamp them with love and far too much water.

Paul had told her, 'Less is more with plants. Thirsty is better than rotting.' But this was ridiculous. She checked the other pots around the house. There were deep cracks in all of them, and many looked pretty moribund, with dark, wilting leaves.

'One thing!' Hope ground the words out between her teeth. 'That's all I ask you to do.'

The dustpan and brush were hanging by the bin, so she swept up the lost earth. But where was the house plant watering can? Well, it wasn't where it should be, that's where it wasn't!

'You alright, Alfie?' She stopped to check him. He gurgled at her as she dribbled a spoonful of apple gloop into his mouth. He showed her his new set of front teeth. Checking all the places the watering can might be only left the places it shouldn't be.

'Aha!' Hope brandished the can at Alfie. The cupboard in the utility room was specifically for all the useful/useless things they'd accrued over the years. All the odd nuts and bolts that no longer fitted anything they had, all the wall hanging fixings, the washers, the dried-up paintbrushes in smeared jam-jars and old spattered trays, the orange-handled Stanley knife that was totally blunt. A man's cupboard. And five bottles of Johnnie Walker whisky. Only one of which still contained some amber-coloured liquid.

Hope shut the door quickly and took a breath. She knew he enjoyed having a drink down the pub with his mates, but this was different. This explained the smell of it on his breath. Secret drinking? And a spirit? This wasn't good. But how would she tackle him?

'I saw all your empties in the cupboard I'm not meant to go in. Care to enlighten me about it? Are you an alcoholic, Paul?'

Don't go blundering in. Harpy voiced accusations, and wild-eyed pointing of fingers might expose more than just his drinking; it might highlight the cracks appearing in their so-called idyllic marriage. And then what leg did she have to stand on?

14

ELE

EPPING FOREST

E le tried enlarging the photo, which didn't help. If anything, it made it fuzzier. It was madness to think it, but could it be possible? Flicking back and forth through all Michael's photos revealed nothing else. Only this one photo, the face in the distance, amongst a throng of strangers, but there was no doubt in her mind. Ransacking through her memories, she searched for clues, for evidence of what she actually knew.

After Michael had left, each day had stretched interminably in front of her, which was so strange as she now knew forever didn't exist. She'd fallen down the rabbit hole. How could any of this be real? When was the Queen of Hearts going to materialise? *Off with his head!*

Since she'd given up cleaning any part of the house in Hackney that wasn't specifically hers, she nearly missed the letter, lying amongst the filth, unread bills and old flyers that had accumulated behind the front door. Was it from Michael? Begging forgiveness, swearing undying love for her, the words on the sheet *screaming* that it'd all been a terrible mistake, an aberration, a hallucination even, something... But she didn't recognise the neat script on the envelope. Ripping it open, she read:

We are so sorry to inform you that our son, Hu Sung, died. We are having a private burial, and our family hopes you will respect our wishes and never contact us again.

Just like that. It was well known that they disapproved of their familiarity, their friendship. They wanted Hu to take over his father's firm and marry a Chinese girl from a well-respected family. A business merger. She'd always wondered if they believed that something more was going on between herself and Tiger, but she had Michael and Hu, well, he had whoever.

Dead? Rereading the words, they were still in the same order, still meant the same thing. Ele clutched at the wall, though her rubber legs collapsed beneath her. Dead? Was this a sick joke, for God's sake? How? What the hell had happened to him? It was so hard and clinical. Did these people have no emotion? Or were they so overcome with grief that to write any more would've broken them into countless pieces? From what Tiger had told her about them, she doubted it. Ele held a hand to her chest. Was her heart still beating? Michael and Tiger. Ripped from her life. The small black room was always there, and now there was no one to help her find the door. And now no chance to say the words that she'd repeated a million times in her head in a million different ways.

Her hand had hovered over the phone so many times, except she'd been unable to dial their numbers, speak to any of them. Especially Michael. But the first call was to him.

'Have you heard? Tiger's dead.'

There was a sharp intake of breath. 'Ele? What are you talking about? Tiger's not dead.'

'I've received a letter from Hu's parents, enlightening me that their beloved son is dead. It's in front of me now. Shall I read it out to you?' The letter fluttered in her hand.

'*What?*' It was practically a scream.

Ele read the unkind words out loud. Did that make them more real, shared with another human being who'd also loved Tiger?

'No, it's not true. I can't believe it.' Michael's voice resonated with pain. 'I only spoke to him a couple of weeks ago.'

Ele didn't respond. Of course, he had. Spoken to Tiger but not to her.

'Are you sure it's real? Not some terrible joke or something?'

'No. It's real.'

'How? I mean, what the fuck happened to him? They didn't tell you anything else?'

'Nothing.'

'Ele? We have to do something. We have to see the others.'

'Do we?'

'You know we do. This is Tiger we're talking about. Have you told them yet? I know I haven't seen you in a while, and it'll be difficult, but he was your best friend and my...'

'Your?'

'My friend too.'

If only he could see the war raging in her head. Friend? Best friend? He'd be recoiling, stupefied until he was cowering from her. But the voice that answered him was calm.

'I'll be there.'

Ele shook her head. Why were all the memories surfacing now? Had the message from Michael and the sudden appearance of Ange triggered something in her? She was beginning to think that Maria was right. She was going to need her, but it could be sooner rather than later.

'*Carida?* Ele, it's me. Are you in there? Hiding?'

The tapping on the door was insistent and annoying.

'I don't want to see you, Maria.' Ele had drawn all the curtains, let the blind down over the kitchen window, locked the front door, so yes, she was hiding.

'You know that's a lie. You always want to see me. Let me in.' Wheedling as usual. As though that would make her let Maria in.

'Sometimes, you sound like you're a vampire. *Let me in.*' Ele slunk to the door, making a face as she spoke, even though she knew Maria couldn't see it. 'As if you ever need permission.'

'I don't need permission, I need a key, then I can let myself in, can't I.' There was a heavier thump on the front door that made the letterbox rattle.

'Then I won't have any privacy.' Ele's hand was on the lock.

'Concealing yourself in a dark room isn't privacy. It's reclusion.'

'Is that even a word?' The lock was sliding.

'Maybe, but you know what I mean. It's not me who is the vampire; it's you.'

'Jesus wept! Okay.'

As the door opened, Maria grinned and gave her a kiss on each cheek. 'I come bearing gifts.' She waved a large Waitrose carrier bag at Ele. Wow, she must be doing well to be able to shop there.

'Gold, Frankincense and Myrrh?'

'Better than that. Bocadillo, Serrano jamon and olives, a pot of sun-dried tomatoes and Manchego cheese. I bring you *home from home.*'

Ele closed the door slowly and admitted a dignified defeat. 'I'll put the coffee on. It's from Machu Picchu. Is that Latin enough for you?'

'It'll have to do.' Maria cleared the small table of clutter, found three plates and a knife.

As she assembled the food on the larger of the plates, Ele sighed. 'You always make that look like an art form.'

'Is it not, then? Surely how your food is placed, how you perceive it visually, how it smells and looks is equally important to simply shovelling it down your throat as fast as you can? Or are we only fat pigs with no aesthetic consciousness?'

'Shovelling usually works for me.'

'Then we have to work on you. Mind now, the coffee is bubbling.'

They sat in silence and ate. Finally, Ele turned to Maria.

'Why are you here again. Do I need you?'

'You tell me. What might possibly draw me here?' Maria turned the full spectrum of her eyes on Ele until she felt as though she was drowning.

Should she tell her? It might bring out the nest of snakes that were already squirming in her gut. There was always a mixture of exhilaration and abject panic when Maria visited.

Maria cut another slice of the cheese and placed it on a crust of the bread. She was waiting.

Do it. 'Michael has contacted me about the pact. He says he's organised it.'

'Uh, ugh.' Now she wasn't making eye contact. Was that a good or bad sign?

'He wants us all to meet up.'

'Not all of us.' There was a sly tone to her voice, which Ele didn't trust.

'No, obviously, but...'

'But what?'

Ele licked her lips. 'I looked at all his photo albums on his Facebook page.' She took a deep breath. 'I saw something.'

'Something? Or someone?'

'Someone. I think I saw Tiger in one of his shots in San Francisco.'

Maria became a statue. Ele couldn't see if she was still breathing. 'What?'

'Tiger. It looked just like him.'

'Tiger is dead. So, you're right, it was someone who looked like him.'

'You remember what he did? After Michael... left.'

'Oh yes. Always there with his not so wide, welcoming shoulder for you to cry on. Your best friend, proffering Kleenex, a bottle of tequila and a box of Belgian truffles. How kind and considerate of him.' There was an essence in her voice, similar to poison gas creeping across the floor to suffocate her. Such sarcasm, *such hate.*

'My best friend forever. I told him that Michael and I were poles apart. I told him that I thought that Michael couldn't see me anymore. I bared my soul to him.'

'What did he say to that?'

'He said that Michael was working through stuff, that he'd come round. He said that Michael would come back to me because I was his "forever love". He even cried with me, and I believed him, Maria. I truly thought he was looking out for me, that he loved me.'

'So sympathetic. Why didn't you believe him? As he said, you were Michael's forever love.'

'I did at that point, until...' Ele looked away, but Maria pulled her chin up sharply.

'Until?'

'Until I saw what he'd done to me.'

Maria grimaced. 'Yes, we need to come to that, don't we. How and why these things keep happening to you. How and why you don't fight back.'

'I don't know how to.' Ele felt the anxiety coiling out of her, palpable, a miasma of shame and guilt.

'You don't think about it. You just do it. *Shazam, bam, wham!*' Maria clicked her fingers. 'They've done this to you all your life, and who has protected you? When you were preyed on as an innocent child? Later in that terrible house? I should have come to you earlier, then maybe we wouldn't be in this state.'

'I'm glad you came at all.'

'I won't let this happen again. I'm not going to let them hurt you. That's a promise.' Maria licked her lips. 'Will you go to meet them all again? I can understand you might want to catch up with Hope, but Michael and Sabine?' Maria made a derisive sound. 'And let's not forget Paul, although I really want to. I wonder if he is still an idiot?'

Ele grinned. 'Come on, Paul's been a good dad, and I think he and Hope are really happy.'

'So you're actually considering this?'

'I can't make a decision yet. I've said yes, but it's too much to take in.'

'And then some.'

'Do you agree with me that it couldn't have been Tiger in that photo? That he's really dead?'

'You've just been contacted by Michael about the pact, so it's bound to be dredging up old memories. I think you saw someone who looks similar, and it brought it all back. I don't for a second believe that this person was Tiger.'

Maria scooped the last olive from the bowl. 'Not for a second.'

15

LIANG

LAMB TO THE SLAUGHTER

'Personal use,' Liang rasped as they waited for the drugs to come out of her.

'We advise,' said a woman guard who spoke English, 'that you contact a consular officer of your home country immediately.'

Liang did that and waited. A red-haired man, liberally sprinkled in freckles and doused in sweat, came to visit her in her tiny cell. He held a crumpled Panama hat in his hand and wore a wrinkled cream linen suit. A caricature of an English ambassador. Better than if she'd contacted the Chinese one. Luckily, she still held a dual passport. She really hoped she'd chosen well that day.

'I can recommend a Thai lawyer for you and can set you up with a translator,' he said.

'Thank you.' Liang had to swallow as if there was a lump of concrete stuck in her throat. 'Is there anything else you can do for me?'

'Not really. Because of jurisdictional limitations, it's difficult for us to do much more than this. I'm sorry.' He wiped the sweat from his tangerine brow with a large, light-blue hanky. 'I'm afraid you must accept that even as a tourist in Thailand, you are still subject to the laws of this Kingdom. As you should know, there is no such thing as ignorance in the eyes of the law.'

'I know.'

'That's it entirely. Did you know? If you did, then you chose to do this, and quite frankly, we in the British Consulate have little sympathy for people wishing to make a...' he rubbed a drip off the end of his nose, 'a fast buck as they say in the States.'

'I have my reasons.'

'Then, if you have any information that might help you here, please tell me now.'

'I'd dearly love to tell you how I ended up here, but then everyone I know will cease to exist. Do you understand what I'm saying?' She tried not to cry, though tears fell regardless.

'You've been threatened? Your family has been threatened?'

Liang nodded.

'But you can't say for fear of reprisals?'

She nodded again.

'Didn't they ask for a ransom? They usually do with, how do I put this, the more high class of their victims.'

'My father wouldn't pay them.'

The ambassador looked taken aback.

'You must be very upset by that.'

Liang looked up at him. 'Have you a daughter?'

'Two. Near to your age.'

'Would you have left either of them in their hands just for the sake of money?'

Rubbing at his neck, the ambassador turned away. 'No.'

'So how do you think I feel when my father did. I hate him so much already, and I think this is just the beginning. But you must understand that I can't risk the lives of my sisters and my brother. I must take what's coming to me.'

'I'm sorry, my dear,' he said quietly, 'then you are well and truly shafted unless we can somehow wrangle a prisoner transfer with Britain. It will be difficult if you don't give us anything to go on. You'll be regarded as a simple criminal who spun the wheel of fortune and lost.'

'How poetic.' She smiled at him, although she thought her smile might've been twisted.

'There's nothing poetic about being locked inside one of Thailand's notorious women's jails, I can assure you.'

How right he was.

How do you explain to someone that you'd just spent seven years in a Thai prison? That her father's rejection and his disinheritance of her had made her feel as though he'd stolen her life, unable to see her little brother and sisters, banned from speaking to her own mother, wiped clean from the surface of the Earth. She'd walked into that situation because she was focused only on what she thought she'd lost; never realising what she was about to lose made it all so petty and childish in comparison. It wasn't even the seven years. It was what she'd seen and heard. Much as she'd like to, she couldn't unzip her skull and wash away the images, the stench and the horror. They haunted her every time she let her guard slip, and especially when she slept.

16

HOPE
SECRETS

'Mum? Mum, the phone's ringing.' Mia walked in, waving the phone around.

Hope glanced up briefly. 'Then answer it, sweetheart. Mummy's busy with Alfie.'

Why did the phone always ring when she was up to her elbows in baby poo? Cleaning bottoms was a way of life to her. At least that's how it felt.

'Hello? Yes.' Mia clutched the phone to her chest. She was in a kangaroo onesie, big floppy ears falling down the side of her head.

'Ask who it is, Mia.'

Mia nodded energetically. 'Who is it?' There was a pause. 'It's Grandma.'

'Okay, give me a moment.' Wiping her hands, Hope took the phone.

'*Hope?*' It was Liesel. '*Hello, darling. Have I caught you at a bad time?*' Her English was perfect, but she had a distinctive accent that twenty years in England hadn't wiped out.

'When isn't it a bad time.' Hope scrunched her eyes shut.

She hated landing her negativity on Liesel. 'Sorry, I'm changing nappies.'

'How is our beautiful little boy?'

'As sweet and cute as ever. Less stinky than a few minutes ago.'

'Mia?'

'Yep, looking like a little kangaroo. She's enjoying the holidays. I think the last part of the term was too much for her.' It'd been too much for all of them. George's latest escapade had popped their balloon. It didn't so much feel Christmassy as funereal. Not that it had affected George one bloomin' iota, except Paul was fuming and pretty shaken up by the thought of what he'd done. Of the possible consequences.

'They get tired quickly. I think we send children to school far too early and then pile the work on them. There's now the debate about homework. I'm sure you're keeping tabs on that.'

'Oh yes.' Hope wedged the phone into her neck and finished rubbing Sudocrem across Alfie's bottom. Poor little mite suffered terribly from nappy rash. 'If they extend the school day to include time to work on set homework, then I will be dancing in the street.'

'From that, I gather that you're still getting the texts from George's school?'

'The last part of this term was horrendous. One practically every night, and he even accrued so many that he was double-booked, and the worst part is, he doesn't understand why. He wasn't a happy bunny, I can tell you.' Paul had warned her not to mention the flare. This was something they would have to drip-feed his parents, although Hope craved to be able to talk to another adult who wasn't accusatory. Who might give advice that helped.

'I expect you had to deal with the aftermath of that?'

'I don't want to be that complaining parent, but I think they need to sort out their SEN policies. Giving a kid such as George endless detentions doesn't stop the behaviour. He can't connect his actions with the consequences.' No matter how many times they explained or tried to show him, it didn't bridge the gap.

'*Where is he now?*'

'Can't you hear? He's killing a bunch of sword-wielding maniacs on the rooftops of what looks similar to Venice. I'll probably be labelled a bad parent, but if it keeps him out of mischief for a bit, then I'm all for it.'

'*Venice? Really? I thought all these games were set in New York and were full of drug dealers and carjackers.*'

Hope laughed. 'So did I. We didn't want to give him any more ideas than he's already got. From the look of it, he'll be more widely travelled in his virtual world than we'll be in our real one.'

'*What a strange concept. That makes me feel very old. Now, darling, on to what I'm calling about. I don't know if you've spoken to Paul yet, but we were wondering if you're coming to us for Christmas?*'

Hope stopped moving. 'Coming to you? What in Dresden?'

'*You know the Christmas Market will be on in the Altmarkt Square. You haven't seen it yet, have you? It's a sight to behold. All the stalls are full of traditional Christmas gifts and amazing toys. The children would love it, I'm sure.*'

'It sounds wonderful, Liesel, but–'

'*We've got the world's tallest Christmas pyramid and the biggest nutcracker!*'

'The world's biggest nutcracker? Oh Liesel, you do know how to tempt me.'

'*No, no, don't laugh. The streets are decked out with lights. It's beautiful, and listen, we can all walk along the banks of the Elbe. Now, doesn't that sound more tempting?*'

'Yes, that does. But it's very close to Christmas.'

'We can go to the Semper Opera House. We can take Mia. She's a cultured little soul. Leave the boys being boys. Not sure who'll be looking after whom. I'm sure we can find tickets for you all.' There was a pause. 'Hasn't Paul mentioned you might be coming?'

'Not a word. Has he arranged something then?'

'No, I just thought...' Liesel cleared her throat. 'Well, I hoped, I suppose, what with...'

'What with what?'

'Don't you know?'

'Know what? It's very hard having conversations about things you don't know.'

'Then it must be a surprise.' Liesel sucked on her teeth. The sound made Hope wince. 'You didn't hear me say that.'

'What is? Liesel, you can't say things like that and then leave it all hanging in the air.'

Liesel's voice moved from the phone, so she was probably looking around. 'Axel will kill me if I tell you, and it's meant to be a secret.'

'I'll kill you if you don't. Work out who you're more scared of.'

'Well, put like that... Paul asked for a loan. His father gave it to him a few weeks ago. I naturally assumed that he'd use a bit of it to get you all here.'

'A loan?' Hope also glanced over her shoulder, although she knew it was unlikely that Paul had come home that day early. Mia was watching *Frozen* in the living room for the umpteenth time. George was still killing things in his bedroom on his X-Box. She lowered her voice. 'I don't know anything about a loan. Do you mind me asking how much?'

'Let's just say it's enough. Hope, darling. Please don't say anything to Paul. He must have other plans for the money, and I'm sorry if I've ruined any surprise. You must look as if it was a surprise. Can you do that for me?'

'Of course, I can. Maybe we are coming to you, and he'll tell us closer to Christmas.'

'I hope so. I'd love to take you shopping through all the little hand-made craft stalls. You'd love it.'

'I know I would. Don't worry, I won't say a thing to him. But I hope he's got me something nice. After all this baby poop, I think I deserve it.'

When the line clicked dead, Hope kept the phone to her ear. It gave her the impression that she could still hear Liesel speaking. Liesel and Axel had become surrogate parents to her over the years. Initially, she'd been wary of their reaction. Their golden-haired, blue-eyed boy bringing home a black girl? Hope smiled. Yeah, they were shocked. No hiding that. But she assumed her charming personality and the fact that she very soon after gave them their first grandson had won them over. Her own father had run at the first sight of a pregnant belly, and her mum had died of a heroin overdose when she was nineteen. At least she wasn't forced into a children's home or foisted off on foster parents as so many kids she knew. But she'd always had Paul. It was funny how the little things could build up until they swamped you, yet the big things, such as love, could be lost in all that thrashing about to bail out the boat.

Hope put the phone back in its holder. No denying it, she still loved that man to bits. A detail not to be forgotten. Now to the important thing. How much money had Paul borrowed, and what was he planning to do with it? She wasn't good with surprises. She'd had a few in her time, and none of them had been pleasant. She worked better if she'd been primed. Forewarned was to be forearmed. How could she find out without him knowing?

17

ELE

EPPING FOREST – 10 DAYS AND COUNTING

To say that Ele had kept up with Hope and Paul was a bit of an exaggeration. She knew that they were still living the dream. Happily married, three kids, nice home with a garden and she suspected a trampoline in it. Ele seemed to have a concrete patch out the front with a tramp in it. There was also a slab of concrete in the back with her shed crushed into a corner, where she made her board games. One large terracotta pot with slightly yellow, rather bald bamboo straggling from it filled the remaining space. But she wasn't grumbling. It was a wonder she'd even got that, all things considered.

She'd always speculated about Sabine. She was the opposite of Ele. Tall and bone-thin, hair akin to spun rose-gold, eyes the colour of new-mown grass. A broad chin for a woman, especially when she was in her teens, a difficulty, possibly bordering on masculine but great for her hope of becoming a model. She even had the ubiquitous mole above her pouty fat lips that every model seems to covet.

Michael had always been a little naughty. 'If I was her, I'd get that small garden mammal evicted a.s.a.p.'

Ele stared at him, watching for tics or "tells" as if they were playing poker. 'So you don't fancy her then? Everyone else does.'

'You're my dream girl, Ele. That should tell you everything.' His irises were like mood-stones that changed colour. She couldn't doubt him when he looked at her with those love-hued orbs. But she'd always wondered if there'd ever been anything going on between them. She'd seen covert looks, sly gestures and whispered messages. Her grandmother's warnings always came back to her. 'Some men can't help themselves, Ele. No matter how perfect you try to be, they always want more.'

'Are you having an affair with Sabine?' It'd just fallen out of her mouth one evening when he'd been too tired to make love to her.

Michael rolled over and levered himself up onto his elbow. 'Where has that come from, Ele?'

'I've seen things.' She covered her face with her hands. Don't cry.

'These things are in your mind. They're not real. Sabine is my friend, and that's it. You know I love you, Ele. How many times do I have to say that for you to believe it?'

'A zillion.'

'Come here, *tonta!*'

'Don't call me stupid!'

'Well, you are when you ask questions like that.'

Ele still didn't believe him.

The only thing she knew about Sabine now was that she'd achieved her dreams and got into modelling. Big time. Her cat-face and armpit length legs adorned many top fashion magazines, *Vogue, Elle, Harper's Bazaar* and *Marie Claire*, to name but a few. Most shot on exotic locations that couldn't include inch long ants and tapeworms, where she was wearing clothes that cost enough to make your average wage earners pea-green with jealousy. That was when she was wearing clothes. But all this was well and truly stymied three years ago when she got her heel caught in a grate outside of The Savoy Hotel, darling! She twisted her ankle, and then her lifelong ambition was shattered, not through a physical injury, more of a puncturing of the heart by a little arrow.

How many times had Ele heard her say: 'Men come and go, but modelling is for a tiny, finite few years. I'm not going to let a man get in the way of my dreams.'

So imagine when a French Aristocrat, Philippe, Duke de Montmorency, gently helped her up and wiggled her incredibly expensive Jimmy Choo shoe free. Love at first sight? What a bummer when he whisked her off in a roller and wined and dined her in the most expensive haunts in London.

'She's got her chateau,' said Hope in one of their brief phone calls, 'except it doesn't belong to her. I wonder if they have a prenup?'

'I never,' Ele said, 'thought of Sabine as being wife material.'

Well, didn't the surprises just keep on coming? Ele pushed the person in the crowd from her mind. It was a trick of the light, that's all, played across the face to make them look that way. There was no way that it could be... No way. Even though Maria had agreed with her, now she wished she hadn't said anything. Why hadn't she thought it through? Maria was so protective of her and sometimes went a little crazy if provoked. The question was, had Michael seen the Tiger look-a-like? If he had, what had he done about it?

Googling this Siren Inn place was the next objective.

Ele read it out loud, but Schrodinger didn't seem that interested.

'The Siren Inn is a Grade two-listed historical inn located on

Siren Street in the ancient town of Rye.' She scuffed through the fuzz and fluff in her head, sure she'd been there. She scanned down. 'Although there are sixteenth-century additions, the building itself dates from at least a century earlier. The Siren Inn has a long-standing connection to a notorious gang of smugglers–' An image of Jack Sparrow slid slinkily into her mind. Mmmm! No, hang on. He's a pirate, isn't he? What's the difference?

'The AA Rosette-winning restaurant serves British and French cuisine–' Now that's more like it. Forget the bloody ghosties and ghoulies; bring on the grub. She peered at the pictures. Quaint. Olde-worlde. Dark and scary. Not sure about it all. Why had Michael chosen this place? Do thirty-year-olds come here? She doubted it.

The main thing now was to get her attire for the festivities right. New Year's Eve. Not only New Year's Eve but one where she would meet people she hadn't seen in years. How had they all changed? She looked at herself in the mirror.

'When I stare into your eyes', Michael told her once, 'it feels as though I'm walking into a sun-dappled forest.'

Was that still true? Her eyes hadn't changed colour, but maybe her expression had. Were the tiny lines radiating out laughter lines, or were they from the years spent screaming. Silently. Ele practised smiling in the mirror, but it hurt.

Rummaging through the wardrobe, groaning under the weight of all her charity shop gear gave her no comfort. She checked her bank balance online. Yes, although it'd be tight, she could squeeze a bit more out this month to splash out on something with more "pizzazz" than two years ago Per Una cast-offs. A haircut was in order. She had curls that wandered off on their own walkabout, sometimes never to return. And what about shoes? She re-read the blurb about this ancient inn. It seemed it was up a cobbled street, so wearing six-inch stiletto heels was out. Catching the train meant she couldn't take too much. She began to feel as though she'd licked Schrodinger all over and now had a fur ball stuck at the back of her throat.

Ele was on Facebook again, waiting for Michael's next response. You could almost say they were pally.

He started. *Are you with anyone? I'm not prying. I've booked double rooms for everyone but I need to know how many to book food for.*

Ele thought about this. Was she with anyone? Did the cat count?

I didn't think our pact included partners, obviously, except Hope and Paul. Is anyone else bringing someone then? Is Sabine bringing her Duke?

There was a slight hesitation. *No. It's only us. Like the good old days.*

Not quite. Tiger won't be coming, will he?

Now there was a longer wait from his side. *I know.*

But it was as though the words were not the words he wanted to write. Curious. Ele didn't want to go down this path. It might lead her somewhere she really couldn't go.

18

HOPE

BRIXTON

Paul smirked at Hope. 'He said he's paying for all of us? Then fuck me, we're going.'

'I don't care if Michael's paying. I still don't think this is a good idea.' *Not ever.*

Paul held tightly onto the reins when it came to money. Running his own small business, she knew no one wanted to pay upfront and sometimes that three to six-month time delay could be lethal.

'Which part of New Year's Eve with friends, paid for by one of the said friends, sleeping in a four-poster bed, eating expensive nosh and drinking fine wine has bypassed you?'

'There's something not right. I can feel it.' It was no good saying anything to Paul about "gut feelings" or intuition. His response was derogatory at best or downright scathing.

'A day and a night away from the kids?'

Hope snorted. 'Do you think that'd swing it? Do you think I need to be away from my kids?' She heard the tone of her voice. Please don't let them argue again. It was becoming a daily routine, along with cleaning teeth.

'No, but it'd be nice. A chance for the both of us to be grown-ups, with other grown-ups and not be covered in toddler shit and thrown food.' He scratched at his goatee. 'And let's not forget the delightful arguments with our eldest.'

'I'm the one who is covered, not you. You're the one who goes down to the pub with his mates and plays pool. You're the one who has a life that's grown up.'

'Then all the more reason to come.'

'I don't have anything to wear, and if I'm not mistaken, we haven't got any spare cash to splash out on a new dress. Paul, I look a mess, and I feel old and frumpy.' She waited, watching for signs. Surely now he'd let on about the money?

His arms circled her. 'Come on, you're still gorgeous. In fact, you'd look fabulous in a bin bag.'

Pulling from him, she turned to look at him. 'Is that what I'll be wearing then? Sabine is going.'

'Oh, God! Is this what it's all about? Bloody Sabine de bloody Montmorency? She's a fucking supermodel, and darlin' no one can surpass that. So why worry? Ele will be there. You'd be pleased to see her, wouldn't you? I know you've had the odd phone call. And from all accounts, she hasn't had it so good over the last few years. It's about friendship. About catching up and not about rivalry. You were all stunning back in the day, and I bet you're all stunning now. It'll just be a laugh. We need that.'

'I'll have to ask Monique to take the kids again. It's a big ask as she had them only last week.' Having kids the same age at the same school allowed a barter system. She'd have Monique's kids along with her own to give her a break and then vice versa. It worked, as long as one of them didn't get greedy and tip the balance.

'She adores them, and they'll have a great time, being spoilt rotten and losing their teeth with all the sweets she gives them. Her kids get on with ours. It's one big happy family.'

'I suppose so.' One big, happy family as long as *he* didn't have to look after six kids, one with ADHD and an attitude to rival any street kid in the Bronx, two little "madams", two "boys will be boys" and a teething toddler.

'Anyway,' Paul cricked his neck. The *popping* sound made her cringe. 'Michael said he had something crazy to tell us. I'd like to know what that is.' He stopped, and a strange look slipped across his face.

'You okay?'

He nodded rapidly. 'You remember when we first made the pact? We all said what we'd be doing by the time we were thirty. Michael said he'd crack a scandal such as Watergate and be remembered as the man who saved the world from corruption and tyranny. Maybe he's done it?' Again, that look she didn't recognise. What was it?

'Yeah, and you told him he'd be covering stories on how someone saw Christ in their cappuccino.' Hope heard how cold her tone was, except she couldn't help it. 'Sabine said she'd be a top model and have her own chateau in the country, and she's done that. Now, what did I say?'

Paul took a step back from her. 'Don't say it, love.'

'I said I'd be a doctor.'

'Come on. Out of the six of us, only Michael and Sabine ended up doing what they said they wanted.'

'And you. You went into the internet business, just like you said you would.'

Paul shook his head. 'That hasn't been plain sailing, has it. We're not millionaires. Poor Ele crashed and burned, nearly literally, Tiger died young, and you, well, you've got three fantastic kids. That's more of an accomplishment than all the others put together.'

'You think?' Hope felt tears itching. 'I thought you said being a mother was child's play.'

'That's because I'm a prick sometimes, and to tell the truth, I know I couldn't do what you do every day. I have to go and hide at work, or I'd probably crack.'

'Then can you help me a bit more?'

'I'm on it. So, are we going to Rye, or are we staying here with our beautiful brood? You know I'm always up for a freebie, but if you don't feel you want to go, then we stay put. A glass of snowball to toast the new year in.'

'Wow. You certainly make that sound tempting.' When was he going to tell her about the money?

Paul laughed. 'Alright. I'll throw in some chicken goujons and a couple of packets of Pringles.'

'I'll let him know we're coming. And I'll get down the charity shops tomorrow before they shut. I might be able to pick something nice up.' Talk about baiting the hook and waggling it around. There was no possible way she could load any more brightly coloured lures onto it.

'You do that, love. You can pick up a bargain like nobody's business and still resemble a supermodel. You'll outshine even a real supermodel.' He winked at her, and she resisted the urge to slap him hard.

'You're sure we can't afford for me to go get a dress? Maybe some new shoes? You know, so I don't go to this do looking like a tramp?'

'Listen, Hope. I've told you you'll look fabulous, no matter what. Money's a bit tight right now but don't you worry, I've got plans coming into fruition as we speak.'

Was the money being pumped in to upgrade the business then? She wished he'd speak to her about what was happening, except they'd got into a routine right at the start. Initially, she was so preoccupied with their new baby, she never enquired about how the business was running. She sort of expected it to be chugging along in the background merrily by itself. After that, she didn't get a chance. They talk about the terrible twos, though she had no idea it would be *that* terrible. The moment George could crawl, he was faster than the speed of light, tiny hands foraging, pulling things out of cupboards or off sideboards and low-level tops. After three trips to the hospital, by the time he could toddle, Hope and Paul had done all they could to baby-proof their home. Then the tantrums started. If he didn't get his way, he'd scream until she thought his head would explode, no caring where they were, and if he could, he'd spin round and round until he was sick. Other parents had sucked on their teeth and nodded sagely. They all go through this stage, and you'll look back in relief when he's three. But he got steadily worse.

'ADHD,' the doctor said. 'Attention deficit hyperactivity disorder. Lots of kids have it.'

'Did we give it to him?' Hope turned towards Paul. 'Did we do something wrong?' What she meant was 'is this my fault?'.

'Not at all,' the doctor's voice was soothing. 'It's probably been around for hundreds of years, but now we have a name for it. What you have to look at here is that in the good old days, kids were working sometimes by the age of nine. If they were lucky enough to go to school, they probably walked miles to get to it and then came home to chores. They didn't get a chance to be hyperactive.'

'So we get him working down the mines as quick as we can and then scrubbing floors when he gets home?' said Paul. He wasn't smiling.

'Nearly. You get him interested in anything that will burn off the excess energy, try to keep focused on even little things and give him unconditional love. Do you think you can do that?'

Hope opened the laptop on their bedroom table. George had his own in his room, and Mia had a mini-iPad. This was for their own personal use. Clicking into Facebook, she found Michael's page and messaged him.

We're in. Looking forward to it and seeing everyone. H & P x

There. It was done. But the heavy feeling that was similar to someone pressing down hard on her chest didn't go. Nerves. It was going to be an assault course seeing her old friends. So much had occurred since they'd made that pact, hands cold from clutching their drinks, so young and trusting.

Friendship, that's what Paul had said at the time. But were they still friends? Sabine, the supermodel, hadn't even invited them to *her* wedding. What did that say about their "friendship"? She must need a vault for all the money she'd earned and then to marry a French Duke and have a chateau in the Central Massif, to which, again, they'd not been invited. After Tiger died, which was the last time she'd seen him, Michael had jetted off all over the place. She covered her face. That last time. So beautiful, so sad... so *stricken.*

Hope had read as many of his articles as she could, even though many were marred by splats of orange-coloured baby-goo. They were good, no denying it, and yet she was resentful of his freedom when she was tethered, and in the end, stopped looking out for them. He'd contacted her on Facebook about five years previously, and they'd sent sporadic comments to each other.

Ele was the one person who'd maintained some sort of contact, albeit fairly recently. There had been a time after Tiger's death that had been a bit of a blackout zone for the both of them. Good thing, really. She was too immersed in looking after George by then and trying to ensure he didn't kill himself, and Ele, well, Ele had problems of her own.

19

LIANG
DOING THE RIGHT THING?

Michael had already gone back to England, buying Liang a later flight as there were no spaces on his. Terror at being left behind was insidious, threatening to overwhelm her. How could she miss him so much, having only just met him? It was late December, and most flights were booked up, so they'd been lucky to get this.

Now on the plane, she was anxious, excited and wondering if she was doing the right thing, no longer able to even distinguish what that might be. Would it be possible to dovetail neatly into his life over there, or were splinters and broken promises waiting for her? Who would she meet, and would they accept her?

After the initial safety film that everyone ignored and chatted through, Liang pulled her thin cardigan closer around her neck and huddled into her seat as it was quite chilly. Now her throat tickled. She usually went down with something nasty after a flight, breathing in everyone else's germs through the cycling air conditioning. There was a man squished in beside her, overflowing from his seat to hers, his shirt buttons being tested to their limits trying to hold all that flesh in. How do you get that fat? Has hunger knocked at his door, so when he has a time of plenty, he eats as though each meal will be his last? As she did now. Or is that just sheer gluttony?

'They say,' the man began in a deep Southern drawl, 'that flying is the safest way to travel, but I ain't convinced.'

Liang wanted to say, 'If the plane blew up mid-flight, after everything I've gone through, that'd be the cherry on the cake.' But she merely nodded as if in agreement. It was the "Paradise syndrome". The closer you got to believing you might make it and paradise was within your grasp, the more likely it was that you'd fall down the subway steps and break your neck. Not enough to die but close enough that your little world, all those hopes and dreams would come to an abrupt stop. But you'd still know about it.

'You know, liddle lady, my pappy used to say that if God meant us to fly, he'd have given us wings. I always said back that if that was the case, if God had meant us to drive, where were our wheels?' The man snorted loudly. 'He'd give me a backhander so hard I'd fly across the room. No sense of humour when he'd been drinking, and boy, could he drink.'

Liang had that awful sinking in the gut feeling. Would he talk to her throughout the whole eleven hours about his crappy job, his bitchin' wife and lousy, good for nothing thankless kids? How the world has gone to pot since Obama got into the White House? How Trump was the best President, ever, as he told it as it was...

Liang mumbled something in Cantonese to him and waved her hands, shaking her head. *She didn't speak English.*

What a sneer he had on his face. Did she epitomise all he hated about "foreigners"? Don't they know how to speak *American,* for God's sake?

Liang had the window seat, so she turned from him. Take the hint, *bud.* Hours were spent craning out the window, first watching as San Francisco airport dwindled to a dot. The sky turned from lightest blue to violet and then the deep Prussian blue of night. Stars were liberally sprinkled, obscured now and then by feather clouds. A kid, still sporting his baseball cap, kicked and kicked and kicked the back of her seat and his parents, quietly arguing, were oblivious. She ignored the *thump, thump, thump.* These were all trivial things.

The flight attendant ran her cart along the aisle. 'Would anyone like a drink?'

Liang caught her eye. 'A tea, please. With milk and sugar.' It was handed to her over the bulk of the man next to her, now snoring in the same way as an elephant seal trying to attract a mate. It was amazing how the *pretty* can be so cruel. She should know better, but she was a little bitter.

Klom Prem Central Prison. Houses up to twenty-thousand inmates.

Sentenced to seven years, Liang seriously contemplated suicide rather than endure that, especially after having the horrors of it whispered into her ear at night by other inmates awaiting their fate.

'Seven years?' An Australian girl who had befriended her shook her head. 'Most people hit the wall about then.'

'What do you mean? Hit the wall?'

'Go crazy. They say for most, it's around the seven-year mark. You always gotta make sure you're out of there by then.'

'I've been sentenced, and there's no appeal. As they said in court, I was lucky I didn't get the death penalty.'

'Seven years is not good in a Thai jail. You got to keep campaigning. Are you still sure you don't want to tell them who set you up for this? If they can pin something on a bigger fish, they might reduce your sentence.'

'No. I can't.'

'Good luck, sister.' She hugged Liang like she would be marched off that day to stand before the executioner's guns.

The journey wasn't long in time or miles, though it was a lifetime for her. All the decisions that had brought her to this place went through her mind. How each step, she could've changed her fate, made a different choice. She walked every path that could've been hers, saw the lives she might have had instead of this, remembered the love of a man, and a hundred sharp knives seemed to pierce her. How to cope? The pain was unbearable. As the grey metal doors clanged shut behind her, and the khaki-clad women guards with hard-set faces and heavy hands stripped her of her clothes and tossed her the new dark-blue prison garb, she finally took in what had happened to her. She was either going to go mad or die there.

When the blazing lights of London could be seen on the ground below them, that was when she felt she'd been kicked in the gut, a wrenching cramping pain. As they landed and the tyres bump-bumped on the runway, she couldn't believe she was back in England. They'd arranged that Michael was to pick her up from Heathrow, except there was a moment when she wondered if she'd walk out to the concourse and not see him. She hadn't thought that through, what she'd do if he wasn't there. Getting a flight straight back was the only option but then, what would be the point of that? She had nothing to return to. Clutching her bag, her palms sweated, although she felt a little shivery. Maybe she had caught something on the flight from all that recycled air. Tired beyond belief, she also felt as if she'd eaten twelve chillies in a row. Would he be there? She kept her gaze lowered as she stepped through the doors that said she had nothing to declare. It brought back that other time when she declared nothing and then lost everything.

20

ELE

EPPING FOREST – 9 DAYS AND COUNTING

Constructing hand-made chess and backgammon boards in the shed in the garden, Ele clack-clacked on a treadle fretsaw akin to a toothy demon. Using no energy but what she supplied, it was economical, eco friendly and a touch *steampunk*. It probably drove her neighbours mad, but what the hell. At least she was outside and not pounding away in her flat. Anyway, the neighbour above her was not considerate in his ways either, playing thumping music until gone three weekday mornings. City life. Inconsiderate on so many levels.

The Apple Market in Covent Garden was where you gravitated to if you were a small, totally bespoke craftsperson. Fighting sharp-clawed for a red-painted stall to call her own in the prestigious Apple Market, she'd been allocated one every Tuesday, and if she got her name in the hat at the weekend, she had as much chance as the rest of the market for a coveted slot. Priceless that your business rested on your name being pulled out of a big black top hat! Not exactly famous, but she knew her boards were sat on someone's table or shelf in countries across the world. It gave her a sense of pride, of self-esteem that'd been lacking for so long. Since Michael had gone, in fact.

Tuesday 23 December brought cold, mizzly rain that kept the prospective punters tucked indoors, the cheapskate wimps. Ele needed their hard-earned cash in *her* pocket, not in theirs. And the coffee wasn't getting any cheaper. The weather was another factor that couldn't be controlled and might ruin her livelihood. Even so, this felt like a "good" day, an "up" day.

She never envisioned her life being this way, believing she was meant to be the next great designer until "the fall" and subsequent degradation and atrophy. But she'd hauled herself upright. The games she made were beautiful and rightly stood on their own as "useful art".

Ele caught the tube to Covent Garden and walked until she reached the prominent "finger" signs that pointed the way. Having never learned to drive was never a hindrance in London. In many ways, it was a bonus. Public transport worked well, and she didn't have to worry about the sheer expense of running a car and the horror of trying to park it.

It was too early for tourists. Shops were only beginning to be opened, boards positioned outside, workers donned aprons or dragged tables and chairs onto their front terraces. She'd always been entranced by the colourful stalls and large vegetable barrows in the North Hall, where craftspeople sold eccentric jewellery made from gold, silver and precious stones, artwork, glassware with shards of colour embedded in the glass itself and moulded into extraordinary shapes, ceramics that were individual, unique metal clocks and turned candle holders inlaid with metal. As usual, she lusted over the chocolates in Thorntons, then bought her takeaway coffee from a café called Pontis.

A large black cloth was used to cover the main wooden stall, and she'd built a variety of stepped shelves to make the best possible use of the space. Each day she traded, she hauled her newest boards to the market in battered suitcases, but the rest of her goods she had in a lock-up down one of the side streets close to the market. She set it all up and then morphed into someone else. Someone who had confidence in what she did, was able to talk money out of people's purses and wallets and then when the street acts were done and the light had dimmed, she packed away, hopefully minus something, but not always. She stood on the Sunday Times, not because it was the best, but it *was* the thickest, and it kept her feet warm.

Nodding a greeting to a stallholder setting up her intricate puzzle creations and observing one man placing his wooden automata, she slipped off her gloves and poured that delicious creamy brown hit down her throat. As she did, day after cold snappy day. Glancing to the end of the row, there was even a stall where plump teddy glove puppets were waiting with chubby arms outstretched while the vendor had one sat on his arm. It waved at any passing children and washed its ears. Ele wished she'd thought of that as the teddies practically leapt off the stall to nestle in people's bags.

When Ele finished setting up, she stopped and only then allowed herself to wonder what the hell was really going on. Michael, then Ange? It was pretty weird. And why had Maria materialised back into her life? There was something she was missing, but part of her was too scared to go looking for it. She had a sixth sense that what she might find wouldn't be good.

The market was coming alive. Strains of classical music curled up from the courtyard below in the South Hall, where four musicians had set up and were playing earnestly. Families, bundled up in thick coats, scarves and hats dodged sword-fighting knights battling it out under the high canopy of glass and metal struts, cheered on by the onlookers that'd slowed to watch. Then, as they came outside to the cobbled stones of the West Piazza, they would be enthralled by a magician, the gathering crowd spellbound as he performed a complicated routine that left them all "oooing" and "aaahing". Ele had seen the performance far too many times, and its appeal had faded,

Facing her was a red-haired Argentinean woman called Rosita. She made exquisite enamelled jewellery baked in a tiny kiln at home. She was always stylishly dressed and poised. Her accent was soft and lilting as she'd been in England for nearly thirty years. Sometimes they chatted a little in Spanish.

Next to Rosita was a *proper* cockney called Lorraine, born within earshot of Bow bells. Ele couldn't get over what an extraordinary colour she was. It was true she went on many holidays to Majorca, yet even that couldn't quite explain the unique orange glow that stopped at her chin.

Lorraine told them every morning what her husband and son, both called Reggie, had gotten up to the day before. Ele had garnered from Rosita that Lorraine's boys regarded the market as a hobby for her while they did the real work of robbing other people blind. As she launched into yet another tale, pride palpable in her voice, Ele was startled when someone tapped her on her shoulder. Turning, she came face to face with Ange. Sweet Jesus! Ground... Open... Up... *Now!*

'You lied to me.' Ange's voice was quiet but strained. She looked about her and waved her hands, the bangles clinking. 'Why didn't you tell me you worked here?'

The sharp metallic sound set Ele's teeth on edge. Words were hurtling around her head, but nothing managed to escape from her mouth except a strange whining sound.

Ange shook her head. 'You told me you were a fucking legal secretary or something.' Now she was getting louder, more strident. 'I came back at six and waited for you outside that office, for like, ages. You never came out. I had to look you up. I mean, what? Are you ashamed to be here?' There was the beginning of understanding. 'No, you were ashamed of *me*. You were frightened your snooty nosed friends here might not think so much of you if they knew you hang out with someone like me.'

Ele found her voice. 'I don't hang out with you. Not for years.'

It was as if Ele had smacked her around her face. Hard. 'Not now you don't, but you used to.'

'Yes. *Used to*. Past tense.'

'Ah, I get it. You wouldn't want them,' she nodded over towards the other stallholders, who Ele knew were listening in, 'to know that we used to down a bottle of vodka and a couple of lines of charlie then go out of a night. Oops, have I let the cat out of the bag?'

Ele didn't look over at Rosita or Lorraine. 'I went through a bad time, but now I'm clean. I never drink, and I won't touch drugs.'

'I don't believe you. Why should I? You've already lied your fuckin' face off to me.' She took a step closer towards Ele and stared up at her. 'Have you forgotten who you used to be then?'

'No, I want to, though. Ange, don't you get it? I never want to be that person again.'

'*That* person was my friend. I don't understand. Me an' Dave helped you after that condescending bastard left you in the shit.'

'Helped me? You turned me into an alcoholic. I never drank like that until you two came into my life.'

'Didn't say no, though, did you?'

'My reason for living had betrayed me, had shot me down in flames, so no, I didn't say no. Maybe you thought you were helping me, but it just made it a million times worse.'

Ange gripped onto her arm. 'We had some great times, Ele.'

'We were drunk more than we were sober. How can that be great? We used to fight so much we got barred from most of the pubs in east London!'

'You were like my *sister*. I loved you. And Dave. I miss him so much.'

Was the floor shifting under her feet? A deep ringing sound was resonating out from her ribcage. Her sight was blurring, and the woman in front of her was just a washed-out silhouette.

'Do you want to know something about your precious Dave?' Ele leant down, so she was inches from the other woman. She kept her voice very low. 'One time when you were away at your mother's, he crawled into my room. He put his hands on me, said he wanted to *fuck* me. He wouldn't leave me alone, pawed at me.'

'Shut up! Shut your fucking mouth, you lying bitch!'

'Got what he deserved.'

'What did you say?'

Ele wiped at her face, slick with a sheen of sweat. Blinking, now she could only see Ange's black eyes and red-painted lips. Was the rest of her transparent?

'I said he got what he deserved.' She took a deep breath. 'So did Rab.'

'Oh God! That's a terrible thing to say. They both burned to death in their beds!'

'Dave tried his best to rape me in *mine.*'

Ange's body went rigid, but Ele could see tremors shaking her as if she was being buffeted by an invisible wind and her hands curled into fists at her side. 'Do you know what, Ele Riviera? I spent years mourning him and you. I loved you both more than anybody.' Tears smeared the kohl down her thin cheeks. 'I don't believe you, and I never will. He wasn't like that, not my Dave.' Her face crumpled but not before she spat fully at Ele. 'I hope you die horribly and rot in hell for eternity.' There was a flash of colour and discordant notes, and then all Ele had to contend with were the stunned looks on the faces of her colleagues.

'What was all that about?' said Rosita. 'Ele? Ele, are you alright?'

'What an awful woman!'

'Burned to death in their beds? That's dreadful.'

Words were coming at her through the sound of fast-flowing water. Was she in a river? Fallen into the sea, being dragged up and down the shingle by the force of the tide? The words she heard spiralled and twisted in her head.

'Did she say she'd been raped?' Was that Lorraine's voice?

She was stepping outside of her body, which was now below her as though she was hanging above it. The body below her was sliding to the ground, arms flopping.

'Ele!' An arm encircled her, and more voices joined in. Rosita had her hands under her armpits. 'Help me, someone. Help me get her up.'

Ele fell back into herself. She was being hauled over to her stall. Someone wiped the spit from her cheek. She balanced on the edge, her vision foggy and distorted as if she was peering through driving rain. Her breath was coming in ragged little spurts, and now her heart was out of kilter, a thump here, two thumps there, losing its rhythm.

'Ele?' Rosita hovered in front of her. 'You look dreadful. Do you want a coffee or something?'

'No. Thank you.' Whispered words.

'She needs a brandy more like,' said Lorraine. 'I can nip to the pub and get a snifter for her?'

'No.' Ele roused herself. 'I don't drink.'

'Up to you, but you ain't half a funny colour.'

'Listen, you go home,' said Rosita. 'We can pack your stuff and get it to the lock-up.'

Ele took a moment to register what she'd said. 'Are you sure?'

'No worries,' said Lorraine, as her orange-hued face

wrinkled in apprehension. 'Whatever that was, it didn't sound good.'

'There was a fire.' Ele lowered her head into her hands. She didn't want to remember. 'In our house. Her boyfriend died. I didn't mean... I...'

'Of course, you didn't.' Lorraine shook her head. 'We know that. But, if some bloke had attacked me, I think I'd be quite pleased if he got his comeuppance.'

'Yes but', said Rosita, 'people still died. Not sure if that counts as *comeuppance*.'

Ele raised her head sharply. 'I didn't have anything to do with it.'

'No one said you did, lovey.' Lorraine patted her head. 'God works in mysterious ways, I can tell you.'

'Get going, Ele. We can deal with your stall.' Rosita grabbed her bag for her where it was hidden under her stall, and half shoved her in the direction of the tube.

Ele wanted to go home, to curl up in her bed with the duvet pulled over her head, Schrodinger hugged tightly to her chest. She knew she couldn't and had to deal with this now. She was not allowed to hide.

Blue line. Piccadilly. Crowds of people. Change at Holborn. Red line. Central. More crowds. Upstairs, downstairs, in my lady's chamber. Jostling, umbrellas, briefcases, rucksacks, shopping, laughter. Who could possibly be laughing? A short walk but feet made of stone. Home. An hour. Maybe more, although it felt it had taken forever.

'Schrody?'

He was there, quick to curl into her lap. Purring, snuggling. Soft fur. *What was that?*

Haunted. Yes, that's what it was. Ghosts from her past were now haunting her. Switching on all the lights. Turning the shower on. Sitting in the bath. Sodden clothes. Schrody watching intently from the safety of the toilet seat.

'Ghosts are harder to see in the light, Schrody.'

Headache. Dizzy. Sick.

Why?

Help me.

'Carida?'

Ele heard Maria as if she was miles away, calling down into a deep shaft, and she was at the bottom of it. The echoes went on and on. How long did it take for her to surface? Seconds? Minutes? Hours?

'Maria? What's happening? Where am I?' Shivering, skin feeling like she'd been sleeping in a snowdrift.

'You appear to be in the bath, and you're wet and cold. You have to help me here, as I don't think I can get you out by myself. Hang around my neck and get your knees underneath you.'

Ele tried to command her limbs to move, but they didn't want to comply. Pins and needles stabbed at her. The weight of her head threatened to snap her spindly neck. Somehow, Maria hauled her out of the bath and yanked off her swampy clothes. A towel was rubbed briskly over her until she felt abraded, as if a layer had been sanded off her.

'You're hurting me. I'm raw.'

'What you are is warm. If I hadn't found you, you'd be sick with pneumonia by now.' Maria tugged a fresh T-shirt over Ele's head and pushed her into the bedroom. 'Get into bed. I'm going to make us both a coffee and toast. Then we'll talk.'

Ele's focus came and went. One moment she was in her bed gazing at the wall, the next snapshots of Ange's mouth curling into a snarl, Michael's wide smile, then there was Tiger, making his toasted sandwiches, Dave's leering face and the smell of sulphur, of hellfire, followed by staring at the wall. Round and round.

'Here, *carida,* drink this.' Though she knew it would be sugared and warm, the rich smell of the coffee nearly made Ele's stomach heave. She took a sip.

'I found these in the bathroom,' Maria waved a small pharmaceutical pot with a prescription, but she couldn't read whose name was on the label. The seal was broken. 'These are mine, Ele. You know you shouldn't be taking them.'

'Yours? I thought Mum wanted me to take them.'

'No, *tonta!* They're for me. Now I'm going to do what I should've done a long time ago.'

Maria stood up, flipped off the lid, and Ele heard her enter the bathroom, the sound of the pills scattering onto porcelain and then the toilet being flushed.

'Should you do that? Mum will be mad.'

'Enough is enough, Ele. I don't ever want to see these things in here again. We're stronger than that, you and I. We're sisters, and we look after each other. Understood? And I promise I won't call you *tonta* again.'

21

LIANG

ISLINGTON

'Liang!'

Michael's call made her heart constrict as if his hands were clasped about it, squeezing her lifeblood from it like an old fashioned wringer. How could this man have this effect on her after all she'd experienced these last few years? Her battered heart should be sculpted from a lump of granite, not be a live, beating organ inside of her. It would betray her. She knew it would.

Running to her, he enfolded her in his arms and then let her go far too soon.

'I had a terrible thought,' he said, 'that you might not be on the flight, that you might have changed your mind.'

Liang breathed out slowly. 'I thought you might not be here either.'

'Of course I'd be here,' he said and reached for the small holdall she had with her. 'Have you more?' He nodded towards the baggage reclaim sign.

'No, that's it. I only brought hand luggage. What could I possibly have to bring back with me apart from the baggage I'm dragging behind me.' She buttoned her coat higher. It was freezing in the airport, so what was it like outside?

'Okay. If there's nothing to collect, we can go straight to the Heathrow Express Train. That'll take us to Paddington. We can chat later about "baggage". We all have it. I've got mine too.' She couldn't tell if he was embarrased or not. But on further reflection, she decided his expression was one of guilt. But of what, she couldn't fathom. It was now a distinct possibility that she should have told him about her life before she'd made the horrendous journey here. She had to remain strong. If he rejected her, then so be it. It would simply show it was not meant to be.

From the bustle of Paddington, they took the Circle line and changed at King's Cross to catch the Northern line, jumping one stop to hop out at Angel. They made what she thought was termed "small talk" as the real issues that encircled them were far too big to risk utterance on a train in public.

Tall, straight trees lined his road of Victorian houses, grey and mottled, with bare spiky branches outstretched. So different to how they looked in summer, heavy with bold fluttering leaves and sun-dappled pavements.

'Home,' said Michael, leading her up steps to a house with a large bay window and dark wood door. A small leaded window was at the top. He fumbled with the lock, his hands shaking. Maybe he was as nervous as she was. Liang couldn't meet his gaze as they stepped over the threshold. The floorboards were stripped pine and waxed. Hanging from the white walls were photos of friends, family and strangers who smiled at them as they passed them. Lots of friendly grins but their eyes bored into her as if they'd turned from their poses to watch them walk by. And she didn't think they were smiling so brightly now. The last was a photo of a group of young friends. She stopped and stared. Six heads close together, arms snaked and hung freely around necks and waists, unified against what might come and anticipating their futures, no doubt. She saw someone who resembled her.

'That's–'

'Yes,' he said, tugging her gently by the arm. 'It was a long time ago.'

But it wasn't *her* face. Similar, yes, but different in so many ways. She moved, willing herself not to cry.

'You okay?' He was part way into the living room. She could see a ghastly gilt mirror over his shoulder, which reflected her. She looked like a ghost, haunted by herself. She'd been avoiding mirrors as one glimpse of her real soul might make it crack into a million shards, and she didn't need another seven years of bad luck!

'Tea?' He waved her to an oatmeal-coloured sofa with oversized patterned cushions. She sank into it as though she'd fallen into a bowl of porridge laced with heaped spoons of golden syrup.

'Liang,' His eyes crinkled. 'Everything's alright now.' His footsteps padded into the kitchen. Liang focused. She loved open-plan living. You could see where everything was and, most importantly, where *everyone* was. No sneaking up on you from dark corners.

Their mugs were mismatched. Hers was tall and white with a tiny handle that she could only get three fingers through. The idea that it was strong enough to hold the mug belied belief. His mug had colours she wouldn't ever put together, yellow and citrus green, the sort that makes your cheeks implode as if you've sucked on a whole lemon.

'I'll make sure you have your own space. Sort out in the bathroom and empty drawers, you know? I want you to feel like you have your own areas that aren't anything to do with me.'

Liang motioned at her bag. 'I don't exactly have a lot of stuff. I can probably make do with one drawer.'

'You'll get more over time.' He grinned at her like a little boy. 'I do know a little about women, and I think, correct me if I'm wrong, that they like to shop.'

Frowning, she poked him in the chest. 'That is so stereotypical that's it's beneath you.'

'Oh, come on. I bet you want some new clothes and make-up? Huh?'

'Sure. Who wouldn't but I don't–' She stopped.

'I can–' he also stopped, was considering his words, 'I'll lend you the money, and you can pay me back when you can. How does that sound?'

'Sounds good.'

He didn't want her to feel like a kept woman. He was giving her some autonomy, even if it was only in name. But he was right, she did need some more clothes, even if it was just so she could look presentable when trying to get a job here.

'Right, a guided tour of my castle.' Michael stood up. 'I had the place renovated about five years ago, so the layout's changed, but it's too small to get lost or anything. You've traversed the hall, met the living room up close and personal, the kitchen is there,' he waved to the left of them, 'the bathroom is through that door, and any difficulties with the plumbing need to be written up on the whiteboard in the kitchen, so I remember to do something about it. I'm pretty crap at getting things sorted.'

Feeling as though she had to do something, she heaved herself out of the sofa and wandered into the kitchen area, fingering at the colourful cookery books, searching through the herbs and exotic spices in glass jars along the back wall. There was a terracotta pot with a spindly dead plant straggling from it. A casualty of his time away.

'Perhaps I should point out,' he was now behind her, 'that

this is not all for show. I can actually cook, and my Moroccan lamb tagine is to die for.' He pointed. 'The cooking pans are here, the glasses up there, the crockery in that one and the cutlery in this drawer. Anything you need, just rummage for it. I do believe I've got most things. Not so hot on the washing up, so behind that door is a dishwasher.' He yanked a cupboard open to reveal a slimline machine tucked into the gap.

'Good to see you've got your priorities right.' She could feel the warmth of him as though he was radiating heat like a star that'd strayed too close. 'I haven't really had a chance to cook much recently, but I'm a dab-hand at chicken and Chinese mushrooms in oyster sauce.'

'So, between us, we can cook and more to the point, we're pretty cosmopolitan too,' he said. 'I like that.' There was a movement by her shoulder. He flipped the lid of the bin, and the dead plant was gone with a loud *thunk*.

'Poor little coriander never stood a chance.'

Memories are things that can play tricks on you. She had an image in front of her, except it wasn't a dying plant left behind to fend for itself. Pouring herself a glass of water, she pushed this from her mind. She couldn't go there yet.

Pulling her round and tilting her head up, Michael said, 'I know it'll be strange at first, but we can make this work.' His breath tickled her face.

'I'm here, aren't I?' She swallowed. *'You yuan qian ll lai xiang hui,* which means "fate brings people together no matter how far apart they may be." I think that's apt for us.'

'Yes. It is.' Nodding, he peered over his shoulder. 'You can have the bedroom–' He must've seen the look on her face, 'and I'll have the sofa bed.'

'No.' She held her hand out and glanced along the hall to the front door. 'I'd rather have the couch.'

'So you can get out quicker?' He also looked pointedly at the door.

'Yes.' She shrugged her shoulders. There must always be an escape route.

'I can jump to all sorts of conclusions about what's happened to you, but I bet they'll all be wrong. The door is open anytime you need to go but promise me one thing?' He leaned down, so he was only inches from her. 'Let me know? Will you do that for me at least?'

'I will.'

'Okay,' he let out a whoosh of air as if he was a balloon that's been squeezed too hard. 'Fancy a walk around the area? It's nice around here, not too frenetic, especially at this time of day. We can pick up some ingredients, and I'll *wow* you with my culinary skills tonight.'

As they passed the photo, she tried not to look at it.

Although the couch that night was uncomfortable, Liang didn't complain. She'd had much worse for years, and this put everything from that point into perspective. Waking from a dream she didn't wish to remember, she shook her head and sat up. Light poured in through the warm, biscuit-coloured curtains and soft floating voile nets. Focusing on the room, painted white, with rustic dining table and chairs and simple furnishings, she realised it was not overtly masculine. What had she been expecting? Black leather sofas and heavy, metal industrial furniture? Wooden shelves groaned under the weight of hundreds of books that she knew would be well-thumbed, with broken spines and lost bookmarks. Incense and holders were on one shelf, masking *The Complete Works of Shakespeare*. There were

African carved heads, golden statues of a fat and smiling Buddha, hanging wooden puppets in elaborate gold and deep red Thai costumes and headdresses. She had to turn her head away.

Retrieving her clothes and folding the duvet neatly, she crept to the bathroom to wash and dress and then put the kettle on for a cup of tea. The kitchen window overlooked the next-door neighbour's garden, and Liang could see a small set of swings and a red and blue plastic slide. Balls were scattered around, kicked into bushes or left where they'd been dropped when the user had been called in to supper. How old were these children? Or maybe they were for grandchildren?

'Liang?'

She jerked and slopped some of her tea. 'Oh, sorry, I didn't hear you get up.'

'I didn't mean to make you jump.' He grinned. 'Next time, I'll whistle or something.'

He was in boxer shorts and a *Simpsons'* T-shirt. His hair stood up on end, and the growth of stubble on his chin had darkened considerably overnight.

'Can I make you a coffee?' Liang was already reaching for the percolator.

'Sure, but then how about we go out for breakfast? I know a wonderful café around the corner that does all sorts of different stuff. Their kedgeree is the best in town.'

'Michael, it's Christmas Eve tomorrow. Don't you have plans? I mean, people to meet or see? And what about Christmas itself?'

'Don't worry about that. This Christmas is going to be all about us. I've got loads of stuff already in the freezer, enough drink to keep a drunken monkey king happy, and we can pick up whatever else we need today or even tomorrow. We don't have to leave the flat if we don't want to for the duration. We can slob in

The Pact

our jammies, watch all the crap Christmas telly and eat and drink until we explode. How does that sound?'

'Rather like heaven. I'm in.' Liang returned his smile and raised an eyebrow. 'Our jammies? Is that a real word?'

'Would you prefer jim-jams? PJs? I'm easy.'

'Go get dressed. I'm starving.' She pushed him out into the living room. 'Your coffee will be ready when you are.' She cocked her head. 'Is that your phone?'

'I'll get it. I've taken Christmas and New Year's Day off, so I hope it's not work.'

His phone was out in the hall. The exchange she heard was muted, and she concentrated on the spluttering of the coffee pot, but she knew he'd turned his body around to muffle it further. That didn't look good.

He didn't put the phone back on the table but held it in his hand.

'Is everything alright?' Liang hovered in the hall doorway, the mug of coffee ready. There was a strange look on his face. Was he angry? 'Please tell me your paper isn't sending you somewhere?'

'No. It wasn't my work, it was... an old friend. Nothing to worry about.' He headed to the bedroom. 'It'll take me a minute to get dressed.' He took the phone with him.

Michael moved around her all through that day as if she was made from spun glass, fragile and easy to break. But she'd been broken and what was left was more like it'd been arc welded back together. Which was good considering that evening he told her of his own *baggage*. She didn't know she could be so possessive, so *vicious*.

So that explained the phone call.

133

What? Did she expect him to be a monk until she practically fell into his arms? But now, there were pictures in her mind, a 3D film that she didn't want or need. They were getting stronger, threatening to smother her with their taste on her tongue and a physicality that she could actually feel. Had she made a terrible mistake coming here?

'I'm sorry,' he said, and she could see the worry in his every movement and look. He was regretting coming clean about "her". 'Maybe I shouldn't have said anything.'

'No,' Liang lied, 'it's better that we know the truth about each other.'

'So we're okay?'

'Always.' Her pretend smile seemed to go unnoticed. Michael looked relieved. But she could feel the little bitter kernel deep in her soul. How could he? *How could he!*

And then he said it. 'I've told you about me, so I think you need to tell me about you.'

22

HOPE

BRIXTON

There must be a reason that Paul was keeping quiet about the loan. Was there a big holiday on the horizon? Where can you go with three kids in tow? So maybe the Galápagos Islands were out of the question. Watching David Attenborough's series had made Hope yearn to see exotic climes, even if that meant getting eaten alive by bugs. She'd kept that longing on the back burner, ready for when the kids were at university, and they were hopefully still young enough and fit enough to be able to enjoy it. And rich enough.

Or jewellery? Paul had presented her with an expensive watch on her wedding day. It'd worked perfectly for eight years, then, *ping*, had died on her. Changing the batteries was daylight legal robbery, and after research, she'd found it'd cost more to get it fixed than to buy a new one. She'd picked up a self-wind watch in her local Marie Curie charity shop. It did the job, told the time, except there was nothing aesthetically beautiful about it. Spending money on such a luxury item was frivolous, to say the least, but she'd had enough of economy, scrimping and "making do".

Her fingers hesitated. Access to their joint account was no

problem. Money in there was reserved for bills, with a little extra for emergencies. The business accounts were more tricky. He'd never shared his passwords for that.

'That's my job, so leave it to me,' he'd said.

Halifax Online. It was allegedly unbreakable. So they said. But security information is only as good as the person who supplies it. And Paul wasn't that imaginative. Was she betraying his trust by snooping? How could this be snooping? She was his wife, for crying out loud! But she still hesitated. If she got in and found something she didn't understand, or worse, something she didn't want to know, how could she explain to him how she knew?

Hope tapped her teeth with a biro.

'Mum?'

Hope jumped as though she'd been poked with a cattle prod. The lid of the laptop slammed shut.

'Wow. Sure made you jump, didn't I?' Her darling eldest slouched against the doorframe, his left leg jiggling. Baggy jeans that were too long for him, (worn and frayed at the hem because of the modern fad of wearing the waistband around your hips, so the kids trampled them), a somewhat grubby sweatshirt, Bob Marley hair, eyes the colour of the new day.

'George. I didn't know you were in. I thought you were round Mark's place.'

'Well, his mum asked me not to come back.'

'Mrs Mancini asked you not to come back? Now, why would she do that?' Hope knew the insidious feeling that was sliding over her skin like an ill-fitting wet suit. She'd experienced it each time that George came to explain *something* to her.

'Think I might've pissed her off.'

Hope chewed the skin off the sides of her thumb. That was allowed, in the circumstances. Fewer mothers were willing to have him around. The "something" always happened.

In as neutral a tone as she could muster, she said, 'What was it this time?'

'It wasn't my fault.'

Hope never raised her voice. What was the point? Shouted words tended to fly over his head but quietly spoken, sometimes they filtered in. Depending on what mood he was in.

'Just tell me what happened.' Then she could decide if it was a red alarm bell situation with the need to call Paul home or if she was on amber and could deal with it herself.

George banged his forehead against the door jamb. 'You see, it was like this.' The banging increased.

Words such as: *calm down* were meaningless. 'That's fine, George. Tell me when you can.'

'I didn't do anything.'

'I know you didn't. But I do need to know so I can fix it.' She changed tack. 'You like Mark, don't you? Surely you want to see him again?'

'Yes, yes, yes. Is that Alfie crying?' George pelted into the baby's room. Hope could hear his breathless chat. 'Hey, Alfie. Woo, you don't smell good. Look at this. It's your favourite teddy-dog thing.'

The bell around the soft toy's neck tinkled. Hope followed him in.

'If you pick him up, you must be very careful, you remember?'

'Yeah, course.' George leant over the crib railing and hauled the toddler out. Hope braced herself in case George fumbled. Of all the things he did, he was always careful with his little brother and holding him often made the mood swings less pronounced. Bouncing the baby on his hip, George turned to her. 'What?'

'George, you were over at Mark's house, and something happened.' Repetition was good. One of the most challenging things they'd had to overcome was the fact that kids with ADHD appeared to be unable to listen to or carry out instructions. Initially, they'd thought him naughty, disobedient, *wilful*. Diagnosed at age five, George had been prescribed Ritalin, but Hope had refused. 'He'll grow out of it, and I don't want my son dependent on drugs.'

'He's driven us bonkers,' said Paul. 'Don't you think it'll be worth it?'

'What you're saying is that using this drug will actually be for our benefit. Not his.'

Paul couldn't meet her eye after that. But there were times when she wondered, secretly, if she'd made a terrible mistake. The symptoms weren't abating; they seemed to be getting stronger. She'd read that this could follow them through into adult life. Constantly changing what he'd be doing, losing things all over the place, talking over anyone else who was speaking, as he'd said, pissing people off. Had she done him a disservice?

'What?'

'Mark's place?'

'Oh yeah. See, it's like this.' His gaze slid sideways, and Hope moved fast to take Alfie from his arms. He'd never dropped him before, but he'd been distracted by a mobile hanging above the cot. It had moved in a sudden draft. Cradling Alfie, setting him in his usual position on her hip, she took a breath.

'Mark. You were with Mark?'

'I didn't mean to smash her stupid window. We were just playing baseball, you know, that American game with bats, well we were using his cricket bat and the ball hit it, and it broke.'

'Where was this?'

'In Mark's living room. You should've seen his mum. She went mental. I mean, *really mental*. I laughed till I was nearly sick.'

'You were playing a ball game in their living room?'

Hope had to swallow the anger that was bubbling up her

throat, ready to scream at him that yet again, they would have to pay for what he'd broken.

'His mum shouted at me, told me to get out and something else. I can't remember.' He turned to her but didn't quite make eye contact. 'It wasn't my fault.'

'Did she say anything to Mark?' It was funny how it *was* always George's fault, and all their little sweethearts had been led along by their stupid little noses. But she didn't dare say that in front of George, in case he repeated it. No, it was easy to blame everything on the crazy ADHD kid.

'Dunno. Yeah, she shouted at him too, went a funny purple colour. I had to get out, or I think she'd have whacked me one.'

'How big was the window?' She waited. 'George! How big was the window? Was it the main one?'

'Yeah, the really big one. Brilliant hole in it and cracks all over the place. It looked cool.'

Hope clamped her mouth tightly shut and counted down from ten. 'We'll go around tonight and get it all sorted. Stay away from Mark's house for a bit, eh?'

'Yeah, yeah. Can we have macaroni cheese tonight? I love that.'

'I expect so.'

'I'm going to play on my X-Box now. Bye Alfie.' He was away into his room. Told that he shouldn't shut his door completely, he left it slightly ajar, and the machine-gun fire and heavy male shouts roared out of the gap. Maybe letting him play these games wasn't helping, though occasionally, it was the only time he was utterly absorbed, lost in the game as opposed to merely being lost.

'Goddamn it, George,' she whispered, 'that window is going to cost us the earth.'

'I've read that kids such as George often have little or no sense of danger,' she'd said to Paul when George had been diagnosed.

'That doesn't mean that he'll be like that.' Paul came and put his hands on her shoulders. 'Try not to read too much about all this, Hope. You'll be looking for things and might end up seeing things that aren't actually there.'

'I know, I can't help myself. It's like reading a medical dictionary and then realising you have every symptom there is.'

'Exactly. If we believe everything we read, we'd all be pronounced dead by now.'

Hope thought about the flare incident. He'd never done anything so dangerous before. Maybe next time, the police would be called. What would they do then?

After wrestling Alfie into his high chair and cutting thin slivers of soft banana for him to chew on, she started to prepare the macaroni cheese. George's condition didn't necessarily mean that future children would also have it. It didn't work like that, she'd been told. She'd stopped reading the articles, but she hadn't stopped watching the other two.

23

ELE

EPPING FOREST – CHRISTMAS EVE

'*Carida?*' Maria was curled at the foot of the bed, with Schrodinger tucked in her lap. 'Feeling better?'

'Couldn't feel any worse, that's for sure.'

'Best not say that, sweet.' The look on Maria's face said that there may still be a way to go.

'What time is it?' Ele yawned.

'Far too early. It's more night than day. What do you remember?'

Ele pulled the duvet up tighter around her; still, Schrodinger managed to crawl into the gap and snuggle, purring into her neck. A sense of relief enveloped her. 'Ange was there, at the market. We argued. After seeing Ange, getting home from the market was a series of images, as if I was looking at snapshots in a photo album, with nothing in between.'

'How did Ange find you?'

'I'm on the net. My work address is on the website.'

'I warned you to change your name.'

'I told her about Dave. I never meant to hurt her like that, but I'd been shoved into a corner and had no place to get out.'

'You're not a mean person, quite the opposite. Her image of

Dave has been tarnished, and she's angry with you, though you need to understand she came to find you. You didn't do this on purpose; you tried to hide it from her, so don't beat yourself up over it.'

'When we discover things about the people we love that go against everything we believe, then it makes us distrust ourselves.'

'Well, you know that more than all of us.' Maria stretched, as flexible as the cat.

Ele reached out. 'Look at it this way. If it hadn't have been for Dave, I would never have met you.'

'Not the best way to meet, though.'

'No, but you saved me, and for that, I'm eternally grateful. You know that, don't you, Maria?'

'Always.'

***

Now Ele had always respected Dave, and she felt she loved Ange. But there are lines you don't cross over, areas you don't venture into. Maybe she'd shared the same ten-pound note with him when snorting her coke and drunk from used glasses covered with his DNA, as cleanliness wasn't a particular priority, but you just don't do what he did and get away with it.

The memory had not faded over time. Someone had come quickly into the bedroom. Ele woke up only enough to know that there was a person in there with her but was not sure *who* it was. She knew who it wasn't. Michael.

The room was pitch black as she had thick velvet curtains and a pelmet that obscured all light from outside. A prickle of fear went down her spine as she realised that she was naked, and now there was heavy breathing, quite low down, punctuating the darkness. Whoever it was, they were near the floor.

'Eleeee?' A very eerie voice crept across the intervening distance.

It took a moment for her to realise who it was. '*Dave?*' Ele grabbed the quilt up around her ears, 'You shouldn't be in here, so find the door and leave now.'

'But I want to sleeeep with youuou.' His voice was sing-songy and still close to the floor.

What had he been taking this time? she wondered. 'Dave! What the hell are you doing in here? Please go now.'

'But Ange is staying with her mother and I'm lonely, Eleee.'

'So?' Ele could feel prickles of fear like fleet-footed mice running over her skin. 'What has that got to do with me? What are you doing in my room? *Get out now!*'

The crawling sounds were getting closer and closer. The hairs on the back of her neck stood on end, and she slithered as far away as she could in the bed, scrunched in the corner.

'I want to sleeeeep with youuou,' he whined.

'Oh dear God! Dave, Ange is coming back very soon, and this really is not a good idea, is it? Please, find the door and go.'

There was a pause as if he was thinking.

'Come on, Ele. I know you want me. I can feel it when we're together.' His voice was nearer than before.

'No. Categorically I don't. Now get out of my room, Dave, before I scream the place down.'

'And who'd come running? Rab?' He let out a long sigh that sent goosebumps popping out all over her skin. 'Mmmm, Rabbie boy's out on the piss, and if I remember correctly, he's not your best pal, is he? Not after you made him so angry, he beat the crap out of you. Michael? Ah, beloved Michael. Now, where's he? Oh yes, he left you.'

'Fuck off out of my room!'

But she could feel the duvet moving. He was pulling it off her. 'Ele.' His voice was now only inches away from her, and it'd dropped an octave. They say that when tigers roar, they hit a sonic point that induces abject fear in their prey. She felt the same that night. Huge hands fumbled up under the duvet and wiggled between her legs. She nearly froze, then a woman's voice said: *'Kick him! Kick the bastard!'* So she did, lashing out with all her strength.

'Aaargh!'

Ele didn't know which part of him she'd caught, but it sent him flying backwards. 'Fuck off! Just fuck off!'

'You stupid *bitch!*' He was at her again.

The woman snarled, 'Kick him again harder.'

Ele drew back her legs and struck out. Dave grunted noisily.

'Bitch!'

Crawling sounds receded, and she could hear him slapping at the walls and furniture. Then there was a burst of light from the door, followed by the sounds of Big Dave rolling down the small flight of stairs that led to his room.

'Let's hope,' said the voice, 'that he ends up with a fine set of bruises.' It was weird, but she had a strong Spanish accent.

'Who are you? Where the hell did you come from?' Ele pulled the duvet up. Her body was twitching and shaking uncontrollably.

'I'm Maria. I came in behind that bastard. I know him. He's on stuff, and I got a bad feeling about what he was going to do. Now get dressed.'

The light *clicked* on. A tall girl with long dark hair was stood in the middle of the room. She was already raking through Ele's drawers, picking out things to wear.

Ele pulled on her clothes as quickly as she could, aware that she wasn't embarrassed to be naked in front of this other woman. 'You know, I thought I'd be safe here.'

'If I were you, from now on, I'd hide the breadknife under your pillow, just in case.'

'Shall I call the police?' Ele took a step closer.

'Hmm,' Maria cocked her head and turned to Ele. 'Do you really want the police to come here? You do have a history with this man, don't you.'

'How do you know that?' Ele straightened. 'I'm sorry? Who are you again?'

'Maria.'

'Are you a friend of Ange's then?'

'Sure.'

'So you know about me through her. Should I tell Ange about this? I mean, what he tried to do, that's not acceptable.' It brought back other memories she dearly wanted to forget. A wave of emotion swept over her. *Rage*. Her voice was ragged. 'I want to kill him for what he's done, for what they all do.' She slid to her knees on the carpet. *'I want to kill them all.'*

'No,' said Maria. 'Let it rest for now. We'll get our own back in time.'

'We'll? Does that mean you'll help me?'

'I'm here now, aren't I?'

Ele pulled her hair over her face, but Maria bent to sweep it back.

'Don't hide your face, *carida mia.*'

'How will we get our own back on them?'

Maria smiled. 'Leave that to me.'

'Thanks for... Well, for saving me.'

'I didn't save you' She sounded puzzled. 'You saved yourself.'

'I would've frozen if it hadn't been for you.'

'Maybe.'

'Maria? Why are you here?'

'I'm going to make everything all right for you.'

Ele suddenly pinged into the "now", focusing on Maria, fidgeting on the end of the bed. She could never remain still for long.

'What are you going to do about Christmas?' Maria finally pulled an old blanket around her shoulders and crept into the kitchen. Her voice rose, and Ele could hear her swishing out the coffee pot. Not cleaning the pot after using it drove Maria bonkers. Ele winced.

Maria called, 'Go home to mummy and daddy dearest?'

'They've persuaded me to go home as Mum's cooking traditional Spanish fare.'

'Bribery, eh? I presume you'll go after work tomorrow? Or maybe that's today by now.'

'Yeah.'

'What about the damn cat? Do you want me to pop by and feed him?' The percolator was thumped on the stove. Maria stuck her head around the door.

'No, it's already arranged. The top flat adores Schrody and they've offered to look after him while I'm gone. They've got a spare key.'

'They obviously haven't met him properly yet.' Maria grinned, then her expression changed, and she took a breath. 'Have you asked the parents if *he'll* be there this year?'

'If he is, then I won't be going.'

'If he is, you might find it in your heart to stick a large knife into his.'

'I don't think Mum and Dad will be pleased about that.'

'Fuck them. Fuck the lot of them. They let that happen to you, oh yes, not so quick on the uptake there when you desperately needed their help but oh so quick with the accusations when you finally hit rock bottom. I don't know how you could even consider going to them. You remember how they reacted to you after Michael? Made out you were an alcoholic–'

'That's because I *was* an alcoholic.'

It wasn't as though she had just launched into being an alkie. No, that would've been too easy. It crept up on her with silent padding feet and nudged her down the road of self-destruction with a gentle hand.

Ele scrunched back against the pillow. 'Mum and dad didn't know how to respond. Poor things. I feel so miserable now when I think of what I put them both through.'

'What you put them through? Where were they when your beloved Uncle Jose was doing *that* to you? Snoring, oblivious in the next-door bedroom.'

'I'm sure if they'd known, they'd have done something about it.'

'You tried to spare them, spare their feelings, except they got it so wrong, didn't they. About Jose. About Michael. And about dear sweet Tiger.'

'I couldn't tell them about it. I couldn't even tell myself. I bottled it up, all the hurt and rage, the shame and contempt and put a stopper on the top and labelled it: "Never to be opened in this lifetime or any other." No, I couldn't face what he'd done to me. What they'd all done to me.'

'Come home, *carida*,' said her mum after Michael had gone. 'I know you must be going through hell. Come home, and we'll look after you.'

'*Joder!*' said her dad, ever the one with words. 'What a mess.'

They never asked what'd happened. Simply assumed that Michael had left her. They would never be able to believe that *she had left Michael*, although he never knew it. That she loathed him from the hair follicles on his head to the cheesy bit around his toenails. If they'd ever been on top of a cliff, she would've shoved him off with all her strength and then clapped like mad.

Articulation became a problem between them. *They* spoke with soft words and arranged their faces into compassionate looks of pity. She held her breath so as not to rage and froth and rip those looks from their faces. Her own parents. They compounded it all by believing that she was a vulnerable creature to be nurtured and coddled. Another reason why she stayed in that house in Hackney.

When Ele did venture home, the bottles of beers progressed onto wines, and then the spirits nudged their way in through the door.

'Ele?' Her mum oozed concern, 'We think you're drinking too much.'

'What gives you that idea?' Slurring possibly gave it away. 'The big bottle of vodka that's on my bedside table?'

'You never used to drink like this,' said her dad. He patted at her shoulder as if she was a rattled dog. 'Drink doesn't solve any problems. It makes it worse, sweetheart.'

'No shit!' she said.

'Perhaps we can sit down and talk about it?' Her mum looked as though she was going to cry. 'We've all experienced a breaking heart, Elena. We can help you through this.'

'A breaking heart?' Ele laughed in such a way that they both took a step away from her. 'You have no fucking idea!' She packed her rucksack and walked out of the house, ignoring their entreaties to stay.

'Maria? Is it a load of crap about coffee keeping you up all night?' Ele sipped and made a face. 'I mean, did you put the whole packet in?'

'I'm off in a bit, so I made a strong one to keep me awake. Sorry.' Maria smiled. 'Don't drink too much then. You've got a long day ahead. Christmas Eve is a biggie.'

'Do you have to go?'

'This time, yes, but don't worry, I'll be back again soon. You can't survive without me. You know that now.'

Ele nodded, set her cup on the bedside table and wriggled down further into the bed. 'Good night, Maria. Thanks. For everything.'

'No problem.' Maria's long hair swept her cheek as she bent down to kiss Ele on the brow. 'Sweet dreams and good luck. I hope you sell everything, and your wallet is bulging with money.' There was laughter in her voice. 'I need a new pair of boots.'

Ele didn't hear the front door close, only softly spoken words drifting towards her. 'Remember, don't mention me to Mum and Dad tomorrow.'

'Get off my head, Schrody.' There were times when Ele needed his warmth, but her sleep was already full of fitful images of leering faces and sibilant words. She couldn't afford to be late, not *this* morning, although every chore took twice as long as usual. Working Christmas Eve was a necessary evil if she wanted to survive into January, but it didn't make it easier. God knows what time Maria left, although the coffee pot was washed up on the side, ready for the new day, even if she wasn't. Ele was glad she was back in her life. Initially, she'd baulked against her, believing she could make it by herself. Now she could clearly see that she didn't have to be alone. It might be topsy-turvy and a bit of a rollercoaster with Maria, yet at least she wasn't atrophying.

ELE

NANA MARIA

'Are you alright, Ele?' Rosita held out a solicitous hand. 'That was a nasty little episode, wasn't it.'

'I'm fine. Thanks. It was a shock, that's all.' She swallowed. 'To see her again. It brought it all back.'

'I'm sure it did. Well, if you need anything, just shout.'

'Thanks. And I want to say thanks for sorting my stall out for me. I really appreciated it.'

'*No pasa nada, guapa.*'

Ele prepared her stall. Money seemed to flood into her money belt, and her boards dwindled, so less to pack away. Good. What was the last thing Maria had whispered to her? Maybe a new pair of boots were on their way. Her smiles were false, but they did the trick. Even though it was Christmas Eve, they still plied their trade until the sky was a deep ultramarine, and the stars were beginning to show themselves above the imposing projecting portico of the actors' church.

She had to catch the last train back to visit her parents. Presents for her mum and dad were stuffed unwrapped into her wheeled, lightweight suitcase, along with some clean clothes and her wash gear. Ordinary day-to-day decisions seemed to be twice as hard to make. Rubbing at her shoulders, she noted she ached from head to toe. That would explain it. On top of everything else, she was going down with a lurgy. The bane of every self-employed person was the holiday bug.

It took longer than she expected to arrive at Charing Cross station. The train would be pulling out in five minutes.

'Mum?' The phone felt hot in her hand. 'I'm not feeling so well, and I don't want to give you or Dad anything. Maybe I shouldn't come home?'

Her mother reassured her that it happened every year and they were expecting her.

'We'll be having our main meal before we go to the midnight mass,' her voice was a little crackly. 'We've got *Pavo trufado de Navidad* – turkey stuffed with truffles. Your favourite.'

'Is Uncle Jose going to be there this year?

'No. He's with his new girlfriend in Madrid.'

Ele felt the relief skim over her. No need for the big knife, then. 'Okay, I'm there.'

'Dad'll pick you up at the station.'

The journey was familiar, and Ele put on her iPod, blasting out album after album, so her mind couldn't wander into areas she didn't want to venture.

The old, low-slung blue Citroen was waiting in the car park by the side of the station.

'Don't kiss me, Dad. I might be infectious.'

'Don't be silly. I never get anything, so give me a big hug and a kiss.'

Ele could smell the cigarettes on him. She noted his hair was now more silver than brown. When had that happened? Was that her fault? They say stress can whiten a person's hair overnight. But no, this had been over time. Old age was catching up with him, and only now could she recognise it. She didn't want to let him go.

Her dad wiped a dirty looking chamois cloth across the windscreen. 'The windows have misted up, so we need to give it a minute. How was today?'

'My boards practically leapt off my stall. I can feed the cat for a while longer.' Ele smiled at him as he checked his mirrors. 'How's Mum?'

'You know your mum. Had to clean and dust every surface, wash all the duvet covers, shine the silver, make all the food from scratch. In fact, I think she even polished the lightbulbs.'

'If it makes her happy. Maybe she can pop round to mine later.'

Ele watched her father grimace. He'd seen the aftermath of Michael and Tiger as if they'd been a hurricane that had laid waste to Ele. When it was apparent that she wasn't going to visit them anymore, her parents took the initiative and came to her, trying in vain to mask their shock. The mess in her room had grown exponentially, and she had no idea how it happened. Crisp packets, old tins of Nutriment, usually chocolate flavoured but now growing various species of mould. Still wearing the same clothes from the week before, often discarded and then when nothing was left, worn again. Alcohol, stale and reeking on her breath when she kissed them. Eyes puffy and swollen, with skin that even Max Factor couldn't disguise. Fingers thin and grasping. Those were his memories of her. But she was not that person anymore. She'd shown them she'd changed, experienced a metamorphosis from the raging, unhinged beast she'd been into a clean, hard-working woman.

The drive in the dark was comforting. She knew the bends, where the lights petered out as they wound down the country lanes, saw the sign to the village proclaiming a warm welcome to visitors. While her father parked the car in the garage, Ele stared up at the house. She glanced sideways. Semi-detached. New neighbours and a different colour on the door. After she split with Michael, it was his parents who'd moved, returned to southern Ireland and their roots. For that, they were all thankful.

Wafts of roasting turkey with sweet undertones hit her as she walked into the house.

Hanging her coat on the hook and slinging her case into the corner, she pushed the kitchen door open.

'*Hola, Mami.*'

'Ah, *bonita!*' Ele was wrapped in her mother's arms as though she was a small child again. Her head was hauled down, and many kisses were scattered over her face. Her mum was smaller, and rounder, and Ele clung to her, breathing in the warm homely scent of her.

'Dinner smells so good. Do you need any help?'

'No, go speak to your father. He needs someone else other than me to speak to. I think he's had enough of me talking about truffles.' She indicated the fridge with her chin as she wrestled the golden-crusted turkey out of the oven. 'There's lemonade and fruit juice if you want anything.'

'I'll get something when we have dinner.'

Ele undid the button on her jeans. 'That was great, Mum. I can't believe three of us could eat so much.'

Bowls containing remnants of food were piled on the table. Ele took one more spoonful of each, straight from the dish. 'I know I shouldn't, and I think I'll explode, except I can't seem to help myself.'

'*Gracias.* That's a nice compliment. Don't you cook Andalusian food anymore? You used to.' Ele noticed a covert look pass between her parents. Were there topics that should be avoided?

'That was before. When I had a reason to.'

Her mum nodded. 'We got the card from Michael and one from his parents. They seem to be well.'

Ele wondered if she should say anything. Was it any of their business?

'Michael contacted me on Facebook. I don't know if you remember, but when we were kids, we made a pact to meet again when we were thirty. It seems Michael has arranged something.'

'Really?' said her dad. 'Are you going to go to it?'

'I've said yes, though that doesn't mean I have to.'

'It might be just what you need after all this time. Cathartic.' This time, neither one made eye contact.

'Maybe.'

Her mum coughed delicately. 'Will that include your other old friends? I remember that lovely girl. I think her name was Hope?'

'Presumably.'

'That'll be nice.'

Ele thought for a moment. Standing suddenly, she went to the fireplace in the open plan living room. On the mantlepiece was a photo of a tiny woman with eyes as black and shining as a small bird's.

'I really miss Maria–'

'*Maria?*' It was nearly a shriek.

Ele spun. Her mother had risen from her chair so violently that it'd been knocked back into the cabinet behind her.

'Nana Maria.' Ele pointed at the photo. 'I miss Nana Maria. Are you okay, Mum?'

'Yes, I just thought, well...' She straightened her chair, but Ele saw the colour had leached from her mother's face. She looked ten years older in a heartbeat.

'I don't mean *her.*' It was barely a whisper.

Her father cleared his throat. 'You haven't seen... Maria recently, have you *carida*?'

'No. Of course not.' Ele held out her hands. 'Not for a long time. You know that.'

'You would tell us,' said her mother without actually looking at her, 'if she ever came back?'

'You know I would. Anyway, she can't, can she. You put paid to that.'

'It was for the best.' Her father started to clear the plates. 'She was a bad influence on you.'

A headache was beginning to build. Stupid! She should know better than to talk about either Maria in front of them. It always set them off.

'Tsk!' said her mother, glancing very pointedly at her watch. 'We'd better get ready for the service.' She paused. 'You are coming, aren't you?'

Before Ele could respond, her father said, 'Have you got your coat, Ele? It might be cold tonight.'

Ele stared at them. 'Why exactly do you still go to mass? Neither of you are devout Catholics.'

'Tradition,' said her dad. He held both palms open wide.

'Keeping in touch with God, just in case,' said her mum. She glanced over to the photo but quickly looked away. 'Perhaps we're more believers than you think.'

'You mean,' said Ele, 'you're keeping your options open.'

Her dad smiled. 'Can't hurt, can it? To let God know that you're still interested.'

'Ha!' said her mum. 'It's really that we love the ceremony and the smell of incense.'

'Are we going walkabout after the service?'

'Not this year,' said her dad. 'I know it's traditional but we're not in the mountains with a crisp cold night sky and bars open for slugs of brandy. It's too damn cold and wet here.'

'We could play scrabble?' said her mum. '*Esta noche es noche-buena, y no es noche de dormir.*'

'Tonight is Christmas Eve,' said Ele by rote, 'and it is not meant for sleeping.'

'When', said her dad, 'is this meeting with Michael?'

'He's arranged it for New Year's Eve.'

'*Noche Vieja.* You mustn't forget your grapes,' said her mum. 'For good luck.'

'I can't take a bunch of grapes with me.'

'No, *guapa,* you can take a box of raisins.'

'And we'd love,' said her dad, 'to see you on the sixth. Our *Fiesta de Los Tres Reyes Mages* wouldn't be the same without you.'

'I know. As long as there are plenty of sweets.'

'Always. You never grow out of catching the sweets.'

That night she dreamt of Nana Maria.

Michael had gone, Tiger was dead, and her world had spiralled into the top of a vodka bottle, right down to the dregs in the bottom.

'We're worried about you, *carida.*' Her mum was on the phone, in truth, her lifeline. 'Nana Maria is coming over from Granada. She wants to see you too. She's getting on, you know. This might be the last time you'll get to see her.'

'That's called blackmail, Mum.'

'I know, Ele, but it's true. Nana's been diagnosed with cancer. She may not have too long to live.'

'Are you blagging me? Because if you are, that's a terrible way to do it.'

'Would I lie about something as horrible as that? My mother is dying, Elena and I think it only right and proper that you see her before the end. Pay your respects.' Ele knew she was telling the truth as the fear and pain made her voice thick.

'I'm sorry. I'll come to you.'

When the line went dead, Ele still held the phone to her ear, as if she could hang onto the sound of her mum's voice a little longer by not putting the phone down.

Most people gargle with mouthwash in the morning, but she washed her mouth out with vodka and didn't bother spitting.

The mirror in the bathroom was not complementary. 'You look like shit,' she said to her reflection, and she, bless her, bared her teeth and snarled.

Borrowing money for the train fare was the only option left to her. She'd spent her dole before she'd even got her bony fingers on it. But if Nana Maria was leaving this world, she had to see her. She had to say goodbye.

Ele's room hadn't been touched. Her parents must've been told to keep things as much the same as possible, for familiarity, for stability.

'Nana Maria,' she said. Her mum wasn't lying.

'You look terrible,' said Nana.

Ele opened her arms and hugged her nana tightly, although all she could feel were her tiny, fragile bones and her heart beating through her ribcage into hers. She actually felt as though she was cradling a dying bird in her hands.

'Thanks,' Ele said. 'You're not looking so hot yourself.'

'*Ele!*' Ele heard the anguish in her mother's voice. 'How can you say such a thing!'

'Because,' said Nana Maria, 'she tells it as it is. We neither of us are looking our best, and that's the truth. *Verdad?*'

'Hell, yeah.'

'Come, *carida*,' she said, 'come and talk to me. You two,' she waved at her helpless parents, caught between fear and sympathy, unable to cope, 'leave us alone to talk awhile. I have many things I need to say to my most beloved *nieta.'*

Her parents left them, speaking in low tones from the sanctuary of the kitchen while Ele sat beside her dying grandmother on the sofa and listened to her words.

'Never let anyone take you from yourself. I know something dreadful has happened to you, but it's not what your *madre* and *padre* have told me, is it?'

Ele shook her head.

'Your soul has been overwhelmed, but you must now be strong. You must find that which is hidden inside of you, bring her out, this strong woman who will deliver you from evil. She is in all of us. I found her many years ago. I said, "I will not live a life that I don't believe in. I will not be subservient, especially to a man." It was hard, don't ever think it wasn't, my *nieta,* but it had to be done. I had to leave all I had ever known, throw my life to the wind and hope it led me to where I could be me. I could be free. Well,' and Nana Maria winked at her, 'I think you know the rest, eh?'

'You were very naughty. You did exactly as you pleased, and as far as I know, you were, most definitely, free.'

'I lived my life by my own rules, Elena. I couldn't bear to be someone else's property, as it was with Spanish wives in those days, knowing that your husband must have at least two mistresses or he is not a real man. Phewee! That was not for me. I worked across Europe, finally settling in England, where I met your grandfather Bob. What a man. We smoked, drank and laughed our way around the world together. I was his equal in everything.' She cupped Ele's face in her claw-like hand. 'Do you understand what I'm trying to tell you, Ele Riviera? You have to fight for your own freedom, your own life and your own identity.

No one else can do it for you.' She kissed the tip of her nose. 'You smell bad, *carida,* go and have a bath before dinner.'

'Yes, Nana.' Ele smiled at her. 'I mean *Abuela* Maria.'

Ele lay in that bath and thought about all she'd said. Autonomy over her own life? Was that possible? Nana Maria. Yes, she'd been everything she could've possibly been and more. She'd sang, painted, been a sportswoman, got herself into local politics as an anarchist, marched in demonstrations, lived alone when all her contemporaries were trawling for eligible men, drank whisky and smoked cigars. She wore unimaginably high heels with stockings that had a black stripe drawn down the back of it with eyeliner. She lived through the Spanish Civil War as a child, hating the fascists that killed most of her village. She was a nurse in the second world war, attending to the dying soldiers across Europe. She'd lived, all right.

It was as though she'd come all the way over to England specifically to speak to Ele. She'd imparted her knowledge of the world as she saw it, and having done what she'd set out to do, her most beloved Nana died that night.

Ele stood at the end of the bed and stared at her. It appeared as if she was still sleeping, but there was no rise and fall of her chest. She tip-toed to the side of her and leant down.

'*Gracias, mi abuela,*' Ele whispered to her and kissed her waxen brow while her parents held each other's hands and wiped tears from their faces.

'She's gone,' sobbed her mother.

'Mum? She spoke to me, and I heard her. You don't have to worry about me anymore.' Ele said.

Her mother clutched at her chest. 'I love you, Elena. Don't you ever forget that.'

Waking up in her old bed with her childhood posters and moth-eaten teddies staring at her was always disorientating at any time. Now other memories tried to force their way in. *Just like he had.* Ele kicked them out. She never wanted to think about him. Maybe she should have said something at the time, but he'd threatened her, made it seem she was the one in the wrong, like she deserved it. He'd told her her dad would be angry with her, and she couldn't bear to make him angry. He said to her that her mother would think she was a dirty girl, and she'd be sent away. Forever. And she'd believed him.

She clung to the remnants of the dream of Nana Maria, held onto the words spoken, the strength imparted. Kept the image of her Nana brightly in her mind. It wasn't enough.

'*Joder!*' Her father's voice rumbled from downstairs.

'You should stop swearing,' said her mother, 'it's not becoming of a man of your age.'

'I burned the toast again. When are we going to get a new toaster? I always burn the toast under the grill. Guaranteed.'

The smell wafted up the stairs and made her gag. The bile rose up her throat so fast, she barely made it to the toilet. Retching loudly, she waited until the spasm had passed. A burned-out carcass of a house and ambulances with sirens stilled. Vivid in her mind. Dirty girl. Dirty Ele.

'Ele?' Her mum tapped on the bathroom door. 'Are you alright?'

'I think I ate too much last night, or else I really do have a bug.' The images were slowly fading.

'Listen, stay in bed this morning. I'll bring you up something simple to eat.'

How nice it was to be pampered. How normal. But the thought was still there. Why hadn't *they* protected her from *him*? Why hadn't *Michael* saved her from *them*? Why did these terrible things happen to her? Did she deserve it all? Was she worthless?

There were times when she wondered if she had the right to breathe the air, walk on the earth, and call herself a person at all. But through it all was Maria. Crazy as a box of frogs, she reminded Ele so much of her Nana. They both had the same carefree and adventurous spirit. Both of them had sawn off the shackles of a Catholic upbringing and emerged as strong independent women. She was still learning from them what it meant to be free. Could you learn to be strong, or was it something you were intrinsically? Could she be as strong as them too?

When she stepped through her front door into her tiny flat, after catching a train the day after Boxing Day, it felt as though she'd never been away. Dropping the suitcase and extra bag of presents, she kicked off her shoes and slumped into the softness of the sofa, pulling the old blanket she had draped over the arm up tight around her. No gaps that'd let the cold in. Schrody was nowhere to be seen, and she missed his soft warmth and musky animal scent.

The thought of meeting Michael after nine or so years of no contact made her queasy. Was he back in England now for good? Had he moved from his flat in Islington? She remembered that flat clearly. The one with the godawful mirror. And everything else! She physically flinched as if she'd been hit.

Michael had moved into a one-bedroom flat in Islington just after they'd split. She was never offered a key, but that's not to say she didn't "acquire" one. She'd had a plan to get him back as she knew they were destined to be together forever. Some part of her was aware she shouldn't do it, but for whatever reason, she did. She'd crept into his flat, not ever thinking that it was an invasion of privacy, as she believed she had the right to be there but... Oh what did she see?

And so came the day when her silhouette was blasted onto the wall. She'd *become* the shadow, the day her love was proverbially and utterly nuked. After that, it was too late, and she really didn't care.

Would she ever be rid of that image, emblazoned in her mind like it'd been etched there? It was as though he'd understood what the very worst thing was he could do to her. Then done it. It wasn't as though he'd known she would creep into his flat, so it must be something he'd done before. Maybe many times, and for that, she felt sick. So she asked herself, did she really want to go to Rye? If the answer was yes, then the next question had to be: why?

It was now the twenty-ninth of December. Decision time. She again made provisions for Schrodinger. Quite frankly, he was so fat, that she thought he could do with a couple of days of fasting, although she knew the neighbours would have their hearts filled with pity when he put on his *Puss in Boots* face with the huge kitten eyes. He was a sod and no mistake.

25

LIANG

REVELATIONS

The days had been passing as though they were on a merry-go-round. Liang saw images flit past the same but different every day. She and Michael were moving closer together at such an infinitesimally slow rate, it was barely noticeable to the naked eye.

His smell in the morning, doused with aftershave and sweet and clean from the shower, made her long for him. But he dressed in his room, and she used the bathroom for privacy.

Today was Christmas Day. The day to be with loved ones, with the people who care about you. Liang wondered if there would be another phone call today. What excuse would he say this time? The truth? Not likely.

A plump duck roasted in the oven, and Michael was simmering cherries and other woodland fruit in a small saucepan on the hob. The roasts were golden, and the orange and sloe berry red cabbage was still crisp and crunchy.

The phone rang. Michael stopped and looked at her.

'Aren't you going to answer it?' Liang kept her voice steady.

'Not today.' He stirred the sauce, although Liang noted he seemed unfocused. What was he seeing?

'You don't regret me coming, do you? Be honest, Michael. I couldn't cope if you lied to me.'

'No. I don't regret you. It's her I regret. A moment of madness, of stupidity. Maybe I shouldn't have told you, but I wanted to start with honesty. Basing a relationship on lies is not healthy and will always come back to bite you. That's just my humble opinion.'

The phone stopped, then a minute later, the ping of a text made them both twitch. Ignoring it seemed puerile, yet what else could they do?

Liang swept her hair back into a ponytail and tried to keep her focus on the "now". 'If I'm your sous-chef, then you need to tell me what to do.'

'Okay, I can do that. More importantly, is the marker past the yardarm yet?' Michael grinned over his shoulder. Liang smiled at him but felt a little confused. She realised that they had to get back to a semblance of normality, but she hadn't understood that last part. Then it hit her. Was this how others felt when she quoted a proverb in Chinese? Maybe that explained their bewildered looks.

'That's a very fetching outfit,' she twiddled at the red apron covered with rubberised images of cheeses. Underneath, he wore only boxers and a T-shirt. 'And what was that strange thing you said?'

'It's hotter than hell in here,' he nodded at the fridge. 'It means if the time is anywhere near midday, we can crack open the bubbly, my lovely.'

'Not while you're still cooking. I remember the last time you drank some vino while cooking; you ended up missing a bit of yourself. And we never found the bit.'

'I think it went into the salad. Added protein, you know.' Sliding the pan off the hob, he turned fully. 'Dinner's nearly ready, and I'd like to make a toast.'

Pulling the bottle out of the fridge, he unwrapped and popped the cork, letting the liquid fizz a bit before he poured into two slim flutes.

'To the future,' he said.

'To the future,' she said. They chinked their glasses, and Liang took a sip. 'To also not looking back.'

Michael nodded. 'That too.'

'I need to get a job in the new year,' she said to him. They were curled on the sofa, fallen together, rag dollies that were so malleable, they meshed. Too much food and wine had made them relaxed. It was the most intimate they'd ever been since he found her on the bridge, apart from when he'd kissed her on the step one morning. She'd gone to buy milk, and he'd opened the door for her as she'd forgotten to take the key. She knew he hadn't intended that to happen; it was more an automatic response.

'I don't want to be a burden.' She stopped, realising the import of her words. His body stiffened. 'I mean, I just want to help, pay my way. You can't be expected to pay for me.'

'I can and will if it helps.' He looked away, and she thought he must be remembering some other day, some previous life. 'I know I fucked up before. I made mistakes, and I didn't help matters.' He cleared his throat.

'We promised not to look back, remember?'

'I know, but some things need to be cleared up. I want you to know I won't do the same to you.'

'There were mitigating factors, and you did the best you could. No one could've done more for her, Michael. She was damaged. We both knew that, and I don't know if we helped her or made it worse.'

'I know. But what else could we have done? I feel so ashamed that in the end, I couldn't cope with all the negativity, the constant need for reassurance. I ran away, didn't I?'

'As I said, you did what you could in the circumstances. Happiness is not something you can hand to someone on a plate. She had to find her own happiness and independence within herself and not rely on you for that.'

'Maybe I should've tried harder. I heard she didn't have a good time after I left.'

Liang shrugged. 'None of us did. Sorry, I didn't mean to come across as flippant.'

'But I can make amends as best I can and at least support you. For however long you need it.'

'That's as may be. I need to pay for myself. It's no reflection on you, Michael. It's more that I need to be independent for myself.'

'So you can leave me?'

'I'll never leave you. I never have.'

'There I disagree–'

'I meant in my heart. You were always in my heart.'

'Then why do you need a job? I have money saved up for the proverbial rainy day–'

'Oh,' Liang waggled her head, 'so I'm a rainy day then?'

'You know what I mean. A day when I can use the money wisely, make good and fulsome use of it. To make things better.'

'Okay.' She snuggled into the angle of his shoulder. 'Make things better.'

He turned his head, and his face was close to hers. His breath warmed her cheek. It'd only take a slight inclination of his head, and his mouth would be on hers. It was as though time stopped. His eyelashes fluttered down like the wings of butterflies, his head moved and then his lips brushed hers, soft, warm and slightly dry.

'I want it to be better for *all* of us. Not only you and me. I want everyone to know about you.'

It was as if a bucket of cockroaches had been thrown over her. She struggled to extricate herself from him. 'No. Not ever. Ever, ever!' Reaching out to hold her, he clasped her hands together and angled his body so she couldn't move. But she'd been held before and not willingly. It was the price she paid.

'Let go of me.' She curled into a ball.

'I'm so sorry, Liang. Forgive me.' He shuffled back until he was scrunched into the other side of the sofa. His voice was quiet. 'Do you want to talk about what happened to you?'

'How would that make me better?'

'It might be a release?'

'Do you really want to know? If I tell you all the horrible things that I've experienced, would that help *you* more? Make you able to understand why I am as I am?'

'I think I do understand. I'm not stupid.'

'I never said you were. But actually hearing the words spoken out loud is a whole different ball game to imagining them. It makes it real.'

'You tell me when you're ready. I won't push you, I promise.'

'Bu bo bu liang, ll bu bian bu ming.' It seems old habits die hard.

'And that means?'

Liang pushed her hair back from her face. 'An oil lamp becomes brighter after trimming, a truth becomes clearer after being discussed. You've told me about her. It's only right that I reciprocate. Better to tell you now than later. If you decide you don't want to be with me, then I'll get the first flight back to the States.'

'That won't happen. I just told you I'll never leave you. No matter what.'

'You can't say that. Listen and then decide.'

Liang couldn't speak for a few minutes. He waited and reached for her hand, but she pulled it away. Before he did. The words, when they finally came, spilt out of her mouth and surrounded them much as a wall. When she finished, his breathing had changed, and his manner was now grave.

'Still want to be with me, Michael?' The pattern on the carpet suddenly seemed so interesting.

'More than ever.' Michael pulled her to him, gripped her like he'd never let her go, digging into her ribs. 'Oh, my darling! I'm so sorry. I should've been with you. What a waste of our lives. All those years. Fuck! Why did I ever let you go.'

'And I should never have walked away from you.'

26

HOPE

HATEFUL SUSPICIONS

Hope knew she shouldn't even grace the idea with a second thought, except the moment it'd entered her head, it was stuck like a limpet to the inside of her skull. Was Paul having an affair? *No, don't go there.* It was as though she'd now got an ulcer at the back of her mouth and just had to twist her tongue as far as she could reach to probe it.

Christmas had passed in a blur of cooking, washing up, cooking some more, washing that all up and then somehow laying out spreads of cold food as if they'd been subsisting on three-week-old oat biscuits and water. This year's presents had been stacked under the squat tree, weighed down by decorations and lights, in the living room. Liesel and Axel always spoiled them with expensive gifts. Once opened, the kids had, thankfully, been content, if not overly enthusiastic, with what they'd been given. Hope wondered what'd happened to the days when you were grateful for the smallest offering? An orange in your stocking, a hand-carved wooden toy, not an X-Box or flat-screen telly that you didn't even have to move for, you could just shout instructions from your sofa or bed. Maybe you had to have experienced what it was to have less than nothing to be able to appreciate what you had now.

Monique and her brood had popped by for a sherry and a cheese straw or two.

'Looking good, babe.' Monique eyed her up and down. What? Was she a prize horse?

'Don't you want to look at my teeth?' Hope drained her glass and then refilled it immediately.

'What's eating you?' Monique held up her hand close to Hope's face and pointed. 'And don't you give me no shit here.' Monique, ever the tactful one, topped up her own glass.

'I need a fag.' Hope motioned towards the hall. 'Shall I get your coat too?'

'Sure.'

Stepping outside into the wild frozen waste of their winter garden, they both lit up, hauling their coats tighter about them.

'So?' Monique raised an eyebrow.

Hope glanced towards the back door.

Monique wagged her head. 'The men are inside watching the sport, so out with it.'

'I can't prove anything, and I don't know what I'd do if I'm right, but...' Her breath caught in her throat. It was so hard to say it out loud. 'I think Paul might be having an affair.'

'Do what?' Monique let out a shriek of laughter and then tried to hide it under a pretend cough. 'Sorry, babe. Listen, I don't think that's an option. He's not like that. He's devoted to you and the kids.'

'You don't know. That's the whole point. You're not supposed to know, are you?'

'What has put this in your head?'

'He's been given a lot of money, and he's not told me about it, even when I pushed.'

'Can't say nothing about that, babe, but I don't think he's putting it about, so to speak.'

'How do you know?'

'I just know. Listen, this money, he might be saving it towards Mia's university education or someink.' Monique flicked the butt into the waiting flower bed, already littered with damp and decaying butt ends, and placed her hands on her hips. 'Girlfriend? If you're that worried, ask him. You'll know then.'

Boxing Day breakfast had been cooked, and yet again, Hope marvelled how any of them could stuff down another mouthful. A plateful of sausages, bacon, hash browns, baked beans, fried eggs and toast later, they were bulging at the seams.

Paul stood. 'I'll do the washing up, and then I'll see if George wants to go to the park, kick a ball around. I'll have my mobile on me if you need anything.'

'If you've got George, I probably won't need to call.' Hope peered guiltily over her shoulder. 'I didn't mean it like that.'

Paul smiled, rubbed at the end of his nose and rolled his sleeves up. 'I know you didn't, though it's true. I'll try and get him to run around as much as possible, see how much of that excess energy I can get rid of.'

'I'll start a bath.' She kissed him near his cheek but didn't touch him. 'See you in a bit.'

A hazy silhouette of a woman had slid unwanted into her mind. She couldn't make out the face, maybe fat red lips, and blonde? Yes, definitely *blonde*. Her head was close to Paul, this unidentifiable woman. She was whispering things to him, and in Hope's mind, they laughed. *They were laughing at her.* Heat stung her cheeks and flared up her neck. Hope ran up the stairs and flopped on the bed until she heard the car roar away.

Sitting at her dressing table in her soft flannel nightie with baby sick stains, she gazed at her reflection. No make-up today; hair cut so short it was only a dark fuzz. No meat on her, all softness sucked dry by her youngest. Not to mention the stress lines that radiated out from her eyes as if they were the scattered ricochets from a thrown grenade, her once pouty mouth more often than not pinched into a hard line. Is this what Paul saw now? A husk of the woman he'd married. She couldn't blame him if he'd sought refuge in another woman's arms. No, that wasn't true at all, was it. *She'd blame him and then kill him.*

Suspicion, especially of your own spouse, was a hateful thing. Was Paul capable of coming home to her every night and pretending to love her? Was it all an act? Oh, dearest God! Hope didn't want to cry but tears slid down her cheeks. She wiped them quickly away. What the hell was she doing? Crying over something that may never have happened and laying blame at the feet of the man she loved, had always loved, calling him a cheat, betrayer. *Adulterer!* The memory lashed at her, making her physically flinch, her stomach beginning to churn. That was her, wasn't it? She didn't plan it, never intended it to happen, although it had happened just the same. It was one night, drunken, yes, but that wasn't an excuse. She'd come back to Paul and lied about where she'd been, who she'd been with. And then there was George...

No, don't go down that road again. Too many years and so many moments in between to wipe it all away. George was definitely Paul's son. He *had* to be. The alternative was too dreadful to contemplate.

'Aaargh!' She ground the heels of her hands into her eye sockets until there was pain. Focus on what she was doing.

Now was a good time to try to break into the business accounts. Paul was out with George at the local park. Alfie was having a much-needed nap in his crib beside their bed. Mia was in her room playing with a cooking set Grandma Liesel had given her this Christmas, although she wished that sometimes the toys were not so gender-based. As a child, she'd desperately wanted to be a doctor. She'd wanted Mia to have that choice, not be brainwashed into thinking all she was good for was cooking and cleaning for some man. She knew Liesel was disappointed about them not coming to visit. Hope could hear it in her voice. Probably nearly as disappointed as she was.

Paul was so predictable. Breaking into his account was child's play. Humming tunelessly, Hope slid her finger up and down the numbers on the screen.

'Ah, got you.' A scary amount of money had been deposited about a month before. But it had gone out the moment it'd cleared. But to where? Also, the numbers didn't add up. There was another regular amount that was coming in. The usual amounts for bills and expenses were going out. Still, there was an alarming chunk of money disappearing monthly that, if her calculations were correct, meant that more was going out of the account than was coming in. How did that work? And where was all that money going? Did Paul have some expensive *love nest* in London, paying for some floozy to live a life of luxury, while his family lived in charity clothes and ate baked beans? How was she going to be able to ask him without him knowing she'd spied on him? Now she was back to where she'd started. She was his wife, and she had the right to know if their lives were hurtling down the pan.

'Mummy?'

Hope swivelled. 'Yes, Mia?' She was dressed in her favourite dungarees, embroidered shirt and pink wellingtons. After asking at the age of four if she could dress herself, Hope had watched in fascination at Mia's clothing choices. She was turning out to be quite the little fashionista.

'Can you watch *Finding Nemo* with me? I'm bored.' Mia twiddled at her halo of curly hair.

Hope smiled at her. 'Of course I can, darling. Just let mummy throw on some clothes, and I'll be down in a mo. Okay?' She had to let all these thoughts go, or it'd drive her nuts, and she knew she'd blurt out some accusation and ruin everything. Maybe he had allegations of his own. Now she felt really sick. Don't rock the boat, as it was already filling, and perhaps they couldn't bail out the water fast enough.

'Can we have some cookies?' Mia opened her eyes wide. She'd learned this trick after realising that if she looked adorable, she seemed to get whatever she wanted. Hope wondered if she'd ever been that precocious as a child.

'Absolutely. Go find the DVD, Mia.'

'Okay.' Hope watched her daughter hop and jump out of the room. Something constricted tightly in her chest. She was so pretty and *so* sweet. Could Paul give all this up for the sake of sex on a stick? Why couldn't she shake this from her mind? Maybe she should be making more of an effort. Why would he stray if he had a hot, sexy wife at home? Bugger him! It wasn't fair. Why should she pander to him? *He should be pandering to her!*

27

ELE

EPPING FOREST – 4 DAYS AND COUNTING

'*Maria?*' Ele was stunned to find her stood in the kitchen, making a cup of tea for a change. 'How did you get in here?'

'Well, that's a nice greeting for your sweet sister, isn't it?' A teaspoon chinked against the side of a mug.

'I'm sorry, it's just that I don't remember giving you a key.' Dropping her bag and kicking off her shoes, Ele thought back. She must've slipped Maria her spare key at some point. How else could she be there? It was as if she read her mind.

'If that's the case, I must've broken in. Go check for smashed windows, why don't you! Of course, you gave me a key.'

'Jesus! Short-term memory loss and then some!'

'Well, my dearest one? What's up?' She handed Ele a mug. How had she known the precise the moment she'd be home?

'Is there something up? You're the one who's come to visit me. So why are you here this time?'

Maria was always here for a reason, and usually, it wasn't a good one.

'Don't you know? Didn't you get a message from our most beloved Michael?'

'Yeah.' Ele rummaged for biscuits, unsure if she could cope with this conversation.

'About the pact?'

'What else?' There was a half-eaten box of Hobnobs. That'd do. 'You already know this.' Taking a biscuit, she handed the packet to Maria.

'It's all been a bit cryptic, hasn't it?'

Ele turned to her. 'We *are* talking about Michael. He's never been anything but cryptic.' She had a whisper of a thought, nothing more, but it made her go quite cold like being lowered into freezing bathwater when she was expecting it to be hot. 'You haven't been over there, have you?'

'Over where?' Maria crunched noisily. Ele could hear the laughter in her voice. She was toying with her as she always did, and Ele felt a bit skittish.

'To Michael's. Have you seen him?'

'You know I have.'

'No, I don't. Why were you there?' It was as if ice cubes were being rubbed up and down her spine. Maria had seen Michael. After all these years. Seen him before she had. She wasn't sure how she felt about that. Jealousy or even dread.

'I'm sure I told you.'

'No, you didn't. So tell me now.'

Maria sauntered up to her, was eye to eye. She slung her arms around Ele's shoulders. 'I don't believe you can't remember. I do.' Her voice was soft, almost sleepy. 'I remember standing across from his flat, waiting, you know, getting my shit together. Oh man, what I was going to say to him. And then I saw who turned up at his flat. I saw Michael let them in, kiss them on the lips, just like old times. Ele. Nothing fuckin' changes does it.' Her eyes were deepening in colour to a vivid glowing green.

Kiss them on the lips. Her words were hard as though she'd physically cracked Ele across her jaw. Ele's head metaphorically snapped away from her. She knew what she was saying, except she didn't want to hear. If she could cover her ears and scream *'la, la, la!'* as loud as she could, if that'd make a difference, she would.

Pulling from Maria's embrace, she needed a moment to assimilate the words. 'What did you do then?'

Did she want to know?

Maria looked down, yet her face betrayed her. 'I went home. What else could I do?'

Ele's heart speeded until she could hear the thumps of it hard in her ears. 'That's what worries me. I know what you can do.'

'Trust me, Ele. You always have done, so why stop now?' Maria laughed, a sweet sound but laced with undercurrents that terrified Ele.

'Maria. I don't mean to be rude, and I know what you're telling me. I need time to think about all this.'

'I'll go if that's what you want. Don't take too long, *carida*. You know you'll need me in the end. You always do.'

28

LIANG

ISLINGTON

The twenty-seventh of December. The day after Boxing Day. For Liang, it felt different from the days before, as though an unspecified something that was blocked had finally dissolved.

There might be snow for the new year. The weather girl on the news had told them the odds, so Liang imagined the English populace would be laying bets. Ten to one or seven to something or other. She was never particularly good at maths, which was another reason her father disliked her so much.

It was late, and the fairy lights on the Christmas tree were switched off, the tea lights and fat church candles extinguished, last curls of smoke trailing. The final mouthful of wine drained. Both of them with stained lips.

'There's only one Ferrero Rocher left.' She held the plastic box out to Michael.

'Do you really think I'd be that mean and eat it? The last one?' He grabbed the sweet and shoved it into his mouth.

'What? Thank you very much, Mr Michael Storm. Such a gentleman.'

Laughing through the chocolate, he pointed to the kitchen.

'I've got another box in the cupboard. It was worth it for the look on your face. I should've taken a photo.'

'You're a bastard. Through and through.'

'A cute one, though, eh?' He danced around her. 'Isn't that so, pretty missy-miss?'

'You're too much, Michael. Go get me the chocolates.'

Michael offered the bed to her again that night but didn't mention that he'd vacate it. They lay without touching, just listening to each other breathe, feeling the warmth from the other's body but allowing a natural space between them. Then they moved closer, softly caressing, talking about their lives. There was no mention of their hopes. They progressed, and now they were kissing, the caressing stronger and more urgent. Liang could bear to be in the dark with him, not frightened of the sounds as she once was, the sounds that meant someone was dying or being attacked for what they had.

Liang woke to weak sunlight sneaking through the curtains. Turning her head, she watched Michael's chest rise and fall, the flop of dark hair that fell across his forehead. A mat of black hair spiralled outwards from the centre of his chest as if it'd been woven and had a weft and warp. Her fingers reached out to touch it.

'Hello, you.' His eyes were open. Sometimes, when she stared into them, she felt as though she'd fallen into a wild sea, swept along in its dark currents until subsumed.

'Hello.' She traced along the line of his jaw. 'One of us needs a shave.'

This new day called to her, telling her that her freedom was real and that she had a chance. She had to take it with both hands and not let go of it.

'I know we said we wouldn't say anything about, you know, *before*,' said Michael, 'but I want to tell you that I'm so happy that you're home with me.' He smiled at Liang. 'I believed you were dead, and now you're here with me like it used to be–'

'Not how it used to be–'

'I know,' he laughed shakily, unsure, pushing himself up onto his elbow, 'you're even hotter than you were.'

'Thank you, but I'm not sure if that's a compliment.'

'I also want to say that I know that we shouldn't mention it, but I love you, whether as a boy or a girl.' He rolled out of bed and walked to the hall wall. She saw him pluck a photo from it. Liang closed her eyes and heard him come closer, the bed bouncing under his weight as he climbed back on, feeling his breath on her face, so he must be leaning in close to her. 'You left me, remember? I would never have left you. I will never leave you now that I've got you back. I swear it.' He kissed her eyelids.

When Liang opened her eyes, she could see the photo in his hand. How young they all looked. How innocent. She doubted that any of them had survived unscathed.

Michael traced his finger over one face in particular. 'I thought I'd lost you all those years ago. I believed I'd never get over you, and now I've got you back from the dead. I love you so much, Tiger. Always have and always will.'

She looked up at him. 'You mean *Liang*.'

29

HOPE
BRIXTON

There were still at least three days when the shops would be open, and she could buy a new outfit, thought Hope. Paul would go into the office on the Tuesday, so she had a window there to exploit. He might even be at work right through to the thirtieth, although she knew George would be a liability if she was going anywhere nice. He seemed to pick and choose the timings of his meltdowns. The bigger the audience, the more attention he got. She knew it didn't really work like that, and he had no actual control over it, yet it felt as if it did. Would she be able to cope with him and Alfie in his buggy while hanging onto Mia and trying to shop for a dress? She had to plan; make arrangements. She stopped for a moment. Should she be doing this? Paul had said they didn't have any money, which was a blatant lie, it had gone somewhere, but maybe he needed every penny they had for something she didn't know about yet. Would she scupper his plans by doing this?

The phone rang. It was Monique.

'Hi, sweet. Listen, just a thought. We've had our new cinema-sized telly arrive, and the bloke is installing it now. We were going to have a premiere, and we wondered if Mia and George might like to come over? We've got popcorn and hot dogs. I know that's not what we should be feeding them, but we thought it was appropriate. What do ya think?'

Hope felt as though a vast glowering cloud had suddenly lifted. She took it as a sign that it was meant to be. 'Monique, you're a real star. I need to go out, and that would help me no end. Are you sure?'

'Yeah, of course. We've got loads of DVDs to keep them all interested. You get them ready and drop them off. The show starts in about an hour.'

'They'll be there.'

It didn't take much to persuade the kids that a day watching films and eating junk food was a perfect idea. Even George was enthusiastic.

That now left the whole day to shop. And shop she would. Alfie was bundled in the buggy, and she'd made sure she was wearing clothes and shoes that were easy to slip out of, as she intended to do a lot of wardrobe changes. Exiting from Brixton tube, she hadn't been out for so long, she felt much as some woodland creature would, emerging from its burrow and blinking in the weak light of a winter morning.

Heading for Market Row, sale shoppers were like a swarm of insects that moved as one, and she ducked and twisted with the best of them, pushing the buggy ahead of her like a shield. How many people could you fit into a shopping centre? Probably everyone in Brixton, it seemed. Shopping is a knack, such as riding a bicycle. You may be a bit rusty, but then it all comes back. Five dresses tried on and eight pairs of shoes, myriad necklaces and shawls later, she exited exhausted but happy and made her way to the café on the second floor. She ordered a cappuccino, picked out an apple Danish, balanced the tray, and nudging the buggy, she sat in the nearest available seat.

Under the buggy was a wire compartment. She reached

down and pulled out a bag. Peering inside, she marvelled at the silky texture of the dress inside. Metallic and shimmering, sexy, and now she thought about it, expensive. Coupled with the silver strappy shoes, a cashmere shawl and a silver necklace, she'd notched up quite a bill. Hope put the bags away quickly. She still had the receipts. But no. She deserved all this and more!

There was a glass barrier around the edge of the café, and customers could see the people scurrying around below. She bounced the buggy gently as she sipped at her drink. Alfie yawned, and smiled.

'Hello, gorgeous. Want a bit of cake?' Breaking a bit off, she put it into his mouth, where he sat contentedly chewing it. 'You've been such a good boy, haven't you?' She grinned at him, 'Yes, you have.'

If she could stay in this moment forever, she thought she'd die happy.

A passer-by leant in to peer at him. 'What a beautiful little boy.'

'Yes, he is.' Hope smiled up at them. 'Thanks.'

All her children were beautiful. Hang on. Why was she so bothered about meeting her oldest friends? She needed to change her stance on this. She was coming from the wrong angle. With a bit of help from Paul, she'd created these exquisite creatures. That was some achievement. They would grow up in a happy and enriching home, which was more than she'd had when she was young. Their children would be set free into the world as fully formed people. One of her kids might go on to become the person who discovered the cure for cancer or worked out how humans could travel faster than the speed of light without dying horribly. Hope nodded to herself. It was going to be alright. And she was going to look fabulous.

Explaining all this to Paul was a slightly different matter.

She'd picked the kids up and was home before he got back. As if a whole day of telly could put them off, they'd had a little snack and were nestled in front of the screen again.

Having cooked Paul a delicious conciliatory supper of Chinese salmon, following one of Ken Hom's recipes and plying him with a fruity bottle of Chardonnay, she showed him her purchases.

Paul's face froze. 'How much did all this cost?'

'Does it matter? I needed to get something new. There's no way I'm going to this party looking like a bag lady.'

'How much?'

'I picked it all up in the sales.'

'Hope?' His voice was rising. Hope shut the kitchen door. *'How much?'*

'Just under two hundred pounds.'

'We don't have two hundred pounds!' Now he was shouting.

'We don't?' Hope stood there, facing him, with her hands curled tightly on her hips. She could feel her nails digging into her palms. 'Really?'

'No, we don't.' He shook his head as though he couldn't believe what he was hearing. 'I told you last week we couldn't do this. Why on earth did you then go out and spend a wedge of money we haven't got?'

'Because we do have it. Liesel told me about the loan.' Hope filled her glass to the brim and took a big swig. 'When were you going to tell me about *that?*'

'Oh right. My mum blurted it out. I bet she was asking us to go home for Christmas? Am I right?'

'She hoped we could, you know after Axel gave you the loan?'

'That's for something else.' His voice was quiet, and all the colour had slid out of his face to his neck, now red and blotchy.

'Something else or *someone else?*' She never meant to say that, but it fell out of her mouth. There was silence for a moment. Hope could hear the tap dripping.

'What's that supposed to mean?' He thumped his hands onto the table. 'Oh God, Hope? You don't think I'm having an affair, do you?'

'No?' Her voice went high and squeaky. 'Yes?' Hope put her head in her hands. 'Maybe?'

'I've never heard anything so bloody stupid in my life. What? Do you think I've got some bird shacked up somewhere that I sneak off and see in the ten minutes I have for my lunch break? Oh, and maybe I fit her in that seven minutes between leaving work and coming home?'

'You're always down the pub, Paul. So you tell me, how do I know for sure? I'm stuck at home with the kids. I'm *always* stuck at home with the kids!'

'I thought you wanted to be home with them?'

'Of course, I do. That's not the point. I don't get a choice. What I want to know is, if we're so broke, how come you can still afford to come back from the pub pissed?' Hope wiped her cheeks. She didn't want to cry as he hated it, and it spurred him on to be even angrier. 'You're always drunk. That must come to more overtime than I've spent today? Tell me, Paul, what am I to you? A cleaner? A babysitter? Your whore?'

'I can't have this conversation now.'

'You can and you will. I'm not leaving it until you tell me what's going on.' And then she blurted it out. 'And I found your bottles of whisky in the utility room. Are you secretly drinking on top of everything else?'

Paul sat down heavily. 'You'd better sit down too.' He sat with his hands lying still in his lap. 'I didn't want to tell you. I thought I could fix it.'

'Fix what?'

'The business got into trouble about a year ago. I couldn't get any money via the usual sources, so I went elsewhere...'

'Oh no.' A cold little shiver tickled down from her neck. He wasn't saying what she thought he was saying, was he? 'Please don't tell me you went to a loan shark?'

He nodded, hunched and deflated. 'I thought the business would pick up, and I'd be able to pay them back with all the interest fast. But it didn't, and I got us more and more into debt.'

'Why didn't you ask your parents first?'

'I was too proud, alright? I wanted them to think that I was successful, that I could support my family. They don't know what it was for, so please don't tell them.'

'Has that wiped the slate clean?'

'Yes, except business is still slow. We're not out of the woods yet.'

'So, no long-legged blonde bimbo squirrelled away in some love nest in Walthamstow?'

'Blonde? No. Walthamstow? Fuck no!' He leant back and breathed in deeply. 'I can't believe you could think that of me.'

Hope hung her head. 'I haven't been making an effort recently, have I? It kinda got caught in my head. I mean, look at me. Perpetually spattered with baby poo or vomit, I look like I haven't slept properly in years, which I haven't, by the way. I don't wear make-up as I can't see the point for a two-year-old or the mothers at the school gates. I felt old and frumpy, Paul.'

'Here.' He stood and pulled her from her chair. 'You are still as gorgeous as the first day I clapped eyes on you. How about you finish your glass of wine while I get the kids to bed and hose Alfie down. Then why not go and get into that mighty fine dress and shoes. We'll let the kids run riot if they have to, and we'll have a night in. Just you and me.'

Hope reached over and raised her glass. 'Sounds good to me.'

Now *he*'d come clean – shouldn't she?

30

ELE

DREAMS OR NIGHTMARES?

E le couldn't shake what Maria had told her from her mind. *I saw who turned up at his flat. Who Michael kissed on the lips.* These words spiralled round and round her mind all day. *Who, who, who.* No wonder she felt exhausted, gnawed down to bare bones by rage and bitterness.

At Covent Garden, the day before New Year's Eve could go either way. The market would either be packed with punters ready to splash their cash – or a trickle of people passing by with their hands deep in their pockets and no intention of getting them out. It was lucky for Ele it'd been the former, as she wasn't in a genial mood for selling.

'You'll need some more stock ready for the new year,' said Rosita. 'Have you got some at home, or will you have to make new stuff?'

'Running pretty dry.' Ele said. 'But I'm not complaining.'

''Ere,' Lorraine handed Ele another Ponti's coffee. That now added up to four so far, and she was feeling a little twitchy. 'Did you say you was going away for New Year's Eve?'

Ele nodded and blew onto her drink. 'Rye. To some old and scary looking inn that's supposed to be haunted.'

'Haunted?' Lorraine grimaced. 'Well, have fun. Doesn't sound like my cup of tea, but each to their own an' all.' She pulled her jacket tighter about her, leaving a smear of orange on her collar. 'I'm off to Marbella for a few days. I need a bit of sun in the winter.'

'Ele?' Rosita came to stand next to her. 'Have you seen that woman again?'

'No, thank God, and I never wish to.'

'It must have been terrifying. Do you mind me asking how the fire started? In your old house?'

That's all it took, and she was there again.

Staring in at the flaming duvet in Rab's room, the tang of the soot was hot and acrid in her nose. Ange had stumbled off down the street, calling for Ele to follow, but she had to check, to absolutely make sure...

'What happened?' she said, her voice barely audible. She was talking to the police officer. Images flashed in her mind like a sped-up Buster Keaton movie. A tea towel laying over the grill, pushed back, so it wasn't really noticeable. A bottle of oil, with the cap half off, at an angle on the edge of the counter, with a drizzle beneath it. *What the hell was that?*

'As far as we know, one of the occupants of the house left something on to cook in the house. The fire started in the kitchen and then spread from there. I don't know if you realise how lucky you are to be alive, miss.'

'Was,' Ele gulped loudly, finding it difficult to breathe. 'Was anyone injured then?'

The officer was young and looked a little green-hued. 'I'm very sorry to have to inform you that two members of the household were killed in the blaze. Neighbours, once alerted, tried to get in, although the fire had taken hold by then.'

'Oh my God!'

'This must be very shocking to you. Have you anywhere you can go? Any friends that you can stay with?'

'Yes, a friend up the road has already asked me.' She sniffed. 'This is too horrible to even think about. I can't get my head around it. Are you absolutely sure that they're dead? Rab and Dave are really dead?'

'I'm afraid so, miss.' He shuffled around. 'We obviously can't let you into the property, as it's far too unstable. If there's anything you need, you'll have to wait until the place is checked by the police and forensics.'

'Forensics? Why should they be involved?'

'They need to make sure this was an accident and not arson. You wouldn't believe the statistics we have on arson attacks, and usually, it's against individuals and not businesses, as you might expect.'

'Oh,' she said. 'I didn't know that.' Was there anything incriminating in the ruin of the kitchen? It was funny how she was conveniently absent that night. Had she been staying around Maria's?

It was a gut instinct, but she was sure Maria had something to do with the fire. She'd been there when Dave had attacked her. Then when Rab had beaten her senseless over something that was out of her control, Maria had said that she'd make them both pay for what they'd done to her. Was this payback time?

'Ele? Oh damnation, I've set her off again.' Rosita was holding tightly onto her arm.

'Stop mentioning that bloody fire then.' Lorraine snorted

loudly. 'You saw what happened the last time it was spoke about.'

'Ele?'

'I'm okay. It was a flashback or something. You can let me go now.' Leaning onto the edge of the stall, she blinked and looked about her. 'Probably too much coffee, and I had a spin-out.'

'I'm sorry.' Rosita looked stricken. 'I should have kept my big mouth shut.'

'No, that's okay. Listen, the fire was started by one of our flatmates, who always came home and put food on to cook and then passed out drunk on his bed. The police said the grill caught fire. They found him in his bed. He'd either been too drunk to realise what was going on, or he'd inhaled too much smoke.' Ele squinted at Rosita. 'We all knew it was dangerous, but none of us did anything about it. The guy was really scary, and no one wanted to talk to him. I suppose I feel guilty that I survived and they didn't.'

'Survivor's guilt.' Rosita nodded. 'That what a lot of people get when they survive a traumatic event. But you shouldn't feel this way, Ele. It wasn't your fault, and you should thank God that you're alive.'

'She's right,' said Lorraine. 'You was right lucky then, wasn't you.' She patted Ele's shoulder. 'Not to be there, I mean.'

'I think I had a guardian angel looking out for me that night.'

'That's lovely, that is.' Lorraine turned to serve a customer.

It felt only minutes later, and she was turning the lock of her front door. The light was on, although she remembered switching it off.

'Hello, Maria.'

'*Hola, guapa.*' Maria was delving through her fridge. 'Not a lot in here.'

'I'm trying not to leave much in there over the holidays. I can't bear to waste food. I've got some butternut squashes in the vegetable tray in the corner. We could make some soup?' She pried off her boots, hung up her coat and flopped onto the sofa. Maybe Maria could wait on her for once.

'Yuck.' Maria made a face. 'How about a takeaway? We can make an order through Just Eat?'

The fire was on, and the living room was a pleasant ambient temperature. 'Go for it. What do you want? Pizza? Curry? Chinese?'

'I never want a Chinese again in this lifetime.' Maria rounded on her. 'And neither should you.'

'I wasn't thinking. Of course, I don't want Chinese. I'd throw up.'

Maria seemed to soften. 'I have a need for chillies, so either Thai or Indian.'

'Thai. I wouldn't mind a green curry.'

'Me too. I'll pay.' She had such an elegant walk. Even three strides across the room showed off her slinky hips and sexy curves. There were moments when Ele was jealous of Maria's confidence and her beauty. As Maria bent to rummage in her handbag, Ele noticed a large, heavy-duty Sainsbury's grocery bag tucked down the side of her computer desk. Constrasting with the bright orange plastic of the bag, was something dark poking out of the top.

'What's in the bag?'

'Oh, just this and that.' Maria eased it further under the desk. 'Nothing for you to worry about.'

'No, really. What the hell is that?' Ele climbed off the sofa and made a grab for the bag. There was a strange tussle, each of them pulling at the bag until it upended. A black wig fell out.

Ele cautiously picked it up with her forefinger and thumb, as though it might snap around and bite her. Long, straight black hair.

'What's this all about?' She waved it at Maria.

'You mean who, don't you?' Maria straightened her skirt and picked at something on it only she could see. She sniggered. It wasn't a pleasant sound.

'Who?'

'Exactly.' She reached over and plucked the wig from Ele's fingers.

On the carpet was a bottle of make-up, but it didn't match either of their olive complexions. There was another bottle tucked at the back. Ele whipped it out. On the label, it read: Fentanyl.

'What's this stuff?'

'It makes dreams come true. For some of us, but not for everyone.' Maria stowed it back in the bag with the wig and make-up. 'For some, I'd say it will be a nightmare.'

'God, are you taking drugs now? That's not like you.'

'Not me, silly. It's for... someone else.'

'What are you up to?' Ele rocked back on her heels. 'I know you're up to something. You've got that look on your face.'

'What look is that then?' Maria licked her lips slowly as if she was savouring something she was about to eat. She winked at Ele and grinned.

'Whatever it is. Please don't do it.' Ele sat back down on the sofa.

'Pretty, please?' Maria shook her head.

'They asked me about the fire at work today. I told them it was Rab and his stupid bits of toast that'd started it. But I keep having these funny little flashes of something in the kitchen. Something wrong with it. Why is that?'

'That kitchen was wrong from top to bottom. A stinking,

filthy hovel. You've certainly lived in some disgusting places in your time.'

'I don't mean that. Did you... did you do something to the kitchen before Rab got back that night?'

'Like what?' Maria pursed her lips, looked puzzled, but Ele knew it was all fake.

'Like move stuff around?'

'Is that a crime now? Moving stuff. Oh,' Maria put on a deep voice, 'excuse me, Madam, but you're nicked because you *moved stuff around.*'

'You know what I'm asking. Did you make it so that Rab would burn the house down?'

'What do *you* think, Ele?' Maria frowned and looked quite stern. 'Do you think I'm capable of a deed such as that? That I could arrange things to facilitate a house fire that killed people? Do you?'

'Not just any old people. They were people who'd hurt me.' Ele felt feelings wash over her: guilt and shame. Why was she accusing her best friend and beloved sister of such a terrible crime? Her voice was shaking, 'Forgive me, Maria. What a really nasty thing to say. I know you didn't have anything to do with it.'

Maria knelt by her side and stroked her hair back from her face. 'I'd do whatever it takes to protect you, Ele. My little Ele. You're so vulnerable and trusting. That's what I love about you. I'm sorry too, *carida,* if I've upset you. Here, let's kiss and make up.' Maria leant down and kissed Ele gently on her forehead. 'As I always say, I'll make it better for you. That's what I do.'

31

LIANG

HOW TO RUIN THE MOMENT!

'Liang?' Michael said. 'We need to discuss something.' He shuffled about in his armchair. The week's papers were strewn around him. The flat smelt of freshly baked bread from the deli up the road, and there was a strong pot of tea brewing. Liang loved it when the bread was still warm from the oven, slathered with butter and maybe a dollop of honey.

'What do we need to discuss?' She felt especially lazy today. With the post-Christmas sales on, they'd spent the previous day buying some new clothes and a phone for her, make-up and deliciously lacy and racy underwear. And two bottles of Merlot that just had to go with the fillet steaks he'd bought. She was feeling a little fuzzy around the edges.

'The pact.'

Liang froze. No words squeezed out. It was as though her head was in the mouth of an alligator, and it was closing its jaws. Some part of her had an inkling that this was still on his mind, but she couldn't even bear to think about it. She never for one second thought he'd go through with it.

'We can surprise them.' He threw the half-folded papers on

the floor and crawled across the living room carpet to sit at her feet.

She gasped out her response. 'They won't forgive me. Ele won't forgive me.'

'We'll tell them why.'

'I can't face them. I can barely face you.'

'Liang. Strong woman.' He was acting as though he was a little boy at Christmas, except didn't he know that Christmas had passed and Father Christmas didn't exist.

Her face felt as if it was set hard like a plaster mask. 'Tiger. Strong man? I don't think so, Michael.'

'We're older. We've all gone through stuff. Look at you. You've gone from a boy to a girl. I mean a woman.'

'Thanks to my open-minded uncle, who paid for the procedure for me.'

'He's gay, isn't he? He understood.'

'That's not the point, though.' Liang willed herself not to shed one tear in front of him. 'Okay, so the others might not have experienced gender reassignment and all the inherent wonder that goes with that, but have we all spent seven years in a Thai prison for drug smuggling? And what about seeing many of your friends, dead, dragged away as if they were only carcasses? Have we all gone through that?'

'You made a mistake, but you got through it. Strong woman?'

'Do you really think it was worth it? None of that would've happened if I hadn't been so blind and stupid.'

'Now you're free. I'll be with you every step of the way.'

'I smuggled drugs. I'll be reviled. They'll hate me no matter what excuse I give them.' She glanced at the door. 'I also left them all believing I was dead. How will they feel about that?'

'We'll explain how it all happened, that the smuggling was because you were trying to help your little brother and sisters, and as your parents had already told us you'd died, you felt you had to go with it.'

She rounded on him. 'And what about Sabine? You were seeing her when you came to San Francisco. How's she going to react to the fact that I'm staying with you? And I'm in your bed instead of her? That's why she hasn't stopped phoning and texting. She doesn't know what's happened.'

'She's married, so I don't think she has the right to say anything.'

'All's fair in love and war?'

Michael had enlightened her about his "relationship" with Sabine *after* they'd arrived back. A stranger would've been easier to deal with, as there would have been no face to go with the jealousy and anger. Not that she had any moral reason to feel angry. She'd willingly given up Michael years before, and he had the right to do what he wanted with his body and his emotions. But it was still there, the sharp-clawed resentment that he'd found happiness in the arms of another. But now, what was worse, was that it was with someone she disliked. Sabine's face swam in her imagination, and she could imagine in graphic detail all their carnal interludes.

'Fair?' Michael practically snorted. 'I was in love with you way before I ever started to see her. And... and most importantly, I thought you were dead. I think it's Ele we have to be more careful of. I know I hurt her dreadfully when we broke up.'

'Did she know about us? I got the feeling that she'd found out somehow. I know it was after you'd left her, but still, it would've hurt her.'

He rubbed his chin. There was three days' old growth, and it made a sandpapery sound. 'After you "died", there was a moment when I wondered if she *had found out*. She mourned you but in a really weird way. Then I lost contact with her. As I said, she went through a bad time.'

'And as I said, that goes for the both of us.' Liang stared at her hands, lying prone in her lap, now manicured and painted a pretty pink. For *him*, not for her. 'That came out wrong. I can't say I've had the monopoly on misery. She loved you so much, Michael. We both loved you. I never meant to hurt her, to betray her friendship. I couldn't help myself. If I'd been in her position, I'd have wanted to kill us both.'

'Let's hope she got over it.' He was trying to soothe her fears, though there was something in his voice that jarred her. He obviously didn't understand about women.

'That's the point. Do you ever? Maybe we should, as they say, let sleeping dogs lie.'

'In case one wakes up to bite us on the arse?' He smiled, and it was warm and comforting but still, a slight chill niggled up her spine. Liang thought, more in case one rips out their throats.

'Please don't go through with this, Michael. It doesn't feel right. *Wan shi du bei, zhi qian dong feng.* Everything is ready, except the East Wind.'

'Do you have a Chinese quote for everything?'

'Probably.' Liang tucked her hair behind her ears. 'You keep saying that Ele didn't have a good time after you left. Do you know what happened to her?'

Michael looked down. 'She was admitted to a regional secure unit.'

'That sounds pretty serious. What exactly is it?'

'It's a medium-security psychiatric hospital.'

'A mental-health unit? Why? What happened?'

'Hope told me about it. It seemed there was a fire at our old place in Hackney. You remember Dave and Rab? They died in the blaze which swept through the house.'

'That's terrible! But what's that got to do with Ele?'

'There was some sort of link between her and the fire. I don't think anything was proved, so no arrest or prosecution. She spent six months in the hospital, but she's fine now.'

Liang was probably sitting there with her mouth hanging open. 'Did we do that?' She couldn't believe it. Ele had been locked up in a mental institution on suspicion of murder? Is that what he was saying? But she's alright now.

Really?

Michael shrugged. 'I don't understand how we could have had anything to do with that. It was long after we'd left.'

'No, I mean, were we the catalysts?'

'She always suffered from depression. We tried to look after her, remember. We can't be held responsible for someone's mental health for the rest of our lives. I presume she had help in this place. Look where she is now. Working in Covent Garden, she's living somewhere nice, and I think she's happy.'

'You think? What if she's not?'

He laughed. 'Trust me. The old gang will be back together, and it'll be great.'

Then it hit her. 'You've already contacted them, haven't you?'

'Yes. They've all agreed to come.'

'But you haven't told them about me?'

'No. It's going to be a surprise.'

Her heart was beating as though she'd snorted a gram or two of finest uncut speed. If premonitions existed, then Liang thought she was experiencing one right at that moment. New Year's Eve was the next day.

32

ELE

RYE – NEW YEAR'S EVE AND NOW IT BEGINS

E le scowled. 'Where have you been? It's getting late.'
There was something different about Maria that afternoon. It was gone six, and Ele was struggling to get her bag packed, although she could've sworn she'd had it all organised. She stopped and stared at Maria, who reminded her of when Schrodinger had somehow unclipped the fridge door and eaten whatever his little furry paws could hook out.

'Look at you, all tetchy and twitchy,' Maria danced around the living room, and her complexion was glowing, like she'd just had great sex, 'while I'm so fine, you wouldn't believe it.'

Ele felt a little smart of jealousy. Who was Maria seeing? She rammed her boots into the suitcase, glad it was wheeled as she didn't relish humping anything heavy up a cobbled street.

'Looks as if you had fun last night then?'

'Not last night. Today – and it was sublime. I would tell you all about it, but I can see you're busy. Oh, *carida*, you're going to have such a wonderful time at this place.'

'Really?' Ele still had swirls of worry gyrating in her stomach.

'I know you will.' Maria twirled up to her. 'I *know.*' Her eyes were luminescent as though she had them backlit with candles.

'Marvellous.' Ele took a last look around and then tugged on her jacket. 'I'm getting late.'

'Don't forget this.' Maria wrapped a scarf around her neck and leant in to kiss the end of her nose.

'My goodness me,' said Ele, 'you are in a happy mood, aren't you?'

'The best. I've merely sorted all your problems out.' She said, spinning a dainty and playful pirouette across the room.

'How?' Ele pulled the suitcase handle free. When Maria said things like that, it made her queasy.

'I've taken something out of the equation, my dearest one. So, don't look at me with such a frightened rabbit face. Go and have fun.'

'What have you done?'

'You'll see in good time. Oh, don't make me frown, Ele. You know it's not good for my wrinkles.'

'Sometimes you're as mad as a box of frogs!'

Maria's expression froze, and then it was as though it was under fire from within. 'Don't say that to me.' There was a snarl in her voice. *'You never say that to me.'*

'I'm sorry.' Ele took a step backwards, 'It was only a joke.'

'That's not a joke to me.' She seemed to soften as if she'd been punctured. 'Sorry Ele, forget this. I'm going to envision you dancing and eating and sleeping in a bed like a queen.'

'Here's hoping.' Ele edged out of the flat. 'You lock up, okay? I'll see you when I get back.'

The train journey was through the English countryside, shrouded in the cloak of early winter. The shortest day had been and gone, and in Ele's mind, they were galloping bravely towards spring. In reality, the trees were not quite skeletal as russet leaves still clung like drowning men to their branches, and her breath didn't "huff" in the air. That was all still to come.

The light had already changed as she left the flat. It was that in-between stage from day slipping into dusk, that point when the darkness always felt too early. Peering through the window, she saw mist drifting in clumps, and where the fields were lit by the low-hanging moon, the palette was mostly a deep violet with sloshes of ochres and dull greens.

What was up with Maria? Gone from so high she was a kite to crabby in a matter of moments. It was like she'd lit the touch paper and then had to run away from the explosion. Wow! She'd never seen her like that. More secrets? Ele shook her head. If Maria had things she didn't want to share, then that was fine by her. The less she had to cope with, the better.

As the train swept into Rye, she had her iPhone out, and a map of the town was emblazoned on its tiny luminous screen. Following its microscopic instructions until she was standing gazing up the moss-encrusted cobbled street, she spied the sign swinging listlessly more than halfway up. Thank God she didn't opt for the stilettos. She went via the pavement as the cobbles were treacherous even in trainers, mired with algae brought to life by a light spattering of rain.

It was as if she'd stepped back in time. Bent timbers, huge steep tiled orange and green roofs, leaded windows through which beckoned white Christmas lights and soft candlelit glows. The sign creaked above her head. Hanging between the heavy wooden frame was a mermaid, with pert breasts and a curled and sexy fishtail. An image of Tiger's bedroom flashed into her mind. Posters of mermaids plastered all over. There was something about them that fascinated him, something to do with their ambiguousness. He was part of the pact all those years ago. He had the right to be here. But what would she say to him if he were? She used to have the words ready, spiky and brightly glowing, but now they had become diaphanous, covered in years of dust, so she could no longer see them clearly. Shaking this vision from her mind, she didn't want to think about him now. Though she would have to, she knew.

The main reception door led into a dark wood-panelled area, where a pretty brunette was standing behind the heavy desk.

'Good evening.' She was as twinkly as the lights around her. 'Welcome to the Siren Inn.'

'Hi,' Ele said, 'there should be a reservation for me, though I'm unsure what name it's under. Possibly Michael Storm?'

'Ah yes, are you Mrs Storm?'

Ele must've shown her shock on her face. 'There's a Mrs Storm?'

'Oh no, I'm sorry. I meant the Storm party.'

'Yes.' She heard herself swallow noisily. Hell! She should be more controlled than this. 'I'm Elena Riviera.'

'Here it is. Room seventeen. That's one of my favourites. A four-poster bedroom.' The girl looked about twelve and still seemed a little disconcerted about her mistake.

'Has anyone else from our party arrived yet?'

'Not yet. You're the first.'

So they were all still in transit. Hopefully, that'd give her a little time to get orientated.

'I'll call someone to show you to your room.' She waved at a young man who was stood awkwardly by the boughs of an impressive Christmas tree. Weighted down with traditional red, gold and silver baubles, it dominated the foyer. He was in a white shirt, black trousers and waistcoat. A shy penguin.

'Can I take your bag, miss?' He reached out, but she kept the suitcase by her side.

'I'm fine, thanks.'

'Oh right. This way then.'

Leading her past the laden tree that was twirled with more tiny white lights, she breathed in that distinctive resin smell. She didn't enjoy the thought of growing a tree and then cutting it down just to hang pretty things on. But then, you never forget the smell of a Christmas tree. She glimpsed communal rooms as they walked by. Fires crackled, and some people sat quietly reading or talking in whispers. She didn't have the time to see much else as they were walking down a long corridor with leaded windows on the right-hand side, old-fashioned decorations and dried gourds tucked on the ledges. Beneath were daubed portraits of what she presumed to be past kings and queens. It was now too dark to see what was outside. They passed a thickset wooden door that opened into a bar where she could hear voices and actually smell woodsmoke. She'd read about this. The Giant's Fireplace or something. Through a door that looked strong enough to stop an enraged rhinoceros, they climbed stairs and then stopped.

'Number seventeen,' said the young man.

'Is it haunted?' She watched for non-verbal signs.

'Not this particular room, as far as I know.' He dropped the key twice in his haste to open the door, which was very heavy, and as she pushed through after him, it was shoving back.

'Doesn't want me to get in,' Ele tried to make light of it, but things like that scared her.

'It's the camber of the room,' he motioned at the windows to their right. 'Everything is squiffy. The floors slope, the walls aren't straight, and even the windows are at weird angles.'

No shit, Ele thought as she peered around her. He flicked a switch, although it didn't seem to make much difference. Two electric lamps gave off the light equivalent to candles. Very atmospheric and all, but far too dark.

'You have lights on either side of the bed and a lamp over there.' He gestured at the heavyset sideboard to the left of them. 'The wardrobe is in here.' He pulled a bit of dark panelled wall, and a triangular closet was exposed.

He then opened a door in the panelling to reveal a modern bathroom with a deep, gleaming, claw-footed bath.

'This is your bathroom.'

Pushing thoughts of secret sliding doors from her mind, she imagined slipping into that bath filled with bubbles, iPod on and a chocolate truffle or two melting in her mouth. The walls were white with blackened beams. It was all pretty magical as long as the plumbing actually worked.

'There's a proper light above the sink.' He pointed.

At least someone must have realised that there's only so much ambience a woman could take.

'Thanks,' she said.

'Mr Storm has requested that you watch a DVD. It's all set up on the side there.'

'What? Does he want us to watch *Ice Age* or something?'

'I don't know.'

'Sorry, that was a joke.'

'Okay. Your dinner reservation is for nine, and the rest of the New Year's Eve festivities will be in the Tudor room where there's going to be dancing. Is there anything else I can help you with?'

'No, that's fine.'

As he scuttled out, the door swung shut before he was through, and it caught his elbow. There was a faint yelp. Ele knew it was to do with weights and angles, but it was as though there was someone in here with her, and they had a mean streak. She looked around. It was *really creepy*. The four-poster bed had narrow lacy cream curtains around it. Red and gold patterned cushions were piled in a symmetrical pattern on the bed, which also had a gold covering. The carpet was the colour of wizened, sun-dried raspberries, the ones that still cling to the bush at the end of summer. A welcome hamper was sat on the sideboard. Was she actually allowed to open it? She saw a selection of biscuits, chocolate covered raisins and a small box of posh tea. There was also a kettle, two cups and saucers, various sachets of tea, coffee, sugars, and tiny milk cartons on a giant silver tray by the TV. Plastic-wrapped fingers of cake beckoned to her. She ripped off the packaging and chewed one. It was deliciously sweet and sticky.

Where should she start? After switching every lamp on and hoping they'd be the ones that get brighter the longer they're on, she unpacked quickly. After hanging her party dress so that the wrinkles fell out, she stashed her wash gear and make-up on a long shelf that ran along the top of the radiator in the bathroom.

She hesitated as she held the DVD. This was all a bit too "cloak and dagger" for her. She didn't enjoy surprises. But she had to put it on. Shock rippled through her. Michael's countenance was lit up as if he'd got a hundred buttercups beneath his chin. He was animated, and his eyes were wild and dark.

'Hey, guys,' he laughed, and his face loomed into the camera. He was doing a "selfie" movie. 'I'm going to be a bit late, so make yourselves at home. There's a tab in the bar under room fifteen, so knock yourselves out on me.' The camera bobbed away, and she recognised where he was. His living room in Islington. The wallpaper was so distinctive, and there was that dreadful mirror his parents gave them when they started living together. They'd always laughed about how truly atrocious it was, but he took it with him when he left.

'I know,' Michael continued, 'you're wondering why I chose this place, but it'll all be clear soon. It's gonna be fantastic. Just like old times.' He blew a kiss, and then the screen flickered off.

He seemed to have cultivated a bit of an American accent that rubbed along nicely with his lilting Irish brogue.

Ele could feel wetness on her cheeks. Was she crying? He looked so alive and happy, on top of the world. But she was a strong woman. Now. She could deal with anything that was coming. Bring it on, Michael Storm. Bring it on!

33

HOPE

RYE – NEW YEAR'S EVE

The light drizzle that had marred their journey so far began to lessen as Hope and Paul walked into the foyer of the inn. They'd parked in the space reserved for them and walked the last bit. Hope didn't know what to expect and had scrabbling things in her tummy, feeling she was an apprehensive child instead of a grown woman. She hadn't realised the extent of her nerves until then. It was over nine years since she'd had any actual contact with these people, if you didn't count the wedding, which was a bit of a blur. Michael hadn't even been there, and she'd barely spoken to Sabine, who, as far as she could remember, had wished her luck and then left early so she could get a flight to the Maldives for an extra holiday. This was *after* Sabine had moaned to Hope that she'd only had four holidays that year so far and was feeling "deprived". Hope had resisted the urge to slap her one. Poor Ele had been in a sad and dejected state, and Tiger was already dead by then. Thinking about it now, Hope wondered if it would be bad form to turn around and drive home. Paul could stay if he wished, but she wanted to throw up and then leg it.

'Are you sure about this?' Paul had stopped walking and was also staring up at the inn's sign, swinging in the slight wind.

Bum! Hope knew that if she said she wanted to back out, he'd go with it and then she'd have ruined the one night that he'd been looking forward to. And why was that? Fear? *Oh yes.* Fear that she'd look old and "motherly" and the other two would be glorious and glamorous. She'd be "Mrs Frump", while they would look pampered and primped. Ele would be telling her about her business, recapping all the stories from the famous craft market, how she'd got contacts across the world, how funny/witty/sophisticated her new friends were. Sabine would be showing them photos on the latest Apple iPhone of her fabulous modelling shoots, the wonderful and exotic places she'd visited, her chateau in the French countryside, her adoring and suave French aristocratic husband. And what would she be doing? Handing pictures of dribbling babies around the table. And could she meet Michael again without a blush to tint her cheeks? Would he recall when they last saw each other?

'Hope?' Paul turned her around and peered intently into her face. 'We can go home right now if you don't want to do this. I know I kind of cajoled you into this, but I'm happy to turn around and go home *right now.* If you want to. Like I said, I'm happy to.'

Dear God. Was fear always going to get the better of her? So what if her only accomplishment in this life so far was three kids? That didn't make her a second-class citizen, did it? Her stretch marks were a badge of honour. *Blow them!*

'No, we're going in, and we're going to have a brilliant night. Like we planned. We can eat, drink and be merry. Let's go.' Now all she had to do was follow through. Her feet took a moment to move up the steps and in through the door.

Hair misted with tiny raindrops, Hope stood and stared. It was wood, wood and more wood. Everything was bathed in a soft amber glow. All the colours were muted and warm, russets and browns, golds and deep greens, rich reds, as if autumn had trailed them in and covered the place with fallen leaves.

'Oh wow,' said Hope, 'It's so beautiful.' She turned to Paul, who was nodding his head. He was like a rat caught in the torchlight by a farmer in his barn.

'Didn't I say that'd it be great?' He smiled, although it only reached his mouth, and he seemed to be breathing very fast. Hope suddenly thought that if she was worried, maybe Paul was too?

'If you want to go, then you can tell me now.' Was he equally daunted at the thought of seeing the great and mighty Michael Storm again?

'No way,' he said, looking around. 'It's kinda creepy, though.'

'Scared of ghosts?' Hope giggled and picked up her bag. She was going to enjoy this if it killed her. 'Come on, we need to check in.'

They were led to their room by a slender, nervy young man, traipsing past several thin corridors swathed in tapestries. 'Number twelve.' He unlocked it and showed them around, then he hurried off as though he couldn't get out of there fast enough.

'Didn't wait long for a tip,' said Paul.

'Was he going to get one?'

'Nope.'

'Look at this place.' Hope motioned around her. The walls were white, with bowed black beams that trailed across the ceiling, but this was offset by vividly coloured curtains of peach and gold, splashed with crimson.

'Oh my goodness.' Hope threw herself onto the golden quilted bed that dominated the room. An array of matching cushions were arranged on the bed. 'A four-poster. This is amazing. We could be King Henry the Eighth and one of his wives in this.'

'What?' Paul sat and bounced on the edge. 'Don't think that's a good analogy, love, considering he did away with most of his wives.'

'You know what I mean. This isn't a replica; it's the real thing.' She tucked one of the orange-hued cushions under her head and stared up at the canopy.

Paul peered into the bathroom. 'Nice. Pretty modern but nice.' He turned to her. 'What did that lad say about Michael wanting us to watch a DVD?'

'Oh yeah. It's set up in the corner there. What is he up to?' Hope wondered if she could stay lying on that big bed all night? The sheets were Egyptian cotton; she was sure of it. And there was a gold embroidered coverlet draped elegantly over the end of the bed that looked so posh, she wanted to nick it.

'You know Michael, he always loved mystery and suspense.' Paul inserted the DVD.

Hope heaved herself upright. It was warm in the room even though she believed it wouldn't be like this in the sixteenth century. She spotted a radiator down one side of the wall that seemed to be listing at a strange angle.

'Paul, this place is safe, isn't it?'

'If it's stood for four or more centuries, I think it'll stay up a night longer.'

They watched the DVD in silence. Paul frowned. 'What the bloody hell was that all about?'

'Search me. This may have been funny when we were eighteen, but quite frankly, I find all this a little bit crass.'

Paul stood and searched through the welcome hamper. 'It's all tea bags and cakes. I need a drink. A proper drink.'

'We've only just got here, and it's pretty early. Can't you wait a bit?'

'Look, he said we can order what we want and stick it on his tab. So that's what I'm going to do. Don't you want anything? For fuck's sake, Hope. It's New Year's Eve. We have the right to some fun, don't we?'

Hope swallowed. 'Okay, I'll have a glass of prosecco. A large glass.'

'That's my girl. You unpack, and I'll get room service.' As Hope hung their clothes, she heard Paul dialling the phone and asking for their drinks. Licking her lips, she hoped that Michael's generosity included the expense of room service because they surely couldn't pay for it.

A waiter in black and white bearing a silver tray arrived and, somewhat ostentatiously, placed their drinks on the side table.

'Number fifteen's paying for it. We're his guests,' said Paul. The waiter did an elegant bow and ran out of the room.

'It's funny how no one seems to like staying in here,' said Hope. 'I wonder why?'

'Nah,' said Paul, 'they're all trained to be servile lackeys and invisible. That's why they're gone so fast. So they're not in your face. That's what happens in places where the rich hang out.'

'Like we know so much about how the rich live.' Hope took her glass. 'To the future. May it be full of wonderful things.'

'And to us.' Their glasses chinked together. Paul downed his glass in three big swallows. His glass was three fingers thick of an amber drink. Was he on whisky?

Hope looked at the table with their order. There was a bottle with the label turned from her, but it had a weird triangular shape she'd never seen before.

'You ordered a whole bottle of this stuff?'

'It's a bottle of Dimple Pinch. It's classic.' He fingered at the shape of the bottle as though it was alive.

'On room service? That's going to cost a bomb, Paul. You can't expect Michael to pay for that.'

'He said, "knock yourselves out", so I am.' Refilling his glass to the halfway line, he went to look out the window.

'This is the time to let our hair down and pretend we're twenty again. We've had kids for a third of our lives, Hope. I'm not saying I don't want that. Still, for one evening, I just need to be twenty again and not have to limit myself because we have to be back for the baby, we have to be responsible adults, we have to remain sober, or someone might call social services and take our kids from us. I want to be hammered and enjoy it.'

Hope knew he wasn't accusing, though it felt like he was. One night. That's all she had to get through, and she should do it happily, then they would return to reality.

'Okay, I'm sorry. It's been so long since we both had fun together, I think I've forgotten how it works.' Hope wrapped her arms around him. 'If we piss off our old friends, it doesn't matter, does it. We haven't seen them in years, so what the heck, eh?' She stood on tip-toe to kiss the end of his nose. 'I love you, Mr Klaus.'

He grunted and pushed his face into her neck. 'Smelling good, Mrs Klaus. Fancy a quickie before we go down to meet the others?'

'We're getting late. We can have a *slowie* when we get back, to celebrate the new year. Now I have to get dressed and try to outshine Sabine. Ha!'

Hope drank her prosecco far too fast. Her head was beginning to spin as if she were on a rollercoaster. It'd been years since she'd allowed herself to drink anything as she was always responsible for the kids. Paul was right. One night of debauchery, that's all it was. They'd never come back to this place, and as long as they didn't end up on YouTube, they'd be fine. For crying out loud! How many times did she have to remind herself that it was New Year's Eve? Weren't they allowed one night off in nine bloomin' years?

'Oi, Paul, lover boy. Pour me a glass of that whisky, will you?'

Paul's eyebrows rose comically. 'Mrs Klaus! Are you getting drunk?'

'Not yet. Listen, the night is young, and so are we.'

'Woo, woo.' Paul poured, and they entwined, dancing to music only they could hear. It reminded Hope of that brief time they enjoyed before they had George. The thought made her sad.

'Do you think we should be getting down there? The party might've started without us.' Hope felt a bit unsteady. She fumbled her way into her dress and decided not to attempt to touch up her make-up in case she smeared the mascara brush across her cheek.

'If it's started without us, then we can make *le grande entrance.*' He cocked his head to stare at her, his glass suspended immobile in front of him. 'God, Hope, but you're gorgeous.'

'Why, thank you, kind sir.' Hope fluttered her eyelashes. Then she realised something. She wasn't alone here. No matter what they threw at her, she knew Paul had got her back.

It was a bit of a maze finding the big bar they'd spotted on the way up to their room. The heat hit Hope as they pushed in through the heavy wooden door. Smoke curled from the crackling and spitting log that filled the massive fireplace.

'Fuck me,' said Paul, pointing. 'That's a whole bloody tree. It's got to be as big as a man.' Heads turned, and a few people tutted.

'What?' said Paul, 'never heard anyone say *tree* before?'

Hope covered her mouth. It felt as though she was wading into fast-flowing water, and she would be dragged under and swept away by the force of the current. Paul was drunk already, and these people looked a right bunch of toffee-nosed pricks. Was she drunk too? Peering around, she couldn't make out the others unless Michael was now that fat and balding bloke sporting a bright-red Christmas-themed sweater with a large dark-green holly leaf on it. Maybe Sabine was the woman next to him, with the low cut dress and a rather wrinkly décolletage? Hope sniggered and then tried to hide it under a cough.

'I'll have a coffee,' she tugged on Paul's arm. 'You go to the bar, and I'll grab those seats by that gargantuan fire.'

She glanced up and saw a massive, blackened and gnarly beam traverse the entire room. The end nearest the bar was dripping with bright green hops, but garlands of Christmas tree boughs twined with tiny, white glittering lights crept up to meet them from the other end.

'Coffee?' Paul frowned. 'I thought we were going to have fun?'

'I am. It's just I've already had more than I normally do in a whole year. I don't want to fall over and show my knickers to everyone.' Hope looked about her and whispered. 'Especially not to this lot.'

'Point taken.'

'And, maybe you should slow down a little too?'

He rolled his eyes and bulldozed his way to the bar.

Placing her bag on the seat next to her, she waited for Paul to return, watching apprehensively for who would be the first of their old friends through the door.

34

LIANG

ISLINGTON – NEW YEAR'S EVE

The arrangement was that Liang would visit her uncle early morning on New Year's Eve, while Michael took the train to Rye to set up the meet. Her uncle had managed to get a flight to London for New Year and had booked into the Hilton. She was to have lunch with him and then make her way back to Michael's flat. She hadn't seen him since she'd left San Francisco, only speaking on the phone. Unable to give her firm notice, she'd walked out, losing her last month's pay in the process. She'd called him to apologise as he'd secured the job for her, but after stating why she'd left, he was overjoyed.

'Trust me, Liang,' he'd said to her, 'You never normally get a second chance at love. If this man is your forever love, then I can only wish you well.'

That morning, while Michael filmed his silly greetings to them all and burned them to disc, she'd watched him from the safety of the kitchen. There would be no point if she'd been in shot. Ruin the big revelation he'd spent so long planning.

'This is so melodramatic, Michael.' She was buttering toast for them both.

'Let me have my fun.'

'You've had to hire three DVD players. That's just weird. Why didn't you merely write them a nice letter instead?'

'A letter doesn't compare to this.' Michael came to her and cupped her face. 'I want them to feel as excited as I do. I want to pique their curiosity.' He took a large bite from the slice she had in her hand. 'Ug, Marmite.'

'Serves you right for eating mine. *Your* toast is on the side there.'

'Honey or marmalade?'

'Honey.'

Michael poured a coffee. 'We'll meet back here at about five or so, then we'll catch the train at six. I've worked out it's much quicker by rail. I'm only using the car to take all the DVDs over there. We can sneak in and then surprise them.'

'Yes, surprise being the operative word. I hope no one has a heart attack.'

'It'll be fine.'

'Will it? Promise me?'

'I promise.'

What a fine and very expensive New Year's Eve lunch it would be with her uncle. Liang was glad she wasn't paying, but aware yet again that the slender, elegant man in front of her wasn't her father, although he seemed to have taken on that role since her own father had disinherited her and forced her from her family. He'd been the one who'd come to her when she needed it most and saved her life in Klom Prem Central.

It lay between them, that dreadful recollection.

'Liang? You have a visitor.' One of the heavyset guards led her to a small room, surrounded by mesh. Sat at the one table inside was her uncle.

'Liang?' He covered his face with both hands. 'My poor sweet child.'

Walking into the room on rubber legs, she held herself up by hanging onto the back of the other chair. 'It's okay, uncle,' she said. 'I brought this on myself.'

'Your father has only just revealed your circumstances. He told me you were off travelling again until I pestered him so much he finally told me. I arranged a flight the moment I knew.'

Liang didn't want to cry, to show emotion as all the guards were watching them through the wire. She took a deep breath and willed herself calm. A image appeared in her mind. Her love, her one true love. Michael. It was his face that always got her through.

'Thank you, uncle.' Liang reached across the table to touch his hand, but a guard made noises that warned her to pull back. She supposed in case he was slipping her drugs.

'I have money for you.' He laid a wad of notes on the table between them. 'Use it as you will.'

'If you give me that, they will have all of it from me in a matter of minutes. Is there any way you can arrange something with the guards? They can take their cut and then give me the rest over a period of time? I might be able to survive then.'

'I'll do that.' He took the money back, and she felt as though she'd been punched in the gut. She was so hungry she was light-headed.

'When you get out,' his look was pure horror, 'I'll be there. I know your father has disowned you because of, well, everything, but you're still my family, and I will not abandon you.'

Then Liang cried as if she'd been flung onto a bed of nails from a great height and been punctured. The precious water flowed out of her like it was nothing. It took a good three guards to pull her from that room as she truly believed she'd never see him again.

Each month, the injection of fresh food that came to her via the guards ensured she made it. When she got sick, she had antibiotics, and once in a while, she received a letter from her uncle. He'd inform her about the little things in his daily world; about her brother and sisters who reportedly missed her terribly. He told her of her mother, who, although she knew wasn't allowed to show any emotion towards her as her father's iron rule did not permit that, longed to see her again. She knew she was a dead child to him, and so her mother must believe that too.

⸻

While waiting for their very expensive dessert, Liang reached across and held her uncle's hand. This time, there were no guards to stop her.

'Uncle? I know you don't want to talk about it now, but I have to say this one thing.' Liang swallowed, but the spit caught in her throat. She took a gulp of her water. 'I told them back then, my captors, "My father is the CEO of Cosorin. If you do this, he'll hunt you down, kill you, and then he'll kill your families," and they said, "Really? Maybe he'll pay a nice ransom for you?" But he didn't. He refused! My father left me there to die and worse.'

Her uncle looked stricken as if she'd slapped him across his face in public. She didn't ever wish to hurt him, except she had to let him know.

'I'm so sorry, my child.'

Liang couldn't stop herself. 'How could he have done that to me? *His own son.*'

'But you weren't his son by then, were you?' Her uncle shook his head and waved his hands, perhaps to ward off unwanted memories. 'Your father is a proud man, high up in the company. When you became a girl, he couldn't comprehend *why*. You were meant to follow in his footsteps. You were *meant* to marry a girl from a good family. How could you do all that as a girl?'

'Should it matter? As a girl or a boy, shouldn't your parent do everything in their power to protect their child? *You* didn't leave me there to fester, yet he did. My own father!'

Her uncle sipped from his tall glass of red wine and dabbed at the corner of his mouth. He leant over the table and whispered, 'I'm gay, child. I believe and hope only you and I know this. My wife and treasured son are unaware of my alternate sexuality. I complied with the rules and did what was asked for by my family, but it never made me happy. You know I run a wine import business that takes me all over the world. I have liaisons that are clandestine and rather furtive. That is all I can do.'

'And if father found out?'

'I would be blacklisted as you were. At least my business does not rely on me being straight. In fact, it's somewhat de rigour to be somewhat effeminate and not overly aggressive.'

'Could he hurt you in any way?'

'Possibly. But I like to believe that my customers are not worried about what someone who manufactures military firearms and ammunition and other delightful high-tech defence products has to say. Especially when they have the reputation of selling missile launchers to any low-life who has the cash.'

'That's something to remember. Thank you, uncle.'

'All I want for you, Liang, is for you to live a long and happy life.'

Liang squeezed his hand tighter. 'That goes for the both of us.'

On the train journey home, all the worries she had crowded like unwanted guests into her mind. No matter which way she played it, the result was always the same. Ele would hate her, Sabine would hate her, Paul would be repulsed by her and Hope, well, Hope had always been the sweetest of them all. Maybe she'd accept her. All Liang could see was a ghastly night ahead and wished she could fast-forward to New Year's Day when they would be leaving to come home. She felt she hadn't quite got here yet. She needed more time to come to terms with having Michael back in her life. It was going to be nerve-wracking seeing them all as Liang, not as Tiger.

New Year's Eve was tonight. That stupid *pact*. She knew Michael had arranged it all, had pooh-poohed her misgivings, and was as excited as a kid as he exchanged messages with their old friends across the internet. He'd finally shared his plans with her, showing her all the messages backwards and forwards. Liang was up to speed with it all, although she didn't like it.

'It'll be great,' he said. 'They'll be so happy to see you again. As I said, what a surprise it'll be.'

'You're bonkers,' Liang said. 'For a start, they'll never get the connotations.'

'That's the point,' he crowed, his face alight with mischievous glee, 'they won't get it until we arrive.'

'Ghosts and smugglers? That bloody mermaid? This is all pretty insensitive, Michael.'

Sometimes she wondered if he had any idea what she'd gone through. She knew that many journalists saw the life around them as if life itself was just one long story to be written down and read. Not to be lived through with all the accompanying trauma. Much as a photographer viewing everything through the lens. It makes it all not *real*. Until whatever you are filming bites you in half.

'Insensitive? It's funny.' He must've seen the look on her face. 'Not for you, but now you can be you, be free.'

'And if they don't understand?'

'Then we'll see them again when we're sixty. They might've mellowed by then.'

'Sixty? Make that ninety!' They both laughed at that. As far as she could remember, that was the last time.

But she still worried. Sabine was a problem for her. She'd been his lover when he'd come to the States to do a job on corruption in sports there. He hadn't banked on discovering her and how this would impact his life, and as far as she knew, he hadn't told Sabine, merely sidelined her.

'Have you spoken to her since we got back?' She knew he hadn't. Avoided her calls and texts. 'You should let her know what's going on. It's only fair.'

'She's back in France with her adoring hubby. I'll talk to her soon, don't worry.'

It was then she realised that was what he'd always done. When something or someone got too much, he'd simply step away and let them flounder and work it out for themselves that he was finished with them. That's what'd happened to Ele. He just stepped out of her life. Understandable in the circumstances as Ele didn't make things easy. But that was the point. Love encompassed the bad times as well as the good, didn't it? When he made his feelings known about her, she didn't hesitate, believing he'd tried his best by Ele, but had he? And she, consumed with guilt, had clung to Ele even more because of it. Okay, Sabine was an adulteress and had no actual leg to stand on. But what about Ele herself? How would she take to the idea that she was now with Michael after being pronounced "dead"? There was a distinct possibility that they wouldn't be best friends for life.

She could envision them in her mind. Hope was a mum of three, so Liang bet she had tons of pictures of her kids and would go on and on about how fantastic they were and how everyone should have at least a dozen. Paul? Well, she was sure he was doing very well, and he'd let them know that as he couldn't help but big himself up at every opportunity. Sabine would be stunning, as what else could she be? And Ele?

Ele had never asked if she, as Tiger, was gay; she'd just assumed.

'Every girl needs a gay best friend,' Ele would say, and "Tiger" never corrected her. But Liang wasn't gay. She was transgender, a girl caught inside a boy's body. At her primary school, she'd confided to some of the other little girls that she wanted to be a girl too. When they teased her and called her names, Tiger was astute enough to keep quiet from then on. But that didn't mean the feelings went away. Her high-achieving parents weren't supportive. Hitting secondary school, she'd decided to act the boy, yet everyone still assumed she must be gay. It was Ele who helped her. Warded her from the bullies. Michael too, but now Liang suspected he protected her for other reasons. With Ele, though, it was more as though they were sisters. In fact, she'd always longed to be Ele's sister, except she still stabbed her in the back with Michael and smiled to her face. She hated herself for that.

If she couldn't forgive herself, how could Ele?

35

LIANG

ISLINGTON – A LOST ANGEL

I t was just gone three. Liang had made good time. She wondered if Michael was home ahead of her. She hoped so, as she didn't want to be there by herself. Her key was in the lock, but she stopped. Something slithered over her skin. She shook her shoulders.

The door opened, her hand still clinging to the keys. Liang saw a shoe first. It was blocking the door and slid across the boards as she pushed into the hallway. Some part of her wouldn't register what she was looking at. He was lying on the floor, both arms flung out. One shoe on, one off where he must've been kicking. She inched in and, fumbling behind her, managed to close the door, which was the only thing holding her upright. Even that couldn't keep her up, her knees buckled, and she slid down.

The acid had dribbled from what was left of his face and eaten into the wood of the floor.

Liang crawled to him, held out a trembling hand to his chest. There was no movement, no rise and fall to denote life.

'Michael?' She was riveted by his melted face, couldn't tear her eyes from what used to be so beautiful but was now ruined beyond recognition. She knew it was him, could only be him, but she had to reject this, else her burning mind might spin out of control, aflame and sparking until there was only ashes left. True, there was a man wearing the clothes that Michael was wearing that morning lying mutilated in his hall, but of course, it wasn't *him*. Michael had nipped off down the shops to buy something else they'd both forgotten. She must've missed him en route. He'd be back any second. He'll know what to do about this stranger on the floor. She could hear her breath stutter.

'M...i...c...h...a...el...' The word, *his name,* dribbled out of her mouth in a long whine. 'Oh God, please help me.'

Now she could see the self-conceit that led her to believe that she could never be broken again. She'd cracked into a million shards. This couldn't be happening! *It wasn't real.* Liang smacked herself across her cheek. Wake up! But he was still there, unmoving. What should she do? The smell made her gag. She didn't know how long she sat there, but she woke as if from a daze. Had she seen him twitch. *Was he still alive?* Again she reached out with trembling fingers and lightly touched his chest. But no, there was nothing.

Tremors battered at her body, and there was nothing she could do. Liang's head cleared for a moment. *Who had done this to him?* She peered around. Nothing seemed to be disturbed. This was not a burglary. Acid in the face? He should've survived that, so he must've been drugged. This is revenge, a vendetta. Who uses acid? A grieved lover. Sabine? Had she seen them?

Hot, acrid liquid burned her throat and spewed out of her mouth. Her stomach heaving, Liang turned her head from the sight of Michael, *her Michael,* lying dead under the grinning pictures of all his friends and family.

'*What the fuck!*' The words tore out of her mouth. '*Fuck! Fuck! Fuck!*' She pounded her fists on the floor, curling them into claws.

'Oh, Michael.' There should be thunder rending the air. Where were the great crackling shards of lightning? Her heart was crushed and bleeding, her mind blown to bits with horror. Pulling her legs up to her chest, Liang curled up and lowered her head till her forehead rested on her knees. Rocking back and forth helped. But how long could she stay here like this? Until the world ended and the sun went dark? It already had. She knew time had passed, though she didn't know how long. A minute, an hour?

Where was her phone? She had to call the police. There seemed to be so much stuff in her bag that she couldn't find the phone. Throwing it all out onto the floor, she was looking down, her hand reaching for the phone, when she heard a sound. Her body froze. A shadow fell across her. Gasping for breath, Liang raised her head.

'What?' But she couldn't move out of the way fast enough. Whatever was in that woman's hand smashed all sense from her; first, bright scalding lights enveloped her and then she sank down into darkness. But she'd glimpsed something, *something awful.*

She was crawling out of a mudslide, gagging for air, mired down so heavily that she couldn't move, the earth holding her tightly in its arms like a lover, pulling her back down. A moment of disorientation, then straight after the memory hit. *Michael is dead.* The pain wrapped itself around her skull akin to having her head on an anvil being repeatedly hit by a hammer. Something wet trickled down the side of her face, but when she tried to wipe it, she discovered her arms remained pinned at her sides, her hands tied behind her back. Dread wormed its way up from her gut. She was bound, lying on what felt like carpet.

There was something sticky covering her mouth and a covering of sorts wrapped around her head. Light filtered in at the edges, and she could partially see if she tilted her head backwards.

'Hello, pretty one.' The voice had a thick, rounded Spanish accent. 'You don't mind if I call you "pretty one", do you?'

Liang stopped struggling. She didn't want to look up. She didn't want to *see*. It would make it real. This could only be the person who'd murdered Michael. *This* was who was going to murder her. That much she understood. But she didn't want to die. Pulling against her bonds, she thrashed and kicked, but whatever was binding her was too strong.

The woman didn't seem to be bothered as Liang watched her feet from under the material covering wrapped around her head, pacing in mid-heeled shoes. Leather. Black.

'That was quite a sight to behold when you came into the flat. All that wailing and crying. *Sweet Jesus,* that's one to put on YouTube. And all over little old Michael. Not looking so good now, is he. Not so much an angel as, hmm, as a dropped bowl of trifle.'

The woman laughed as though she'd made a saucy joke.

Liang heard the words but could barely understand them. How could she be speaking about Michael this way? *Why* had she done this? *Who* was she? She realised she must have been dragged into the living room. Past Michael. Liang started to shake. Michael. Tears squeezed out.

'What? Crying? Are you crying over him, pretty one?' A shadowed face loomed into her view, but Liang shut her eyes. No, she didn't want to see her. 'He wasn't worth it, you know. Surely you know he was a lying, cheating bastard? You should, of all people.'

Liang couldn't breathe through the covering across her mouth. Her nose was blocked, and tiny spangles of light were dancing at the edge of her vision.

Sudden pain in her arm made her cry out. Had she been cut?

'Now listen to me, pretty one. I'm going to take off your gag. If you shout or make any loud noises, I'll slice you again but much deeper next time. That was only a warning scratch.'

Liang could feel something cold and sharp push against her skin. 'Nod once if you'll do what I say.'

Liang bobbed her head. The gag was ripped from her mouth. It hurt, and she winced but made no sound. Hauling in a deep breath that filled her lungs, she wondered what was coming next. None of it was going to be good, was it?

What was she doing now? Liang didn't want to look, except it was as if she was caught by a serpent, mesmerised by their swaying head.

'I could cut you into lots of delicate pieces. I really could, but then you've already been cut, haven't you?' The woman made a grab for Liang's groin. 'Lost a special bit of yourself, I gather.'

Liang shied away, but the woman yanked her back by her hair. The mask over her face slipped. Just enough for Liang to see that the woman now had her back to her and was rummaging in a bag. She had long, straight black hair. When she turned around, she was holding a syringe. A full syringe. Liang focused on that.

'No, no, no!' Her voice was a whisper, even though she needed to scream out her fear. 'Oh please no, whatever you're going to do, please don't.'

'Don't you worry your pretty little head. This is only to knock you out. I have an appointment, and I need to go in a minute. But we're not finished yet. Not by a long way. Yes, we have unfinished business, you and I.'

As the syringe was pushed into her arm, Liang finally looked up.

'Oh my God! *No!*'

36

ELE

E le washed slowly in the bathroom and reapplied her make-up. She didn't dare have a bath in case she fell asleep in it and missed the whole shebang. A quick squirt of perfume but not too much as she hated those women whose scent arrived two minutes before they did. Slipping into the new dress that had cost her half of last month's earnings, she knew it made her look good. Or feel good, but what's the difference? It was bright red, a nod to Santa and her Spanish heritage, highlighting her dark chocolate hair and olive skin. The zip glided up her long black stiletto boots, picked up in a local charity shop, along with a largish clutch bag with a thin gold chain. The box of raisins was crushed inside. It was a ritual she never missed. By adding a handmade necklace and a fairly posh but not too "bling" watch, she was nearly good to go. She wriggled into a little black shrug in case the warmth from the fires she'd glimpsed didn't extend into the corridors. She didn't want to arrive purple mottled and goose-bumpy with cold.

Tracing her steps back, Ele passed the bar.

'Ele!'

She spied Hope, waving at her from a room packed with

men in festive sweaters and women in Marks and Sparks tops and dresses. Ele smiled her practised smile and weaved through, avoiding elbows, bags and tables. Wafts of mulled wine intermingled with the heady wood smoke. Glancing up, some vast black beam, smothered in greenery and fairy lights, went from one end of the bar to the other. It looked as though it was holding the entire inn up.

Hope gesticulated around her and called, 'We managed to bag a spot by the fire.'

Ele saw a few eyebrows rise.

Paul struggled upright and was heading towards her, also negotiating routes through the crowd. His arms were outstretched, and for one tiny moment, she wanted to turn and run.

'Ele, you look a million dollars. As usual.' She was pulled into a tight embrace that smelled distinctly of alcohol.

'Hey, Paul.' Bit lame, she knew, though she couldn't think of anything else to say and anyhow, he'd squeezed most of the air out of her lungs.

'It's good to see you,' he breathed into her hair. She had to pull back. As he released her, he nodded at the bar. 'What's your poison? Remember it's on dear old Michael.'

It was an unfortunate phrase that. Poison.

Paul continued, 'Though where he's got so much dosh to splash about is anyone's guess. Journalism must pay okay.'

'A J2O for me,' said Ele.

His expression was puzzled as if she'd said something in Arabic.

'Pacing myself.' She smiled, willing him to not ask *why*.

'Okay. I'll get them. Go see Hope. She's been so excited about seeing you again since the moment Michael contacted us.' Waving behind him, he said, 'She's just had a coffee but I'm getting her a wine now.'

Paul moved away from her, shoving through the throng milling at the bar. A small bird-like barman took orders and poured drinks with bonhomie and sure-fingered alacrity. Ele felt as if she was a hula dancer as she wiggled through to where Hope was sitting, with the proprietary bags on empty chairs ready for the others to arrive. Each step was like a camera "click". Hope was thinner, but gaunt rather than shapely. Strangely, more meat on her suited her better. "Click", although she was enveloped in silver that offset her midnight skin beautifully, "click", she looked tired, much as a caged animal might, but not surprising. Three kids must have taken it out of her. "Click", Ele knew her dreams of becoming a doctor had never materialised after the first baby was born. It seemed she may not be the only one of them that hadn't lived the life they'd wished for.

'Ele, it's brilliant to see you.' Hope's arms encircled her. Wow! Two hugs in one evening. She must be on a roll. 'You look fantastic.'

'It's good to see you too, Hope. It's been a long time,' Ele said. A set response and she felt terrible that she had no other words to say to her as yet.

'I never thought we'd actually do this after all these years, did you? It freaked me out initially. How about you?'

Ele sat down on a heavy, wooden chair that was difficult to manoeuvre. They were close to the fire, and her skin felt taut in the heat.

'I must admit, I'd stuck it at the back of my mind.' Ele twiddled at her hair and then lowered her hand. It showed she was agitated. 'Yeah. Really strange how he's gone about it.'

'I would've thought we'd meet in a nice restaurant close to where we all used to live or maybe somewhere in town near to our old school. Not a place like here.'

'What? Old and scary? Do you think that's how he views us all now?'

'Charming,' said Hope. 'Do you remember that time when you came over? It was, hang on, yes, just after George was born. We talked about the pact then.'

Ele stared at her. 'I came over? What, to your place in Brixton?' There was no recollection. She looked down at her lap. Nothing at all.

'It was a long time ago, I know, but–' Hope stopped suddenly, her eyes flicked upwards, and deep red spots heated her cheeks. 'Sorry, forget it.'

'But what?' Why had Hope reacted like that? It seemed a bit extreme.

'Nothing. As I said, it was a long time ago.' She shuffled in her seat as though *she* was uncomfortable, not the seat. What was she going to say? Hope then tried to sideline her. 'You really do look fantastic, Ele. In fact, I think you look younger than the last time I met you... oh.' The blush had travelled down her neck.

'What were you going to say, Hope? When was the last time we met?' Suddenly there was a picture in her mind. An end of terrace house. She knew Hope and Paul owned all of it. It was painted a seaside blue and had a neat, trimmed front garden with pruned shrubs. Somehow, she also knew that everything was muted and coordinated inside the house, and there was a baby with deep blue eyes gurgling merrily in his crib.

'You're right.' Ele said slowly, 'I remember your house... and I did see your baby. George, was it? God, I'm so sorry. Such a bad memory.' A slow realisation. 'I stayed with you.'

It was *that* night. She was sure of it. She'd spent the afternoon with Hope and Paul and stayed over. That must mean she hadn't been with Maria. So where had Maria been and why didn't she say anything when Ele had spoken to her about it? And more to the point, what had Maria been doing?

Hope blinked rapidly. 'Yes. Just the one night. We hadn't seen you since the wedding, and you phoned out of the blue and said you could visit. We had a lovely time.' Her words were rushed, breathless.

There was a horrible droning in Ele's head. 'Can you remember the date?'

'Oh, er, it was sometime in February.' Hope had a hooded look, as though she was hiding something that was right in front of her that Ele couldn't see. Had someone jabbed her with a sharp tined fork? What had she glimpsed earlier? Had she really been over there? Why couldn't she remember properly? Oh God, had she been really pissed?

'Can you be a bit more specific?'

'It was the twentieth.' Hope reached over but didn't touch her. 'I'm sorry, I don't mean to dredge up old memories.'

That was the date. A burned-out ruin. Crisped sheets. Ange. 'You mean about my old house. Did I tell you what had happened when I got back?'

'Yes... yes you did. From what you told us, it was a hell-hole, and I don't know how you survived there for so long.' Hope swallowed loudly. 'It was dreadful to hear about, you know, the two guys.'

'Yeah, it was. I still can't believe it.' Ele grimaced. 'It was a bloody awful house all round.' The images were fading, replaced by others she didn't want to see. 'And I don't think I did survive.'

'I'm so sorry, Ele. Are you alright about it all now? I mean, it must've been terrifying to come back to that.'

'Some of it is a bit of a blur.' Ele shook her head. 'Listen, the past is the past, and we all need to move on.'

Hope nodded rapidly, a nervous movement. 'You're right. It's

New Year, and we should have a right old knees up. Paul and I said earlier that we hardly get a chance to enjoy ourselves anymore. God knows I think we deserve it.' She gazed levelly at Ele. 'We all do.'

'Is happiness a given right?' Ele smiled at Hope. 'I'd like to think it is.'

'Me too.' She craned round to search the bar. 'I hope Paul's not chatting to the bar staff, or we'll never get our drinks.'

'I see you have a coffee? Are you teetotal?'

'Nah. Just drank a bit too much, too fast when we arrived. Needed to get my footing back. You?'

'Trying not to. It's hard. You don't think you've got a problem, and that's the problem.'

'You should say that to Paul.' Hope looked like she was deflating slowly. 'Enough whingeing. Are you still at the market? That's the last thing I remember you doing.'

'Yeah. It's pretty bonkers, but I love it there.'

'I'm jealous,' said Hope, 'I'd love to do exactly what I wanted, like you do...' She shook her head. 'Oh, I'm sorry that came out wrong. What I meant was to have autonomy. I know how hard you work.'

'I know what you meant. I bet with young kids, you never stop.'

'You're not wrong there. Sometimes, I lock myself for a couple of minutes in the toilet, just to get a break.' She grinned.

'Hope, I meant it when I said you look great. I can't believe you've had three kids, and you still look like that.'

'Through no fault of my own.' She made a face that looked more a grimace, and then it was like she'd realised she'd done it and reset it. Her smile was brilliant. Ele was obviously not the only one who'd been practising their smile in the mirror.

'Is there anything wrong?' As if Hope would tell her. As if she'd tell Hope.

'No, no. Of course not.' She changed tack. 'What did you make of Michael's little film?'

Ele tucked her bag near her feet then felt foolish. Was there anyone in this place who would steal it? She suspected that most of the couples chatting animatedly were wearing more than half her year's earnings on their wrists alone.

'I thought it was strange. Pretty manic, actually.'

'How are you about seeing him?' Hope leaned forward, and Ele thought she could see pity on her face. There was a flare of anger blossoming in her head, although she squashed it down. In the same position, she'd pity her. Ele glanced towards the bar as Paul shouldered his way through a medley of men in Christmas-themed sweaters.

'It was a bit of a jolt seeing him on that DVD. But it's okay. Nine years is a long time to get over someone. He looked happy, and I'm glad for that. Better than at the end, you know?'

'If you're sure, but let me know if you need anything.' Hope finished the coffee in front of her and pushed the cup to the side of the table.

A movement startled Ele. She'd forgotten there was anyone else meant to be there with them.

'What an amazing fireplace.' Paul placed a pint, a glass of white wine and an orange-coloured bottle with a straw on the table. 'Here we go. We read up on this inn.' He settled on a chair next to Ele. 'What on earth induced Michael to choose here?'

'It sounds like a mystery,' Ele said. 'He said he had a story or something, and we'd all love it.'

Paul grunted and took a long swallow from his glass. Only half remained when he set it down. 'I hate mysteries. Just tell it like it is; that's my motto.'

'Really?' said Hope, fingering at the condensation on her glass of white wine. 'Maybe you should try doing that with me then.' She scrunched her face briefly and pursed her lips. Ele had the impression she hadn't meant to blurt that out.

'Now's not the time, Hope. I thought we'd discussed this?' Paul's eyes narrowed. 'It's New Year's Eve, and we should all be cheerful and carefree, eh?'

'I know. Sorry.' Hope turned away from him, now fiddling with an ornate silver necklace that looked Indian. In that moment, Ele realised they all had their tics. The things they did when they wanted to cover their unease, their *anxiety*. Something was up, but Ele didn't want to know, too busy wallpapering over the cracks in her own life to bother with criticising other people's decor.

'Ele?' said Hope, 'What's your room like? Ours is, well, it's creepy.'

'I'm glad you said that first.' Ele laughed, and when she leant forward, their heads nearly touched. 'I was told my room's not haunted, although it seems a prime location to me. All dark wood panelling and creaky floorboards.'

'Oh, man,' said Paul, downing the remains of his drink, 'those floorboards are something else. No sneaking around here.'

Ele caught a look passing between them. Hope's eyes flickered some sort of matrimonial Morse code and she interpreted it to mean "slow down".

'Listen, my darling,' he drawled, and Ele connected the dots. This was not his second or even third drink tonight. He was way ahead of them and was seriously pissed. 'It's on the house, so I'm merely taking advantage.' He sniffed. 'As I thought you were.'

'I'll have another glass in a bit. As I said, I don't want to show my knickers to everyone in the bar. Not before midnight anyway.'

Ele raised an inquisitive eyebrow. 'Should I leave you two to be alone?'

'Nah', said Paul, 'we're okay. Top up, anyone? No?' Standing up, his movements were the practised ones of the long term alcoholic who can easily compensate. Only another alcoholic could recognise them.

'Talking of which,' he bent down to her level. 'Ele, are you sure you don't want a *proper* drink?'

And there it was. The live bait to a hungry but ultimately stupid little fish that has already been hooked so many times but miraculously wriggled free. Ele could see it, the flash of it, practically smell it, could feel it going down her throat and washing all her sins away, letting her believe that everything was fine and dandy. It'd be so easy to slip back into it, the old ways.

Ele took a deep breath. 'No, I'm fine, thanks.' Feeling vindicated, if only for a moment, because she knew that for a recovering alcoholic, to be surrounded by drink and companionable drinking "buddies" was one of the ultimate tests. She'd had to hammer her willpower on the anvil of life or some such shit like that, but there had been heat and sparks and pain. She didn't think it ever went away.

'Oh my God! There's Sabine.' There was a particular note to Hope's voice.

Ele followed Hope's gaze. A vision in gold had entered the bar, and they were not the only ones transfixed.

'Bonsoir,' Sabine called gaily. The mass of festive-sweatered men and pearl-garlanded women parted as if she was Moses commanding the Red Sea.

Ele was sure the consensus of opinion at this point must be that they were all drab little sparrows to her glorious peacock splendour.

'What a journey!' Sabine air-kissed them in their general direction. A scent that reeked of sophistication and extreme wealth enveloped them like they'd slipped into a first world war trench and been bombarded by Chanel No. 5. until they suffocated horrifically. 'Is Michael here?' She looked around her.

'Not yet,' said Hope, 'but he said he might be a bit late on that film.' She stood up to kiss Sabine. 'Lovely to see you. Been a long time.'

'You look utterly stunning,' said Paul, except Ele noticed he wasn't actually looking at her. 'What can I get you? Wine? Spirits?' He sounded flustered. Ah, he'd forgotten that this is what she did, had always done. How all men turn into mesmerised mice and she was a rattlesnake about to strike, but at least they'd die happy. Poisoned by her toxic love. You could say it was in her genes, her Gallic blood. It was still so easy, and Paul should've known better.

Sabine acknowledged Ele with an inclination of her head. Like royalty. But then, what did she expect? Probably a little demure wave of the hand to go with it and not embraces and tears.

'I'll have a large glass of red wine but not that mulled rubbish. That's sacrilege. Only you British would do such a heinous thing.' Sabine sat on the proffered chair.

'You British?' Ele glanced at Hope. 'You're no longer one of us then?'

'Was I ever?' Sabine's eyes were two emeralds that glinted sharply in the reflected light from the fire. 'I didn't think you were either...' She stared at Ele.

'I still drink tea with milk and sugar.' Ele winked at Hope.

'So, Sabine,' said Hope, smiling, 'how's life treating you?'

'Hmm,' said Sabine. 'We have to say the correct thing now, do we? How are you? You're looking great, even if we all know that's a lie. And that classic one, what are you doing with your life since we made the pact. Since we actually cared and listened to each other.'

'Wow! Say it how it is, Sabine.' Ele wasn't shocked, though.

It'd always been Sabine who voiced what they thought. She said she was merely being *truthful*, as opposed to *tactless*. Ele thought there was a fine line there. She and Tiger used to be so catty behind her back. "Pompous cow!" That's what Tiger had called her.

'Isn't that so?' Sabine raised one perfectly plucked eyebrow. 'I remember the time when we could all speak as friends, say that someone looked shit and then find out what we could do about it. Not go through the motions of friendship.'

'Yeah, I suppose you're right,' Ele shrugged her shoulders, 'but it's going to take a little while to get back to where we were.' She didn't add if they ever could. 'I last saw you at Hope and Paul's wedding. How long ago was that?'

'Nine years or so,' said Hope. 'We read about *your* wedding', she nodded at Sabine, 'in the culture section of *The Times*.' They all knew what she was saying even though she didn't say it out loud. None of them were invited. 'While they dissected your expensive cutlery and crockery and the wonderful marquee in the grounds of that amazing hotel.'

Quite frankly, *now* Ele felt a little taken aback. Hope, their greatest and foremost peacekeeper, had "had a go", as they say. *Well, well, well.*

'The wedding was in Mauritius,' said Sabine. There was a hard line to her mouth, 'and it was just a close, select group who were invited. We couldn't afford to pay for everyone. I always meant to have a little "do" for us, but time slipped away from me, and now here we all are.' She peered around the room again. 'Well, most of us anyway.'

'Still happily married?' Ele asked.

Sabine turned just at the moment Paul thumped a fat glass of red wine on the table. A slosh spilt over the rim and trickled like a thin dribble of blood down the stem.

'Oops, sorry.' He sat between herself and Hope like they

were a barricade. There was something more than alcohol here, except Ele couldn't work out what it was. She'd never been into hunting for clues, and had never, ever worked out "who dunnit".

'Have you watched the DVD?' Hope was trying to cover up her previous comment or Paul's blatant drunkenness.

'Yes,' Sabine brushed something invisible from her dress. It was shimmering so much in the light from the fire that she appeared to be in a sheath of writhing flames. She continued, 'Michael is always so playful, isn't he?' She twisted to look at the bar door as if he'd miraculously arrive on cue.

'It's gone half past eight,' Ele said, squinting at her watch. 'Isn't our dinner reservation at nine?'

Paul nodded. 'He said he'd be late, though.'

'What,' Ele said, 'late enough to miss the meal?'

'Ele?' said Hope. 'Haven't you got his mobile number?'

'No, anyway, we shouldn't call him if he's still driving. It's dangerous.'

'I have his number,' said Sabine, pulling her iPhone from the depths of her Prada bag. 'I'll leave a text message, and then he'll be able to read it when he can. As you say, we don't want him to have an accident.'

Ele saw Hope frown slightly. She probably thought it strange that it was Sabine who was seemingly in contact with him. But she supposed of all of them, she was the most likely. Sabine and Michael had kept up with each other, not let their friendship slip as the rest of them had done. That was what Hope had told her. Ele had always suspected they'd been seeing each other. *The bitch!*

'It's such a shame that Tiger isn't here with us,' said Sabine, as she tapped the front of her phone. 'I'm sure he'd have loved all this.'

Ele froze as though an Arctic vortex had descended upon her.

'*Sabine!*' There was a "snap" in Hope's voice. A mother reprimanding a rude child.

'Oh come on,' slurred Paul, 'it's been years. Surely Ele's over it now?'

'Ele! Your hands are shaking,' Hope reached across to cup them. 'Are you alright?' She could see concern etched across her face.

'Yeah, I'm fine.' Ele pulled her hands from Hope's embrace. 'I just want to talk to him again.' The words in her head could melt lead.

'Of course, you do,' said Hope. 'We understand.'

'Listen, we'll celebrate him tonight as well. Eh?' said Sabine. She lay a warm hand on Ele's shoulder. 'Ele. I didn't mean to upset you.'

'That's okay. It caught me by surprise.' Ele needed to get away from this. She could feel something inching its way up from deep inside her as if she'd eaten a live octopus and it was climbing with its suckered legs up her throat. She silently counted down from ten. She couldn't think about him. Not now.

37

HOPE

RYE – NEW YEAR'S EVE

'I 'm really sorry,' Hope stood, making sure she didn't make eye contact with Paul, 'but I'm nipping out for a ciggy.' She pulled her bag open and tugged out a crumpled box of Marlboros and a red lighter. Funny how even they looked Christmassy.

'I thought you were giving up?' Paul sounded disappointed, and Hope felt like slapping him hard across his self-righteous face. She nearly replied with, *'that's rich coming from the man with bottles of whisky hidden in the utility cupboard,'* but kept her lips sealed tightly instead. Having a scene here was not what either of them needed right now. The idea that they were going to have fun together was being rapidly replaced with the fact that he was extremely drunk already, far outstripping her ability to keep up. It made her feel unbalanced.

'Do you mind if I join you?' Sabine tilted her head but didn't move. 'We social pariahs should stick together, and I won't be able to make it through dinner if I don't have at least one now.'

'Sure,' said Hope, 'It'll be nice to have company.' Damn, Sabine was the last person she wanted to spend quality time with. What on earth could they chat about? They had absolutely nothing in common.

Hope yanked a shawl across her shoulders, pushed through the people and out the heavy wooden door. A blast of icy air cooled her hot skin. She felt rather than saw Sabine behind her.

'Bloomin' heck, but it's cold.' Hope shivered and dragged her shawl tighter around her shoulders, cupping her hands, so it was easier to light the cigarette.

'What a truly horrendous place this is.' Sabine took a long drag, sucking it in slowly. 'Whatever induced Michael to pick here? And where is he?'

'Not a clue. On both accounts.'

'I know he said he'd be late, but I expected him before now. You don't think anything has happened, do you?'

Hope noted a strange mix of general concern coupled with something more distraught in Sabine's tone.

'I'm sure he's fine, just got held up somewhere.'

Sabine tapped her foot on the concrete. 'I really need to speak to him. Tonight. Especially tonight.'

'You've kept in touch with him, haven't you?'

'Yes. We're pretty close. I would say very close... except...' her voice tailed off.

'Except what?' Hope could see glints of gold reflections across her perfect skin as light from a nearby window shone across her. She looked like an angel, damn her!

'I haven't seen him for a while.' There was an indefinable sadness in her voice.

'He'll be here in a bit.' Hope thought it might be a good idea to change the subject. 'How's Philippe?'

'Oh, he's fine. Off on a hunting trip to Africa.' She'd already lit her next cigarette. Hope could see the hot red tip bobbing about.

'Hunting? Hunting what?'

'Lions, gazelles, zebras, you name it. If it can run away from him, he loves to shoot it. Tigers are his favourite because they're so rare. He has a penchant for the unobtainable.' She paused. 'I think that's why he wanted me.'

'That's horrible!' Hope squirmed. 'Sorry, what I meant was I don't condone hunting and especially endangered animals like tigers.'

'Nor do I, although he doesn't particularly listen to me.'

'You're his wife!'

'Yes, I am, yet that's a rather moot point when it comes to his little fancies.'

'Anyway, isn't it illegal?'

'Not for men such as Philippe. They're a breed apart, and I gather the rules don't apply to them. On any account.'

'Well, that's nice, isn't it.' Hope couldn't disguise the contempt in her voice. Yet again, the rich could get away with whatever they wanted but put her or Paul in a similar situation, and they'd probably be sentenced to years in the nick and have a hefty fine. Hope stubbed her cigarette out hard on the grille by the door and posted the butt into the metal box.

'I suppose we'd better get in.' She reached out to open the door, but Sabine pulled her back, looked down and shuffled her feet. 'You've got kids, haven't you.'

'Three.' Hope desperately wanted to get into the warmth of the bar. She tapped her feet to keep warm.

'I presume it changes your life?'

'Forever.'

'That didn't sound good.'

'No, no. It's really hard in so many ways but what you get out of it is worth it a million times over. I love my kids more than life itself. I'd do anything for them, even when they're driving me bananas. And they do that most of the time.' Hope frowned.

'Look, it's freezing, and I'm sure you don't want to be outside here with me blathering in your ear about my kids–'

'I'm pregnant.'

'What?' Hope clapped her hands together. 'Sabine! That's brilliant news.'

'No, it's not.'

'Why ever not?

'Because it wasn't planned. It's come as a surprise even to me.'

'Then you need to tell Philippe *tout de suite,* as you say.' Her attempt at a joke obviously failed. Sabine looked as if she might cry. 'Sorry, I was trying to lighten the tone.'

'He won't be at all happy about this.'

'Oh come on, don't say your fancy Frenchie hubby doesn't want kids?' Hope felt angry enough to punch the wall.

'My fancy Frenchie hubby doesn't know anything about it.' Sabine's eyes were liquid, like looking into a pool of green water. 'It's Michael's child.'

'What?' Hope laughed a little hysterically. 'You are joking, aren't you?' *What?* Sabine was having Michael's baby? No way. She had a sudden urge to embed her poorly manicured nails into any part of Sabine she could reach.

Sabine flicked her cigarette into the grass by the side of the bar door. Hope saw it glowing fitfully, then it winked out.

'I love him.'

'You love him? You're in love with Michael?' Hope glanced quickly at the door. 'I presume Ele doesn't know?'

'Of course not. I think she'd rip my head off. Even though she always said she was over him, I don't want to put that to the test. Hope, please don't say anything to her about this. Promise me?'

Hope put on her practised smile. 'I promise. But,' she waved at Sabine's stomach, 'it's going to be showing soon. Are you going to tell Philippe that it's his? Or...' Hope nodded, 'that's why you need to see Michael tonight. You're going to tell him.'

'I don't know how he'll react. It hasn't been good between myself and Philippe.'

'Did it start before or after you married Philippe?'

'After, of course.' Sabine looked bemused. 'I know it all sounds sordid and dirty, but I truly loved Philippe when I married him. I think essentially, we were too radically different to each other. It's like he's in another world, near to me, and yet I can't get over to him.'

Yeah, I'm sure it's terrible trying to talk to a multimillionaire, thought Hope. 'If the worst comes to the worst, could you pass the baby off as his?'

'Not unless it's a miraculous conception. We haven't slept together in over eight months.'

'Then you have to see what Michael says.' Hope waggled the pack of cigarettes at Sabine. 'And you have to stop smoking and drinking. You can seriously damage your baby.'

Sabine reached into her bag, scrunched up the pack and stuffed it into the bin.

'Satisfied?' Pushing past Hope, she walked back into the bar.

Hope stood alone for a minute more, trying to digest what she'd been told. Sabine was pregnant by Michael. Now there was a twist no one saw coming. Poor Ele. Hope prayed she'd never find out. About any of it.

38

ELE

RYE – NEW YEAR'S EVE

Sabine came back in first, with a look on her face like she'd been sucking on lemons. Hope followed her a moment later and again, with such a strange expression that Ele wondered what they'd been talking about.

'You both okay?' She looked from one to the other, but they were either fumbling inside bags or swigging drinks. Hope mumbled a reply that Ele didn't catch.

She tried again. 'You two look like you had a jolly time out there.'

'It was cold,' said Sabine and stared at Ele with a stern look. 'And I prefer to be warm.'

Ele snapped her mouth shut. Been told there, hadn't she?

There was one of those awkward silences that slowly enveloped them like a warm, heavy blanket. It was finally interrupted when the young man who'd shown them to their rooms popped his head around the bar door. 'Sorry? Is the Storm party here? Your table is ready.'

They all waved. Sabine took control, looking around at everyone. 'Could you,' she shouted across to him, 'hold it for a bit as one of our party, well actually Mr Storm himself, isn't here yet?'

'I can probably hold it until quarter past nine, but I don't think I can do more than that.'

Paul turned to them. 'Where the hell is Michael?'

'I'll call him,' said Sabine. She turned from them and murmured a message into her phone.

At quarter past nine on the dot, the lad was back, hopping from foot to foot. 'If you can't come now, you'll miss your spot.'

'What do we do?' said Hope. 'Surely we can't start without him?'

'Maybe this is part of his surprise, and we're in the middle of ruining it.' Sabine held out her hands, and Ele noticed they were shaking. She had a point, and Ele was hungry. There was also something about Sabine's movements, though, jerky and sharp, as if she was cross. Had she had a row with Hope when they were outside? She resolved to get Hope by herself and probe until she received an answer, especially as Hope wasn't making eye contact with any of them now.

'Let's go,' said Paul. He stood abruptly, and that seemed to be the signal. They straggled after him like baby ducks as they were led out.

39

LIANG

ISLINGTON – NEW YEAR'S EVE

Spiralling up the inside of a twister. Faster and faster until she woke with a start as though she'd been kicked. Pain pounded in Liang's temples, and she realised the gag was back around her mouth. Her arm smarted from where she'd been cut. Was she still bleeding? She was blind, opening her eyes into blackness.

Rolling gently, she managed to get onto her side, and by rubbing her head across the carpet, she dislodged the mask. It was dark in the room, though orange street light crept in under the drawn blinds. Liang slowly got used to the gloom, terrified that *she* would be in there with her, sat watching from the sofa, stood behind the door or lying beside her on the carpet. Inches away. Liang closed her eyes, the fear threatening to overtake her, but she opened them again. Waited. Stared into the darkness. What had been clumps of shadows slowly materialised into the sofa, the sideboards, the shelving units and the side table.

Was *she* still here? Somewhere in the flat? Was she playing a sick joke on her? Cat and mouse? Murderer and murdered? As Liang's heartbeat speeded up, so did her breathing, and now she was having trouble dragging air into her lungs. If she didn't get that mask off soon, she might asphyxiate. Think, *think!* Years of yoga had left her supple. Wriggling sideway to try to reach the sofa, she was pulled back. Not only was she tied up, but she was tethered to something heavy. Close enough to hook her legs onto the sofa, she rested her bum against the base. Kicking off her trainers and sliding off her socks, she bent her right leg and used her toes to grip the material covering her mouth. It was shiny and stuck fast. By careful manipulation, she started to pull it off, enough so that she could breathe properly. Listening intently for any sounds that shouldn't be there, she tugged the rest of it off.

There was a party next door, music blaring, laughter and loud talking. Was it possible to attract their attention? If she thumped on the wall, would they assume she was a curmudgeonly old git and turn the music up louder?

Lying with her head on the floor, she stopped. Michael must still be out in the hall. But just that one slight exertion had left her exhausted. It must be the drug, but what drug? Just something to knock her out, so not poison. Had her assailant given her too little, not expecting her to wake up this early, or was she just about to arrive back? In time to kill her. Surely if she'd been in the flat, she'd have come in by now? The pounding in her head was worsening, and she felt nauseous.

The French-style clock on the mantlepiece had illuminated hands. It told her it was nearly nine. Dinner was going to be at nine, so they must all be there by now, at that inn that Michael thought was so funny. She didn't think it'd occurred to Michael that there might be a problem about three of his lovers all meeting in the same place, probably fuelled with alcohol and not expecting the revelations that would ultimately come out. But then that wasn't going to happen now, was it. They'd be waiting for his arrival and wondering where he was. A vision of Michael lying on the floor filled her mind. Where were the memories that would block this? She had to search for them before she was overwhelmed, had to have another picture of him, happy, laughing, not this atrocity. Then maybe she could find the strength to fight, to try to escape.

When Michael's phone suddenly *pinged* where it had been left on the small coffee table, she jumped as if she'd been stung by a fire ant. It was a text coming through. It must be from one of them. She was sure they were discussing where he was and why he was late, although Liang didn't think "murder" would be at the top of the list. She could feel the fear and pain squirming inside, her shattered heart beating too fast, willing her breath in and out of her body. Tears fell, great wet splots that pumped out of her. Who did that to him? Her beloved Michael. Who could be capable of that? What had she seen, right at the last moment? No, it wasn't true. She must've imagined it.

The tether shortened as she rolled over and over, but then she heard creaking. The oak sideboard and dresser were in that corner. If that was what she was tied to, then if she pulled it down on her, she'd be crushed. All the last remnants of strength seeped from her body, and she drifted off into a troubled sleep. It was only a dream, but Liang was there again. Dreamworlds can be as real as any actual world when you're in it.

40

LIANG

HELL ON EARTH

L iang was back in prison, in her cell. Seventy lost souls packed into a tiny space.

A woman called Heather took her under her wing and each day gave her another way to survive there. 'Think of a special, really happy time in your life, and when all the shit happens, you go hide in that memory. Whatever is happening to your body, leave it there. They can't destroy your mind unless you let them. It's about the only thing you've got that they can't take from you.'

Years passed, and they clung together, laughing and crying through the worst of times, for there were no good ones to speak of. Heather was in for smuggling drugs, as most of the inmates were. The difference between them was, she did it so she could buy more. The threat of relapse was ever-present, the lure of the drug-induced oblivion so powerful.

One morning, when the sun was cool enough to warm you without burning, when the water was flowing, the toilets unblocked, and the showers ran clear and not the customary russet brown, when it seemed everything was okay, Heather said to her: 'This place swallows inmates like a hungry wolf. Don't ever forget that, Liang.'

That was just before Liang caught her stealing her stash.

'Heather?' Liang could hear the shock in her own voice. 'What the *hell* are you doing?' She'd shared fifty-fifty of what she'd got from her uncle.

'What's it look like I'm doing?' Heather's voice was tremulous. She'd stopped, mid-action, as though frozen.

'You could've asked me.' Liang held out her hands. 'I'd have given you anything if you'd asked. I've already given you half of what I've had.'

'It wasn't enough, Liang. Jesus, I got back on the *meow meow,* and now I can't kick it. I've got to score some more.'

'So you're selling my stuff so you can score drugs here? Are you out of your mind or what? You know this drug is dangerous. It'll kill you if you're not careful.'

'Don't you get all high and mighty with me, missy!' Heather's hands were now curling around a fat toilet roll. Worth a lot.

'Oh, that's funny coming from the person who's robbing me!'

'I need it.' She stood there, eyes wild and mouth drawn back in a rictus. 'You've got more than you need. You're alright.'

'I thought you wanted to stay clean for your son?'

She staggered backwards at that as if Liang had actually hit her. '*Bitch!* You leave him out of this.'

'Heather, you've got to get off this stuff.' Liang took a step towards her. Her beloved sister. 'I don't want you to die. Please, listen to me. I'll help you any way I can, but you've got to stop the drugs.'

'I know what I'm doing.' Heather scuttled from her and disappeared in the maze of alleys that ran across the prison.

Liang was working late that day, and when she returned to her cell, she still hadn't managed to find Heather. Probably avoiding her through sheer gravity of guilt. That's what she thought. She knew they'd make up in the morning. They'd talk, shout maybe, but they'd get through this as they'd got through every other thing that'd threatened them here.

Liang was six years in, and Heather had gone past the time when most people lost it. They both thought she'd survived and got through it, but the next day, Liang heard a commotion from the yard. Someone called her name. It wasn't a voice she recognised. Running with the other women, it took her a full minute to realise who the figure was lying on the ground by the wall. She was having convulsions, and then she stopped moving.

'Heather?' Liang looked around at all the women staring. 'Someone get help.' No one moved. *'Get help!'*

A lone woman trotted off to alert the guards.

'Heather?' Managing to roll her onto her side, Liang leaned over and saw her face was blue. 'Oh shit, what have you done?'

'Meow meow.' A Thai girl nodded at her.

Fumbling, Liang pulled Heather's wrist to her and felt for a pulse, searched at her throat. Nothing. *She can't be dead.* She pushed on her chest, forced her breath into her lungs, over and over again. No, no. No! *Heather!* The prison guards finally shoved through the throng, hauled Heather around as though she was a sack of potatoes.

'Leave her alone!' The scream tore out of her throat so ferociously that even the guards stepped back from her. This woman lying broken at her feet had been the one person that'd kept her alive here.

'She dead.' The woman's face was impassive. Life was so cheap here.

Liang hit the ground. Watched as they took Heather away. Dead? She was dead? She shook her head, great waves of anger and fear washing over her as if she was being dragged along by a tidal surge. Heather only had two years of her sentence left. How did she miss this? Was this her fault? If she'd done more, could she have saved her? The knowledge that she might be okay, that one day she'd walk from this place back into the world, was dulled by the knowledge that Heather wasn't there with her, would never be there. Liang wondered if she'd make it without her now. She went back to work and blocked her from her thoughts, only seeing her one last time as they took her out the gate. The look of pure bliss on her face haunted her.

Liang woke with such a weight on her chest that she believed her ribs had cracked. The bed was soft and warm, and the street lamp was shining through a gap in the bedroom curtains. Michael had brought her a child's nightlight to ward off the horrors of the dark, and she could see its warm glow on the wall. She had to remind herself that she wasn't still in Thailand. She was safe. She would creep into the kitchen to make a cup of tea, savouring the fresh milk and sweetness of two sugars. She wouldn't make too much noise, as she didn't want to wake Michael, but... no, that was all wrong. She was lying on the floor, cold and cramped, sharp stabs of pain ricocheting up her legs, across her shoulders when she tried to move. She wasn't safe at all, and Michael was dead.

There were sirens in the distance, a cat wailing at a rival and the sound of a couple, quite drunk as far as she could ascertain, passing in the street out front. Music still blared from the flat next door, voices raised, all the sounds of a great party.

'Help me.' It was barely a croak. 'Somebody, please help me.'

Sleep was tugging at her, insistent. Liang knew that the next time she woke, *she* would be there. The woman who looked exactly the same as *her*.

41

ELE

NEW YEAR IN RYE, 10PM–1AM

The dining room was sumptuous. Black timbers against whitewashed walls, gilt-framed paintings of stiff-faced men and women with dagger-sharp eyes, fleur-de-lis patterned carpets. The table was dressed beautifully, with thin silver flower holders filled with fronds dripping tiny buds like miniature bouquets. Heavy silver cutlery and gleaming glasses were placed on a diamond of pristine white cloth.

'This is posh,' said Hope. 'Please don't let me make a prat of myself.'

Ele resisted the urge to say it wouldn't be her that'd balls it up. It'd be her drunken other half. Strange. As the waiter marched up, Ele waved a hand. 'Excuse me? Why is the table set for six when there's only five of us?'

The young man shrugged. 'As far as I know, all the tables are set up so they look symmetrical. We don't leave things looking bare.'

Sabine was staring at the extra place setting. 'He's not bringing someone else, is he?' Her voice was small and childlike.

'Of course not,' said Hope. 'No one else is included. It's just us.'

'It might explain why he's late, though?' said Paul.

'No, as Hope said, it's only us. I mean,' she swivelled to Sabine, 'did Michael invite Philippe?'

'No.' Sabine swallowed noisily.

Ele smoothed a crinkle out of the snowy white table cloth. 'There you go. It's just us. The old pact crew.'

'Can I get you anything to drink?' The waiter dished out the drinks menu.

'Are these drinks on Michael too?' Paul hovered with his finger on a particular spot.

'Everything is on Mr Storm.' The man waited. He had a French accent, which of course, Sabine picked up on, and they launched into a conversation in French. Ele caught some of what they were talking about, but *her* second language was Spanish. Now she needed to find a Spanish waiter so she could show off. Then she felt guilty that she could think in such a snobbish and pretentious manner. She reminded herself that Sabine was French and had the right to speak her native language with a fellow snail lover. *Oooh, miaow.* Ele realised that she still didn't like Sabine and probably never would.

'To start with,' said Sabine, back in English, 'I'll have the Châteauneuf-du-Pape, Clos des Papes.'

Ele quickly scanned down the menu. £42.00. Nice.

'I'll have the same as her.' Paul snapped his menu closed. 'And a pint of Stella.'

'Paul?' Hope's hands fluttered. 'We're sharing that, alright?'

'Yeah, whatever.'

'I'll have sparkling water,' Ele said.

'Still pacing yourself?' Paul looked unfocused.

'I'm sure I'll get into my stride later. We've still got a way to go to get to midnight and beyond, and I don't fancy passing out on the first stroke. I want to see the New Year in.'

New Year. New beginning. But it was starting to feel

different; now, tonight, she could allow herself to drink again. She was here to celebrate with her oldest friends, not berate herself. Yes, celebration felt right, as if something momentous had been accomplished.

'Yeah,' said Hope, fidgeting, 'maybe you should follow her example for a bit? It's still pretty early.'

'I'm fine, so please don't nag me. You know it makes me doubly bad.'

'Hey,' Ele said. 'We all run at different speeds, and it is New Year.' After all, who was she to judge?

They were handed the menu, and Ele's mouth actually watered at the profusion of yummy, yummy dishes on offer. And for free, considering the hefty price. Usually, she'd barely be able to afford the starter. Could she choose them all, a bit of pick'n'mix? How much was this costing? If Michael didn't turn up for whatever reason, she wasn't paying. She couldn't.

They ordered, and while they waited for their drinks to arrive, they looked around them. Ele noticed there were no glaring bright modern lights that were practically X-ray. Enough light to see, but not to take away the feel of the place.

'You know,' she ventured, 'initially I thought this inn was pretty scary, but it's not. It's just old and quirky.'

'Like me then.' Paul laughed, and Ele could see he was unsteady on his seat. That expensive bottle of wine might cause a severe subsidence in a bit. He drummed his fingers on the table until Hope nudged him. He leant back and started to pat out a rhythm on his knees. Hope closed her eyes. It was a possibility that she was counting to ten. Most alcoholics have two routes from this point on. Ele wondered which one he'd take. The "smiling benignly and passing out on the table cloth" one. Or, the "taking umbrage at every comment and bunching the fists ready for punching" one. Ele was always the latter. She believed she could even piss herself off and cause a fight.

The two bottles of wine were expertly opened, and a snifter was tested.

'That's fine,' said Sabine.

'Zippity doo-dah!' said Paul, one hand on his pint and the other around the bottle. Ele got the feeling he wasn't up for sharing.

Her bottle of water was placed in front of her. It might be a lovely shaped bottle with a posh hand-drawn label, but it was still water. This didn't feel fun, except something deep inside her knew she was having fun, that she'd definitely passed a milestone of some sort, won her victory and could stand tall.

Hope cleared her throat. 'This seems to be more than just about the pact. What do you all think?'

'I know,' Ele said, 'why pick here?' She motioned around them.

Sabine nodded and wrinkled her nose. 'You may think it old and quirky, but we're the youngest here if you look around you. Most of the clientele are well over fifty. I mean, what is he playing at. And where the hell is he?' She was now tapping on the table with her fork. At this rate, thought Ele, if she and Hope joined in, on a pudding spoon and tapping at the flower holder, they'd have their own percussion group. She nearly giggled out loud, though she kept her face straight.

'This is getting beyond a joke,' said Paul. He looked behind him, and his voice raised, shouted, 'Come on, Michael. We know you're in here somewhere.' Paul wagged a finger at them all. 'You know they have loads of priest holes and the like. I bet he'll pop out of one when we're halfway through dinner and scare the fuck out of us.'

Ele laughed. 'I must admit, that is his style, isn't it.'

'Dear God,' said Hope, as her dish was lowered carefully in front of her, 'I haven't had food like this in like, forever.'

'Really?' Sabine dabbed at her painted lips. 'This is not that special.' She poked at her rib of beef. 'You should try the food at The Arch London Hotel. Absolutely divine.'

'Well,' Ele couldn't help but bristle at that, and for a moment, she felt as spiky as a toilet brush. 'Some of us don't have rich husbands who can pay for us, Sabine.'

Possibly she'd overstepped the mark and gone too far, but Sabine did seem to be rubbing her wealth in their faces.

'Well, at least I have a husband.'

Touché!

'Hey,' Hope again galloped to the rescue. 'Stop it now. We haven't seen each other in years, so don't start bickering.' She seemed to level this right at Sabine.

'Man,' said Paul, breaking the tension, 'this food's so good.' Drips of sauce were splotted down his shirt. He was really drunk, appeared stressed, short tempered and agitated. The man hadn't stopped twiddling, drumming or twitching since they all met. He also looked as though he hadn't slept properly in weeks. Maybe things were not so cosy *chez* the Klaus household. Perhaps it was time for Ele to steer the conversation for a bit, but she didn't want to cause a meltdown. She plunged in.

'How are the kids?'

'As delightful', said Paul, 'as two-, five- and eight-year-olds can be.' He picked up one of the rib bones and chewed on it.

'They're the best thing that's ever happened to me,' said Hope. She rummaged in her bag and pulled out her wallet. Photos of gap-toothed grinning kids were passed from hand to hand.

'That's George.' She pointed at her eldest, who would either grow into a ladykiller or possibly just a killer.

Ele peered at the photo. *He looked a right little devil. He'd got those eyes that make you swoon, even when he's strangling you with your own tights*, she thought.

'He's a good-looking boy.' Ele said slowly, 'You know, he reminds me of Michael.' She looked up to see a strange wide-eyed look on Hope's face. 'I mean, he's cute, nothing else.'

'Michael?' Sabine stared at Hope with a peculiar expression.

'Michael?' Paul looked about him. 'Is he here?'

'No,' said Hope. 'Not yet.' She gazed levelly at Sabine.

Ele handed the photo quickly to Sabine, who stared intently at the picture. 'Yes, I see…' She again stared at Hope. It appeared that Sabine was about to cry, which Ele found disconcerting. Sabine was not an Earth mother type of woman and had never shown the slightest interest in children. The photo wound its way around to Paul.

'Ah, good old George.' He waggled the picture at Ele. 'You met him when you stayed around ours one weekend,' said Paul. 'Don't you remember? Just before you went home and found–'

'Paul!' Hope kicked him hard under the table.

'Found what?' Ele turned from Hope back to Paul. 'Ah, you mean when I found my old house had burned to the ground with two of my flatmates in it.'

'That'll be it,' said Paul. 'Sorry for mentioning it.'

'You're joking!' Sabine sat up straight and then leant across the table, riveted on Ele. 'Tell me what happened.'

Hope shook her head. 'People died, Sabine. Listen, it was ages ago. It must be difficult for Ele, so can we leave it at that?'

Ele nodded, the power of speech being hard to come by at that point. She knew she lost time sometimes, but this was incredible. Had she really met up with them and seen their baby? Spent time with them? How could she forget that? Just little snippets left floating in her mind. Was that shock? But she could remember coming home so clearly.

'This is Mia.' Hope waved another photo at Ele, who already seemed to have lost what they were talking about.

'Wow,' Ele said. 'She's definitely a contender for *Britain's Next*

Top Model. She's absolutely gorgeous.' She really meant it, and the fervour in her voice must've rubbed Sabine up the wrong way as she felt her stiffen beside her. *Sod her!* She had her chance and tossed it away for a chateau and a Rolls Royce. *Poor her.*

'And this is Alfie. He's nearly two.'

'He's so cute.' Ele smiled at her, and this time it didn't hurt.

'He's a handful and no mistake. The "terrible twos" as they say.' Hope's face was clouded. 'You haven't got any yet, have you Ele?' Her gaze slid for a second across to Sabine.

'No. I've got a slob of a cat, and he's more than enough responsibility for me. I take my hat off to you. I couldn't cope with one, let alone three.'

Ele swung round to Sabine. 'Are you going to have kids, Sabine?'

Ele watched Sabine's eyes as they practically changed colour. They were mood stones like Michael's. Now Ele thought that was a normal question, but Sabine looked as if she'd just been asked if her bowel movements were regular.

'Maybe one day.' She peered over her shoulder, and Ele had a sudden thought. Is she *already* pregnant?

'I can't believe that Michael has chosen to miss all this,' said Paul, 'why set this up and then not bother to be here?'

But that was it, in a nutshell. He'd spoken their fears. Where was he? There was late, and then there was late for a reason.

'You don't think he's had an accident or whatever, do you?' Paul lay his fork down. He seemed to have sobered up.

'No, don't say that.' Sabine fumbled under the table, and Ele knew she was touching wood. For good luck. She'd been superstitious since a kid. Ele reached under the table too.

'He's fine.' Hope flapped at them. 'Come on, you lot. Don't get all maudlin and melodramatic on us. He's got stuck in traffic, or have you forgotten what night it is? Either that or he's broken down on the motorway.'

'Maybe, but he would've called me,' said Sabine. 'I know he would.' She clutched at her stomach.

'He's okay,' Ele said. 'He'll leap out at midnight wearing a bearskin helmet and playing the bagpipes or whatever. You know what he's like. Calling you or us isn't part of the deal. I'm sure he's fine, and I'm not going to waste another minute stressing about him. He's probably left his phone at home or something and is just trying to get here. I'm sure he wouldn't want us ruining tonight by worrying ourselves silly over him. It's New Year, and *we're* going to celebrate.'

'I'm with you on that one,' said Paul and slid elegantly off his chair. 'Oopsy!' He clambered back on. 'Bit pissed.'

'No shit!' said Hope.

They all stared at each other, and then Ele couldn't help it. She sniggered. It gathered momentum until they were all hiccuping and snorkelling, and the room was filled with their laughter. Ele caught a few slightly angry stares and an outright nod of disapproval. Well, *fuck the lot of you.*

She made a decision. Probably a bad one, but there was part of her that suddenly didn't give a stuff. After being careful for so long, she grabbed one of the long-stemmed wine glasses and held it out. 'I think I'll have a glass of your mighty fine wine if you don't mind.' Sabine poured for her. She watched the ruby red liquid languidly fill it up. Ele didn't drink it straight away. She sniffed it and swirled it around the bowl, letting it coat the surface. A sign of a fine wine. This one was thick and heady.

'What percentage is this?'

'It's a fifteen per cent.' Sabine also rolled her own glass. 'A combination of Grenache, Syrah and Mourvedre grapes. Rather nice, I think.'

Ele raised it up, let it wet her lips. Was she being that stupid little fish again? Could she do this and know when to stop? Did she care? She took a swallow. Oh, how good that felt. Yes, she was definitely celebrating.

'Here's to missing friends.' Ele raised her glass, and the others clinked. 'Wherever they are.'

'Missing friends,' they chorused.

'I wonder,' said Hope, 'what Tiger would've been like now if he was still alive?'

'He'd be fat and bald by now,' said Paul.

'No, said Ele slowly, 'he'd be beautiful. Even more beautiful than he was when we knew him.'

'You think that?' Hope leant back in her chair.

'I know that.' Ele drained her glass.

Sabine cleared her throat and dabbed at her lips. Ele noted her lipstick was still perfect, so maybe it'd either been tattooed on or was lacquered over with clear varnish. She tapped Ele on the arm. 'Hope tells me that you work in a market.'

Maybe Ele was wrong, but she was sure she caught a malicious glint in Sabine's eyes.

Hope made an awkward face as if embarrassed.

'Makes her sound like Del Boy from *Only Fools and Horses*,' said Paul. He fumbled for his glass and nearly knocked it over.

'She's in the prestigious Apple Market in Covent Garden,' said Hope. 'That kind of market.'

'Oh,' said Sabine. '*That* kind of market.'

Ele resisted the urge to point out that "that market" kept the bailiffs from her door, kept her and Schrodinger fed and watered and that she'd done it all by herself without waggling her arse at a rich man like she was a she-cat in heat. Why did Sabine still cause the same reaction: a need to smack her one. The only course was to change the subject or follow through with a deft backhander.

'Paul?' Ele saw him haul himself awake. 'What are you up to at the moment?'

And then it was there. Fear. Ele watched it coalesce on his face, and she turned to Hope, who was now staring at the table cloth.

'Sorry, have I put my big foot in it?'

'No, everything's alright.' Hope flicked a glance at Paul, and then her jaw kind of set. 'Well, mostly, just life stuff. Look, it's New Year's Eve, and most people have moved off to the next room. Wasn't there the mention of dancing?'

'Great,' said Sabine. 'Do you think we'll get as far as the nineties? Or will it be disco, disco, *disco* all the way?'

'Nothin' wrong with disco.' Paul upended the bottle and practically wrung it out. 'A lot of those eighties tracks are classic. *Ring My Bell*, that Sisters one and who could forget Michael Jackson's *Thriller?*'

'Yeah? And where the hell is *our* Michael?' Sabine wiped at her eyes, smudging mascara. 'Why hasn't he called?'

'I'm sure,' Ele reiterated, 'there's a reasonable explanation, and we'll all laugh about it in the morning. As I said, he's probably getting into his uniform and inflating those bagpipes.'

The waiter slid up to them and nodded to the entranceway. 'The party has started in the Tudor room. Would you like me to show you the way? I'm afraid you have to go out the side door by the reception and cross the alleyway.'

They were the only ones left in the room, and the staff were obviously waiting for them to bugger off so they could clean and maybe get home to their own loved ones in time to see the new year in.

'Let's go.' Ele stood and wriggled into her shrug. 'They're waiting for us, and I need another drink.' She caught up with the waiter. 'Is there a bar in this Tudor room?'

'Yes, miss. And you get a glass of champagne at midnight, to celebrate, like.'

There was a chilly nip in the air as they stumbled across the narrow cobbled alley. The Tudor room lived up to its name, yet more dark wood beams, white walls, and heavy timber. The floor here had red-painted bricks. They grabbed what was the last available table and sat down. Garlands and boughs of Christmas trees adorned the heavy timbers that straddled the room, with silver, white and red baubles hung on them. Light came from carriage clocks on the walls and large electric chandeliers that hung above them.

'I read on the internet,' Ele ventured, 'that many of these beams come from ships' timbers. Amazing.'

Sabine wandered over to one and peered at it. 'It's covered in scratches. Actually, I think they're names. It's got graffiti all over it.'

'Hah!' Ele went and looked too. 'So we've been carving our names in stuff for hundreds of years.'

'Thousands,' said Hope, 'didn't the Romans chisel out their names all over the place?'

'I suppose it's a form of immortality,' said Sabine.

'That's pretty deep for a night like tonight,' said Ele.

'That's pretty deep for any night,' said Hope.

'Dig that funky music,' said Paul. 'Mrs Klaus? Come and dance with me.' He pulled Hope upright, and they tottered down the steep steps to the dance area. Couples were swirling around with linked hands.

'You were right,' Ele said to Sabine. 'The DJ hasn't got past the eighties yet.'

'Oh come on,' Sabine held out her hand. 'If you can't beat them and all that.'

Blue flashing lights, followed by spinning red ones and then green rays that arced out and made her dizzy. Not exactly the sort of lights they'd become accustomed to at festivals and clubs, but as Sabine had pointed out, the clientele were a little more elderly.

Couples began to break apart, and there was a sort of *hum* in the air. Ele squinted at her watch. Two minutes left to go.

'Where's Michael?' Sabine suddenly looked really bad-tempered, her mouth practically a sharp line, and her cheeks red and blotchy. 'Fuck him. *Fuck him* and his stupid games.'

'I agree,' Ele said. 'Fuck him!'

'It's nearly midnight,' said Hope, dragging Paul over to them.

'We have to have grapes,' said Ele.

The others stared at her as if she'd just spoken in Klingon.

'It's a Spanish tradition. Twelve grapes. One every time the clock chimes. It's for good luck.'

'Okay, but have you got...' Hope counted, 'forty-eight grapes about your personage right now?'

'No, but I have a big box of raisins in my bag. We've worked out that does just as well.'

'Alright, I'm up for some bloomin' luck,' said Hope. 'I'm going back to the table. You lot coming?'

Ele handed out the raisins. 'Are we ready?'

Waiters with trays of champagne flutes hovered, and they all took a glass. They stood in a tight knot. The countdown from twelve began, and they joined in, popping a raisin in at each count.

'...12, 11, 10, 9, 8, 7, 6, 5, 4, 3, 2, 1...'

'Happy New Year,' they called to each other and to the merry couples around them. Their glasses were downed. Ele had the urge to throw the empty glass into the fireplace, but perhaps that wasn't the done thing around here. She waved it around for some more, although maybe it was a statutory "one glass and that's your lot, mate".

'Where the fuck is he?' Sabine texted again, and Ele could

see her fist clenched around the phone, knuckles white and bony.

'He's alright,' Ele said.

'How do you know?' Sabine's eyes were filled with unshed tears. 'There's more going on than you can ever know, Ele.'

'There always is,' Ele shook her head. 'As to how I know he's okay, he can't be anything but. That's it. You have to believe, or you'll go nuts.'

'Yeah, you're right. I'm sorry, it's just that I'm worried about him. He's been a bit funny with me recently.'

'You've kept up with him, haven't you.' Ele patted Sabine on her arm.

'Until not long ago. I haven't had much… contact for a little while. Only speaking to him through Facebook. And only about the pact.' The tears fell.

Ele frowned. *There's more going on than you can ever know.* What did that mean, exactly?

'I've got to get the delectable Mr Klaus up to our room,' said Hope.

'Great,' said Ele, 'I'm ready for that scary bed in that dark and eerie room.' She pretended to shiver. 'What time is breakfast tomorrow?'

'Between eight and ten, I think,' said Hope. 'Shall we call each other when we're ready to go down or make it a set time?'

'How about nine-thirty or so?'

'Okay by me,' said Hope, 'but Paul might not be up for it.'

'I don't think Paul is going to be up for anything,' said Sabine. 'Do you want us to help you get him to your room?'

'I'd appreciate it.' Hope also looked a little upset. 'He's not normally this bad. We're going through a bit of a… rough patch. Not us personally. I mean the business, and he's taking it hard.'

'Right,' Ele said, 'no need to say another thing.'

Both Ele and Sabine moved to help Hope, who was now

struggling to keep Paul upright. They lumped and bumped him up to their room, dropping Paul onto the bed. Hope wrestled with his shoes and then threw a small coverlet over him.

'Thanks,' Hope said. 'I'll see you at nine-thirty or thereabouts.'

Ele stared at Paul's huddled form. Was this married life then? Perhaps, after all, she was better off out of it.

Ele kissed Hope goodnight, and she and Sabine retreated.

'Poor thing,' Ele said. 'God knows what's happening right now.'

'He's a shit,' said Sabine, 'and she deserves better. She gave up her dreams to be the mother of his kids. You remember all she ever wanted was to be a doctor? That's well and truly over. She'll never get the chance now.'

'She might,' Ele countered, but she knew she was on shaky ground, thin and cracking underfoot. 'When the kids are grown up? She could retrain.'

'That's like saying that I could still be a model. It's over.' Sabine stared at Ele speculatively. 'You might be the luckiest one of the lot of us.'

'How's that then?'

'You were never destroyed by the love of your life.' She pursed her fat lips. 'I know you came close to it, but I think you pulled through in the end.'

Ele lowered her head and breathed deeply through her nose. 'You know nothing, Sabine,' she said very quietly. Then she thought about what Sabine had said. 'Are you saying that Philippe has destroyed you?'

'No, but my true love has.' Sabine kissed her fingertips and waved them at her. 'Goodnight, Ele. Happy New Year.' She sounded far from happy.

Her true love? If that wasn't Philippe, then who the hell was it?

42

HOPE

NEW YEAR IN RYE

'Did I look good tonight?' Hope slipped off her dress and hung it on a hanger in the cupboard. She placed her shoes carefully on the shoe rack.

'You were a goddess.' Paul's voice was slurred.

Hope nodded and undid her necklace. 'So it was worth it?'

'Absolutely. I do truly love you, Mrs Klaus.'

'I should hope so.' She felt as though she was already asleep and in a dream state. Should she tell Paul about Sabine and Michael? Not tonight as he was too drunk, and he'd either not remember or blurt it out later when he shouldn't.

'I love you too, Mr Klaus.' Pulling on a silky little nightdress she'd bought especially for this night, she snuggled in beside him but had to turn her head away as his breath was similar to a distillery. But the one thing for her was how glad she was that Michael hadn't appeared.

New Year? New Beginning?

Hope woke to the sound of Paul being sick in the en suite. She sat on the edge of the bed and stared at the dial on her cheap charity shop watch. The tiny glowing tips told her it was nearing three in the morning.

'*Oh fuckety, fuck, fuck.*' Hugging himself, he slid back into the room.

'What is it, Paul? I know there's something else going on.'

'Women's intuition?' He rolled onto the bed. The springs barely moved, not like their knackered old mattress at home that had two human-sized indents on either side, with a noticeable gap between them that said it all.

'How much do you love me, Hope?' There was a tone to his voice she'd never heard before. Forlorn. Lost. It made her shudder. Paul was always the strong one, and now this unnerved her.

'How much do I have to love you?' she whispered.

'Enough that if I've been a really stupid prick, you could forgive me?'

A deep buzzing started in Hope's head as if a million trapped bees were beginning to wake up. 'Haven't you already been a really stupid prick? Is this a new adventure that we're about to embark on?' She actually didn't want to know. Peaceful ignorance was alright by her.

'Yep.' Levering himself onto his elbow, he stared at her. 'Do you remember when I said I'd got it all sorted? That we were going to be okay. That wasn't only to do with the loan from Dad.'

'Hmm.' She knew it was a non-committal sound, but she couldn't help it. 'What *was* it to do with?'

'Last year, when I was right at the end of my tether, I found out something, and I used it. I mean against someone I shouldn't have. I'm not proud of myself.'

Hope suddenly had an inkling as she perceived something like a cold hand shimmying down her spine. 'Is it to do with Sabine?'

'Oh hell. It was that blatant?'

'No, more like I found out something tonight.'

'Does it begin with an "M" by any chance?'

'And then some. What did you do?'

'I sent her a blackmail note. I was desperate but obviously not as desperate as she was to keep it all hush, hush. She paid up. I think old Philippe, le Duke de Fucktard Montmorency, wouldn't be that chuffed to find his wife was diddling around with a mate from school. He has quite a reputation, me thinks.' Paul's head was lolling. 'I'm so sorry, Hope.'

A stellar explosion was unfurling in her mind. Her husband, the father of her children, was blackmailing one of the richest supermodels in the world. Add to that the fact that Philippe de Montmorency had been linked to the French version of the mafia. If he was found out, at best, she'd be visiting him in prison, or he'd be buried in a large vat of cement somewhere and never be heard of again.

Paul fumbled behind him and switched on the bedside lamp. 'You need to breathe now, Hope.'

'You're right. You are a stupid, *stupid* prick,' she hissed. Her jaw was clamped, and she could barely get air into her lungs. Hot tears squeezed out and rolled down her cheeks. 'If you're caught for this, you'll go down for it. I'm not bringing our kids to see their father in prison.' She wrenched away from him as he tried to reach out. 'Get off me, you idiot.'

'I know. I was desperate. I wasn't thinking. I... I saw it as an opportunity.'

'An opportunity? Dear God! An opportunity is when someone you know and trust opens a new business and offers you a partnership. Not this. Not getting on the wrong side of people who have reportedly killed other people! He's a dangerous man. I got the feeling from Sabine that she's petrified of him, and she's *his wife*. Do you know the git is off shooting endangered animals as we speak? It's what he does. Can you stop the payments? Can you get out of this?'

'I can tell her I won't say anything and that it will stop. I don't know what else to do. I know I've been a fucktard, Hope. I was trying to keep us all above water.'

'Surely anything would have been better than this. Why didn't you speak to me? Don't you trust me?'

'It's not that. I didn't want you to see that I was weak, that I wasn't able to look after you all. I couldn't bear to see the look of contempt on your face.' Hope could hear the fear in his voice. 'Do you hate me now?'

'I'm not condoning what you've done,' said Hope slowly, 'but I know you did it for the right reasons. I'd also like to add that I've always hated Sabine, and quite frankly, she deserves what she gets. She always got what she wanted, had it all given to her on a plate. So, I know it was wrong, except now we have to make sure there are no links to us.' This was not the time to think about the possible consequences of his actions.

His voice was like a child's. 'Thank you, Hope.'

'And you need to stop drinking. Promise me you'll stop?'

'I only started 'cos I thought I was going to kill myself.'

'What?'

'When I started the business, I took out Life Insurance to cover you and the kids. I started drinking 'cos I was planning to have an accident. A pretty fatal accident. Then you'd get the money and be able to pay off these bastards and still be okay.' His breathing was stuttering, and then he began to cry. 'I'm such a fucking coward. I couldn't even do that properly. I'm so sorry, Hope.'

There was a terrible crackling sound in her head. 'Dearest God! Tell me you won't ever do something like that. Not for any reason, do you hear me? *Not for any reason.*' She grabbed hold of his shoulders and shook him, leaving red half-moon indents in his skin. His head lolled from side to side.

'Hope, stop now. Stop.' He reached up and grasped her wrists. 'Not even for the best reason in the world?'

'Not even for that. We'll get through this, Paul, but you get that idea clean out of your mind.'

'Okay. I didn't really want to die. I couldn't bear the thought of leaving you and the kids.' Rubbing his face of all the tears, Hope realised that he was just as vulnerable as the rest of them. She should never have expected him to be the strong one, to be superhuman.

'I'm sorry too,' she lay back down on the bed and stared at the dark-hued canopy that felt heavy and claustrophobic above her. 'From now on, you tell me everything.'

'I promise. I hope to God we'll have nothing more to tell.'

'Oh, by the way. Sabine is pregnant by Michael.'

'What!' Paul nearly fell out of bed. 'You're kidding!'

'No, she told me when we were outside for a fag.'

Paul fell back against the plush pillows. 'That's why she was so mental.'

'I wonder what really happened tonight? What possible reason would Michael have to set all this up and then not be here?'

'Maybe one of his many ex-lovers has finally come to their senses and killed him.' Paul held open his arms. 'You must be the only woman on this sweet earth that hasn't shagged Michael Storm.' He frowned. 'At least, I hope you haven't, and if you have,' he added quickly, 'I never want to know.'

Hope lay her head on his shoulder, hearing his heartbeat inside her head. She stroked the hair on his chest. Was her heart beating faster than it should? Reaching across him, she flicked off the lamp and kissed his shoulder.

'We are going to be alright, aren't we?'

'Promises aren't my forte at this moment in time. All I can say is Hope? I hope so.'

After all the revelations that night, Hope knew there was still one more, and she prayed it would never come to light.

43

LIANG

HELL HATH NO FURY...

Liang surfaced again. Less groggy than the last time, but the residue of the drug and being tied into this one position had left her feeble. Great sobs built up inside her until her body convulsed.

Perhaps she should've jumped off that bridge and missed all this fun in between. But she hadn't, and now here she was. Her father's expectations had been pumped into her as if he was blowing up a bicycle tyre and not a human being. She was such a disappointment to her father, right to the point when he told her to her face that she was dead to her whole family. Now she wished she was.

There was something achingly familiar about the woman she'd glimpsed. But so frightening too. Long black hair, dead straight and the same length as Liang's own hair. It was as though Liang knew her intimately, yet she was a stranger. How could this be? Her mind showed her a picture. Ele as she was at eighteen. No, please, no. The quiet voice in her mind told her the truth.

Liang knew that Ele would've welcomed her as her sister if she hadn't slept with her boyfriend. No, worse than that; the man she'd expected to marry. Liang realised that Ele had known about Michael and her. There'd been one day in his flat. She and Michael had been in the bathroom, but not using it for what it was intended for. They'd been in the throes, so to speak. She'd been wearing the long black wig he liked to shag her in and gripping onto the edge of the bath, eyes closed. But she'd heard a sound, no, a whisper of a sound. Liang had turned her head and thought she'd seen a shadow at the door. She'd always wondered if it'd been Ele. Michael said afterwards that she didn't have a key, so how had she got in. Liang remembered looking at him with incredulity, as this was the difference between them. She thought with a girl's mind. He was all bloke.

'She'd get one,' Liang said simply.

'Ele wouldn't do something like that behind my back,' he said.

Liang laughed. 'Of course, she would. You don't really know her that well, do you.'

'She's not like that.'

'She's losing you, and she doesn't know why. She'd murder the Queen of England if it would give her an answer.'

'It was a trick of the light, seen through guilty eyes, a mirage to whip yourself with.' He smiled, and it was as though the curtains had been pulled back, allowing the sun to shine in on her. And she knew this was what Ele had lost. Lost to *her*. But now she thought Ele had seen them, and that sound was her soul leaving. With that same perception, Liang knew that Elena Riviera was capable of murder, and she was aiming to drag her down with her.

The woman was Ele, and she was, for whatever reason, pretending to be her. Her best friend and sister was going to kill her as she'd already killed Michael.

What's that saying? Hell hath no fury like a woman scorned.

44

ELE

NEW YEAR'S DAY

Sunlight was trying to sneak past the heavy drapes and glinting off sections of the dark wood panelling in Ele's room. The frilly valance around the top of the bed was spangled with circles of light, the four-poster bed had crisp, white cotton sheets, and the actual bed made her feel as if she'd died and gone to heaven.

Waking in a strange place can be tricky at any time, but rolling over to the view Ele had that morning was indescribable. Tweaking the richly patterned and thick curtains open, she peered out of the diamond panelled window that was so bowed, it looked pregnant. In the tiny courtyard below was a fountain, with a green copper mermaid sitting languidly with her tail raised. The steep, deeply shelved and curved roofs were covered with splattered mounds of soft moss and grey lichen. The glowing sun had reached the apex of the roof and was turning it to a burnished orange, crawling slowly down the tiles. A bright and glorious New Year's Day.

The glare through the window hurt her eyes, and a headache began to wrap itself tightly around her temples. Who'd have thought it, eh? A hangover on New Year's Day. But it was okay, not like the ones from before, where every movement was painful, the brutal daylight skinned your eyeballs, and your stomach was roiling like you've eaten twenty bird's eye chillies for the fun of it and washed it down with a bottle of washing up liquid. She felt a little bleary and red-eyed, but she could walk, and she thought she could talk, although she hadn't tried it yet.

The previous night, before going to sleep, Ele had set her alarm for an early start so that she could have the luxury of that deep, claw-foot bath. Filling it high, she squeezed in a bit of the posh bubble bath they'd kindly left for her on the side. *It's taken for granted that you swipe all the accessories.* She'd already tucked them by her wash bag, so she didn't forget them. Scrubbing off yesterday's make-up, she was ready to apply some more in a while. She twiddled her hair into a topknot and slid into the hot, soapy bath. The floor was faux slate tiles. Maybe genuine tiles would've been too heavy on these old floorboards, and the bathroom might cave in. She'd worked out her room was above the dining room and could hear the muffled burbling of voices below. She prayed that this was not the moment that the bath did crash through the floor and she'd end up on someone's breakfast table. All the fixtures and fittings were silver, with the bath and shower bits on the side, so you didn't lean back and bash your head on them. Glancing upwards, she saw the thick, fluffy white towels hanging ready over the rail. It might be winter in a sixteenth-century inn, but they sure knew how to keep it warm. No wind whistling through the uneven gaps.

An image of Michael raced through her head. There was something wrong with it, and she shook her head to flip it out. What was that? She'd been trying not to dwell on him and was hoping that he'd be downstairs when they met for breakfast with tales to tell and wide-grinned apologies. "Arrived far too late to wake you all," he'd say to them. "Reasoned I'd surprise you in the morning." Yes, that was what'll happen, she thought.

Ele didn't want to doze off, so she reluctantly stood, careful not to crack her head on the beam above, and let the water out. If the people below were expecting a quiet breakfast, then they were seriously mistaken. What a noise.

Slipping on a nice top and trousers, her trainers and a thin cardigan, she checked her watch. It was nearly 9.30am. She applied her make-up as she dared not go down with just her naked skin, and anyway, she had to cover up last night's excesses. That under-eye concealer worked a treat. You'd never guess she'd drunk nearly a bottle of wine last night. Not bad. For her. But this had been one hell of a party, and she wouldn't have another drink. She promised herself. New year's resolution. Again.

As Ele worked her way back to the dining room, she saw Hope sitting with a coffee in front of her. It wasn't steaming, so Ele presumed it, and she, had been there a little while.

'Paul still in bed?'

'Paul's been throwing up most of the night. Oh joy.' There was that hooded look that she'd seen last night. What secrets was she hiding?

'It's New Year. We've all done it at some time or other.' Ele sat down. At least her reptilian brain had been kicked back into its box.

'I want to go home now.' Hope shook her head. 'That sounded so rude. I'm sorry, Ele. I've really enjoyed seeing you all, *you* especially, but I miss my kids. They're at my mates' house, so they'll be spoiled rotten by the time I get my hands on them again, and I'll have to retrain them.'

It was as if she'd finally seen her coffee. She took a swallow and made a face. 'Yuck. It's cold.'

'We'll get some more.'

The young waiter was already on the move. He handed them the breakfast menu. 'Would you like tea or coffee? Fruit juices and yoghurts are on the side there,' he pointed, 'and there's also a continental breakfast if you'd like anything before your cooked one.'

'We can have all of it?' Ele winked at Hope. 'Is that sheer greed? Especially as we, hopefully, won't be paying for it?'

'Of course,' said the waiter, 'choose whatever you wish.'

'Right, for now, we'll both have some coffee and then order breakfast when our friend gets down.'

A tall, ornate silver coffee pot arrived on the table, with a matching milk jug. Ele poured for the both of them. 'I had a really good night. Thanks, Hope.'

'So did I.' Hope shook her head. 'Weird and full of surprises but still good.'

'If you don't mind me asking, are you and Paul okay?'

'We've had a few ups and downs, but I think we're back on an even keel.'

'Sabine was acting strangely last night, sort of hysterical.' Ele plopped another sugar cube into her coffee.

On cue, Sabine walked into the room and waved. She looked tired. Ele expected that none of them were looking their best.

'Any news yet?' Ele asked, though she already knew the answer. She could see it on Sabine's face. She sat heavily.

'I don't know what to make of it all.' She swept her hair up and bound it in a ponytail. Like that, she didn't look any different to how Ele remembered her when they were at school. Ele covered her face with both hands. The tears were now coming.

'What a fucking fiasco.'

'Ele!' Hope pulled Ele into her arms.

Even Sabine patted her shoulder. 'Don't you start now, or you'll get the rest of us going. Everything's alright. We'll find out what Michael is doing, and then we'll brain the bastard.'

Ele sputtered out a laugh. 'I'll be right behind you on that. I might even be ahead of you there.'

'Yeah, the bastard,' repeated Sabine, her fingertips straying to her stomach. Rousing herself, she turned to Ele. 'It's New Year's Day. Michael was going to drive you back, wasn't he?'

'That was the plan as there are no trains or buses today. I might have to go look for a room in another place for tonight and get home tomorrow.' Ele didn't relish this suggestion, but if she had to, she had to.

'Don't be ridiculous.' Sabine practically snorted. 'I'll drive you home.'

'We can too,' said Hope. 'We're much closer than you are. In fact, wouldn't you be heading in the opposite direction if you're going back to France?'

'I'm not going back to France. I've got a flat in Camden Town near to the lock. It's my... I suppose you'd call it my bolt-hole.'

'You need a bolt-hole?' Hope frowned. 'Ah! Yes. Right.'

'*Right,*' said Sabine a little too pointedly.

'Well, if someone can drive me back, that'd be bloody marvellous,' Ele said. She'd noted that Sabine and Hope seemed to be on an alternate wavelength to her. A niggle skittered over her. Why wasn't she included?

'We need to work out what to do about the bill,' said Hope, and Ele saw the fear she felt reflected back at her. If she tripled her allowed overdraft, she didn't think that'd cover it, especially as she'd forked out for new clothes before Christmas.

'I'll pay.' Sabine rummaged through her bag and pulled out her monogrammed leather wallet. Ele saw the initials on it: *S d M*. How bloody ostentatious was that?

'I'll get it back from Michael,' said Sabine, 'when I see him.'

Sabine got the short straw. Or maybe it was Ele, as she'd have preferred to drive back with Hope and Paul. The journey to Epping Forest should've been uneventful, small talk and inconsequential catching up of the bits they omitted last night, the final daubs of paint on the canvas, the missing jigsaw pieces that completed the picture. Well, Ele got the missing jigsaw piece, alright. She should've kept her mouth shut, tearing homewards in Sabine's silver Ferrari as if they were on the tippy-tip of a tornado.

'Are you pregnant, Sabine?'

Perhaps a sensitive question on the M23 at ninety-five miles an hour is not the way to go.

'What!' Sabine practically ripped the steering wheel off. Her knuckles were white, her skin stretched thin and bloodless where she was gripping the wheel.

She turned to Ele, and her expression was wild. 'Who told you that? *Who told you?*' Her voice was nearly a scream.

'Look at the road, Sabine.' Ele waved frantically in front of them.

'Who was it?' Her jaw was set hard, a chunk of granite. 'Was it Hope?'

'No one. I guessed as you kept patting your stomach. So, *are* you?'

Ele didn't know if she was going to yell at her or cry. 'Yes, but I don't want anyone to know. Promise me you won't tell anyone else?'

'Okay,' Ele said, 'but aren't you pleased?'

'It's complicated.'

'Does Philippe know? Doesn't he want kids then?'

'No, Philippe doesn't know, and I want it to stay that way. We decided to have kids when we were older, not now.'

'So, no congratulations.'

'No. I haven't worked out what to do yet.'

Ele nodded, though she supposed Sabine couldn't see that as she was finally concentrating on the road ahead. So she wasn't sure if she wanted it, but the little Ele knew of Duke Philippe was that he'd go apeshit if he found out she'd aborted his child without his knowledge.

'I hope you get it all sorted, Sabine.'

'Thanks, I don't think it can get any worse.'

Now Ele knew that was always a statement that should be avoided.

Their parting was sombre. Dropped outside her flat, Sabine declined Ele's offer of a coffee. Too busy pondering an uncertain future.

Ele waved her phone. 'Do you want my number? You know? Then you can let me know if you hear anything from Michael?'

'Sure.' Sabine punched in the numbers. 'I'll call you now, so you also have mine.'

Sabine kissed her twice. 'See you, Ele.' Then she was off in a streak of silver and a screech of tyres.

As Ele descended the stairs to her flat, she noted the light was on. Maria must be here, waiting for her, and Ele suspected, more than eager to hear how the festivities had gone.

'I've had the craziest night.' Ele hugged Maria, who was making butternut squash soup on the hob. Warm buttery, slightly curried smells hung in the air. Just how she loved it. Peering into the pan, she slung her arm around Maria's neck. 'Told you that squash would come in handy.'

'You seem pretty upbeat, so tell me about your crazy night.' Maria sprinkled some salt and ground black pepper into the bubbling mix.

Ele hunted through the cupboard and found an unopened pack of custard creams. 'You don't mind if I have one. I promise I won't ruin my appetite.' She handed Maria the biscuits and then went to perch on the sofa. 'We all met up on New Year's Eve as we were told to, but it was bizarre because Michael wasn't there. We kept making excuses as to why he didn't turn up, but none of us have heard from him. Sabine dropped me off. *You* haven't heard anything, have you?'

'Why would you think I have? And you need to fill me in some more on what Sabine's been up to.'

'Sabine's pregnant. I have a sneaky suspicion that it's not Philippe's.'

'Interesting,' said Maria. 'Then whose is it?'

'She didn't say.'

A nasty little thought coalesced in Ele's mind as though a red-painted devil had whispered in her ear: if Sabine didn't want Philippe to know about her pregnancy because it wasn't his child, then the next question had to be: whose was it then?

The devil jabbed at her with his pointy pitchfork.

It's Michael's.

Ele tried not to think about her conclusion. After all, weren't presumptions the mother of all fuck-ups?

'Tell me what you're thinking.' Maria's voice was neutral.

The soup was being ladled into Ele's best ceramic bowls. It smelt so earthy and comforting that she didn't want to ruin the moment.

'Come on,' she repeated. 'Tell me. I know something is whizzing around that sweet head of yours. Is it about Sabine?'

'It was the way she was acting last night. All dramatic and emotional. She was a real bag of nerves and kept going on about Michael.'

'And you said the baby wasn't Philippe's? Do you have any idea whose it might be then?'

Ele blinked rapidly. 'I think the baby might be Michael's.' Ele heard her own words. Michael's baby. Surely her head was going to implode?

'Are you telling me you think that Sabine is having Michael's baby? Really?'

'I... I don't know. I might be jumping to conclusions, but it kind of fits.' She gulped a full spoon of soup, burning her throat. 'Ouch, shit, shit, shit.'

'So,' said Maria, very softly, as if she knew that Ele was hurting, 'if you've just worked this out, how do you feel about Sabine and her impending "bundle of joy"? Are you really happy for her? Do you send your heartiest congratulations?'

'*Hell no!*' Even Ele was shocked by the ferocity of her tone. 'If Michael was going to pass on his genes in perpetuity, then it should've been with me.' Jumping to her feet, she stumbled towards Maria. 'That *fucking* ring didn't materialise, the white wedding was vaporised, and the happy gurgling of a newborn was never heard, except in my dreams.' She felt like throwing the soup bowl at the wall.

Maria's voice was velvet. 'It's been years now. Surely you're over it.'

'It's the principle, isn't it? We never, *ever* shag our friends' ex-partners, no matter what. It's tantamount to sacrilege, like having sex with a sibling.'

'Especially her. Especially Sabine.' Maria's eyes changed colour. 'You've always hated her. I expect she's *gloating* about it.'

'This must be the story of my life. How could this have happened twice with my so-called friends?' She had to calm herself, or she'd pop. She sat down on a kitchen chair.

'What about Hope?' Maria's eyes were darker still. 'I bet she's got some darling kiddies?'

'Beautiful. That George, only eight but he's going to be a good-looking boy when he's older.'

'Did he *look* like his daddy?'

'Paul? Not particularly, more like...'

'More like who?'

'It's weird, but he kind of reminded me of Michael as a kid. We lived next door to each other before we ever got to secondary school. I mean, he looked like Michael when he was that age.'

Maria sucked on her teeth as though she was thinking. 'George couldn't be Michael's son, could he?'

'What? Don't be ridiculous, Maria.'

'As you say, it's ridiculous, but then, who'd have ever thought that Sabine and Michael would be proud parents soon? Life is strange, eh?'

'No way,' Ele frowned and pushed out of her chair. She started to pace the tiny living room. 'Hope was engaged to Paul by then. She wouldn't do something like that. Not to me and especially not to him.' Her pacing got faster. 'No, no. She wouldn't.' She stopped abruptly. 'Would she?'

'Michael was no angel, as we both know.' She left the connotations of her words hanging in the air between them. 'Well, we'll rise to the challenge and re-write the ending of your story.' Maria winked at her, a co-conspirator, but of what, Ele didn't know.

'How will we do that? Bash bloody Sabine de Montmorency's head in with a blunt instrument? Go and accuse Hope of adultery? Because I can tell you, that's how I feel right now.'

'That's my girl.' Maria pulled Ele into a tight hug. 'Now you've got it. Don't let the bastards drag you down.' Maria looked at her. 'Maybe you should go and speak to Sabine first. Sort things out, once and for all. Oh, and take a bottle of wine with you, for old times sake, eh?' She laughed throatily. 'Here's one I prepared earlier, and Ele? Try not to drink it yourself. Give it to Sabine. She needs it more than you do.'

45

ELE
SECRETS

Ele phoned Sabine. 'Can I come over? I feel like we need to talk.'

'Okay,' Sabine said. 'Why not?' She sounded as if she'd already started on the wine. The bottle that Maria had given her wasn't a Châteauneuf-du-Pape or whatever it was called. Anyway, it'd have to do. Don't they say that screw caps are actually on a par with bottles with natural corks, and aren't they saving the planet, one cork tree at a time? Anyhow, both she and Maria were on a budget, and money didn't grow on trees, cork or not.

The number thirty-seven on Sabine's front door was gold but a little tarnished. The paint had chipped and been painted over with a different green, so now it looked camouflaged. Ele's heels clicked on black-and-white diamond-shaped tiles as Sabine led her into the kitchen, patting her way along a wall.

'I brought this.' Ele pulled the bottle from its bag and left it on her black marble countertop, flecked with gold and green.

'Thanks. Running a bit low.' Sabine was gripping onto the sink, and her knuckles were white.

'Are you okay?' Ele touched her gently on her shoulder. She jumped as though she'd accidentally scratched her.

Silver-framed photos adorned the wall. Front covers from *Vogue* and lots of shots from all the other glossy magazines that Sabine had posed for. Hired by the best agencies and photographed by the brightest up-and-coming young things. Dear God, she was amazing; face painted and enveloped in the most fabulous creations against exotic backgrounds. Ele had only glanced at them before on the newsstands and shop shelves. She supposed that jealousy had blinkered her. And Sabine had given all this up for a man? Dumb or what? She must've loved that man, or maybe Ele couldn't comprehend how rich he was.

It was all open plan and very modern. A sleek beechwood cupboard swung sideways, and a wine rack was exposed. Pulling the last bottle out, Sabine kicked the cupboard closed, leaving a scuff mark on the wood. An expensive-looking bottle opener pulled the cork out. She leant her head against a door and stopped moving, but Ele needed that drink.

'I'll find a glass. Sit down, Sabine.' Spying tall stemmed glasses on a shelf to the left of the cooker, she tweaked one down and poured herself a liberal amount and then took it and the bottle back to the living room. Sabine was slumped at the table, twirling her glass, unaware that some had spilt out across the wooden surface and stained it. Her eyes were unseeing, and Ele knew she didn't want to go where Sabine was now.

Ele sat down quietly and took a sip of the wine. So much for new year's resolutions, but then a pledge like that shouldn't include betrayal like this. Or maybe it should, except her willpower wasn't that strong.

'Is it Michael's baby?'

Sabine gulped in a breath. 'Did Hope tell you?'

'Hope knew?' Yet more betrayal. That's what they'd been discussing outside.

'You said you were over him. Last time I saw you at the wedding. You told me you'd rather die than be with him again. As far as I remember, you told anyone who'd listen. I took that as gospel. I'm sorry if I've upset you.'

Ele grabbed Sabine's wrist to pull her around so she could see her more clearly.

Sabine twisted from her. 'You're hurting me.'

'Sorry. Sorry, Sabine.' Ele let her go, belatedly aware that she'd left finger marks in red like a bracelet around her thin wrist.

Sabine rubbed at the welt. 'I've called him over and over, so he must be ignoring me. I can't explain it otherwise.'

Ele knew she was avoiding looking at her. Is that because her fear would be mirrored in Ele's eyes? 'Unless something's happened to him. That's what we can't face, isn't it?'

Sabine's voice was faint. 'Yes.'

Ele lowered her head to her arms and let it wash over her. It came from the deepest part of her, rising up from her core, sweeping all other feelings out of the way, enveloping her in pain so excruciating it actually physically hurt. Breathing became her focus now. In. Out. In. Out. In. Out... How easy it'd be to just let this breath out and not suck one back in.

'Ele?' Sabine's voice was flat, all emotion crushed from it. 'What do we do now? Go around there?'

'I don't know.' Ele couldn't surface yet, couldn't show her face. 'No, not yet, at least.'

'Then what? Call the police?'

'We don't actually really know what has happened, do we?' Ele finally pulled herself upright and stared at her. 'What would we say? Our friend didn't turn up for a party, and he's not answering his phone? Do you think that's enough for them to act? Don't they usually need at least twenty-four hours for a person to be reported missing? Not that we know he is. Do you see what I mean?'

'Oh, sorry, Ele. I'm feeling really weird right now. I've just come off the phone from speaking to Philippe.'

'How's that going, or don't you want to talk about it?'

'How do you think it's going?' Sabine rubbed her stomach. 'I haven't told him yet. He's still abroad, and I'm pretending that everything is fine when it's not. He's a proud man. Being cuckolded is not something he'd ever envision happening to *him*. I've seen him laugh with utter scorn at other men, ridicule them and feel superior that his *little* wife was where she should be and always would be.'

'I also take it that he doesn't know about this place?'

'I bought it when I first started modelling. No matter what, I knew I had to have a place that was totally mine.'

'I get that.' Ele was beginning to slump in her chair.

'It's worse than that. Someone found out about Michael and me ages ago. I've had to pay them to keep quiet, or Philippe would've killed me and then divorced me.' She sniffed loudly. 'In that order.'

'You're being blackmailed? *Fuck!*' Ele twirled her glass in her hand. 'Do you have any idea who they are?'

'If I did, what could I do about it? Go to the police, and then Philippe would find out. Again, no more Madame de Montmorency.'

'This is getting too complicated.'

'I know. I'm not supposed to be drinking, what with the bump and all, but I can't seem to help myself.'

'My mum drank all through her pregnancy with me. We're not English are we. Wine flows in our blood, and after everything else that's happened, I wouldn't beat yourself up about it. Remember in the fifties, you were expected to *drink and smoke* during your pregnancy.'

'Ha. Then I'm truly foreign.' Sabine poured them a refill that skimmed the rim.

'Here's to...' Ele stopped and shook her head. 'What do we toast, Sabine?'

'Here's to life.' She raised her glass, and some wine splashed across her hand.

'To life,' Ele said, and they chinked their glasses.

'He will divorce me.' Sabine pulled her fingers through her uncombed hair. 'I know he will. The family are one of the oldest in France. They've had their share of scandals through the years, but they got past it all by distancing themselves from anything that threatened them.'

'Nice,' Ele said. 'There's nothing like "for better or for worse" then?'

'No, only better and even more better. I wouldn't put it past them to put a "hit" out on me.'

'A hit? You mean they'd have you killed? No way. They're posh aristos, not the bleeding mafia!'

'Really? You don't know these people, Ele.'

'If you're worried, go to the police.'

'And what would they do? Waste expensive resources on a cheating wife? I don't think so.'

'Stop worrying. It's a waste of time.'

Sabine lowered her face to her hands. Tears splashed and wet the tabletop.

'I'll get that other bottle.' When Ele turned the cap, she realised that it'd already been opened. Weird.

Sabine was wiping her face when Ele returned. Her own glass was still relatively full, and Maria's words came to mind. 'I don't want to mix, so I'll top mine up in a minute. You ready for another glass?'

'Like you wouldn't believe.' She held out her glass. 'I know everything's been shot to pieces, Ele, but I'm glad I've met you again. Back in school, you were the "it" girl, and I so longed to be like you. I never got close to you because I wanted everything you had. It's taken me a long time to come to terms with how jealous I was. I'm so sorry about that. I just needed to say that I think you're a great person, Ele.'

Ele's hand gripped that bottle so hard, she thought it must shatter into a thousand sharp pieces. Bright white spots wavered before her eyes as if she'd got fireworks popping inside her skull. How could she say that to her now? But she pulled back from the edge.

'Thanks, Sabine,' Ele whispered, as her voice had curled up around itself and hidden like a mouse in leaf mulch. 'You're a great person too.'

Ele poured Sabine another glass and finished her own. 'I'll let myself out.'

Maria was there again, pulling the wig from under the bed where it'd been stashed. Dead straight and dark, not dissimilar to her own hair but different enough. The make-up was under the sink in a little seagrass basket. The bottle of foundation had a yellow tinge to it, and smears coated the glass, as though it had been used in a hurry. Ele didn't like the look of it, though it suited Maria when she was wearing the wig.

'Where are you going now?'

'Out?'

'Out where?'

'For some fun. I never get any fun anymore, Ele. And anyway, some things need to be done.' She'd changed into her new clothes. Ele hadn't touched them as Maria warned her not to.

'Did you take that bottle of wine as I told you? Did you give it to Sabine?'

'You don't think I'm capable, do you.' Ele hated her when she was like this. She made her feel inadequate, useless.

'Oh come on, my sweet, don't get all mushy on me. I'm simply asking.'

'Yes, I gave it to her.'

'Did she drink any of it while you were there?'

'I gave her a glass when I left. I didn't have any myself as you said.'

Maria nodded. 'Do you think she'd have had more? I mean after you left?'

'From the way she was slugging it back, I expect so.'

'Ah.' She sucked on her lip and looked over Ele's shoulder. 'Good. Yes, that's very good.'

'What is? What are you doing?'

'How many times have I told you that I'm here to make things better?'

'Zillions?'

'Exactly.'

'I know, but sometimes it's scary, Maria.'

Maria's eyes glowed, reflecting the light from the kitchen lamp. 'Trust me.'

'Okay. Don't stay out too late.'

'You're not my mum, Ele. I'll come home when I'm good and ready.' Maria tweaked the plastic-coated cook's apron off its hook and rolled it into a plastic bag.

'What's that for? Are you going on a cookery course?'

'Of sorts.'

46

LIANG
FOREVER

Liang wondered how many days had passed. She'd been unable to control her bladder any longer and had wet herself. Humiliation was swamped by terror. Her throat felt swollen, parched and as dry as a sun-baked stone. Licking her lips seemed to make it worse. They were cracked, and when they'd split, she could feel spurts of hot stuff that tasted metallic. Blood then wet her lips. All feeling had left one side of her body. She could no longer move in case she pulled the dresser down on herself.

Images were swimming in her mind. Snapshots from her past. The times with Ele and the others intermingled with sudden blasts of memory from her time in prison. Heather's gaunt face would morph into Ele's and then slip into Sabine's or Hope's. Michael would be there, laughing and playing around as he did, then it was as if she'd been cracked over the head when a picture of his destroyed face came unbidden. Heather's death had nearly torn her apart, yet she continued to exist. Could she survive this?

'Michael,' she moaned. 'I'm so sorry.'

What happened? Did she bring this to his door? Was he

dead because of her? After all this time, she'd lost him again, and this time it was forever.

Curled and shaking, she remembered how his lips felt on hers, how strong and sensual his hands were, how gentle he was with her. The tattoo on her shoulder; yin-yang, the same as he had, identical. They had them done at the same time nine years ago. To show their love. And then she saw what they'd done to Ele, and she couldn't bear it. She told Michael that she'd love him for the rest of her life, except she wasn't going to be *that* person. He'd railed against her, told her that she was stupid to throw their love away because of guilt, exhorted her to reason and to realise that if she left him, then none of them would "win".

And now, none of them had.

47

HOPE

BRIXTON – SECOND OF JANUARY

How was Hope going to find out if Sabine knew that it was Paul who'd been blackmailing her? Even indirect questions would lead to suspicion. Did Michael know about it, or had she kept quiet? If he did know, had he planned the meet so he could accuse them in public? Shame them in front of their oldest friends by calling the police and watching smugly as they were handcuffed and marched to a waiting police car? But that hadn't happened. Was it to come?

Were there any clues on his Facebook page? Hope snapped open the laptop and waited while it booted up. Paul was out at football with George at their local club. He played with a team and was a natural, though even if he'd had two left feet, they'd have tried to get him running around to expel some of all that energy that was bottled up inside him. Nervously tapping on the table, she watched Mia playing with a doll and a toy polar bear, dancing them around and speaking for the both of them.

'We're going to have lots of babies,' said the polar bear to the dolly. The dolly responded that she loved babies *very* much.

Hope smiled. 'Maybe they'll come out a little furry too?'

'Don't be silly, Mummy. Babies aren't furry.' Mia pointed with the toy at Alfie, sat in his playpen. 'Alfie's not furry, is he?'

'No, but then his daddy wasn't a polar bear.' Hope clicked on the Facebook icon and searched through her list of friends until she found Michael's name. He had loads of albums, but they were all dated. The most recent one seemed the logical one to start with. Photo after photo of all the places she wished she could have visited, all the strange and beautiful landscapes, the smiling inhabitants in bright and bizarre costumes.

'You lucky, lucky... man.' She glanced over at Mia, who was now telling Alfie her own potted version of the plot of *Frozen*. How she'd managed to keep her promise to never swear over these last few days was anyone's guess. Sometimes, all she wanted to do was beat her fists against the wall and scream as many profanities in as many languages as she could remember. Scanning the last few photos, she nearly missed it. There! Dearest God! Staring at the picture, she shook her head. It couldn't be, could it? Was that Tiger?

Hands shaking, she dialled Paul's mobile. 'You need to come home as soon as you can. I've found something, and I think it could explain it all.'

Waiting for Paul was interminable until eventually, he was examining the photo, their heads close together. 'Really? You think that's Tiger?'

'Look. It has to be.'

Paul turned as there was a crash from the living room. 'George, put that down.' He turned back to Hope. 'So what exactly does this explain?'

'This is the mystery.' Hope couldn't help the excitement that tickled over her skin. 'This is what Michael was going to tell us. Tiger's not dead. Don't you see?'

'Nope. This is quite a long shot here.'

'What if Michael spots Tiger, then threatens to expose him.

Let everyone know he's still alive? Maybe Tiger's not up for that. Maybe it's Tiger who stopped him from coming to Rye. To keep him quiet.'

'Stopped him coming by doing what? I mean, how can the diminutive Tiger stop great big hulking Michael doing anything he wanted?'

'Whacked him over the head with a frying pan. I don't know, but I think we need to let the others know.'

'That we think we've spotted a dead guy in the mob in the States, and we think he's murdered Michael with a frying pan? Plausible? I think not.'

'Mermaids!'

'What?'

'Tiger always loved mermaids. That's the connection. It was a joke, a pun. We weren't supposed to get it until he told us.' Hope looked up at him. 'I think we should contact Sabine right now. I've got her mobile number, and she said she'd still be here until mid-January. I think we should go around to Michael's place together.' Hope keyed in the numbers, but there was no dialling sound. 'I don't like this. I'm going now to see if she's okay.'

'Just because her phone's dead doesn't mean anything's happened to her. It simply means she forgot to charge it.' He looked sideways at that while Hope waited. 'Yeah, you're right. A woman such as Sabine always charges her phone. Are you alright going? I can stay with the kids.'

'I'll call you when I get there.'

Anticipation. Hope could imagine that Sabine would react with derision and mockery at their idea. Having parked up the road, walking up the well-kept street, Hope slowed her steps. Most of the properties were whole houses and would be worth millions. Even those sliced up into flats would probably cost twice as much as their four-bedroom house in Brixton. Jealousy is a snide and nasty emotion, and she knew it should be beneath her, but Hope let it envelop her. There was no condoning what Paul had done, never in a million years, though if they got away with it, she wouldn't feel that bad. When had Sabine experienced one day of poverty? Had there ever been a time when she wondered if she'd eat that day? If she could pay the essential bills to keep a roof over her head and remain warm? She doubted it.

The door that belonged to the address on the note in her hand was a lot more shabby than she expected. Rapping sharply, Hope waited. Nothing. She banged again, this time harder. Glancing up and down the street, she hunkered down and lifted the letterbox. Once her eyes had adjusted to the gloom, she peered in. 'Sabine?' Hello?'

Looked like she'd come all this way for nothing... Except, what was that she could see, where the hall led into the living room? Squinting, Hope made out a shoe, but there was something connected to it.

'Oh, Shit!' Hope stumbled backwards, and half toppled down the steps to the pavement. Breathing fast, she crawled back up and *pinged* the letterbox open. Willing herself to look, she focused on the shoe. There was a leg attached to it. A leg that wasn't moving.

'Sabine?' She must've had a fall. Was there another way in? Backtracking round to the next side road, Hope counted the houses. The ground floors of each terraced building opened out into a garden. When she got to the one she thought must be Sabine's, she unlatched the gate and crept in. Would anyone challenge her? Sabine was on the first floor and had a decent-sized balcony that jutted out over the neighbour's garden. An emergency ladder was lying across it, but it could be hooked down using a bent coat hanger hung on a nail in the wall. It crashed down with such a clang that Hope winced and prepared to run. There was either no one in, or they were stone deaf.

Climbing the ladder carefully, Hope inched her way over the industrial-looking railings onto the balcony. Too cold for winter pruning, the surrounding gardens were empty. Hope cupped her face to ward off the glare and peered through the large glass window into Sabine's living room. At first, all she could make out were large pieces of furniture, a modern table and leather-backed chairs, a brown sofa, also leather judging by its sheen and how expensive it looked. A chic-looking sideboard. Photos on the walls. Shifting further up, her viewpoint changed.

Sabine was lying with her arms flung out as though on a cross. Although partly obscured by the table, it couldn't conceal the blood. Deep crimson splashes had sprayed up the walls and soaked into the cream-coloured rug.

'Oh my God! Oh my God!' Hope reeled backwards, hanging over the railings, vomit bursting out her mouth and nose. Wiping her mouth with her sleeve, she fell to her knees whilst retching and gasping. Could Sabine still be alive? She had to break that window and get in. A wrought-iron chair was tucked in the corner. Hope picked it up. It was heavy, so when she swung it, it crashed through the window, leaving great shards like giant teeth half hanging out of the frame. Kicking them in, she crept carefully through the gap.

'Sabine?' Hands held out, she slid stealthily forward, one step at a time. 'Oh, God!'

Gaping cuts were opened up on her wrists, but much worse was the deep gash across her belly, as if she'd been gored by a wild beast. Had a creature done this to her? Hope peered around her. But no, if she'd been fighting some escaped animal, then she wouldn't be in such a posed position. This was on purpose.

Hope dragged her gaze from the wound on her stomach. Her thoughts were leading her to where she didn't want to go. Was the person who'd done this still here? She couldn't run without checking if she was still alive. There was no movement, no rise and fall of the chest and her eyes were open, staring up at the ceiling with a look on her face that looked more like amazement than fear.

Whispering, *'Oh God, oh God, oh God, oh God–'* Hope crawled towards Sabine. Stopping, she reached out to feel for a pulse at Sabine's throat. There was nothing. Focusing on her chest and trying not to look at the ripped hole in her belly, Hope felt for a heartbeat, then hovered her hand over Sabine's mouth. Still nothing. Hope shook her head and crept backwards, a low moan escaping from her lips. This was *murder.* Cold and bloody. What was going on?

Scrambling to her feet, Hope ducked through the broken window. When she got back to the balcony, she tipped her handbag upside down, watching the room and preparing to run if she saw anything move. With shaking fingers, she dialled Paul.

'Paul?' Her breath was jumping out of her. 'Paul... Something terrible has happened to... Sabine.'

'Hope? Are you alright? What do you mean?'

'There's... blo... blood over everything. I think she's dead.'

'Dead? *Did you say dead?* Call the police and an ambulance, Hope. Did you hear me? Call the police and come home now.'

'I have to warn Ele. Someone's killed Sabine. It might be him. It might be Tiger. She might be next.'

'Get away from there now, Hope. *Get out now!'* The alarm in his voice transmitted itself through the phone.

Half climbing and half falling, she tottered through the garden.

'I'm out in the street.' Hope clung to a signpost that showed it was a one-way street.

'I'll get in touch with Ele and then call you back. Now call the police, as I don't know what her address is.'

999.

'Please help me. My friend is injured, maybe dead. She's in her flat. I broke in. I think someone's murdered her.' Sobs rose up from inside her. She could no longer speak, no longer hear the voice, calm and authoritative on the other end of the line. She knew she had to state where she was. Coughing, she read the address from the scrap of paper in her coat pocket.

'Yes, I'll stay here.' She waited, flinching at every movement.

The phone rang. She saw Paul's name lit up.

'Hope! I called Ele and told her about Sabine, and she said she was on her way to Michael's. She wouldn't listen to me, said she had to see if he was alright. Bloody hell! This is all madness.'

'If Tiger is there... Oh God, Paul, I have to get there first. Keep calling her. Make her understand that she's in danger.'

'You're not going over there. No, no, no! Hope, listen to me. If Sabine is dead, then there's some madman running around. I know it was a joke, but maybe he's done Michael and Sabine. We could be next. He's trying to silence us all. You come back right now!'

Hope was already running to the car when she heard the sirens blaring in the distance.

48

LIANG

'Hello, pretty one.'

Liang woke with a start. She'd missed the key in the lock, the footsteps down the hall. She must still the thumping of her heart. Listen.

The woman in front of her made a great show of sniffing and waving her hand under her nose. She bent down, unwound some of the rope tying Liang and pulled her up into a sitting position. Her hands were smeared with something dark. 'Not smelling so good today. Nearly as bad as him.' She nodded over her shoulder and made a passable imitation of the Wicked Witch of the West. 'I'm melting, I'm melting!' She mimicked.

Liang shuddered.

Ele was staring at Liang as though she'd never seen her before. 'You look... different.' She turned away suddenly, as if the image in front of her was too much to bear.

'As do you.' No denying it. Same gold-flecked green eyes, except this Ele was concealed behind a disguise.

Ele reached out to touch her face, almost gently. 'You make a lovely woman. She always knew you would. It never occurred to her that's what you wanted, even though, thinking about it, it was all there in front of her. She's never been any good at reading between the lines, watching for clues.'

'Who is *she*?'

'Why Ele, of course.'

Liang realised that whoever was in front of her was not Ele. There was someone else looking out of her eyes. 'No, that was Michael's penchant.'

'Always on the lookout for a mystery to solve. Never realised that might be you.'

It was *her* voice, even if it wasn't the face she remembered, hidden behind a wig and make-up. Liang couldn't find her own for a few seconds as it'd fled in sorrow.

'Ele,' Liang croaked. 'It's me. Tiger.'

You could hear the grass growing in the silence that stretched between them.

'I'm not Ele.'

'Who are you then?'

'You know who I am, sugar.' There was a soft drawl to her words, more Spanish than Liang had ever heard her and deeper as though she was talking from her gut. 'I'm Maria, Ele's sister.'

'Ele hasn't got a sister. She's an only child.'

'Only in your view.' Maria knelt down in front of her. 'And as far as I know, Tiger's dead.' She said it matter-of-factly. No emotion.

'Yes, he is.'

'Then who are you?'

'Liang.' She'd know if she lied to her, even after all these years.

'Liang, eh? Is it true you faked your own death and had a sex change?'

'I didn't fake my death.' Liang tried to swallow, but it felt as if she'd stuffed pins down her throat. 'My parents disowned me and told everyone that I'd died in an accident. They said I'd brought dishonour to their family name, so I left.'

'Boo hoo. Poor you.' Maria squinted at her. 'Was that because you'd had a sex change? Daddy dearest didn't like that?'

'Yes.'

'Hmm. You're no longer the mermaid. That's why you loved them? Sexless creatures with no "bits", isn't that right?'

'Yes, I hated what I had. I wanted what you had. I wanted, well, I just wanted.' Her breath caught in her throat.

'You mean you wanted what *she* had, what Ele had. Your best friend.'

'By then, we weren't best friends, were we? There was a distance between us.'

'I wonder why that was?' Her voice was cold enough to turn boiling water to ice. Liang had seen that on a YouTube clip, in Russia or wherever, a bloke pouring boiling water over a balcony, aware of the people passing below. Yet as they gasped and scorned him, the water trailed off and fell as ice. It was similar to that now, the ice creeping across the carpet to freeze her soul. 'Care to enlighten me?'

Liang's eyes watered further, tears hanging on her lashes, although she didn't want Maria to see she was crying. 'You know why. You have done for years. I couldn't cope with the guilt. I loved you, Ele. You must know that.'

I'm not Ele. Get that through your pretty little skull.' Maria lunged forward, and Liang felt a sharp sting down her left calf. At first, there was only a pink line, then blood welled out of the cut and dribbled down her leg, dripping onto the floor. The cooking knife was now lying in Maria's lap, a thin smear of bright red coating the edge, but the blade looked rusty, coated with something brown.

'So,' said Maria, 'you loved Ele enough to steal her boyfriend. Yeah, that's love, all right.'

'I loved him too.'

'Oooh, yes. Ele saw how much you loved him.' Maria pumped her hips and grunted, her face contorted, mouth open. 'Yeah, just like this.'

Liang turned her head. She didn't want to see this. She tried to roll the rope down from her wrists. Her hands were small-boned and fragile. The pain was excruciating, but she had to keep going with it, even if it scoured off all her skin.

'How did you meet again? Ele saw the photo of you on the Golden Gate Bridge. She couldn't believe it. Did you recognise him first? I want to know which one of you instigated all this.'

'No, he spotted me as I was trying to jump off the bridge. Some part of me regrets that I never made it.' Then, she thought, none of them would be here now. Michael would be alive, and Ele? Well, she'd probably still be crazy.

'He stopped you from killing yourself?' Maria laughed raucously. 'As you say, shame he did. And then what? Did he blackmail you? Did he threaten to tell the world all about you?'

'No,' Liang smiled at her, even though it hurt her to do so, 'he asked me to come back to England to live with him.'

Maria's hands clenched. 'He did? Why?'

'Because he loved me. Had always loved me. You know that. Or at least Ele did. As you say, she saw us. All those years ago. I broke her heart. I was her best friend, and I stole her lover right out from under her nose. I felt bad, except I couldn't help myself. He was so beautiful. It wasn't my fault that he chose me over Ele.'

It was a terrible gamble, and Liang knew she was risking her life. By goading Maria, she hoped she'd make a stupid mistake, one that she could utilise to her advantage. Already weak and suffering from dehydration, she wouldn't last much longer, but the ropes were easing off her fingertips, even though her hands felt formed of glass and could shatter at any moment.

'He didn't choose you. How could he? You were a boy, for God's sake.'

'That's where you're mistaken. Ele assumed I was gay. That I wasn't a threat.'

'No,' Maria said slowly as if coming to this realisation for the first time, 'She assumed Michael was straight.'

'He was.'

'How do you work that one out? He was fucking you, wasn't he? You're a boy, so that makes him gay.'

'I was always a girl. I merely had the wrong bits. He saw that, saw what I really was, not the outer parts but what was inside of me.' At least this part was genuine.

'Oh, how poetic.' Maria's voice was beginning to lower as though she was a barometer, but instead of being linked to warmth and rain, she was linked to emotion. 'Michael saw the real you, eh? I think he saw your arse, your tight little balls. That's what he saw. Funny, from what Ele saw, weren't you in a wig? So you looked like...?' Her eyebrow rose.

'Looked like Ele? Why would I want to look like her?'

'Didn't Michael want his "boy" to look like her?'

'No. He wanted me to look like myself, like a Chinese girl, with long straight black hair. It's funny, but now you seem to look more like me.' Liang shook a lock of her glossy hair at Ele.

'Forgive me if I find it all disgusting. Just the thought of you two together makes me want to puke.'

'Each to their own,' Liang said. 'But he told me he'd love me forever.'

'You stole him from Ele. Thief.'

'I did that. But the best girl won, didn't she.'

There was a sudden movement and agonising pain across Liang's cheek. Warmth spread down and dripped onto her lips, slid down her neck.

'Not quite so pretty now.'

Liang licked the blood from her lips. 'Did you kill Michael because of me?'

'I was going to give him a chance, but then I saw him with you that morning. It was déjà vu. Same old, same old. I couldn't let her meet him again after that. Twice in one lifetime? No.'

'Why kill him like that? Why not a clean, quick death?' Liang was sobbing openly now. How he must've suffered, and now she was wondering if she'd die the same way.

'I couldn't let him continue like that. So beautiful, he lured them all in like he was one of those anglerfish with a light to trap the little fish. Like you, not so beautiful now.'

Liang flinched when a phone rang. It wasn't hers, so it must be Ele's. Maria crawled to where her bag was slumped on the sofa. The screen blinked out as she pulled the phone out.

'Hope.' Maria shrugged sharply, as though she was irritated. 'I wonder if Michael has been up to his bollocks in her too? Why not diddle the lot of you, eh? Four for the price of one. Maybe he had a bit of Paul as well? Do you know, Tiger?'

Maria made a noise, somewhere between puzzlement and revulsion. 'You're not the only bitch to have been under our beloved Michael, are you? Did you know about *her*? It's funny, but she didn't know about *you*. She was quite upset about it when I told her but possibly more upset when I killed her.'

Liang froze. 'Who did you kill?' She already knew. A wave of dizziness threatened to suck her under.

'Why should you care about her? You and Ele used to take the piss out of her all the time. I did you a favour. I mean, what an arrogant cow, and she really deserved what she got. I was the hand of God, Tiger. I punished them both for their sins.' There was another pause, maybe a second. 'Don't cry, now baby. It's all for the best. Are we having fun yet? I sure am.'

'Sabine?' Liang needed to know, needed to understand how

far this Maria persona would go. 'Are you saying you've killed her too?'

'Dead as a dodo.'

'What was her sin?'

'You don't know, do you? Oh my, oh my.' Maria snorted air through her nose. 'The delectable Sabine de Montmorency was pregnant. And who do you think the daddy was, eh?'

In Liang's mind, there was a supernova exploding; broken shards of colours that flamed brightly. She closed her eyes, but they smarted as if she'd had a handful of salt thrown into them. So many calls and texts. Now she knew why. To tell him she was pregnant, to ask if he would step up to be the real father, to see if she had to abort and kill a bit of him.

'Ele told me all about it, how crazy she was acting when they all met up after Michael didn't show. *Whining* his name over and over again. We could have told her not to bother, Tiger. We should have told her what he was like.'

It was all so clear. Liang whispered, 'She presumably stole what wasn't hers? Is that why you killed her?'

'That baby should've been Ele's. Oh, the heartbreak. She wanted it so desperately, and he squandered it on a lying cheating bitch. Sabine was married in the eyes of God, and yet she threw that all away and then took what wasn't hers to take. There had to be retribution.'

Maria stood unsteadily. Then Liang saw the great streaks of reddish-brown down Maria's dress, and she knew what was all over her hands. Blood. Sabine's blood.

Liang wriggled and thrashed to get away from her.

'You're a monster! How could you do this to them?' Liang looked up at her. 'You've murdered an unborn *baby!*'

'Sabine paid the price for her infidelity and Michael for his betrayal.'

'You're mad, you crazy fucking psycho bitch!'

'*What did you call me?*' Maria reached over and slapped Liang hard across the open wound in her cheek. The pain ricocheted over her skull. 'You know, I really don't like it when people say stuff like that. It's downright rude.'

Liang took a deep breath. Was this her chance? 'Ele ended up in an institution, didn't she. Padded walls, one of those nice shirts that do up behind you–'

'What the fuck? What are you playing at?' Liang could hear the stress curling at the edges of her voice.

'Ele's mum and dad had her sectioned. Don't you remember that? Was that because they met *you*, Maria?'

'Sectioned? You're the one who's mad, whatever you're called now.'

'Liang. My name is Liang. Maybe you're ready for another stint inside that mental institution. Sort out your head.'

There was a snarl in Maria's voice when she finally responded. 'My head's fine and dandy. Not so pretty one, you should think about what comes out of your mouth in case I decide to cut out your tongue.'

'Hell hath no fury like a woman scorned. Is that where you fit in?'

'Me? I'm her real guardian angel. She didn't need another one once she found me.'

'So you've been looking after her?' Liang held the rope tightly. 'For how long?'

'Long enough to have made a difference. Long enough for her to be finally happy until that prick Michael came back into her life and ruined it all. And you. You were with him. I saw it. I was going to talk to him, find out where we all stood before I allowed her to see him. And there you were. This is all your fault, you know. You may not be the one who did the deed, but you were the catalyst that started all this.'

'No, it's not true.'

Maria picked up the knife and stared down at the blade. 'Are you happy now, *Liang?* Michael's dead because of you.'

'No!'

'Sabine is dead because of you.' She looked momentarily sad. 'That poor little baby is dead because of you.'

Don't cry anymore. That's what she wants. She must be an emotional vampire, sucking up all the bitterness and grief until she's gorged with it. Liang wouldn't give her that satisfaction.

'Remember Maria, if you kill me, then I get to spend eternity with Michael.'

Liang saw the flash of the blade as it sliced across her chest. The pain hit her a few seconds after that, threatening to make her pass out.

'What's the matter? They're not real, are they?'

Liang screamed. Her head lolled back as agony wrapped itself around her.

'Oh, I'm not going to kill you fast. I'm going to slice and dice you and savour each little bit that I take from you. I might let you live your life as a *freak*. So goodbye to eternity with old Mickey-boy.'

Warmth spread in a wave down her chest. 'Why do you look like me, Maria?'

'I've set you up. Neighbours saw you go into Sabine's flat. I made sure of that. A Chinese girl with long black hair. I wore dark glasses, because I couldn't get your face quite right.'

'I understand you have to punish me. I do.' Her glass hands were coming back to life. She had to focus all her fear, all her pain, so that she could act. Dying here wasn't an option.

'Yes, I do have to punish you.' Maria nodded. 'More than any of them. None of this would've happened if it wasn't for you.'

'All I wanted was to spend the rest of my life with the man I loved. Is that so hard to understand?' Something was rising up from deep inside in Liang, something that longed to rip this

Maria's face clean from her skull, smash her, tear her to shreds. *This creature had murdered Michael, killed Sabine and her unborn child.* 'And that was all he wanted too, you bitch!'

Maria shook her head slightly, 'No one loved Michael as much as we did.' She smiled gently at Liang. 'You, of all people know that.'

'Fuck you,' Liang struggled upright, but both of them stopped moving when the phone rang again, an insistent sound. If it was Hope, then it sounded as if she really wanted to talk to Ele. Had someone discovered Sabine? Put two and two together. Please get here in time. Please. *Ele. She was the one she had to talk to.*

'I want to speak to Ele.' Liang screamed. *'I want to speak to Ele. Where is she? I know she's in there.* Ele!' Liang dragged her arms out from behind her back and lunged at Maria, except it was as though she was swimming through treacle, her body moving in slow motion, far too slow to stop Maria from throwing herself backwards. Liang saw Maria's fist rising.

'Shut your mouth!' Liang's head was snapped back by the force of the blow. Drifting in and out of consciousness, it was then that the doorbell rang, and there was a smart rap on the door.

49

HOPE

ISLINGTON

Hope now wanted to chuck her phone across the road and then go and jump up and down on it. What was the point of owning a phone and then not answering it? It'd gone to voicemail so many times that she must've filled up Ele's memory by now.

'Just answer the effin' phone, Ele!' The few pedestrians on the same side as her crossed over and watched her warily, eyebrows raised.

It'd taken far too long to get to Michael's flat. At that moment, when she'd stopped speed-dialling Ele, her own phone rang. But the incoming call was from Paul, not Ele.

'Paul? What's happening? Have they got to Sabine yet?'

'Hope, I'm getting the kids over to Monique's. She sounded pissed off, but I told her it was an emergency. I'm coming over, and I've grabbed a taxi. You need to tell me what the address is, then I'm going to call the police. On no account do you go there on your own. Do you hear me? Please, Hope, wait for me.' There was a scratchy static sound, and Hope could make out Paul cajoling George to get in the car.

Hope told him the address.

'I'll call again when I've got them all safely to Monique's.'

'Please be quick then,' Hope added, 'I need you here.'

Hope stood outside the flat. A small but leafy bush blocked her view of the main window from the street. She peered around it and saw a shape flit past the blinds, which were open a crack. Hope was transfixed. What should she do? If she waited for Paul and that was Ele in there, she could be in grave danger. What if Paul arrived too late and they got inside the flat to find that Ele had been murdered, just as Sabine had been?

'Oh God help me,' she whispered. Marching with what little confidence she could muster, she poked at the doorbell and thumped once on the door. The bell chimed inside the flat. Then she stepped back.

'Hope?' It was Ele's voice. 'Is that you? Oh, thank God you're here.'

'Ele! Let me in. Are you okay? I have to talk to you.'

As the door opened, Hope heard muffled shouts coming from the living room, just as a godawful stench hit her. Holding her hand over her mouth, she'd barely registered who was standing in front of her, before she felt herself being yanked in through the doorway. The door slammed shut.

'Who the heck...' But under that strange wig and ghastly-coloured foundation, Hope could see that the woman in front of her was Ele. 'What's going on?'

The shouting was becoming more distinct. 'Get out, Hope. *Run!*'

As Hope peered down the corridor, she was transfixed by the man lying on the floor, arms outstretched in the same position as Sabine. But whereas Sabine was recognisable in her horror, this melted thing was not. Hope reared back and hit the door.

'Oh, God! Is that... Michael?'

'Dearest Michael, yes.' The woman who wasn't quite Ele spoke with a broad Spanish accent. She sighed loudly, and then

Hope saw the knife in her hand being lazily spun about as she spoke. 'Hope, Hope, Hope. What a shame you had to pop over now. But then, here we all are. The old gang back together.' The knife was now pointing at Hope's throat, which had gone very dry, as if she'd eaten a handful of sand.

'Ele?' Her voice was hesitant.

'Not Ele, not Ele. How many fucking times do I have to tell you people that?' She made a sound in her nose that sounded familiar to Hope. It was the same noise that Hope made when exasperated by one of her kids. 'I'm Maria. Got that? Now, there's someone else I think you might be interested in seeing. Come on, don't dilly-dally.' The knife led her on.

'Look who has arrived. Hope, you remember Tiger, don't you?'

Hope struggled to find her breath. They'd got it so wrong. Tiger was trying to lever himself off the floor but was half-blinded by blood pouring from a deep gash across his forehead. There was something different about him. Even under all that blood, Hope could see that he was feminine. He seemd to be in a dress. Another cut had slashed his cheek to the bone, and his clothing was glistening with glossy red stuff.

'Tiger?'

'Hope? I tried to warn you.' Tiger spat a mouthful of dark stuff out. 'My name is Liang now. I'm a girl.'

'*What?*' Hope was now of the opinion that she'd fallen through some sort of inter-dimensional portal. 'What the hell is going on?'

It was too much to take in. She'd come from a room filled with blood to another room filled with even more blood. Unsteady, as a wave of dizziness threatened, she clung to the mantelpiece over the fireplace. An ornate silver candlestick focused her attention.

'This is so much fun, isn't it?' Maria was grinning. 'The blue fairy granted our little Pinocchio his wish, but she made him a real girl. That was always his wish, wasn't it? Be a real girl and take what wasn't his.' Maria spun. 'Sit down, Hope. You look a little pale. Take your coat off and make yourself comfortable.'

Slipping off her coat, Hope didn't think her legs would hold her up any longer anyway. There couldn't be much left in her stomach, but whatever was left was still smouldering up her throat and making her eyes water.

'*Shitshitshitshit!*' Words under her breath.

Her phone rang from inside her bag. Hope made a grab for it, but Maria knocked it out of her hand.

'*Paul!*' Hope was screaming now, panic overriding all other emotion. '*Paul!*'

'Paul, schmaul,' said Maria. The handle of the knife cracked Hope on her jaw, and she was tipped viciously to one side. 'You keep quiet now. Liddle old Pauly isn't coming for you. It's just the three of us. You, me and the girl-boy. In fact, we were just discussing if you'd also shagged the delightful Mr Storm senseless?'

Hope felt as though her head had been wrenched off, and there was a deep sonorous ringing in her ears. Upended onto the carpet, she tried to work out what the hell was happening. Surely this couldn't be real...

'Have you?' The blade tickled at her throat, as Maria leant forward to stare at her.

'What?' Hope swivelled to stare up into Maria's eyes. The question coalesced in front of her. 'No.'

'Really? Ele told me about the photos of your kids. It seems George is remarkably like Michael. Peas in a pod, she said, although a touch darker. Care to explain, Mrs Klaus, how your firstborn looks more like Michael than his so-called daddy? Does Paul know he has a pretty little cuckoo in the nest?'

'Don't be absurd.' Hope felt as though she'd lost her footing. 'Ele, what are you doing?'

'I'm not Ele.' Maria raised her hand again, but Tiger's voice cut past them.

'Leave her alone, you *nut job.*'

Maria swung back. 'You still opening your mouth like you're someone?'

Hope saw the flash of the blade. She didn't think; she acted. Lurching to her feet, she grabbed the candlestick and launched from the side of the sofa, shoving Maria, who stumbled and fell heavily next to Tiger. The blade skimmed Hope's collar bone, and she dropped the candlestick. Hot blood spurted, and pain shot up her neck. How badly was she hurt?

Tiger also kicked out, catching Ele on her hip. She yelped. The knife swished through the air. Hope watched as Tiger flinched and tried to turn, but he was obviously weak. The blade hacked into him, and he screamed.

The blinds shot upward as something crashed into the window. A figure was grappling with the wooden slats and *roaring* Hope's name. *Paul.* He'd come for her.

Hope realised that he would be looking out for Tiger, that he wouldn't regard Ele as the threat. 'Watch out!' she bellowed. 'It's not Tiger, it's Ele. It's *Ele!*'

As Paul emerged from the tangle at the window, clutching a child's bike and blinking in the gloom, Hope saw Maria turn. She looked from Hope to Tiger, who wasn't moving. It was as if white static was building up in Hope's mind, blocking all conscious thought. Was Maria contemplating which of them to kill?

'Poor Hope. You shouldn't have come.'

As quickly as Hope could crawl backwards, Maria moved faster. The knife loomed. Hope lifted both arms to ward the blow, then she saw Paul fall on top of Maria, yanking at her hair.

'Get away from her, you bitch!' The wig came off in his hand.

'What are you doing?' Maria spun and clutched for the wig.

'What the fuck! *Ele?'* He must have seen her properly for the first time. Paul made another grab for her, but she was already snaking out from beneath his hand. The blare of sirens coming up the road made him falter, just for a second. Hope couldn't breathe. It was all happening too fast. Maria's eyes looked a deep red in the gloom of the room. With her back against the wall, Hope saw the knife coming at her and Maria's enraged face as she tried to stab her. Paul caught Maria round the neck and dragged her backwards. Maria slipped her hand behind her, and they fell, Maria's arm pinned beneath Paul's weight.

'Paul?' Hope scrabbled towards him. *Where was that knife?*

His eyes flickered open. 'Hey, darling. I think I might have cut myself.'

Maria rolled and was trying to get upright. Tiger was kneeling beside them, his hands were shaking uncontrollably, but he was clutching the dropped candlestick.

'I love you, Ele and I'm so sorry I did all this to you.' Tiger smashed the candlestick over the back of her head. Maria slumped onto Paul, who groaned.

Dark-uniformed figures were fighting their way in through what was left of the window and there was the sound of the front door being caved in.

'Holy shit!' A man's voice from the corridor.

'Police,' shouted a voice. 'No one move.'

Hope waved her hands above her head.

'I said, don't move!'

'Help us!' Hope struggled to shout at him. 'My husband has been stabbed. Please help him.' Hope looked over to where Tiger was curled over. 'And him... I mean her.' Hope tugged fearfully at Maria's prone body. 'Paul? Oh God, Paul, please don't die on me. *Paul!'*

'Hands above your head!'

Hope raised her hands, sucking in breath after breath. 'Please help him.'

'Okay,' one of the police officers said, 'someone find a light in here, and you two, get her off of him. But be careful; I don't know which of them is dangerous.'

'She is, *she is!'* squealed Hope, pointing a finger at Maria.

On rolling Paul over, Hope saw the knife was embedded up to the hilt in his side. *'Do something!'* She clutched at the officer.

'Calm down, miss. We're doing the best we can. Sergeant Davies? Come here and put pressure on this man's wounds. He's losing blood. Where's that ambulance? In fact, call for another one.'

'We've got a body out here,' said a tall, burly man, poking his head into the room. 'I'd say been dead for a few days now.'

'We need to call in a Senior Investigating Officer. Get the coroner's office on the line and a police surgeon down here asap. Everything needs to be photographed and examined. This is now an official murder investigation. Everyone has to be very careful not to disturb any evidence.' He directed his men. 'We need to secure the vicinity, get these people to the hospital and then get their testimonies.'

Paramedics in high-visibility jackets and green uniforms were now in the room, bending over Paul, pushing Hope firmly out the way. She saw them go to Liang, who was lying silently on the floor.

Hope clung to Paul. 'Is he going to be alright? I'm his wife.' She tried to get closer to him.

'We're the people who are trying to save his life, and you need to give us the room to do that.' They examined the wound, and Hope screwed her eyes shut. Spasms shook her body as though she was being buffeted by hurricane winds.

Paul groaned and tried to lever himself up. 'Hey there, sweetheart, don't fret now. I'm fine.' He peered at her. 'Hope? Is that your blood?' Trying to push himself up, he shouted at one of the paramedics. 'Christ, man. My wife's been hurt. Look after *her.*'

'We'll get to her in due time, sir, but we need you to be calm. We have to prioritise. You're losing blood.'

Paul was hoisted onto a mobile stretcher and an intravenous drip inserted into his arm, before he was partly rolled and carried down the hall. Hope followed, aware of Michael, now an exhibit, police treading carefully, not to disturb the scene, either shocked or impassive. Hope supposed that not many had seen such horror before. She didn't want to look, but she whispered, 'Michael,' as she cowered past his body. *Such horror.* Please let this be a dream. Please let her wake up now. But the pain radiating down her neck and through her jaw spoke otherwise. An officer trailed her out.

'Hope?'

An electric shock passed through her body, all her senses opened up, *she* was still here, she was still going to try to kill them all. Hope turned slowly.

Maria was stood up, a female paramedic guiding her up the hall behind her. Another officer behind them. No, she knew that look, that vulnerability, that sweetness. Oh dear God. It wasn't Maria, *it was Ele.*

'Where am I?' Ele's voice was like a child's. 'What's going on?' She stared at the body spread-eagled by the broken door. 'Who... who is that?'

'Ele?' Hope felt all the emotion rushing up inside of her, like a geyser about to burst out. 'Don't you know? Don't you remember?' The trembling increased, such terrible winds tearing her apart.

'Remember what? Hope? Who is that?'

Paul was being bumped down the steps; she was losing him. 'That's Michael. Maria killed him. *You killed him.*'

'Michael?' A sound mewled out of Ele. 'Maria did that? No, no, she couldn't have.'

Hope buckled, hanging onto the wrecked door frame. 'Maria killed Sabine too. Don't you get it, Ele? You're Maria, look at yourself.' Screaming now, face contorted. *'Look!'*

Spinning around, Hope rushed to be with Paul as he was being loaded into the back of the ambulance. As she climbed in the door, she saw Ele on the steps.

'You did all of this.' A great throbbing rage swamped her, filled her lungs, took her breath away.

Ele stumbled out. 'I don't understand.'

'Look in the mirror. I can't bear to even see you after what you've done. I have to be with my husband.' The paramedics slammed the door, and the ambulance, sirens caterwauling, took off down the street just as more police cars arrived.

50

ELE

Ele reached out to steady herself. The world was a kaleidoscope of colours. She must be on a boat, as whatever was under her feet was heaving up and down.

'You're alright now, miss,' said an unfamiliar voice. The woman was wearing such a bright yellow vest it hurt her eyes. Somebody was holding onto her elbow. Ele blinked and tried to focus. Leaning heavily on this person, she peered around her, then wished she'd kept her eyes sealed tight. Carnage, that's what she saw. There was what looked like blood-daubed walls, crimson-sodden carpets, a tattered blind hanging forlornly, glass shards glinting sharply. Claustrophobic with the sheer amount of people in the room. Dark clothes, heavyset faces. Had a bomb gone off? A plane crashed?

A gurney carrying a man she did recognise was nudged past her. 'Paul?'

Walking was a problem. Her feet weren't responding as they should, and now she felt a dull hammering pain start at the back of her skull until her head was clamped in the unstoppable jaws of a vice. Was that Hope following behind Paul?

'Hope?' But her voice was crushed, and only a strange sound came out of her mouth.

'You must wait until we can get you medical attention,' said the fluorescent person next to her.

'That's my friend.' Ele pushed past and patted her way up the wall, aware of being closely followed.

'Hope?' This time, Hope turned. Ele couldn't understand why Hope was looking at her like that. It morphed from fear to revulsion. 'Where am I?' Then Hope's face crumpled, and Ele could see a wave of grief or sorrow sweep over her. 'What's going on?'

Ele looked past her. The door had been shattered, great teeth of wood bent inwards. Her gaze travelled from the entrance to the floor. Was it Halloween? Or Guy Fawkes night? A dreadful, poorly-made Guy was sprawled, arms akimbo, one shoe on and one kicked aside. But no, that wasn't a dummy. That was a real person. Ele held her hand over her mouth.

'Who... who is that?'

Hope shook her head, her face smeared with tears. There was a glistening red graze on her chin, nestling in a swollen mass of blue and purple. Ele wondered if she'd been hit or something.

'Don't you know? Don't you remember?' Hope's voice wavered. Ele felt the fear rising from the pit of her stomach.

'Remember what? Hope? Who is that?' Ele whispered.

'That's Michael. Maria killed him. *You killed him.*'

'Michael?' Hope didn't know what she was saying. How could that awful thing be Michael? 'Maria did that? No, no, she couldn't have.' Maria was many things, she knew, but she wasn't a murderer. There was no way...

You killed him. What the hell did that mean?

'Maria killed Sabine too.' Hope's movements were clumsy, uncoordinated. 'Don't you get it, Ele? You're Maria. Look at yourself. *Look!*' As she turned, Ele saw the blood welling from a nasty cut across her neck, staining her red dress a deeper colour.

Through the gap, Ele saw two ambulances and several police cars at skewed angles in the road. Men with yellow-and-black tape were cordoning off the area, directing passing cars back the way they'd come. Others were stepping into white suits. Ele watched as two burly paramedics got Paul into one of the ambulances. As Hope climbed into the back with him, she looked over towards Ele.

'You did all of this!' Hope's hands were clenched. Loathing. That was what was on her face now.

'I don't understand.' Why did Hope hate her? Why was Paul going to the hospital?

'Look in the mirror.' Hope pulled back. 'I can't bear to even see you after what you've done. I have to be with my husband.'

Ele felt as though her world was caving in around her, the ground was quicksand tugging at her feet, and the sky was sulphurous and acrid. As the sirens blared, Ele thought it must be the end of the world.

Maria killed Michael? Maria killed Sabine? Had Hope gone mad? What was she talking about? Look? Look at *herself*?

'Miss?' The person was still grabbing at her arm. A paramedic. 'You need to be checked out. You've a nasty cut on your head.'

'We also need to take your statement,' said someone in a dark uniform.

'I have to see something.' Ele shouldered past them and tottered to the mirror. A flash of recognition. That was the mirror his parents had given to them when they'd first moved in together. Michael's parents. Michael's flat? That body out there was Michael? The face that glared out of the mirror at her made her cringe back. Who was that woman? It wasn't her. Why did she look like that?

'Ele?' A soft voice, filled with subtle nuances. 'Ele? Do you know me?'

Ele dragged her eyes from the woman in the reflection and focused. Yet more paramedics were tending to someone lying hunched on the floor. Police were huddled around. All of Ele's senses were assailed. Hot coppery smells coupled with the stench of old men's toilets. The brightness of the paramedics' jackets. The flaking russet coating embedded in her fingernails and that covered her hands. The taste of acid in her mouth and old charred wood.

She crept closer. The woman, stained and stinking, a bib made of blood, with mats of red on her clothing, turned her head slowly and gazed up at her.

Ele crunched to the floor. 'Tiger? Is that you?' Ele made a sound. 'Of course, it's not. Silly me...' She tried to swallow, but the spit wasn't there. 'Tiger died years ago.'

'I'm so sorry.' A hideous gash sliced Tiger's swelling cheek. Ele had to ignore the rest, or she thought she'd pass out. Sobs slid out of him in soft waves. 'Sabine is dead, Ele. Don't you remember?'

'Sabine de Montmorency?' The officer nodded. 'We were called to her flat earlier. We found her body.'

'What are you talking about? Sabine's not dead.' Ele heard the stridency in her own voice. She held her hands wide. 'I only saw her yesterday. We drank wine together. She was fine.'

'You killed her, Ele. At least, Maria did.' Tiger pointed a shaking finger at her. 'What's that all over your hands, Ele? All over your clothes?'

'I don't know. I don't know where I am or how I got here.' Ele went to cover her mouth, vomit threatening, but saw the red streaks and the darkness underneath her fingernails. What was it? 'How could you ever say that.'

'Who is Maria, Ele?' Tiger was being laid out on a new stretcher. 'You need to remember. Who is she?'

'She's my sister.'

'No, Ele. Think. You don't have a sister, do you?'

'Not my real sister, but my friend sister, you know?' The police officers were listening, holding out phones, recording.

Tiger cried out as he was moved. *'She's you, Ele.* You have to understand that Maria has a hold over you that you can't control. That she murdered the man you loved and punished Sabine. See what she's done to the rest of us.'

'Shut up, it's not true. She's not me. You're lying, as you've always done to me.'

She couldn't bring herself to face the truth. She felt as if she might crack. If she let the pain rip out of her mouth, it would form a howl that'd make them believe that it was the end of the world!

51

LIANG

CHESS PIECES ON A BOARD

Liang knew she only had moments left. She'd told the principal investigating officer her version of events. He looked sceptical, and Liang knew that even she doubted the veracity of her own words.

'You're telling me that the woman over there is not the woman who's done all this, but there's another woman inside her that did it?'

'Multiple personalities. *That's Ele.*' Liang nodded over towards Ele. 'She doesn't know that she's also Maria. She thinks Maria is a real person.'

Liang winced as a paramedic examined her wound. 'We have to get this woman to the hospital now.'

The officer grimaced. 'What you're telling me is very strange. We'll have to take all your testimonies, but if this is true, which one of them will we be arresting?'

'Maria. I think she's subdued right now. Locked somewhere in Ele's subconscious.'

'Then how do we get her out?'

'She comes out when she thinks Ele is under threat or when she's goaded out.'

The officer turned to the paramedic. 'Have we time to do this?' He nodded at the gash running red along Liang's ribs.

'I'm binding it now, and I'll get a drip into her. Then with or without your permission, I'm getting her to hospital.'

'Do your best.' The officer nodded at Liang and swivelled to watch Ele.

'Ele,' Liang called, 'listen to me. Maria drugged Michael and then poured acid over his face and then watched him die in agony.'

'Shut up. Shut up.' Ele waved her hands in front of her. Was it to ward off the terrible words?

'She murdered Sabine and then made sure she killed Michael's baby.'

'No, no, no, *no!*'

'You know she did. She's attacked me and beaten Hope. She's stabbed Paul. Maria did all this.'

'Stop it! Why are you doing this to me?' Ele fell to her knees, her arms hugged around her body.

'Maria's a murderer. You know she is. She's forced you to do dreadful things. Where is she, Ele?'

'I don't know.'

'When do you see her?'

'At home. She didn't kill anyone. I know her.'

'Has anyone else seen her? Tell me, Ele.'

'Loads of people... I... I can't remember.'

'She's been using you. What kind of friend does that?'

'She's my best friend. She's looked after me since you all left me.'

'She's killed in your name.'

'No, no, no! You're lying to me. She wouldn't do any of this.'

'You know I'm not lying, Ele. She and *only she* can be held accountable for these heinous crimes.'

Ele twitched violently. Her head lowered. Everyone in the

room stopped whatever they were doing. When she raised her head, Maria smiled at her adoring audience.

'She and *only she?*' Ele's voice had finally changed. There was no denying that a different persona was in front of them now. Her accent, her body stance and movements, even her facial expression had changed.

'To whom am I speaking?' The officer's voice was quiet but controlled. Was he thinking that any sudden noise or movement might make her bolt? Liang noticed him slip his gun from its holster. It was held low by his leg, ready.

'I think I am the "she" that old Tiger is speaking about.'

The officer held out his hand slowly toward her. 'Maria? Am I speaking to Maria?'

'Of course, you are.'

Tiger called out, 'You've looked after Ele for a long time now, haven't you?'

Maria rounded on her, and the officer stepped between them, raising his gun higher. 'Did you know she was raped over and over again by her Uncle Jose? Her parents didn't protect her. I've looked after her since she was beaten up by a psycho and nearly raped by a druggie bastard. No way, *Jose,* that I'd let that happen to her again. I dealt with it.'

Her accent was rich and round and deep. Liang wondered at this Maria who had no fear. This version of Ele, who stood as her champion.

'Go on,' mouthed the officer to Liang, when she looked up at him.

Liang spoke to Maria. 'Are we talking about Robert Dalgleish and David Barnes? Did you set up that fire in the house she shared in Hackney?'

Maria nodded and grinned widely. 'They had to be taught that they couldn't treat her the way they did, that there would be consequences.'

The officer butted in. 'And Michael Storm?'

'He was a cheating bastard. He also had to be taught a lesson. He deserved what he got.'

The officer continued, 'And what about Sabine de Montmorency?'

'Sabine was married. Swore her oath to God himself. Well, we can't have people breaking their sacred vows all over the place just to get their leg over. There had to be a reckoning.'

'Did you kill her?' Each word was enunciated clearly.

'Of course, I did. She guzzled down that bottle of red like she was dying of thirst. A bit of Fentanyl in it made sure she was nice and compliant when I arrived.' She looked around her as if searching for something. 'Took back what wasn't hers.'

'And Liang here?' The officer indicated Liang.

'She has the weight of all these deaths on her shoulders. It has nothing to do with me. I was only justice. It's all her fault. Not mine.' Maria blew a sweet kiss over to Liang.

The officer straightened his shoulders. 'I am arresting you for the murders of Michael Storm and Sabine de Montmorency.' He pulled a set of handcuffs out. 'You do not have to say anything. But, it may harm your defence if you do not mention when questioned something which you later rely on in court. Anything you do say may be given in evidence.'

Maria pulled from him. 'Not me, you fool. Arrest her. Weren't you paying attention? I was only the hand in this. She was the one who was the catalyst. She was the one who started it all those years ago.'

'I'm sorry,' said the paramedic, 'but now we have to get this woman to a hospital.'

There was movement and Liang felt herself hoisted gently onto a gurney.

A soft, cool mist began to obscure Liang's vision. She lay her head back and watched as the ceiling rolled past above her. She knew they were trying to get the gurney she was lying on over Michael's body, but she didn't look down. That husk wasn't the man she loved. He was enclosed within her heart; a heart that weighed as heavy as the centre of the sun. She could feel the fear and pain squirming inside, filling her head with visions she didn't want to see, her crushed heart beating too fast, willing her breath in and out of her body. Where were the images of him laughing, the remembrance of his wide, warm smile, the touch of his hands? Not this thing that haunted her.

'Forgive us all,' sobbed Liang.

'*I won't forgive you!*' A spasm of rage contorted Maria's beautiful face, making her hideous and deformed. The knife was in her hand, and she was running towards her. All Liang could see were the startled looks of the paramedics and the police officers, already moving to shelter her, arms held out, except it wasn't them who saved her. It was as if Maria had been caught and held by someone behind her. She pulled up, practically rearing back, although there was no one there.

'Tiger?' There she was, still a lost and helpless child. She looked down at the knife in her hand. The police officers were now moving, but they were too slow. Ele looked back to Liang, flipped the knife and plunged it into her own chest. A sharp *crack* pierced the air a second later, and a deep red stain flooded out from Ele's stomach.

Liang screamed.

Muted light and shapes played across her closed eyes. Surfacing back up from somewhere leaden, that had undulating shadows making terrible keening sounds that tried to grab hold of her and drag her down.

Was she rolled in cotton wool? She felt cushioned and warm, but some part of her knew she should be cold and dead.

'I think she's waking up.' A familiar voice, although she wasn't sure whose it was. Female, that was all.

Eyes opening, only a crack. Sticky and wet. Opening a little more. Something wiped across her face. The wafts of disinfectant mingled with a soft scent.

'Can we have a moment, please?' The familiar voice. Who was it?

'Call me if you need anything?' A different voice, then footsteps were heading away.

'Liang?'

A figure standing near but not too close. Softly spoken words. 'Liang, you're in a hospital. You're going to be alright.'

Closed blinds over the windows, one light above her but not harsh. Machines beep-beeping with coloured moving lines.

Recollection. Flooding in as the dam burst. 'Hello, Hope. Is Ele dead?'

'Yes, the police shot her. She tried to attack you.' Hope crept forward. 'They saved your life.'

'No,' said Liang, 'Ele saved me, and I think she saved herself.'

'What do you mean?'

'Right at the end, when Maria was running at me with the knife, something pulled her back, made her stop. It was Ele. It was like she couldn't let Maria do this one last terrible thing. She couldn't let Maria kill me. I saw her come out.' Tears obscured her vision, but she could still see it all clearly in her mind. 'Ele killed herself, one second before the police fired, but I know she was taking control back from Maria. Maria didn't win.'

'None of us won, did we?'

Liang heard a chair being dragged closer, the sound of someone making themselves comfortable.

'No. I think we were chess pieces on a board. Moves set out, only certain places we could jump to. It's weird, but we all had our part to play in this.' Liang shifted, aware now of drips and lines radiating from her body. 'I'm sorry, I should have asked after Paul.'

'He's stable now. I've been with him until they said for me to go get a bit of air. Told me to. Been hovering and doing their heads in, I suppose. So, here I am.' Hope slipped off her jacket. 'Paul's parents are flying over from Dresden. They'll be here in a couple of hours, and a good friend is looking after our kids.'

'How about you? You were cut badly too.'

'I think I got off lightly, all things considered. Just a little scar on my throat. A few bumps and bruises.'

Liang reached up, aware of a drip in her wrist, and gingerly touched her cheek. A padded bandage covered her face. 'I think I might have more than a little scar.'

'I'm so sorry.'

'It doesn't matter. Vanity is a moot point now. After all we've experienced, it's a wonder any of us are still alive.' She breathed in deeply. 'I would've loved to have met Ele again, the real Ele. I saw her briefly, at the end.'

'It's all unbelievable. I still don't understand what happened.'

'We happened. All of us together, entwined somehow, but we didn't even know it.'

'And that stupid pact, all those years ago.'

Hope shuffled, and Liang could hear her shoes squeak on the linoleum floor. 'Liang? Please don't say anything to Paul about what Maria said? You know? About George?'

'So it's true then.' Liang felt a weight on her chest lift. A part of Michael would live on.

'It was after you died. I mean, we thought you'd died. Paul was at his parent's place in Dresden. He hadn't seen them in ages.' Hope swallowed noisily. 'Michael called round. He was in such a state about you. Even then, I didn't twig about the two of you. We talked, and he cried and then we found the whisky. It's no excuse, but we were pretty pissed.'

'Let me get this right. Straight after I'd supposedly died, Michael was crying on your shoulder and then one thing led to another, and he shagged you. Is that right, or did I miss something?'

'You were dead.' Hope's voice was broken. 'And Ele was out of the picture.'

'And Paul?'

'I don't know what to say. I never meant to do that, but it was Michael. You must know what that's like?'

'The anglerfish...'

'Sorry? I don't understand.'

'That's what Maria called him. An anglerfish who lures in all the other pretty little fishes. Maybe that's the truest thing anyone has ever said about him. I don't think he could help himself.'

'I don't think we could help it either.'

Liang turned her head to look at Hope. 'I won't say anything about George, I mean, you don't know for certain.'

'Oh, I know. You can't mistake those eyes, and he's got the same wildness that Michael had when he was a kid.'

'Do you think Paul suspects?'

'Maybe, but I think a part of him couldn't ever allow himself to believe that I would cheat on him with his best friend. If he did suspect, he's hidden it deep inside. Mia and Alfie are different. They're similar to Paul; all of them are excitable and full of childish wonder.' Hope smiled. 'Especially Paul. George has a strange Machiavellian streak in him. Like Michael did. You remember? We all loved him so much, and we accepted how he got what he wanted because he was Michael.'

Liang nodded slightly, but it hurt. 'That's it, isn't it. Because he was Michael. But I'm still glad that a little Michael exists in this world.' Liang held out her hand to Hope, who took it in both of hers. 'It's over now. I don't know how but we have to keep on living. We have to move on.'

'I've still got my family, and for that, I'm eternally grateful. Paul's done some questionable things, too, so laying blame at each other's doors won't help us. But I love him so much, always have done, and he came through in the end. He saved us both. You're right, though. We all have to move on and live the best we can.' Hope held Liang's hand tighter. 'But what about you? Didn't you come here to be with Michael?'

'I lost him a long time ago. I lived with that then. I will live with that again. I've paid for what I did in the past. I believe what I have to learn now is that I have a right to live and be happy. We all do.'

'We'd love to see you when Paul gets home, and we get a semblance of family life back.'

Liang shook her head. 'Not yet, maybe later. Thanks. I don't think I could cope with seeing a little Michael at the moment. I wish you luck, Hope. You've a good man. I saw what he did to save us from Maria. Hang onto him.'

'He's not getting away from me. We've had our upsets, but I truly believe we're stronger because of this. There's nothing like the deaths of half your friends and the attempted murder of the rest to clarify what's important in life.' Hope shook her head. 'Maybe that sounds flippant, but I sure know I want a long and carefree life with Paul and my kids.'

Liang nodded slowly. 'Have you heard of something called string theory?'

Hope frowned. 'I presume it's nothing to do with vests or musical ensembles?'

'String theory is the idea that there are many universes and many versions of you that live in them.'

'Many versions of me?' Hope said, 'Doing what?'

'All the things you ever could. If in one life, it all goes terribly wrong, in another one, you're happy and successful.'

'I like that,' Hope said.

'What I'm trying to say is that in one universe somewhere out there, we're all alive, we're all happy, and we're all friends. None of this happened. No deaths, no fear, only friendship and love. That's what I want to believe. Somewhere out there, it turned out okay.'

THE END

ACKNOWLEDGEMENTS

I would like to thank my publishers, Bloodhound Books and their dedicated team for believing in me and my work. So, thanks to Betsy, Fred and Tara, and thanks to my hard-working editor, Caroline, who has steered me straight through choppy waters. Also, many thanks to the lovely Hannah, who has answered all my stupid questions with kindness and bonhomie.

Thanks also to Cornerstones Literary Consultancy, who have critiqued my work and taught me invaluable lessons along the way.

My thanks are extended to Pam Newman, who has read all my work and is perhaps my Number One Fan (but not in an Annie Wilkes sort of way.)

Thanks to my partner Malk, who also lives and works in his own box (he's a musician), while I live and work in mine. We meet for coffee in the garden.

And last but by no means least, thanks to my mum and dad (who have now both passed on), as they never wanted me to let go of my dreams and told me to do whatever I wanted with my life. I did, but I wish they were here to see it.

So again, thanks to everyone who has helped me on my journey here.

Website: www.hillybarmbyauthor.com
https://www.instagram.com/hillyollie
https://twitter.com/Hilly_Barmby
Facebook: Hilly Barmby Author

A NOTE FROM THE PUBLISHER

Thank you for reading this book. If you enjoyed it please do consider leaving a review on Amazon to help others find it too.

We hate typos. All of our books have been rigorously edited and proofread, but sometimes mistakes do slip through. If you have spotted a typo, please do let us know and we can get it amended within hours.

info@bloodhoundbooks.com